Mark Billingham has twice won the Theakston Old Peculier Award for Crime Novel of the Year, the Sherlock Award for the best detective created by a British writer and the Crime Writers' Association Dagger in the Library Award. Each of the novels featuring Detective Inspector Tom Thorne has been a *Sunday Times* bestseller. *Sleepyhead* and *Scaredy Cat* were made into a hit TV series on Sky 1 starring David Morrissey as Thorne, and a series based on the novels *In the Dark* and *Time of Death* was broadcast on BBC1. Mark lives in north London with his wife and two children.

ALSO BY MARK BILLINGHAM

The DI Tom Thorne series
Sleepyhead
Scaredy Cat
Lazybones
The Burning Girl
Lifeless
Buried
Death Message
Bloodline
From the Dead
Good as Dead
The Dying Hours
The Bones Beneath
Time of Death
Love Like Blood
The Killing Habit
Their Little Secret
Cry Baby
The Murder Book

The DS Declan Miller series
The Last Dance
The Wrong Hands

Other fiction
In the Dark
Rush of Blood
Die of Shame
Cut Off (Quick Reads)
Rabbit Hole

Digital originals
Dancing Towards the Blade
and Other Stories
Thorne at Christmas

Audio original
The Other Half (with My
Darling Clementine)

Non-fiction
Great Lost Albums
(as co-author)

MARK BILLINGHAM

What the Night Brings

SPHERE

SPHERE

First published in Great Britain in 2025 by Sphere

1 3 5 7 9 10 8 6 4 2

Copyright © Mark Billingham Ltd 2025

The moral right of the author has been asserted.

*All characters and events in this publication, other than those
clearly in the public domain, are fictitious and any resemblance
to real persons, living or dead, is purely coincidental.*

All rights reserved.
No part of this publication may be reproduced, stored in a
retrieval system, or transmitted, in any form or by any means, without
the prior permission in writing of the publisher, nor be otherwise circulated
in any form of binding or cover other than that in which it is published
and without a similar condition including this condition being
imposed on the subsequent purchaser.

A CIP catalogue record for this book
is available from the British Library.

Hardback ISBN 978-1-4087-1714-1
Trade paperback ISBN 978-1-4087-2639-6

Typeset in Plantin by M Rules
Printed and bound in Great Britain by
Clays Ltd, Elcograf S.p.A.

Papers used by Sphere are from well-managed forests
and other responsible sources.

MIX
Paper | Supporting
responsible forestry
FSC
www.fsc.org   FSC® C104740

Sphere	The authorised representative
An imprint of	in the EEA is
Little, Brown Book Group	Hachette Ireland
Carmelite House	8 Castlecourt Centre
50 Victoria Embankment	Dublin 15, D15 XTP3, Ireland
London EC4Y 0DZ	(email: info@hbgi.ie)

An Hachette UK Company
www.hachette.co.uk

www.littlebrown.co.uk

For Luca Veste, who told me I had to do it.

I do solemnly and sincerely declare and affirm that I will well and truly serve the King in the office of constable, with fairness, integrity, diligence and impartiality; upholding fundamental human rights and according equal respect to all people; and that I will, to the best of my power, cause the peace to be kept and preserved and prevent all offences against people and property, and that while I continue to hold the said office I will, to the best of my skill and knowledge, discharge all the duties thereof faithfully according to law.

The Police Constable's Oath of Attestation

PART ONE

NOBODY LIKES US

ONE

It was funny, how a certain sort of man's attitude changed dramatically when he was the one staring down the barrel of a gun.

Or happily, in this case, several of them.

It wasn't the first time Thorne had witnessed behaviour so seemingly out of character when someone got nicked. When they knew their future was no longer looking as rosy as it had before half a dozen armed officers crashed into their front room. There might have been the odd one who had to be dragged away spitting and lashing out, but in Thorne's experience they were the minority and, even then, it had all felt like a pantomime staged for any family, friends and business associates who happened to be around at the time. A last, if pointless hurrah.

A lot of it was down to movies and TV dramas, Thorne reckoned. A cliché every bit as tired as the detective faced with one last, dangerous case before retirement. The hard man who went down fighting, vowing revenge on all those doing the nicking and swearing that no prison could hold him, even if statistically the majority of His Majesty's bang-ups made a fairly decent job of it.

Thankfully, Nick Cresswell was showing rather more restraint.

Thorne watched as the armed officers withdrew from the room and one of the uniforms led Cresswell's dumbstruck wife out into the hall. While two other local uniforms kept hold of the prisoner's arms, Thorne nodded to DI Dave Holland, who stepped forward to recite the caution.

Thorne studied Cresswell's reaction, such as it was to begin with. It wasn't as if the man hadn't been arrested before, though Thorne knew that few of those arrests had amounted to very much and, more importantly, none had been for murder.

Cresswell looked across at him when Holland said the M-word.

Thorne smiled and nodded. 'Yeah, sorry, Nick. What ... did you think we'd gone to all this trouble because you'd not taken your library books back?'

There was a glimmer of anger then, a narrowing of the eyes, but for the most part the man in the khakis and the ratty cardigan just looked disappointed, sorrowful even. For a moment or two, Thorne wondered if Cresswell might be experiencing something strange and confusing, like empathy. Was he finally able to understand just how helpless and terrified all those people he'd pointed a shotgun at over the years had felt? What a twenty-four-year-old security guard named Jordan Wainwright had been feeling three months earlier, right before Cresswell had blown his face off?

Was he fuck, Thorne decided.

He waited until Cresswell had been led from the room, then followed the guard of dishonour out of the house and across the moonlit front garden towards the road. There were a good few smiles and handshakes. Yes, there would certainly be a drink or two taken in the Oak after his shift tomorrow, but more than anything, Thorne felt a huge sense of relief. Relief that the intel had been sound and that the arrest had gone without a hitch, which was important when the hitch could easily have involved Cresswell being armed and shots being fired.

It bothered Thorne more than slightly that the shitehawk who had provided the crucial intelligence – one of Cresswell's own crew – had done so in exchange for a place in Witness Protection. Such compromises were necessary, of course, but it rankled all the same and he couldn't help hoping that the man in question didn't find himself quite as protected as he was banking on. Thorne imagined spending an evening in one of the less salubrious pubs on Cresswell's manor a few months from now and blurting out the informant's new name and address a little too loudly after one too many.

Or after none at all.

Thorne watched as Nicholas Cresswell was ungently bundled into the back of a van, then turned and walked away.

Two squad cars were parked close together across the entrance to the cul-de-sac, and the four uniformed officers – two men and two women Thorne did not recognise – who had been stationed to ensure no pedestrians entered were leaning against their vehicles, chatting and laughing. Gathered beneath a streetlight, they were drinking coffee and snarfing doughnuts, which Thorne found more than a little irritating because he hadn't snarfed anything since lunchtime.

'Sir.' The taller of the two male officers licked his fingers and had the decency to look slightly embarrassed.

'Looks like that all went off a treat,' his colleague said, between mouthfuls. 'Job done.'

Thorne nodded towards the half a doughnut in one of the female officers' hands. 'Any more of them going?'

'Sorry, there were only four in the box.'

'Great,' Thorne said.

'I'd normally buy enough for everyone,' she said. 'These were a freebie, though. Someone left them on the car.' The woman reached for the empty box on the bonnet of the squad car and held it up so that Thorne could see what had been scrawled on it.

Thanks for everything you do!

The tall officer grinned and raised his coffee cup in salute. 'Who says nobody likes us?'

'Yeah, well, I'm very happy for you, but it's no good to me, is it?' Thorne watched the woman pop what was left of the doughnut into her mouth, then squeezed between the two vehicles and walked away, muttering. I mean, she could have offered him *half* a bloody doughnut, couldn't she? What happened to basic human decency and, more to the point, did rank count for nothing these days?

Thorne looked at his watch and saw that it was after three a.m.

He'd be lucky to find a kebab shop that was still open.

Someone was screaming in Thorne's dream, ragged and desperate and, just when he'd decided that the terrible noise was coming from him, he opened his eyes, took a second to remember where he was and realised that it was his phone doing the screaming.

He reached for the handset on his bedside table, saw who was calling and sat up. It was just before one o'clock in the morning. He answered the call and mumbled a hello.

'Tom . . . ?'

Something in the way DCI Russell Brigstocke had said his name made Thorne sit up a little straighter, wide awake now. 'What?'

'The Cresswell arrest the other night.'

Thorne immediately began to wonder what he'd done wrong. 'It was by the book, Russell, I—'

'There were four uniformed officers from Wood Green station working the wider scene, managing the neighbours, whatever.'

'Yeah, I spoke to them,' Thorne said. 'Afterwards.'

'So, each of them was rushed into hospital at various points over the last couple of days.'

Thorne threw back the duvet and felt Helen shift next to him. '*What?*'

'Convulsions, vomiting . . . all sorts. Poisoning looks like the best bet, but who knows—'

'Doughnuts,' Thorne said. 'They were all stood around eating doughnuts when we brought Cresswell out.'

Brigstocke took a few seconds. 'OK . . . but how on earth—?'

'They were a present. Someone left them as a thank you.'

'Oh, Jesus,' Brigstocke said.

'How are they doing?' Thorne waited for an answer, and the catch in Brigstocke's breath as he said nothing gave it to him. 'You're fucking kidding me.'

'Three of them died in the last few hours and there's a young woman in a coma who's looking very much like she's going the same way.' The DCI's voice broke a little before he cleared his throat and let out a long sigh. 'Three dead coppers, Tom, maybe four by lunchtime.'

Now it was Thorne who had nothing to say.

He was trying to remember their faces.

'You'd better get in here,' Brigstocke said.

When he'd put the phone back on the table, Thorne sat up and moved slowly to the edge of the bed. The room wasn't cold, but he was starting to shiver as he remembered just how much he'd wanted one of those doughnuts. He thought about how – if he'd been just a little pushier – he might have maybe snaffled half a one.

He felt the mattress move beneath him, then, a few seconds later, Helen's fingers against his shoulder. She asked him if he was all right, who it had been on the phone. She pressed herself against his back.

Try as he might, Thorne still couldn't remember the tall lad's face, but sitting there in the dark he could still picture the goofy grin, the coffee cup held aloft in mock-triumph.

Who says nobody likes us?

TWO

Christopher Tully.
Asim Hussain.
Kazia Bobak.
Catherine Holloway?

Thorne stared at the names scrawled on the whiteboard; the felt-tip roll-call of the dead and dying. The question mark was a handy, if morbid reminder that the final name on the list belonged to the woman who remained in a coma and was, as of now at least, a victim of attempted murder. Thinking of little else at the time but how hungry he was, Thorne hadn't clocked the ID tags on their stab vests, so couldn't be certain, but he felt instinctively that Catherine was the one who'd done most of the talking in the street two nights ago. Who had cheerfully brandished the empty gift box that dozens of her grieving colleagues were now working overtime to find.

The one whose half a stupid doughnut he'd coveted so much.

Russell Brigstocke stood up, took a breath and kicked things off. 'Three murders and one attempted, but let's make no mistake, this is *one* case, and it's our case. I'll be SIO on this and I want everyone in this room working it every minute that they have available.'

There were murmurs of assent, of determination.

Thorne was sitting next to Dave Holland towards the back of the incident room at Becke House. In the seat immediately in front of him, DI Nicola Tanner sat alongside DS Dipak Chall and DC Charita Desai. Every other seat was taken, including a good few extra ones that had been brought in from offices and corridors, and when Thorne glanced behind him he saw a row of grim-faced uniformed officers standing along the back wall, having requested permission to attend.

'Don't get me wrong,' Brigstocke said, 'I'm not saying that other cases will be pushed on to the back burner, because that would be unprofessional, but I'm sure most of you don't need telling that, save for a killing spree in Brent Cross Shopping Centre that leaves at least a dozen dead, this case takes priority.' He sighed and took off his glasses. 'I'll be saying much the same thing to DCI Jeremy Walker from Wood Green any time now, when he bowls up shouting about how *he* needs to run this one because the victims were from his station. When he—' Brigstocke stopped when he saw Thorne getting to his feet.

'Not happening,' Thorne said. 'I was running the Cresswell operation.' His eyes were on the whiteboard behind Brigstocke's head. 'This happened on my watch.'

'Don't worry about it, Tom.'

Thorne sat down again. He wasn't worried, because although he'd managed to twist Brigstocke's arm once or twice over the years, they'd been working together a long time. He knew better than anyone that when the DCI decided to dig his heels in, he wouldn't be shifted, whichever station the person trying to shift him happened to be from.

'It goes without saying that there's no way to keep a lid on this,' Brigstocke said. 'In terms of the media, I mean. We won't be releasing the precise manner of death, but everything else is online already like as not, and it'll be all over the evening papers and on every front page tomorrow. On balance, I don't think that's any bad thing.'

'Nice to have a more positive story for a change.' A voice from the back of the room.

'*What?*' Brigstocke glared. 'Positive?'

Thorne, along with everyone else, turned to stare at DC Stephen Pallister, a newish addition to the Major Investigation Team who had been transferred from somewhere south of the river a few months previously. Pallister – skinny, balding, in his early forties – immediately began to redden. 'No, not *positive* . . . that came out wrong. I just mean something that reflects a bit better on the force generally, that's all. Officers killed in the line of duty and not just another story about us dropping the ball.'

'Are you being serious?' Thorne said.

'I'm not saying it isn't a tragedy, but—'

'Maybe you've been smoking something.'

Nicola Tanner offered the man a thin smile. 'By "dropping the ball" you mean Metropolitan Police officers being convicted of murder, or maybe a string of rapes? That the kind of bad press you're talking about?'

Someone shouted, 'Wanker.' One of the uniforms leaning against the back wall.

Pallister raised his hands and spluttered, trying to formulate a response, before making the very wise decision to keep his mouth shut, largely because he couldn't fit any more of his foot into it.

'I think we should move on,' Brigstocke said.

Half an hour later, sitting in Brigstocke's office, the DCI said, 'He had a point. Pallister . . .'

Thorne just sniffed. He worked his tongue at something stuck between his teeth and continued to stare out of the window at a view of Hendon that never failed to make a grim day feel that little bit worse. The congregation of cranes, severe against a grey sky; the arches of the RAF Museum like a sheet of corrugated cardboard beyond them and the pulsing ribbon of the M1 curling around and creeping north. He'd said his piece back in the incident room, but he'd known what Pallister and now Brigstocke were getting at.

'He could have put it a bit more sensitively maybe,' Brigstocke said, 'but I'm betting there's people in the media office jumping up and down right now.'

Thorne finally nodded. 'A good day to bury bad news, right?'

Brigstocke looked at him.

'OK, I could have put *that* a bit more sensitively.'

However much certain elements might have wanted to, the Met was now under close public scrutiny having been unable to bury more than its fair share of *seriously* bad news. One officer convicted of murder, another unmasked as a man responsible for almost fifty rapes and more than five hundred officers currently under investigation for domestic and/or sexual abuse. The Casey report had concluded that the force was institutionally racist, sexist and homophobic, leaving coppers on the street with a worse rep than Premier League footballers. The Met had been placed under Special Measures and senior police management talked of little else but how desperate they were to make changes and demonstrate improvement.

These efforts had certainly not been helped when, only a month previously, a PC named Craig Knowles had been sent down for twelve years; revealed to be only the latest in a horrifically long line of rapists with warrant cards.

The motto used on Met Police signage had never seemed more ridiculous. *Working together for a safer London.* Almost as ridiculous as the new recruitment advert Thorne had spotted on the tube a few days before. *A career to take pride in.*

Thorne couldn't remember the last time he'd felt even remotely proud.

'What are you thinking?' he asked.

'Aside from early retirement, you mean?'

'Yeah, well, we're all thinking about that.'

'I'm thinking someone's got a grudge.'

Thorne shook his head. 'That's putting it mildly. I've got a grudge against the bloke next door because his cat keeps pissing against my bin, but I wouldn't kill his entire family.'

'A more general grudge against the police,' Brigstocke said. 'I mean, it's possible it was only one of them the killer had it in for, but that's quite a sobering thought.'

'Right.' Thorne wasn't going to argue, even if he'd hunted

down a number of individuals in his time quite capable of such a scattergun approach when it came to committing murder. 'God forbid he'd try and kill four officers just because one of them had nicked him for an out-of-date tax disc.'

Brigstocke grimaced. 'Obviously we'll check out all the recent cases each of the victims was working on, see if anything jumps out at us, but let's assume it's something more general until proved otherwise. There are several ... groups out there.'

'Not the kind of groups you'd find on Facebook?'

'Not really. The serious cop-haters tend to get together somewhere a bit less public.'

Thorne knew what Brigstocke was talking about. During his last major investigation, Thorne had needed a degree of guidance in navigating certain corners of the Dark Web that were even more disturbing than most, so he knew exactly who to approach for help this time round. 'There's a good bloke at the DFU,' he said.

'Great. Let's get Tanner briefed and she can handle that.'

'OK.'

'I'll get Holland to accumulate all the CCTV footage from the area around Cresswell's place, and when he's not doing that he can get the search for that doughnut box stepped up. It might well be in a landfill by now and I seriously doubt our poisoner's left us a nice handy fingerprint, but you never know.'

Thorne held out his arms. 'Are you telling me I can have the rest of the day off?' He looked at his watch. 'I might make it home in time for *Loose Women*.'

'I'm telling you to shift your arse and get yourself down to Hornsey Mortuary.'

'Course you are,' Thorne said. 'What was I thinking?'
Brigstocke was already up and on his way out. 'Your mate Phil's going to have an even busier day than the rest of us.'

THREE

Seeing no real need to sit through a trio of back-to-back post-mortems, certainly not when each of the victims had died the same way, Thorne had ducked out once the procedure had been completed on the body of Christopher Tully. He trudged up the road to a café he'd visited countless times on such occasions and spent the rest of the day drinking coffee, talking on the phone to other members of the team and poring over hospital reports and statements from family members on his laptop.

The man behind the counter knew exactly where Thorne had been and who he was waiting for. He didn't bother asking if Thorne wanted anything to eat.

Still stinking of formaldehyde, Phil Hendricks breezed in late afternoon and immediately ordered the all-day breakfast. He carried a mug of tea across and dropped into the seat opposite Thorne. 'I could eat a scabby dog on a bap.' He looked across at the man behind the counter. 'Don't suppose you've *got* any scabby dog?'

'Fresh out,' the owner said.

'I'll stick with the breakfast, then.'

Thorne closed his laptop. 'So . . . arsenic?'

'I usually just go with ketchup,' Hendricks said.

Thorne shook his head and looked across at his friend; the collage of tattoos and the fearsome array of facial piercings including a chain running from ear to lip which Thorne couldn't remember seeing before. 'Do you still think it's arsenic?'

'Yeah. I smelled garlic on all three of them, so unless they all happened to have had Italian food at the same time, my money's on arsenic. Arsenic trioxide's your best bet, I reckon. You make an incision in your doughnut, whack in half a teaspoon of that, because guess what, it looks like sugar anyway, and Bob's your uncle. *His* uncle . . . the killer's uncle. You know what I mean.'

'OK, so where would someone get hold of that stuff?'

'Well, you could get it shipped over from the US and there's a few places in the far east, I think, but over here . . . a lab or a chemical manufacturing firm, something like that? A hospital maybe, because they actually use it to treat leukaemia, in a very different form, obviously . . . which is ironic as it goes, because it can actually cause cancer. Oh, and FYI, it was once used to treat syphilis.'

'I'm not sure that helps,' Thorne said.

'You never know, it might come up in a pub quiz.'

'Pubs are for drinking in.'

'Agreed.'

'But thanks anyway.'

Hendricks rubbed his hands together as his all-day breakfast was laid in front of him. He added a sizeable squirt of ketchup to his plate and began buttering bread.

'Anything else?' Thorne asked.

Hendricks laid down his knife. 'Yeah. Kazia Bobak was pregnant.'

'Oh, Christ . . .'

'Very early stages. I'm not sure she'd even have known, but either way you'll have to inform the next of kin, right?'

Thorne nodded. The conversation with Kazia Bobak's partner was certainly not one he was looking forward to, but he had no choice. The pregnancy would come out at any subsequent trial, and if there was one thing guaranteed to cost him the trust of a victim's family it was holding information back. Much as Thorne would have liked it to, this new information would make no difference to the charge when it was finally brought. The killer could not possibly have known about the pregnancy, besides which no *destruction of a child* charge could be brought before a child had actually been born, despite the sterling efforts of pro-life nut-jobs to amend the law.

Thorne sat and watched Hendricks eat.

He was glad of the few minutes' silence, even if it was . . . unusual. Having a mouthful of bacon and egg had never stopped Hendricks gobbing off before and, despite his jokiness a few moments earlier, Thorne sensed that his friend wasn't quite firing on all cylinders.

'You all right, Phil?'

'Yeah . . . I'm sound.'

'You sure?'

Hendricks folded a slice of bread and butter then sat back and ran a hand across his shaved head. 'I don't *always* love what I do, you know that, right?'

'You and me both,' Thorne said.

'Even if I am frighteningly good at it.'

'Goes without saying.'

'I mean, I don't want to blow my own trumpet.'

'No?'

'Trust me, I would if I could, but I'm not supple enough.' He tried for a cheeky smile, but couldn't quite pull it off. 'Multiple victims is always a bad day at the office, that's all.' He turned and nodded back towards the mortuary. 'Them three in there... none of those poor sods was even thirty yet.' He turned slowly back to stare at Thorne. 'That was a bastard.'

Thorne waited. He knew that Hendricks would shrug it off, because he always did. He knew there'd be another joke or a filthy comment or a football-related dig coming soon enough.

There'd be something to change the mood.

'Down to you now, though, mate.' Hendricks sliced a sausage in half, speared the biggest piece and pointed with it. 'Your mission, Jim, if you choose to accept it, is to get out there and catch the scumbag responsible.' He stared at the end of his fork. 'This sausage will self-destruct in five seconds.'

'Nothing too difficult, then,' Thorne said.

'No, not for a successful and highly experienced copper who's insightful yet tenacious. Whose cunning is matched only by his deep understanding of the criminal mind and formidable powers of deduction.'

Thorne sighed, waiting for it.

Hendricks grinned and jammed the sausage into his mouth. 'So yeah, *you* might find it a tad tricky.'

FOUR

Tanner had visited this particular Digital Forensic Unit hub before, so once she'd shown her warrant card at the reception desk of the nondescript office block in Wembley, she dispensed with the offered escort and made her own way up to the third floor. The man she was here to see was sitting at a corner desk of the vast, open-plan office. He looked up and waved at her as she walked across.

'Greg ...' Tanner dragged a chair across from an unoccupied desk nearby and sat down next to the chair Greg Hobbs was in. The much larger one, with wheels.

'Nice hair, Nic.' Hobbs removed his headphones, took a closer look and nodded approvingly. As always, he was dressed immaculately; a tweed waistcoat over a crisp white shirt buttoned to the neck. His beard was perfectly trimmed and the assortment of silver earrings gleamed as if they'd been freshly polished.

The first time they'd encountered Greg Hobbs, Thorne had been astonished to discover that a nerd could also be a hipster.

'Suits you,' Hobbs said.

'You think?'

Tanner immediately began fiddling with her hair, still not sure if she was doing the right thing. The blonde highlights had made their first appearance almost nine months before when she'd started seeing a woman she'd met on a dating site. She and Fiona were still seeing each other, on and off, and even though Fiona's tastes in the bedroom were a little less vanilla than Tanner's own, the semi-casual arrangement seemed to suit them both.

OK, a lot less vanilla.

'Freaky Fiona', Thorne and Hendricks called her.

Tanner watched as Hobbs began to type and a series of pages appeared one by one on the three huge screens in front of him. They were predominantly black with plain white type, though Tanner knew this was not why it was called the Dark Web. Hobbs continued clicking and scrolling, navigating his way rapidly through a slew of sites with which he was clearly familiar. Tanner had spoken to him on the phone a few hours before and let him know what she was looking for, so perhaps he had begun looking straight away and found something already.

Hobbs clocked her look and guessed what she was thinking. 'I've made similar searches before,' he said. 'That's all.'

'Really?'

'Well, bearing in mind some of the stuff that your lot's been up to, it's not a big surprise that a few of the Met's bigger cheeses are keen to keep an eye on what their critics are saying.' He peered at the centre screen. 'I say *critics*, but we're not talking about the kind of people who write strongly worded letters to *The Times*.'

'Activists,' Tanner said.

'That's putting it politely. The powers that be have requested that some of them be ... monitored. The more dangerous-sounding ones.'

'Not closely enough,' Tanner said.

Hobbs grimaced. 'Obviously not. Nasty business, those four PCs.'

'So, you know where to look?'

'I know where to start looking,' Hobbs said. 'There's no shortage of this stuff. You could likely nick a fair few of them for hate speech straight away, but you'd have to find them first, which takes some doing. One of the benefits of the Dark Web.'

'We'd best crack on, then,' Tanner said.

'OK, cool.' Hobbs called up a fresh page and peered. 'How's Phil?'

Tanner sighed. 'Oh, much the same.'

'Glad to hear it,' Hobbs said. 'There's not too many like him.'

The words *small* and *mercies* leaped into Tanner's mind, but she chose to leave them there. Having met not long after she and Thorne had first visited the DFU, Hobbs and Hendricks had quickly become extremely matey which came as something of a shock to those who were present at the time. Predictably, Hendricks had refused to do as most others probably did and tiptoe politely around the issue of Hobbs's disability. He had pointed out that tiptoeing around a disability that had cost a man the use of his legs was at best ironic and at worst downright tasteless, then proceeded to gleefully trample all over it in heavily studded size ten Dr. Martens.

Having casually asked how Hobbs had wound up the way he had, he'd grilled him about his sex life, then asked if he could borrow his blue badge before helpfully suggesting a variety of ways in which Hobbs might 'pimp' his wheelchair.

Go-faster stripes and cup holders. A flashing blue light on the top ...

And Greg Hobbs had loved it. He'd laughed like a drain the whole time and, most impressively, given every bit as good as he got.

'I'll tell him you said hello,' Tanner said.

'Here we go.' Hobbs nodded towards the centre screen. A page with the heading *Social Networks: Message Boards; Hidden Answers; Intel Exchange*. 'Some of this might not make for pleasant reading,' he said.

'I think I'll cope.'

'And like I said, it won't tell us anything about who these people are. I mean, I'm good, but if people have taken the proper steps to stay hidden ...'

'I'm not expecting to leave with anyone's name and email address,' Tanner said.

Hobbs began to navigate various sites and mini-sites, tunnelling his way deeper into the dark until he found the anti-police message boards he was looking for.

FUCK THE FILTH

STAB UP DA COPZ

BLUE CLOTH, BLACK HEART

Hobbs had been spot on; it didn't make for comfortable reading. There was little that hadn't been said to Tanner's face at one time or another, though, even before the recent upswing in serious criminality among Met officers. In truth, she had little argument with many of the sentiments expressed and, more importantly, she saw nothing that suggested serious criminal intent or might even prompt others to move in that direction.

People were angry, simple as that.

They were venting and Tanner couldn't blame them.

Towards the end of the day, after a break for coffee during which Hobbs had shown Tanner umpteen seemingly identical photographs of his cat, they found themselves studying a message board Hobbs had never come across before.

'All manner of nooks and crannies in here,' he said.

ROASTING THE PORK

Much of it was, by now, dispiritingly familiar. A litany of complaints and abuse, a frenzied outpouring of shock and disgust. A post from three months earlier caught Tanner's attention and briefly stopped her breath. A winged avatar and a simple message from a woman calling herself ButterflyGrrrl.

> *I was raped six months ago by a copper. Too scared to go to the police.*

Tanner looked at Hobbs. 'There's no way . . . ?'

He shook his head. 'All this stuff's relayed via multiple computers. The browser . . . well, it's not even what you'd think of as a browser . . . is encrypted and the circuit is automatically refreshed every ten minutes. These things are virtually untraceable. Sorry, Nic.'

Hobbs continued scrolling.

There were no further messages from ButterflyGrrrl, but towards the end of the final page was a post from only three days ago that brought Tanner to her feet. A simple statement which made her think that, despite the cat photos, the trip to the DFU might turn out to have been worthwhile after all.

'What?' Hobbs asked.

A message from someone calling him or herself LoveMyBro.

Two names that Tanner recognised, for very different reasons.

Chris Tully and Craig Knowles. Two peas in a pod.

'I need you to print that out for me,' Tanner said.

FIVE

The forty minutes or so it took Helen to get her son Alfie bathed and into bed gave Thorne time to get dinner sorted. He'd never been much of a cook and rarely put much effort in if he was eating alone, but pasta was easy enough and it didn't take very long to knock what looked like a decent carbonara together. He began dishing it up when Helen came in, then paused when Alfie shouted from his bedroom and she immediately went out again.

A few minutes later she was back, and as soon as she'd poured herself a large glass of red wine and Thorne had opened a bottle of Peroni, they sat down and started to eat.

'He OK?' Thorne asked.

'He wants me to tell you to say hello to "Spiky Uncle Phil".'

'I will. I saw him today, actually.'

Helen nodded, knowing exactly what that meant, as she twirled spaghetti around her fork. 'And to tell him that Arsenal are rubbish.'

'That's definitely not a problem.' Thorne couldn't be doing with the twirling business and was busy cutting his spaghetti up into manageable pieces. Had there been a bottle in the fridge, he'd have happily added some brown sauce which – while knowing that most foodies would consider it monstrous – he deemed perfectly acceptable, considering he was basically eating bacon and egg.

'This is good,' Helen said.

'Really?'

Helen nodded and took another mouthful.

'Well, I don't think I'm ready for *MasterChef* just yet.'

'It's all good,' she said. 'You cooking me dinner, that's a shedload of Brownie points for a kick-off. And you know ... you being here.'

Thorne looked at her in mock-amazement. It was the first time she'd said anything quite so ... couply since they'd become a couple again. It hadn't been an immediate thing. They hadn't fallen weeping into one another's arms and neither had needed to ask why they'd ever split up in the first place.

Thorne knew the reason had been him.

Helen had been there for him when his last relationship had ended in circumstances that Thorne preferred not to think about too much and what had begun as plain and simple comfort had eventually settled into an easy familiarity and, finally, the committed relationship that they'd clearly both missed a great deal.

That wasn't to say that the first time they *had* shared a bed again was much to write home about. Not even worth a postcard.

'I'm not sure I can remember what you like,' Thorne had said.

'Don't worry.' Helen had winked and rubbed his arm. 'I'll tell you.'

Now, she looked across at the smile creeping across Thorne's face. 'Come on, don't you think this is good? The two of us.'

'No argument from me.' Thorne thought it was way better than good, but hearing it from Helen was by far the high point of his day, so he was happy to let her make the running.

'Better than last time, I reckon.'

'You think?'

'When last time wasn't terrible, I mean.'

'Probably because I'm not here quite as much,' Thorne said. 'If I was around any more than I am, I'd soon start getting on your tits again.'

'Maybe.'

When they'd first been together, Thorne had divided his time fairly equally between his own flat in Kentish Town and Helen's in Tulse Hill, but second time around he didn't take the nights spent at her place for granted. It remained something to look forward to and he knew that the arrangement suited them both. There was Alfie to consider, of course, the school two streets away, but one thing that hadn't changed was the need they both had for space. For precious time alone, a few nights a week, at least.

'Be honest,' Thorne said, his smile widening. 'It's really about the cooking dinner thing, isn't it?'

'Oh, I could certainly get used to it,' Helen said. 'But I do think you're different. I mean, we both are, obviously, but you're definitely a lot less stressed.'

Thorne stared down at his plate. 'Yeah, well, that might be about to change.'

They ate in silence for a few minutes, and when they'd finished, they carried their drinks across to the sofa.

'The murdered PCs,' Helen said. 'That's why you saw Phil today, right?'

'Arsenic, he reckons.'

'He's usually right.'

Thorne nodded. 'Someone went to a lot of trouble, getting hold of the stuff, working out the best way to use it. That's a lot of planning.'

'Someone who wanted to make a statement.'

'A *serious* statement,' Thorne said. 'Four dead coppers. Well, three dead and one as good as.'

Helen sipped her wine. 'It's hardly a surprise, though, is it? Plenty of cops got attacked in the US after what happened to George Floyd. Sarah Everard was our George Floyd moment, so now it's our turn.'

Thorne said nothing.

'There's a thousand Met officers on suspension at the moment. Enough coppers to police a small town have been deemed unfit to serve, and I'm not even talking about the ones who've been convicted.'

'I know,' Thorne said. 'I know all that.'

'I'm just saying, it's not a big shock that plenty of people don't like us.'

'*Us?*'

She smiled and shook her head. 'It'll take a while ...'

Having spent a number of years as a DI on a Child Protection Unit, Helen Weeks had quit the Job a month or so after she and Thorne had got back together. Knowing that the horrors she'd dealt with on a daily basis could make Homicide seem like a cushy option, Thorne had fully supported what had been a difficult decision. These days, she had more time to spend with her son and, without childcare to pay for, it was easy enough to live off her police pension, while volunteering two days a week at Citizens Advice.

Even if Thorne wasn't convinced he was any less stressed than Helen thought he'd been before, he was damn sure that she was.

'It's not going to be easy,' Helen said.

Thorne raised his beer bottle to his lips, having momentarily lost the thread of their conversation. 'What isn't?'

'To turn things around. To start with, you need to come down hard on any copper that thinks they're above the law. To be *seen* to come down hard, not just these stupid suspensions on full pay.'

Thorne couldn't argue. For every dodgy copper that might eventually get prosecuted, there seemed to be hundreds more sitting on their arses at home and getting paid every month for the privilege. There was plenty of big talk from the Independent Office for Police Conduct, but they seemed rather more reticent when it came to actually putting anyone away.

'Then you need to do whatever's necessary to win back the public trust, and that's not going to be easy.'

'What *I* need to do is catch this maniac.' Thorne stood up, trudged across to the table and began clearing away the dirty plates. 'There's no guarantee he's finished.'

'Yeah, obviously,' Helen said.

He carried the dishes through to the kitchen, rinsed them and began loading the dishwasher. He actually began *re-loading* it as, to his mind, Helen was somewhat cavalier when it came to the task. He rearranged the dirty cutlery so that all the forks were facing the same way. He imagined how outraged Nicola Tanner would be at the chaos and how delighted she'd be at his efforts to restore some order.

He shouted back through to the living room. 'I tell you what we *do* need . . .'

'What?'

'You're out of brown sauce.'

SIX

'First off, thanks to those of you who were due a Saturday at home for coming in.' Brigstocke sighed and nudged at his glasses. His greying quiff was uncharacteristically lifeless and he obviously hadn't shaved. 'It is what it is.' Not unexpectedly, a blanket clearance of overtime had been authorised, even if no financial incentive was actually necessary to further motivate any of those present. The murders of three of their fellow officers was always going to trump a visit to the garden centre or a football match.

'So.' The DCI leaned down to activate the laptop connected to the screen behind him. 'Developments . . . '

The key members of the team were gathered in a meeting room, one floor down from their MIT offices: Thorne, Tanner, Holland, Desai and Chall. The only unfamiliar face belonged to the man they had been expecting and to whom Thorne had been briefly introduced on his way in. DCI Jeremy Walker sat bolt upright in an expensive blue suit, wearing a predictably grim and frustrated expression which was somewhat at odds with the bright red tie and matching pocket square.

Brigstocke hit a key and an image appeared on the screen behind him. The gift box Thorne had last seen in the hands of Catherine Holloway was crumpled and sealed inside a plastic evidence bag, but the message she'd been so keen to show him four nights before was still clear enough.

Thanks for everything you do!

Thorne thought about the conversation he'd had with Helen the night before. Now it was all but impossible not to focus on the hideous deeds of some, encompassed in that seemingly generous message to all.

Everything . . .

'It was found stuffed into the rear footwell of one of the squad cars,' Brigstocke said. 'It's unbranded, as you can see. Just a bog-standard paperboard box. It's gone to the lab, obviously, but I don't think we should hold out too much hope, because of *this*.' He clicked again and turned to watch the short, grainy black and white video, which immediately began to play. 'This is from a security camera on one of the houses opposite.'

Thorne leaned forward, but there were simply no details to pick out. A dark figure in a hoodie hurrying across the road, depositing the box on top of the squad car and quickly disappearing out of shot.

'As you can see, he's wearing gloves, which take prints out of the equation. We've talked to other homeowners in the street, and as a few of them had been woken up by the activity around the operation at Cresswell's place, we've managed to find a couple who saw the same figure.'

'Is that a man or a woman?' Chall asked.

'Difficult to tell,' Desai said.

'Doesn't look very tall,' Tanner said. 'I suppose it could be a woman, but he's walking like a bloke.' Everyone watched as Brigstocke played the video again. When it had finished, Tanner sat back. 'Yeah, that's a bloke.'

'Unfortunately, none of those neighbours we talked to could give us any information that isn't on that footage.' Brigstocke zoomed in on the figure in the freeze-frame. There were no identifying features. 'So, not a lot of help.'

'Looks like he's aware there are going to be cameras,' Thorne said.

'There's always cameras.' Holland shrugged. 'He's just being careful.'

'No, it's like he knows where they are,' Thorne said. 'Which houses have got them, so he can always keep his face out of the shot. Let's presume he'd scoped the street out beforehand.'

'I'll go with that,' Tanner said. 'But it does beg a fairly important question.'

Thorne knew exactly what she meant, because it was a question he'd been asking himself since the murders. 'It's clearly not a random attack, right? It's not like he was just walking the streets with a box of poisoned doughnuts, waiting to spot a police car.'

Brigstocke was already nodding. 'So, how the hell did he know we'd be there? That was a need-to-know operation, so how did he know about the raid on Cresswell's place?'

There was a long silence.

'Radio scanner?' Chall suggested.

'Maybe,' Brigstocke said.

'Could just be that someone on the operation got a bit gobby,' Holland said. 'Told someone who told someone else.'

'There *is* another explanation,' Thorne said. 'What if he's a copper?'

Now there was a longer silence as those around the table struggled to process what was, by any measure, a shocking possibility; to come up with any reason at all why a police officer should have murdered three of his colleagues.

'Let's park that one for a minute,' Brigstocke said, eventually. 'Because we also have this.' He leaned towards the keyboard again and called up another image. 'Nicola came across it on a visit to the DFU yesterday, posted on one of the Dark Web message boards.'

Chris Tully and Craig Knowles. Two peas in a pod.

'Obviously, none us need reminding who Chris Tully is, and I would hope most of you are aware that PC Craig Knowles was convicted of multiple counts of rape just over a month ago.'

'Convicted of raping his wife.'

Predictably, it was DC Stephen Pallister who had spoken up. Thorne turned to him. 'Are you trying to demonstrate your detailed knowledge of the case or do you have something to say?'

'No ... just that's what it was, right?'

'Rape is rape is rape,' Brigstocke said. 'I'm assuming you believe that, DC Pallister. Or do we need to have a private conversation in my office afterwards?'

'No, of course not. I mean ... yes, I believe it one hundred per cent.'

'Good to hear,' Brigstocke said. 'So ... '

He turned to the screen and everyone stared at the printout

of the message posted on the Roasting the Pork message board by LoveMyBro.

'Interesting,' Holland said.

At the end of the table, DCI Jeremy Walker huffed, glaring at the statement as though it was a photograph of someone shagging his wife.

'It's certainly something worth looking into,' Brigstocke said.

'Seriously?' Walker sat forward quickly and pointed accusingly at the screen. 'A random message from some online nutters' forum? Some troublemaker ...'

'It doesn't look very random to me,' Thorne said. 'It's pretty specific.'

Walker turned to glare at Thorne instead. 'It's a vile accusation against a dead man.'

'Not an accusation anyone here is making,' Brigstocke said.

'Even so—'

'But somebody is, and precisely because Chris Tully *is* one of our murder victims, it's an avenue of enquiry we need to pursue.'

'It's a dead end,' Walker said. 'You're wasting your time.'

'I don't think so,' Brigstocke said.

'You remember who George Oldfield was, don't you?'

It was clear from Brigstocke's face that he remembered very well and that he knew exactly why Walker was reminding him; where he was going with it. Seeing the recognition on Brigstocke's face, Walker turned to address the other detectives around the table.

'For those of you not quite old enough, Oldfield was the copper who chose to believe the "Wearside Jack" tape that arrived during the Yorkshire Ripper investigation. Who believed it was genuine and not just something sent in by a "nutter" or a "troublemaker". He was the officer who decided it was an "avenue of enquiry they needed to pursue" and diverted the investigation to Sunderland, which almost certainly cost the lives of two more women who were murdered in, surprise surprise, Yorkshire.' He turned back and stared at Brigstocke. 'Don't be George Oldfield, Russell.'

Thorne watched as the fists held tight against Brigstocke's side slowly unclenched; as he took a few moments to breathe and regain his composure and fight the urge to take on his opposite number from Wood Green.

Then he turned calmly to his team.

'First and foremost we need to look for any connection between Tully and Knowles. Did they ever work together? Did they drink in the same pub? Were they in the same five-a-side football team? And at the same time, let's have a good hard look at Christopher Tully. Home life, service record, notable arrests in the last few years . . . anything that might suggest—'

Brigstocke stopped when Walker stood up suddenly, his chair rocking back as he gathered his things. Everyone in the room watched as the man adjusted his bright red tie, turned the ID on his lanyard to the front and walked slowly around the table towards the door.

He opened it and spoke without turning round. 'I don't think there's anything else I need to hear.'

Brigstocke barked out a laugh. 'Oh, well, that's—'

'Or *care* to hear come to that.' Now, Walker turned round. 'I'll be waiting in your office.'

SEVEN

<<*I think we're on for tonight if you're still up for it.*>>

<<Seriously?>>

<<*I don't joke about this stuff.*>>

<<I'm not sure I can.>>

<<*OK. Sorry.*>>

<<What do you mean?>>

<<*Thought you wanted to.*>>

<<Yeah but it's scary.>>

<<It's cool. I've sorted everything. Found a good place and I know he's on shift.>>

<<Tonight, though? I need to think about this a bit more.>>

<<It needs to be tonight. Well, in the early hours of tomorrow if you want to be exact.>>

<<I don't think I can do it. Too soon.>>

<<Up to you but not sure he'll be the one turning up if we do it another time.>>

<<I don't know. I'm shitting myself just thinking about it.>>

<<Trust me it'll be fine.>>

<< . . . >>

<<You still there?>>

<<Yeah.>>

<<He needs to know he hasn't got away with it, right?>>

<<I suppose so.>>

        <<That you're going to do something. We talked about this.>>

<<Yeah talked, but I didn't know you were going to really arrange it.>>

        <<You know I take this seriously. What it means.>>

<<I just don't know how I'll feel seeing him again.>>

        <<I'll be there, so he can't hurt you.>>

<<Things are different now, though. Those dead coppers. Didn't you see it on the news?>>

        <<Yeah, I saw it.>>

<<So he might not be on his own.>>

        <<If he isn't we call it off. We leg it, or you come up with some story. I think he will be, though.>>

<<Let me think about it. Just for a few hours.>>

<<If you want.>>

<<Don't think I'm not grateful because I am.>>

<<Nothing to thank me for. You're doing this for you.>>

<<Yeah.>>

<<You've just got to say your piece, that's all. Let him know his time's up and he's going to prison where he belongs. And I'll be with you, so there's really no danger.>>

<<I do want to.>>

<<So we're on then.>>

<<Just panicking here because it's so sudden.>>

<<No reason to panic.>>

<<Easy for you. It wasn't you it happened to.>>

<<My bad.>>

<< . . . >>

>>*Sorry. Didn't mean to be insensitive.*<<

<<*Didn't mean to sound touchy.* 😊>>

>>*I'll send you the details about where and what time.*<<

<<*Yeah, I suppose, if you really think it'll be OK.*>>

>>*We can meet up somewhere before to go through it. You need to trust me.* 👍👍👍<<

<<*I do, but it doesn't make me any less scared.*>>

>>*Once you've done this, you won't have to be scared any more.*<<

EIGHT

Thorne waited no more than five minutes after Brigstocke had wound the briefing up before knocking on his door. The knock was not a request, because he didn't bother waiting to be invited in, and nobody could have described it as polite. It was, in Thorne's head at least, a warning.

'What can I do for you?' Brigstocke was seated at his desk while the man Thorne was really there to see was sitting opposite him. They might have been discussing the weather or the increase in petrol prices, because it certainly didn't seem confrontational; not as confrontational as Thorne had hoped, anyway.

Walker looked at him, waiting.

Thorne said nothing, doubting himself suddenly, wondering if he had quite as much credit in the bank with his boss as he thought he did.

'I know it's a bit beneath your pay grade,' Walker said. A thin smile appeared suddenly, like a crack in plaster. 'But if you've come with the offer of coffee, I take it black with no sugar.'

Thorne opened his mouth, then closed it again and swallowed. For a few seconds he considered leaving well alone, telling himself that, on this occasion, discretion might well be the better part of valour.

Then he remembered that he didn't have a great deal of either.

'What do you *want*, Tom?'

'I wanted to tell DCI Walker that there's really no need to let anyone know he thinks he should be running this investigation.'

'Is that right?' Walker said. 'Thanks for the heads-up.'

Thorne stayed focused on Brigstocke. 'No need, because it was written all over his face in the briefing. A face which, now I come to think about it, didn't so much look like a smacked arse as one that's had seven shades of shit thrashed out of it.'

Now, Walker turned to Brigstocke. He held out his arms and shook his head, as if to ask his fellow DCI if he was really going to allow one of his detectives to talk to a senior officer like this.

'But more importantly, there's no need because there really isn't any point.'

'Oh, is there not?'

'No, because DCI Brigstocke has already approved the investigation's command structure with officers who've got a few more pips on their shoulders than anyone in this room.' He turned to look at Walker. 'It's a done deal. Sir.' Back to Brigstocke. 'Isn't it, sir?'

'It is as far as I'm concerned,' Brigstocke said.

Walker got to his feet and when he started to talk – his voice raised a little, but not too much – there was a good deal of pointing. 'Whether it's done or not, it's certainly not the *right* deal. Those three dead officers … all four of those officers were based at my station.'

'Yes, but they were seconded on to an operation that *I* was running,' Thorne said. 'I spoke to them while they were ingesting the arsenic that killed them. I as good as watched them being murdered and I'm going to be part of the team that catches the man responsible.'

'Your operation, but my officers. That should count for something.'

'What, you're going to tell me you're thick as thieves with all the uniforms based at your station? I know how all that works, because I know exactly how many of the uniforms in *this* place are pally with plainclothes. It's still "suits" and "lids" however much we try and pretend it isn't. It's still the glory hunters poncing about up here and the men and women at the sharp end, strapping on stab vests a couple of floors down. You come marching in here with all this "blue brotherhood" crap and I'm betting you didn't even know all those dead coppers' names until a couple of days ago—'

'*Tom* …' Now Brigstocke was on his feet.

Walker was statue-still and unblinking. To anyone else he might simply have appeared stunned, but Thorne saw only a predator waiting for its prey to get near enough before it strikes.

He had said his piece and tried to look calm as he walked towards the door, even if he was anything but.

He said, 'I'll see if I can get that coffee organised for you.'

Half an hour later, Thorne emerged from the Gents to find Walker waiting for him. A little nonplussed, he gave a cursory nod and moved to walk past, but the DCI stepped to block his way.

'What you said to me before, that was out of order.'

'I don't think it was.' Thorne stood waiting for Walker to move. 'Look, if you think I'm going to apologise you'll be stood there a while.'

'Oh, I'm damn sure you won't.'

'Right, then.'

'Even if, from what I've heard about you over the years, you've got plenty to be sorry about.'

Thorne shrugged, hoping his not-giving-a-toss smile looked genuine. 'Listen, dob me in to HR if you're feeling all offended or emotionally abused or whatever. Send a strongly worded email to the Chief Constable. I really don't care. What I do care about is what's best for this investigation, so that's why I said what I said—'

Walker stepped towards him. 'What you said was wrong, though, and you need to know that. What you were suggesting. I knew every one of those officers. I know the names of all their kids. I've had dinner with Asim Hussain's family and I've been out drinking with Catherine and Chris plenty of times. I was at Kazia Bobak's wedding, for pity's sake.'

Thorne tried not to look as taken aback as he was. 'Well, that's good to hear.' He couldn't think of much else to say and knew that now he probably should express some degree of regret for his outburst in Brigstocke's office, but he simply didn't have it in him. He said, 'I'm sorry for your loss.'

Not an apology, but it was meant.

Walker nodded, staring, and when Thorne moved to leave he did not step aside. 'It's a shame, because yeah, I've heard some iffy things about you, but I've heard one or two good things as well. Even so, I'm very glad you're not on *my* team.'

'Well, at least we're on the same page,' Thorne said.

'I feel for Russell, I really do,' Walker said. 'Because honestly, I can't think of anything worse than being your DCI.' Then that thin smile appeared again. 'Although, having said that, being your girlfriend doesn't tend to end up very well either, does it?'

NINE

Dave Holland began scraping away with a knife at the burnt bits of lasagne around the edge of his bowl. 'One of the things I was hoping might have changed while I was away was the lunchtime menu in this place.'

Holland had returned to the Met less than twelve months before, having spent several years in Bedfordshire and more latterly Buckinghamshire, where he'd earned himself a promotion and acquired a fiancée: now his wife, Pippa. He'd come back to be closer to his daughter Chloe, whose mother – Holland's ex-wife – had never approved of his career choice and who had hated Tom Thorne in particular, seemingly for no other reason than Holland had aspired to be like him.

Back then, at least.

Thorne had always thought it was a laudable ambition, but understood why others might disagree. 'Well, you're an idiot, then,' he said now. He stared down at the sorry-looking slice of gammon on his own plate, the congealed egg sitting on top.

'Maybe that lot in Thames Valley were a bit quick to bump you up to inspector.'

'Oh, shut up and stop being an arse,' Tanner said.

'I'm not sure he can do both,' Holland said.

They were sitting at a corner table in the Oak, the pub of convenience if not of choice. As usual, its proximity to both Becke House and Colindale station meant that there were plenty of coppers in there eating lunch. It was far from being the nicest pub in the area and it certainly didn't provide the best food, but it was definitely the least likely to get robbed.

Thorne looked across at a group of uniformed officers sitting at a table on the other side of the room. One of them caught his eye and nodded. Thorne nodded back, remembering what he'd said to Jeremy Walker.

Suits and lids.

He'd been in a black mood most of the morning, largely due to his confrontation with the DCI from Wood Green. The work that had needed doing meant that he'd got his head down and had been largely able to mentally gloss over his rant in Brigstocke's office, but it had been somewhat harder to forget what Walker had said to him outside the toilets afterwards.

That *fuck you* smile when he'd said it.

'So, what are we thinking?' Holland asked.

Thorne did not want either of them to know what was on his mind at that very moment, so was happy enough to discuss progress on the case, such as it was. 'I'm thinking there's bugger all to talk about, but that we should definitely talk about it anyway.' He speared a chip like he was putting it out of its misery. 'Then this becomes a working lunch, and we might be able to claim some of this shit on expenses.'

'Toxicology confirms it was arsenic,' Holland said.

Thorne grunted and ate the chip. He'd never doubted that Hendricks would be right.

'Charita and several others are phone-bashing, chasing down all the likely sources, but I can't see it throwing up anything useful.'

'It won't throw up anything at all,' Thorne said. It was already obvious to him that they were looking for someone who planned and prepared carefully. Wherever the killer had got the poison from, he'd have taken care not to leave a paper trail. 'I'll talk to Russell, but I think we should give up on that.'

'I spoke to the lab that's working on the doughnut box.' Tanner poured the last of her sparkling water into a glass. 'There *are* prints and we'll obviously run them, but we know our man was wearing gloves, so chances are they're from whoever was working in the shop he bought it from.'

'From someone in the Amazon warehouse more likely,' Holland said.

'Right.'

'Something a bit more promising.' Tanner leaned forward and lowered her voice. 'I've been able to establish that Tully and Knowles did know each other.'

Now, Thorne and Holland leaned forward, too.

'They joined up in the same year, same intake, and even if it doesn't prove they were best mates or anything, we now know they were at Hendon together.'

'We should talk to other coppers who were there with them at the same time,' Holland said. 'See if we can find out just how pally they were.'

'D'uh, Dave.' Tanner shook her head. 'I hadn't thought of that.'

'Yeah, that's definitely promising,' Thorne said.

'Promising ... *ish*,' Tanner said. 'It could easily be coincidence, or it could just be that LoveMyBro is someone who *knows* Tully and Knowles trained together. Remember what you said about our man maybe being a copper himself?'

'It was just a suggestion,' Thorne said. It hadn't been an idea that had really taken hold, although maybe that was just because it was so hard to process.

'Yeah, well, if he is, maybe he was at Hendon with both of them.'

'Whatever,' Thorne said. 'It's somewhere to start.' He knew it would never convince the likes of Jeremy Walker that they weren't wasting their time, but what Tanner had discovered was enough to tell Thorne they should keep on wasting it. 'What about Tully?'

'Steve Pallister's been flat out on that,' Holland said. 'No red flags on his arrest record and as far as his service record goes, there's nothing to get worked up about. No disciplinary concerns, no complaints from members of the public, just ... sod all, basically. Christopher Tully was a model copper.'

That in itself was enough to bother Thorne more than slightly, because the only model policemen he'd ever come across were in toyshops.

There was always something.

'What about his domestic set-up?'

'Same thing,' Holland said. 'Nothing to frighten the horses. Happily married with two little lads and a wife who's apparently in bits.'

Thorne knew that in itself meant next to nothing. He'd seen it up close often enough to know that the wives and girlfriends of men who preyed on women were usually oblivious. Women who would live the rest of their lives feeling guilty because they wrongly believed that they should have known.

That said, Thorne saw the expression on Nicola Tanner's face, and he could guess what she was thinking. What if Walker was right and they were looking for dirt where there was none; casting baseless suspicion on a wholly innocent murder victim? What about the grieving widow and the two fatherless children?

In fact, though Thorne could not know it, she was thinking about what she'd seen when she was scrolling through those anti-police message boards with Greg Hobbs. That simple, shocking statement from someone calling herself ButterflyGrrrl.

As Thorne sat back and pushed his half-eaten lunch away, he saw two of the four uniformed officers he'd noticed earlier approaching the table. He'd seen both of them around but was struggling to put names to faces. 'Lads . . . '

The taller of the two PCs hooked his thumbs inside his belt. 'Don't want to disturb you while you're eating, but just wanted to say . . . we know you're working on the poisonings and if you need any extra help with anything at all, you know, donkey work or what have you, give us a shout.'

'Cheers,' Tanner said.

'If you need spare bodies, you've only got to ask.'

'You might be sorry you've offered,' Holland said.

'No chance,' the PC said. 'Anything we can do. We're all Job, aren't we, especially when something like this happens. We're a team, or at least we should be.'

Thorne nodded along with the others, but despite everything he'd seen in Tanner's face – the very reasonable doubt and the concern – something in that anonymous message still nagged at him, still felt as though it was demanding to be taken seriously.

Two peas in a pod.

'We're all on the same side, right?' the PC said.

Thorne watched the two officers step away from the table, saw the thumbs-up before they turned and walked back across the pub.

Thinking: *Some of us.*

TEN

Thorne was relieved that he'd be sleeping in his own bed. He didn't want the vestigial ugliness of his day's mood to spoil Helen's evening and, though the prospect of his own company was not a particularly attractive one, a few hours alone still felt preferable to enduring anyone else's. A few hours' much needed brooding time. There were also the remains of a takeaway from the Bengal Lancer in the fridge, not to mention the welcome opportunity to watch *Match of the Day* without interruption and, even if they were not the main reasons for spending the night in Kentish Town, and despite the fact that Spurs had only managed a goalless draw at home to Aston Villa, Thorne was at least guaranteed an hour or so of enjoyment at the fag-end of an otherwise shitty Saturday.

He had just settled down with a beer in front of the TV and was humming along contentedly with the rousing theme tune when his phone rang.

Teeth gritted, he pressed pause and answered the call.

'What's up with you, then?' Tanner asked.

'What, *now* you mean?'

'No, not now—'

'You're keeping me from my date with Gary Lineker for a start.'

'You were miserable all day. More miserable than normal, I should say, and there's no point keeping it to yourself. You know I'll get it out of you in the end.'

Thorne was in no doubt that she would, that there was any point pretending she'd got it wrong. 'I had a run-in with Jeremy Walker.'

'Yeah, I watched you marching into Russell's office.'

Thorne could have left it there and might well have got away with it, but he saw no good reason to hold back. 'No, after that.' He took a swig of BrewDog and let his head drop back. The conversation was about to veer into troublesome territory and even if he wouldn't – *couldn't* – go too far into it, he suddenly felt the need to share his anger with someone he knew would understand. 'He mentioned Melita.'

'*What?*'

'Not by name, but it was obvious who he was talking about.'

'What did he say?'

'Just some snidey crack about how things don't end well if you're my girlfriend.'

'Shit, Tom . . .'

'Yeah.'

Melita Perera had died nine months earlier, at the hands of the man for whom she had betrayed Thorne; a man who had himself died shortly afterwards, in circumstances which Thorne preferred not to think about very much.

'Walker just wanted me to be aware that he knows, that's all. He was laying down a marker.'

'That he knows ... what, exactly?'

'That she died,' Thorne said. '*How* she died, maybe.' Walker could not know any more than that, Thorne was sure of it. If he did, if anyone did, then someone Thorne and Tanner both knew very well would certainly have been in prison by now. 'Look, it's not a problem. I'm fine. It just took me by surprise, that's all.'

'Well, if you're sure. That you're fine, I mean.'

'I've got a belly full of dhaba lamb, a beer in my hand and *Match of the Day* lined up, if you'll bugger off and let me watch it.'

'I don't know what you're so excited about,' Tanner said. 'Nil-nil, wasn't it? Spurs –Villa.'

'Since when do you look at the football results?'

'Fiona's a Brentford fan.'

'Bloody hell, she's freakier than I thought.'

'I'm going now because you're being a twat, but ring me later if you want to talk.'

'Won't you be tied up with Fiona? Or maybe tied up *by* Fiona ... ?'

''Night, Tom.'

'Thanks for calling, though, Nic. Seriously.' Thorne reached for the remote. 'Thanks for ... caring.'

'Oh, I don't care,' Tanner said. 'I'm just nosy.'

Five minutes later and the teams were just coming out for the Liverpool–Brighton game when the phone rang again.

'Why aren't you watching this?'

'Nic just called me,' Hendricks said.

Thorne sighed and pressed pause again. 'Right ... '

There was a very long silence while the things they'd chosen not to discuss crackled in every breath and were finally swallowed. Their unspoken agreement to leave certain incidents unexplained, certain crimes unsolved.

'You good, mate?' Hendricks asked eventually. 'Nic said you were, but she told me what that prick said. So, there's every chance you're not.'

'Yeah, I was pissed off,' Thorne said. 'I wanted to lamp him, but I didn't want him to see how much he'd wound me up.'

'That sounds very sensible.'

'It does, doesn't it?'

'Which means you're definitely not yourself.'

'Look, it was a big deal ... what happened with Melita. What happened to *him* afterwards. I'd be amazed if every copper in the Met didn't get to hear about it, some version of it anyway, but right now they've got better things to worry about.'

'Like getting done for rape,' Hendricks said.

'Or getting killed for rape.'

'That what you reckon's happening, then?'

Now they were on safer ground, even if *safer* was relative when they were talking about multiple counts of murder. 'It's one possibility, that's all.' Even as he said it, Thorne was remembering what Walker had said to Brigstocke that morning. He was thinking about George Oldfield. 'We've found a connection between Tully and Knowles ... I don't know.'

'Tully might have been the target, that's what you're saying.'

'Maybe. It's still a bit tenuous ... more than a bit.'

'Whoever poisoned those four PCs was only after one of them?'

'Sounds mental, doesn't it?'

'Right, and all the killers we've had dealings with over the years have been so nice and normal.'

There was another sizeable pause after that, the silence finally broken when Hendricks let out a loud belch. 'You're welcome,' he said.

'Am I going to get a chance to watch the football, or what?'

'Fill your boots, mate,' Hendricks said.

Thorne took another slug of beer and picked up the remote. 'You not interested in seeing Arsenal lose again, then?'

'It was a dodgy offside decision from what I've heard. Besides, Liam's on his way over, so I'll be kicking off myself in a minute.'

'If I can stop you there, I really don't need any of your football-slash-shagging analogies.'

'You sure? Might cheer you up a bit.'

'I'd rather be miserable.'

'So, I can't talk about my lethal finishing if I get round the back?'

'Hanging up now, Phil . . .'

Thorne had spoken to Helen when he'd got home, but by the time he'd finally finished watching *Match of the Day* it had gone midnight, so he decided against calling again. He sent a text, letting her know that he'd speak to her in the morning, then went to bed.

He lay awake in the dark, thinking about Tully and Knowles and peas and pods; about Catherine Holloway still hovering somewhere between life and death and Kazia Bobak's partner who had lost both a wife and an unborn child. He thought about the last words spoken to him by a man who was anything but nice or normal.

'You got me, you got me . . . or is it the other way round, Tom?'

When his phone rang again, it felt as though he'd only been asleep for a matter of minutes, but when he picked up the handset he saw that it was just after four a.m. He sat up and spoke quietly so as not to wake Helen, before remembering that he was alone.

'Russell . . . ?'

'We've got a body in Hendon Park,' Brigstocke said. 'Male, multiple stab wounds. I'll meet you there.'

It wasn't totally unheard of for a DCI to attend a crime scene, but it didn't happen very often. 'Something I need to be aware of?'

'He's wearing a uniform.'

ELEVEN

Sunrise was still a couple of hours away, but it wasn't hard to spot where the action was. A trio of powerful arc lights had already been set up and anyone watching from the top floor of one of the houses opposite might have presumed they were seeing a movie being shot. A cordon of uniformed officers at every entrance was there to prevent anyone getting close enough to realise that was not the case and, though there *were* cameras, the footage being shot was purely evidential.

Nothing here was fit for public consumption.

Thorne wound his way through the assembly of police and CSI vehicles, including one squad car that had been coned off, with plastic evidence markers placed at each corner. He showed his ID to a uniform who nodded and swallowed, glassy-eyed. Shivering a little, he hurried into the park, past the café and tennis courts towards the taped-off area. He grabbed a coffee from the urn that had been set up on a trestle table and stooped to pick up a bodysuit and gloves from the box underneath.

There were maybe two dozen people on site already, carrying equipment, taking measurements, doing jobs they had all done countless times but, though Thorne had attended more murder scenes than he could count, something in the way these officers and civilian staff moved and interacted seemed unusual. As far as he was aware, they were dealing with a single victim, but the strangely heightened atmosphere gave it the feel of a major incident. It wasn't panic, not quite that, but it was as though they were dealing with the aftermath of a terrorist attack and were concerned that a second bomb might be about to go off.

'Tom.'

Fastening his bodysuit, Thorne looked up to see Brigstocke walking towards him, lowering the hood of his own. He could not remember the last time he'd seen the DCI looking quite so shaken.

'PC Adam Callaghan.' Brigstocke raised his voice a little, fighting the hum of the generator. 'Pronounced dead twenty minutes ago.'

'Do we know what he was doing here?'

'A woman made a 999 call just after three, said that a man was threatening her in the park, getting aggressive and following her when she tried to leave. Callaghan was four hours into a night shift, having his dinner at a Turkish place just over there, same as always apparently.' Brigstocke pointed back towards the main road. 'He was the nearest officer, so Control instructed him to attend. "Task not ask", right?'

Thorne nodded. There was a time when the call would have gone out requesting the assistance of any officers willing and able to respond. Now, with the GPS functionality in police radios allowing control rooms to pinpoint every officer's location, policy dictated that those who were closest were given no choice.

'He was on his own?'

Brigstocke nodded. 'Single crewing.' Another recent initiative which, for reasons nobody could quite fathom, was officially termed 'safer crewing'.

'In what universe is it *safer*?' Thorne asked. 'I mean, certainly not now, right?'

'I think that particular policy might be about to change.' Brigstocke looked as if he'd bitten into something sour, and turned to spit the bad taste out. 'So, he arrives at the park ten minutes after the emergency call comes in, maintains radio contact for several minutes after that, then suddenly nothing. Another crew gets sent out to see what's happening and they find the body at quarter to four.'

Thorne thought about it. 'If this bloke the woman said was threatening her killed Callaghan, what happened to the woman?'

'No idea.'

'Unless it was the woman that killed him, in which case . . . '

'Maybe there wasn't any bloke in the first place.'

'Just a story to get a police officer out here,' Thorne said.

'We could stand around all night speculating, but I haven't had a chance to listen to the 999 call yet. So . . . '

'Bodycam?'

'Yep, still on him, so we can look at that as soon as we're done here.'

Brigstocke turned to stare towards the body, now partially obscured by those working to ascertain how it came to be there. 'I'd better get back,' he said. 'Try and get ahead of this before the news gets out and everything goes stupid. I'll see you in a couple of hours.'

Thorne watched Brigstocke stride away, fighting to tear his bodysuit off as if the material was burning him, then walked towards the lights and ducked beneath the tape.

He couldn't help but glance around as he got closer.

Waiting for that other bomb to go off.

The body of Adam Callaghan was splayed out on a dirty bed of mulch and black earth, ten feet or so into the trees. His right leg was raised and flopping, suspended across a dead branch. One arm lay across his face, while the other stretched out to the side as though grasping for the hat which lay just beyond its reach on the ground.

The arc lamps picked out every streak of mud on his stab vest and the cracked screen of his radio. They lit up the blood, which pooled around his collar and had already begun to soak into the fallen leaves at one side of his neck.

A CSI was taking pictures of what looked like footprints in the mud as Thorne squatted down next to the figure murmuring into a hand-held recorder. He raised his head and stared into the darkness beyond the lights while he waited for Hendricks to finish.

'So ... ?'

'Well, VAR's ruining football and Brighton's centre-half is seriously fit, but I'm guessing you want to know about the body.'

Thorne just nodded. He understood that Hendricks was obliged to make the tasteless joke, to clutch at that straw, but he could tell that his friend's heart was not really in it this time. 'Anything you haven't already told Russell?'

'I don't think so. Two, maybe three stab wounds ... *here.*' He placed two fingers gently against one side of his throat and then the other. 'Stab vests are all well and good until someone sticks a knife in your throat. No defence wounds as far as I can see, which would suggest he didn't see what was coming, but I'll know a bit more once I've got him laid out and we can wash all the blood and muck off him.' Hendricks reached across to delicately pick away a leaf fragment caught in Adam Callaghan's hair. 'He's been dead about an hour, but you already know that.'

'Yeah.' To be fair, they knew rather more than they usually did at this stage of the game. 'Cheers, Phil.'

'I'll call you when I'm done,' Hendricks said.

Thorne stood up, snapped off his gloves and walked back the way he had come, clambering out of his bodysuit as he went and stuffing it into one of the bins by the café. At the exit, the same officer who had checked his ID stepped across before Thorne had a chance to turn towards his car.

'The fuck's going on?'

Thorne stared at the PC, whose badge identified him as M. Healey. He was mid-thirties and stocky, and Thorne could see that he was fizzing with adrenalin. It might just have been the understandable buzz of the crime scene, but it looked rather more like fear. 'I wish I knew, mate.'

The officer nodded back into the park. 'I knew Adam a bit. Not well, like, but I knew him.'

'Good lad?'

'He was a top lad.' There were a few seconds of nodding. 'A cocky sod every now and again, but yeah.'

'I'm sorry,' Thorne said.

Healey straightened himself up and tugged down his stab

vest. He touched his radio as though it was some kind of lucky charm. 'So what ... are we all targets now, then?'

Thorne glanced around and saw that several of the other PCs guarding the perimeter were looking expectantly at him. 'It's my job to find whoever's responsible,' he said. 'That's all. I'm not sure panicking is going to help.'

The officer squared his shoulders and jutted out his chin. 'Yeah, well, if there *are* people who fancy coming after us, bring it on.'

'You serious?'

'Some of us have started to think about it, all I'm saying. Every arsehole you nick for speeding, every bloke kicking off outside the pub at chucking out time ... he might be another one with a knife or whatever, decides you're the enemy, thinks you're fair game.' Healey turned to exchange a long look with one of his colleagues standing a few feet away, then turned slowly back to Thorne. 'How else are we supposed to react?'

Thorne looked back at the cluster of uniformed officers gathered around the coned-off squad car which had been driven there by Adam Callaghan. He saw only blank expressions and plumes of breath hanging in the air and wondered how many of them had begun to think the same way.

Would refuse to be fair game.

There were some seriously bad apples in the Met, it would be stupid to pretend otherwise, but the simple fact was that an awful lot more were just idiots. More worryingly, some of those idiots were authorised to carry firearms. Thorne did not know for sure that the murder of Adam Callaghan was connected to that of Christopher Tully and the others, but he was starting to wonder if, as far as catching those responsible went, time might not be on his side.

He turned back to the bullish PC. Healey's eyes were wide, scouring the street for movement, a hand on the butt of his Taser like he was ready for anything.

Thorne was cold and tired and irritable.

'Maybe some of you deserve to be fucking targets,' he said.

TWELVE

'Police. What's your emergency?'

'I'm in Hendon Park, near the tennis courts . . . and there's this man. He started talking to me and I thought he was OK at first, but then it all got a bit weird.'

'Can you tell me your name, love?'

'He was saying things, being dirty, like I was a prostitute or something.'

'It's all right, love, just try to stay calm and tell me—'

'I tried to leave and he wouldn't let me. He tried to grab me, so I had to run. I'm hiding now because I don't know where he's gone. Fuck . . . fuck, I think he's still in the park.'

'So, you're by the tennis courts?'

'Yeah, and there's a café. I'm hiding in the trees, yeah?'

'That's the Queens Road entrance, is that right?'

'You need to send someone, now. You need to get some police here. I'm scared . . . '

'Someone's already on their way, OK? You can stay on the line until an officer gets to you, if you want to—'

'No, I need to move.'

'It might be best if you stay where you are, so the officer can find you—'

'Shit, I can hear someone. It can't be the police already, can it . . .'

'Are you still there, love . . . ?'

Brigstocke hit the button to stop the playback. He leaned away from the computer and turned, eager to hear from those members of the team who were sitting in a semicircle around one of the desks in the incident room. He looked to Thorne first. 'Tom?'

Having left the park a couple of hours earlier, Thorne had gone home to shower and grab something to eat. He'd arrived at the office just after seven, and while dozens of uniforms began a fingertip search of the area where the body was found and went door to door on the surrounding streets, he and the other detectives had been called into the incident room to listen to the 999 call.

'She certainly sounds scared to me,' Thorne said. 'Breathless too, like she'd been running.' He looked to Tanner, Desai and Chall. Nobody seemed to disagree with him. 'If it *was* a set-up, she made a good job of it.'

'We don't know that yet,' Brigstocke said.

'What was she even doing in the park at three in the morning?' Chall asked. 'It's a bit late to be walking a dog or whatever.'

Desai shook her head. 'Does it matter?'

'Anyone hear an accent?' Brigstocke asked.

'Not a strong one,' Thorne said. 'London, though, I reckon.'

'Agreed,' Tanner said.

Brigstocke stood up. 'Right, well, let's hope we can get a bit more from Callaghan's bodycam.'

The rest of the team got to their feet and followed the DCI to a different desk, to a computer with a bigger screen. The camera had been removed from Adam Callaghan's stab vest and a civilian technician had already slotted it into a dock on top of the desk. The contents were downloaded quickly, and the technician began scrolling through footage from the first few hours of the dead policeman's shift. He stopped once Callaghan was stepping out of his car at the entrance to Hendon Park.

As they were moving chairs into position and sitting down ready to watch, Thorne leaned across to Brigstocke. 'Where's Dave?'

'He was called out in the HAT car.' Brigstocke waved at the technician to let him know they were ready. 'Likely suicide in Finchley.'

'Likely?'

'More than likely. Some poor sod chucked himself off Dollis Brook viaduct.'

The job of any on-call detective working with the Homicide Assessment Team would simply be to decide if a death was suspicious. In almost all cases it was a straightforward call, especially where suicide was the most obvious cause. Thorne knew that Holland would do his job, but also knew he would have resented the demand on his time, especially now. Whether or not it turned out to be connected to the poisoning of Tully and the others, he would have wanted to be working the Callaghan murder.

'Here we go,' Brigstocke said.

The members of the team leaned forward as the footage began to play.

The final minutes of Police Constable Adam Callaghan's life, as he would have seen it ...

It's predictably jumpy, with Callaghan on the move and in a hurry. The date, time code and officer ID are displayed in the top right-hand corner of the screen, the Metropolitan Police logo in the bottom left.

He walks quickly into the park past the shuttered-up café. The light from the camera illuminates the path, perhaps fifteen feet of it ahead of him as he walks. He keys the radio attached to his shoulder to let control know that he's at the location and looking for the caller. Control acknowledges the message.

There is a rhythmic clatter as his stab vest judders against his chest.

He looks right and left every few steps and the camera shows the tennis courts on one side, a thick cluster of trees to the other.

He stops and shouts, 'Police.' He waits, but there is only the sound of his own breathing, so he moves on again.

Half a minute later he emerges on to a large open space. There is a semicircle of trees across from him, black against the slate sky, and he moves towards it, shouting again as he picks up speed.

A voice shouts back, high-pitched and desperate.

'I'm here ...'

He begins to jog towards the woodland, his breathing heavier, the stab vest bouncing noisily against him as he moves. The picture freezes momentarily and shifts: dark grass, the trees up ahead; a glimpse of his boot as he runs and lights from one or two of the houses beyond the trees.

He mutters, 'Fuck,' as he slips, straightens up and starts to run again.

Half a minute later he is into the trees. He slows and begins to move more cautiously, stepping across large branches and around thick patches of mud. He stops to shout, 'Where are you?' and there is movement away to his right. He turns and the camera catches a flash of silver among the branches.

He walks slowly across to where a figure is crouched behind a large tree, arms wrapped around knees, head bowed. He says, 'Are you injured?'

The head, covered in a thick woollen cap, shakes.

'You reported a man,' he says. 'Is he still nearby?' He spins slowly around to scan the immediate area and when he is facing the figure again, we see that it's a young woman who is now getting slowly to her feet. She's wearing jeans and a silver Puffa jacket. She's breathing heavily.

'It's OK,' he says. 'You're safe now. Are you sure you don't need any medical attention?'

She shakes her head again and steps away from the tree.

He keys his radio. Says, 'I've located the caller and she appears to be unhurt...'

The young woman smiles. 'Unhurt? That's actually quite funny.'

'Sorry, why is it—'

'You seriously don't recognise me, Adam?' She takes another step towards him and removes her cap. 'How about now?'

There are a few seconds of silence before PC Adam

Callaghan's hand is raised quickly towards his camera and the footage abruptly ends.

'Shit,' Brigstocke said.

Thorne had nothing more incisive to add.

While other members of the team exchanged bemused looks, Brigstocke instructed the tech to take the footage back until the screen was filled with a nice clear shot of the woman after she'd removed her cap. Then he stood and leaned back against the desk. 'Well, not ultimately as helpful as it might have been, but we do at least have a decent picture of our prime suspect. We need to get this out there as widely as possible. We need to hit all the papers and every local TV news outlet and make sure it's distributed at every station roll call for the rest of the day.' He turned to look back at the image of the woman in the Puffa jacket. 'Let's find out who she is.'

The team began to disperse, but both Thorne and Brigstocke stayed where they were. Thorne looked across and Brigstocke's expression told him that the DCI was thinking much the same as he was.

Yes, they needed to identify the woman, but it would be the answer to an altogether different question which might ultimately prove to be more valuable.

Why the hell had Adam Callaghan turned off his bodycam?

THIRTEEN

Dave Holland was shown into the living room by a female Family Liaison Officer and watched as the woman who had just become a widow rose from an armchair to greet him.

'No, please,' Holland said, gently urging her to stay seated.

'Let me go and get you some tea or something,' the woman said. 'You look like you could do with warming up.'

'I'm fine, honestly.'

'I'll get it,' the FLO said.

'Oh, all right then.' The woman sat down again. 'Thanks, love.' She nodded her gratitude as the FLO closed the door behind her, then looked across at Holland and produced a shaky smile. 'It's definitely getting colder, isn't it?'

Karen Sadler lived in a semi-detached house in Southgate, only a few hundred yards from where she worked at a local opticians and less than five miles from where her husband had been found, lying broken and bloody beneath the Dollis Brook viaduct several hours before. The body of Daniel Sadler had been discovered on the otherwise deserted B-road that ran beneath the bridge by a still-traumatised driver who had been forced to swerve to avoid running it over.

'I thought it was just a bag of rubbish at first,' he'd told the attending officers.

Holland sat down on a small sofa and formally introduced himself. Karen Sadler was, he guessed, somewhere in her early fifties. A slight, fine-featured Black woman wearing furry slippers and a thick blue dressing gown, the same one – Holland presumed – that she'd been wearing when she'd nervously answered the door to two police officers a couple of hours before. 'I'm sorry for your loss,' Holland said.

The woman nodded quickly and waved a hand as though condolences were the very last thing she needed. 'I'm glad you're here, because we need to talk about all that,' she said. 'Try and clear it up, you know?' She leaned forward and lowered her voice, nodding towards the kitchen. 'She's very nice and everything, but you're obviously . . . *senior*, so I'm hoping we can get to the bottom of things.' She leaned towards Holland. 'I mean, it's obviously been a stupid mistake, because whoever the poor soul was they found under that bridge, it can't be Daniel.'

Holland wasn't thrown, because he'd seen this before. Denial and desperation; a grasping for that last sliver of hope in the face of what was all too dreadfully obvious. He'd witnessed every variety of response from those in the same awful position as Karen Sadler. He'd seen shock transmute into a terrible stillness that bordered on catatonia; rage and hysteria that had resulted in him being slapped more than once as well as getting kicked and spat at. There was no such thing as a normal reaction, no behaviour this situation could prompt for which Holland was unprepared.

'I'm sorry, Mrs Sadler, but there's been no mistake. They—'

'It's Karen.'

'I'm sorry, Karen, but—'

'No,' the woman said. Simple and brooking no argument. 'No.'

'There will need to be a formal identification, obviously, although we can wait until you're ready. But the officers on the scene found your husband's wallet on his body.' Holland knew these were the same two uniformed officers who had then had to deliver the death knock, as though their Sunday morning had not been hideous enough. 'His motorbike was found nearby.'

It might have been the mention of her husband's motorbike, but for whatever reason the tears came then. There was no noise to go with them, no sobs or sniffles. The tears simply ran down her face as she spoke. 'It was his pride and joy, that bike. I mean, he'd always been into his bikes, but he really loved that one and it was brilliant that he'd found a job where he could ride the daft thing all day long, you know?'

Holland didn't know. 'What did your husband do for a living?' He leaned down to the box of tissues on the low table between them and handed them across.

'He was a courier. Delivered all sorts on that bike.' She dabbed at her eyes and looked at Holland. 'Where did you say they found it?'

'It was on Crescent Road,' Holland said. 'In Finchley.'

'That's near this viaduct, then, is it?'

'It's not far.'

'So, how did he . . .'

It was a single branch line, carrying tube trains between Finchley Central station and Mill Hill East. There was an eight-feet-high metal fence just yards from where Daniel Sadler had parked his bike. Once he'd climbed over that, he'd have needed to clamber up a grass bank, then walk the hundred metres or so along the tracks until he reached the viaduct which, at sixty feet, was the highest point on the whole network. At that time of the morning there would have been no passing trains to spot him and nobody to alert anyone.

Holland knew how much effort and determination it would have taken because he'd made the journey himself before coming to Karen Sadler's house; scaling that fence and climbing up that steep, muddy bank to get to the tracks. If the woman had spotted the nasty-looking graze on his palm or the stains on his trousers she hadn't mentioned them.

'He just walked along the line,' Holland said.

'It still doesn't make any sense.' Now, the crying had taken hold, her words spluttered out between sobs. 'We'd been talking about a few days away somewhere, a bit of winter sun or whatever. He'd been looking at places online and he was excited about it, and you don't do that if you're planning to ...' She balled up a handful of tissues and pressed them to her face. 'You tell me if that makes sense.'

Holland couldn't, because it didn't, but he knew very well that sense, or what most people thought of as sense, didn't come into it if the balance of someone's mind was sufficiently disturbed. Yes, it seemed bizarre that anyone could take their own life when they were so clearly planning ahead, when they had an outing to the theatre underlined in their diary or dinner booked at a nice restaurant. Why on earth would someone book a plane ticket to Barbados for Monday and then kill themselves on Sunday night?

Because they did. It was as simple as that. They just did.

'I can't,' Holland said. 'I'm sorry.' He waited until the sobbing had eased a little. 'How did he seem the last time you saw him?'

'He seemed fine. Just ... himself, you know, but I was half asleep to be honest, because this would have been three o'clock in the morning. I woke up and there he was out of bed, getting dressed.'

'Did he say where he was going?'

'Well ... we know where he was going, don't we?'

Holland nodded, thinking about Daniel Sadler trudging along those tracks in the dark towards the viaduct. 'Of course, I'm sorry. What did he tell you, though?'

'He just said he had to meet someone. That it was some work thing and that it was important.'

'Had he ever had a work thing at that time in the morning before?'

'No, never. I mean, sometimes he worked until the early hours, got in after I'd gone to bed, but he'd never gone *out* at that time. I suppose I should have asked him about it, but like I said I was half asleep. He told me he wouldn't be very long, so I wasn't to worry. Then he gave me a kiss and told me to go back to sleep. I must have gone straight off again, because I don't even remember hearing the front door shut or his bike revving up ... '

Holland watched her for a few moments, knowing that now she was remembering that last kiss; that she would always remember it, lying awake and seeing his face and thinking about what it had meant. That her husband had been kissing her goodbye.

There were things that could never be forgotten.

Some memories that bled and would never stop.

'How long were the two of you married, Karen?' he asked.

That shaky smile appeared again. 'Feels like ages, but it's only been ten years ... eleven in a couple of months. Second time round for both of us, you see. Daniel's got a couple of kids from his first marriage, and I've got a grown-up son, but everyone gets on and mucks in. All round here for Christmas ... well, every other year, anyway.'

'Sounds nice,' Holland said.

'It is.' The smile vanished and Karen's face crumpled. 'It *was* ...'

Holland stood up. 'Why don't I see how she's getting on with that tea?'

Karen Sadler was already turning to reach behind her, leaning to lift a framed photograph off the window ledge. She held it out for Holland to take. 'See?'

Daniel Sadler standing next to his motorbike, posing proudly in full leathers with a crash helmet under his arm and grinning like an idiot.

'Daniel was happy,' she said. 'Perfectly happy. I know he was. We had our ups and downs, course we did, because everybody does. But he loved his job and he doted on his kids and on me, and ... we had a good life.'

The door opened and the FLO reappeared, bearing a tray. 'I didn't know how everyone wanted it,' she said, 'so I brought milk and sugar.'

'Thanks,' Holland said.

Karen Sadler did not seem remotely interested in tea. She reached to take the photograph back and stared down at it. 'A good life.'

FOURTEEN

The man who, in certain circles, called himself LoveMyBro sat down at his computer and logged on. The bedroom was a decent size, even if – the tiny bathroom aside – it was the *only* room, but when he'd rented the flat, in a name that was no more real than his online alias, he'd known it would do the job. He didn't need any more space, besides which his benefit payments wouldn't stretch to anywhere with a higher rent.

He'd had some savings back when he'd started, but they'd all gone on equipment over the last year or so and that was fine, because he'd needed it. He looked at the array of screens and scanners set up on his desk, the lights on the shiny black computer towers pulsing on either side, and he didn't regret a single purchase.

It was money well spent.

There had been one or two other miscellaneous costs, of course – certain niche chemical ingredients that hadn't come cheap, as well as other, rather more basic bits and bobs – but the tech stuff was always going to be core to the mission. In the last few months, a lot of his time had actually been taken up by doing nothing more high-tech than poring over court records and newspaper stories, though he was able to do at least some of that sitting in his car. He'd spent quite a lot of time in his car, because when he wasn't gathering the necessary evidence he was parked up and staring at the front of numerous cop shops, carefully studying the comings and goings of various boys in blue and taking copious notes. Yes, it was donkey work, but it had needed doing. Most importantly, it had paid off, because all that information had eventually been transformed into detailed spreadsheets which had been the basis of everything in the end, and it was those hours in front of a screen, seeing it all come together, that he enjoyed the most.

Using one of his many disposable operating systems, all activity hidden by a Virtual Private Network that was not commercially available, he opened the Tor browser ...

Getting to the right spot always felt a bit like finding a hidden corridor in some big old house in the woods that only a few people even knew was there. You went in through the main entrance, but then you had to move between floors and navigate a series of interconnecting passageways before getting to a door that didn't even look like a door. That got you into one room, but there was always a secret way out of that room into another and another, each one smaller and darker than the last, until you eventually found yourself where you needed to be.

The quiet place he'd created, where the two of them could meet and talk.

<<You didn't seem very happy afterwards. I'm a bit confused.>>

<< . . . >>

<<It went exactly the way you wanted, didn't it? The way I thought you wanted, anyway. Talk to me . . .>>

<< . . . >>

He checked his watch to make sure he'd got the time right. They'd agreed to leave it a while before catching up and that had turned out to be very sensible. Buzzing as he was afterwards, he'd fallen into bed as soon as he'd got back from the park and had spent the next eight hours dead to the world.

Not as dead as some, obviously.

<<Hellooooo . . . ??>>

<< . . . >>

She'd definitely been a bit weird with him right at the end, no question. It wasn't like he'd been expecting a high-five or that they'd go somewhere to open a bottle or anything, but he'd thought she'd be happier. As it was, she couldn't wait to get away. Maybe she hadn't understood, but as far as he was concerned it had all been pretty bloody obvious.

What had she thought the set-up in the park was all about?

She certainly wasn't stupid and all along she'd seemed every bit keen as he was, every bit as up for it.

> <<What did I do? I don't understand.>>

> <<...>>

> <<I mean, his face was a picture, didn't you reckon? His mouth hanging open like that because he knew he was fucked.>>

> <<...>>

He knew that nobody was going to be as committed to all this as he was or would do quite so much to put things right, but it wasn't like she didn't have a serious bloody grievance. Not as much as him, obviously, but she definitely had skin in the game.

> <<Come on, I can't piss about waiting for you.>>

He sat back and stared at the winking cursor and told himself that if he never spoke to her again it wouldn't be the end of the world. This had never been about making friends. It was about finding allies, that was all. Hooking up with those who felt broadly the same as he did, whatever their reason. It was a shame, because she was nice and her pain had sat together nicely with his, but it couldn't be helped. Fighting a campaign like this, there would always be losses on both sides.

He'd give her ten more minutes, then knock it on the head. He had stuff to do.

FIFTEEN

Thorne had not found the opportunity to exchange more than a few words with Dave Holland after he'd got to the office at lunchtime, so via a series of short and snappy text messages they'd arranged to get together at going home time; to catch up over a drink which, by then, they both knew would be seriously needed. Tanner was only too happy to tag along.

'Not the Oak, though,' Thorne had said. 'Somewhere there's a chance we might be the only people in the room with warrant cards.'

They drove in separate cars to the Stag in Belsize Park. It was a half-hour ride away, but was at least in the right direction: south towards Kentish Town, to Holland's place in Clerkenwell and Tanner's in Hammersmith. It was too cold to sit upstairs on the smart roof terrace, so they nabbed a table in the bar, sitting beneath a blackboard displaying a tempting range of food on one side and an extensive wine and cocktail menu on the other.

'This is a cut above,' Thorne said. He touched his pint of Guinness to Holland's 'bold and hoppy' IPA then to Tanner's wine glass. 'Closest you get to a cocktail in the Oak is lager and lime.'

They drank in silence for a minute or two, taking in their surroundings while listening to snippets of conversation from the nearest of their fellow drinkers. Thorne reckoned that the three of them had upped the average age of the customers considerably and if there *were* any coppers in the place, they were all deep undercover as models and media types. The music wasn't too bad, though: Tyler Childers giving way to Margo Price. It wasn't Hank or Johnny, but you couldn't have everything.

Thorne opened his mouth to speak but could do no more than stifle a yawn.

'Yeah, me too,' Tanner said.

It was just after nine o'clock and they'd all been working for seventeen hours straight.

'She wasn't alone,' Thorne said. 'The woman in the park.'

'The bootprints, right?' Holland sipped his drink. 'It's not a lot.'

'Never said it was.'

'All sorts of people could have been tramping about in those trees,' Tanner said.

'Not that recently, though. They look pretty fresh to me and they were very close to Callaghan's body . . . a mess of them, you know?'

Holland considered it. 'Like Callaghan and whoever was wearing the boots were struggling.'

'Wasn't much of a struggle,' Thorne said. 'Not once that knife was in his neck.'

The prints, discovered and photographed by CSIs at the scene, were more or less the only evidence of any sort that might eventually prove useful. The fingertip search had turned up nothing of interest, the door to door had been no more productive and the murder weapon – which Hendricks had identified as a seven- or eight-inch serrated kitchen knife – had not been helpfully disposed of in any nearby drain or litter bin. The woman they'd seen on Callaghan's bodycam had been picked up on CCTV just a few minutes after his body had been discovered – that silver Puffa jacket moving quickly along Queens Road towards Hendon Central station – but had not been seen again after that.

'She said there was a man in the park when she made the 999 call.'

'Just maybe not a man she was scared of,' Tanner said. 'More like a man she was working with.'

'I think that's a strong possibility,' Thorne yawned again. 'Easy enough for him to leave the park a different way to her. The south end, maybe. He picks up a car he's left somewhere he knows there's no CCTV and he's away up the North Circular in five minutes.'

Tanner nodded as she took a drink.

'Which one of them killed Callaghan, though?'

'Maybe she was the one wearing those boots,' Holland said.

Thorne closed his eyes while he considered that, and it wasn't until a minute or so later that he opened them again when a glass clattered loudly on a nearby table. Tanner was grinning at him. 'Thought you'd gone off,' she said.

He shook his head fast and widened his eyes, decided that a little more Guinness couldn't possibly make him any more tired than he already was, then nodded across at Holland. 'How did your suicide go?'

'The wife's refusing to believe he killed himself,' Holland said. 'Doesn't want to believe it, whatever.'

'Sounds pretty standard,' Tanner said.

'Yeah, I know, but all the same there's one or two things bothering me about it. For a kick-off, I know the drop from that viaduct is a pretty sure-fire way to get the job done, but it isn't an easy spot to get to and I know because I did it myself.' He held up his hand to show the graze, which was redder than it was before and had begun to swell. 'I mean, surely there are other ways to do it.'

'No point bringing logic into this,' Tanner said. 'People spend hours getting trains and buses to Beachy Head even when they've got cabinets full of tablets at home.'

'Granted, but who the hell goes to bed for a couple of hours, then gets up to top themselves?' He waved away Tanner's response before she could make it. 'Yeah, I know suicides can do all manner of odd stuff ... but he told his wife he had to go out for a work thing, which is weird enough in itself at that time because nothing like that had ever happened before, on top of which we can't find his phone.'

'Why's that a problem?' Thorne asked.

'Well, it's *not* necessarily. Except it wasn't on his body and it's strange that we can't find it anywhere else because his wife says he always had it on him. I mean, what if he *did* get a call telling him he needed to be somewhere and whoever made that call doesn't want there to be a record of it?'

'Talk to his mobile provider,' Thorne said.

'Already on it,' Holland said. 'Well, I've put the request in, but we all know what an arse-ache that is. It's most likely a waste of time anyway.'

'So, what are you going to do?' Thorne asked.

Holland stared into his beer. 'I don't know ... maybe I should just sign it off as done and dusted and get back to these murders.'

'I tell you what you *should* do.' Tanner grabbed Holland's wrist, brought it towards her and studied his palm. 'You need to get that hand looked at.'

Fifteen minutes later they were walking down Fleet Road towards their cars when Tanner took a call from Russell Brigstocke.

Thorne and Holland strained to listen over the noise of passing traffic, tightening their jackets against the cold. They heard Tanner say, 'When?' and watched her expression become serious. When the call had ended, they looked at each other, fearing the worst.

'A woman walked into a station in Clapham an hour ago and said she was there when Adam Callaghan was killed.' Tanner slipped her phone back into her bag. 'She was wearing a silver Puffa jacket.'

'Fuck,' Holland said. 'So ... '

'Said she was there?' Thorne waited. 'That's all?'

'Russell sent the footage across to make sure and it's definitely the woman we saw on the bodycam.'

'Are they bringing her to us or are we going down there?' Thorne asked.

'She's coming to us,' Tanner said. 'First thing tomorrow. Russell said she's not going anywhere, plus a night in the cells won't do her any harm, so it can wait until the morning. He said he'd been thinking about heading over there himself then thought better of it, because he's dead on his feet, same as the rest of us.'

'Some sleep *would* be nice,' Holland said.

Thorne couldn't argue, thinking that if this was the break in the case it sounded like, they might actually get some.

SIXTEEN

Karen knew it would be freezing in the garage, because they kept bottles of water and Diet Coke and stuff in there and when they brought them into the house it was like they'd been in the fridge, even when it wasn't as cold outside as it was now. So she was wearing gloves, as well as thermals underneath her joggers and a thick, padded jacket. She had one of Daniel's woolly Chelsea hats on and two pairs of socks.

She stepped in through the side door from the dark of the garden and reached for the switch. The strip-light immediately began to flicker and she remembered that Daniel had promised to replace it. She knew that he would have done, because he was always good about that stuff. He wasn't lazy like a lot of men or happy just to say whatever would shut her up. If he said he'd do something, or get whatever needing fixing fixed, he'd do it.

She smiled, thinking that she *might* have had to remind him . . .

The strip-light came on properly just then, and the smile broadened because it was like he was winking or wagging a finger at her.

You cheeky sod!

She walked across to where the little stepladder was hanging up. All the tools were displayed on the wall around it, their outlines drawn around them so everything got put back exactly where it was supposed to. There was a little plastic cabinet underneath them with the drawers labelled for all his screws and nails and washers and what have you. She'd always reckoned he was a bit OCD or whatever the name for it was, but he wouldn't have it.

It's called being organised.

She reached to get the stepladder down. It wasn't even a proper ladder really, just one of those fold-out things with three steps which they used if paintwork needed touching up or they were getting bits and pieces down from the top cupboards in the kitchen. Tupperware and all that.

She unfolded it, dusted off the top step and sat down.

She stared at Daniel's motorbike.

There was mud on the wheels and a bit more spattered up the sides and she knew how much he would have hated that. Obviously it got dirty all the time, because he was delivering stuff around town in all weathers, but he always cleaned it whenever he'd finished work. Got the jet-washer out and sprayed all the muck off.

The police had delivered it back a few hours before. She'd watched them bringing it home from the front window, seen it rattling down the road on a low-loader. They'd brought Daniel's crash helmet back with them too. He'd left it sitting on the saddle, by all accounts, so as soon as she'd wiped the dirt off the visor and given it a bit of a polish, that's where she'd asked them to place it, once they'd wheeled the bike into the garage.

She stood up, walked across and straightened the helmet for him.

You know, me too bloody well, love . . .

Back in the house they'd be wondering what the hell she was doing, most likely, but Karen didn't really care. Her son had come over straight away of course and Daniel's eldest girl a little bit later, but they could look after each other and, to be honest, she wanted to be on her own, just for a bit anyway. She knew there'd be lots of things to organise, all the horrible jobs, and she'd be grateful for the kids' help with that because she couldn't think straight. Didn't know if she'd ever think straight again.

She took off one of her gloves and stroked the saddle.

The leather was cold, but it was nice to feel the cracks and the dips in it.

She put the glove back on and stood there for a minute or two with her eyes closed, just taking in the smell of it. The oil and whatever else, because it was also the smell of him a lot of the time. Then she turned to walk slowly back to the stepladder and sat down again.

She still wasn't having it, the idea that he'd done it to himself. She hadn't said as much to that detective because it felt sort of selfish, but the fact was Daniel never would have done that to *her*. Simple as that, really.

He wouldn't have left her alone.

Course not, because you couldn't cope without me.

It was true all the same, and even though the policeman had been very kind, she knew he'd been thinking that she was being a bit daft. That she was bound to think he'd never have done what they said he did, because anyone's wife would, wouldn't they? Anyone's other half.

There was a knock, and her son Nathan put his head round the door.

'You all right, Mum? You must be freezing in here.'

She nodded and waited and, once he'd closed the door again, she sat back to look at the bike for a while. She wrapped her arms around herself, thinking that her husband had loved his stinky, stupidly noisy 'hog' almost as much as he'd loved her. There was another smile, there and gone, when she thought that there probably hadn't been very much in it and it was a good job she'd never actually asked him the question.

She'd forgotten to bring any tissues with her which was a bit stupid, but she was all over the place to be fair, and the gloves didn't help much because they weren't very absorbent, so in the end she stopped bothering to wipe the tears away.

Come on, love. Don't be so daft . . .

She just sat there and wept and stared at what there was left of him.

SEVENTEEN

According to the ID she'd produced at Clapham Town station the day before, Emily Mead was twenty-seven years old, but the woman sitting opposite Thorne and Tanner in the interview room at Colindale could easily have been a good few years older than that.

Not that people in her situation ever appeared at their best.

It might just have been that she was make-up free and exhausted after a sleepless night in the cells. It could have been down to the harsh overhead lighting, which was rarely flattering. Or perhaps something else entirely had taken the colour from her face, hollowed out her cheeks and produced those premature lines around her mouth and blue-black shadows beneath her eyes.

It might just have been her life.

Whatever had derailed it.

Tanner stared across the table as she recited the caution and reminded the suspect that she had waived her right to a solicitor and that the interview was being recorded. The young woman did not raise her head. The fingers of one hand beat out a nervous tattoo against the steel tabletop while those on the other moved back and forth through her short, straw-coloured hair.

'Do you understand?' Tanner asked.

Emily Mead's head stayed down, but she eventually mumbled a 'Yes'.

Since arriving at the station first thing, she had barely spoken, aside from repeating what she had told the officers in Clapham, stating again that she had 'been there when Adam Callaghan was killed'. This time, though, she had been keen to add a somewhat crucial caveat.

'But it wasn't me that killed him. I didn't know that was going to happen.'

'Tell us about the man in the park, Emily.' Thorne waited. 'When you made the emergency call you said a man was harassing you, but that's not what was happening, was it?'

She shook her head.

'For the tape, please.'

'No, it wasn't.'

'So, who was this man?'

'I don't know his name.' Her voice was low and quiet, every bit as colourless as her face. 'I'd never even met him until the other night.'

'How did you know him?' Tanner asked.

'It was all online,' she said. 'This secret group called Roasting the Pork.'

'To be clear ... that's an anti-police message board on the Dark Web, correct?'

'Yeah ... that one. He messaged me so that we could talk privately.'

'What did you talk about?' Thorne asked.

'What do you think?'

'Specifically.'

It took her a few moments. 'He really hates you lot, I mean, properly hates all of you.' She had begun to raise her head, but just for a few seconds at a time. 'I mean, nobody in that group likes the police very much, but he's serious about it. Like he's obsessed, you know?'

'Are we talking now about the individual who uses the online alias LoveMyBro?' Based on the message Tanner had seen, it seemed like a reasonable assumption.

Emily nodded. 'Yeah, that's him. Once we started talking, he just kept banging on about making you pay, about coppers getting what they deserved after what they'd done.'

'And what was it exactly he said they'd done?' Tanner exchanged a look with Thorne. 'That *we'd* done?'

'He never told me.'

'He just wanted you to help him.'

'Yeah, obviously that's what was really going on, but I didn't know that then, did I? It was supposed to be all about him helping me.'

'Helping you with what?' Tanner asked. She waited for the woman to raise her head again. 'Why did you need his help?'

She asked again, but Emily Mead's head stayed down.

'OK, let's talk in more detail about what happened in the early hours of yesterday morning,' Thorne said. 'You made the 999 call to lure Adam Callaghan to the park, is that right?'

'Yeah . . .'

Thorne's mobile vibrated. A message from Russell Brigstocke who was watching via video link from the floor above.

How did they know it would be Callaghan?

'Emily . . . how could you or the man you were with be sure that it would be PC Callaghan who would attend?'

Now, the woman looked up, a little more animated. 'He knows all that stuff. He studies these coppers for weeks, their shift patterns or whatever. He knew Callaghan was on nights, where he ate when he was on that shift and exactly what time he'd be there. He knew it would be him, and if anything did go wrong and for some reason it wasn't him, he just told me to blag my way out of it and we'd try again another time.'

Thorne glanced towards the camera. 'Right. So you met this man in Hendon Park and then you made the call.'

'Well, we met up before that, before I called 999.'

'Where was that?'

'Still in the park, but at the other end. Not the bit where . . . Callaghan was killed. There's this wooden footbridge near the railway line and we just sat there for half an hour, smoking fags while he talked me through it all. What was going to happen. Well . . . what I thought was going to happen. That was before I knew what he'd done, though, you need to know that.'

'What he'd done?' Tanner said.

'I had no idea it was him—'

'What did he do?' Thorne asked.

'I really didn't know, I swear I didn't.' She looked in desperation from Thorne to Tanner and back again, a film of tears across her eyes as her breathing began to quicken. 'I didn't know he was the one who poisoned those coppers.'

Thorne looked at Tanner, then raised his eyes to the camera. The fact that the three dead officers had been poisoned was one they had not yet released to the press.

Emily clocked their reaction and began nodding. 'Right, yeah ... that was him. That arsehole fed arsenic to four coppers and there was only one he was actually bothered about.'

'Are you talking about Christopher Tully?' Tanner asked.

'Yeah, Tully.'

'Wait a second.' Thorne pushed his chair back. 'Interview suspended at ... 9.17 a.m.' He stood up and walked towards the door, turning back to talk to Tanner. 'Give me two minutes.'

Holland, who had been watching alongside Brigstocke, came haring along the corridor looking every bit as confused as Tanner had been when Thorne had left the interview room. He held out his arms, revealing a dressing taped across his palm.

'What's going on? You were just about to get—'

'I'll still get it,' Thorne said. 'But we need to send a small team of officers down to that footbridge she was talking about, pronto.'

Holland hesitated, trying to work it out.

'She said they were smoking, right? When they met up.'

'Cigarette ends,' Holland said, getting it. 'Good shout.'

'We know he's careful, don't we? No prints or DNA on anything up to now and maybe that's because he's in the system.'

'Makes sense.'

'He doesn't know Emily Mead's here, though, does he? He doesn't know she's told us about their pre-murder chit-chat at that footbridge. As far as he's concerned, nobody would know he was ever there, so ... '

'No reason for him to be careful with his butts.'

'That's the theory,' Thorne said.

'Worth a try,' Holland said.

'I mean, I haven't given it much thought, and it might be too late already if there were cleaners down there yesterday.'

'On a Sunday?'

Thorne nodded, relieved and delighted that the day of rest enjoyed by employees of Hendon council's Parks Maintenance Department might yet give them a chance. 'Let's get every fag end anywhere near that footbridge collected up and sent straight to the lab on an urgent.' He turned back towards the interview room. 'See if we get lucky.'

Emily Mead had calmed down a little by the time Thorne had sat down again, let Tanner know that he'd fill her in later and the interview was recommenced.

'You've told us that this man confessed to the murder of three police officers and the attempted murder of another,' Thorne said. 'Fed them arsenic, that's what you said.'

'Yeah, well, that's what he said. He was sort of bragging about it.'

'When was this, Emily?'

She looked a little confused. 'When . . . ?'

'When did you know that this man you met online and were now hanging around in the park with in the early hours of the morning had already killed three police officers?'

She was beginning to look uncomfortable again. 'It was after he'd killed Adam Callaghan, and like I've already told you, I had no idea that was going to happen.'

'Yes, you've made that very clear,' Tanner said.

Thorne's phone buzzed with another message from upstairs:

How did he know where those officers were going to be? The poisonings.

Thorne showed the message to Tanner and asked the question. 'This man who'd confessed to poisoning the police officers, did he tell you anything about how he'd planned it?'

Emily shook her head.

'They were part of a highly confidential operation,' Tanner said. 'So, how did he know those officers would be there?'

'I've got no idea,' Emily said. 'He knows all sorts of stuff, though, I told you. He's got special computer programs or whatever; he's got fancy equipment.'

'A scanner?'

'I don't know. Maybe.'

'OK, let's move on,' Thorne said. 'Talk us through what happened after PC Callaghan arrived in response to your emergency call.'

Emily gave a small nod. She sat up a little straighter and took a few deep breaths. 'He was hiding in the trees,' she said. 'The man I was waiting there with. Callaghan was calling out as he got closer, trying to find out where I was, and as soon as I started shouting back the man got out of the way.' She stared at Tanner, helpless. 'He was just there to protect me, that's what he said, which was fine because I could never have gone there on my own, except I didn't even know he had a knife. He told me he was there to make sure nothing bad happened.'

'Something bad did happen,' Thorne said. 'I'm fairly sure that's how Adam Callaghan's family would see it, anyway.'

'Go on, Emily,' Tanner said.

'When PC Callaghan was ... close to me, the other man came out of the trees. He came charging out suddenly, from behind, you know? Callaghan heard the noise and turned round, but it was too late, because the bloke already had the knife in his hand.' She swallowed hard and began to tremble a little, staring past Thorne and Tanner, her gaze fixed on the wall behind them. 'I would have started running then... I know I *should* have, but I couldn't really move. I just stood there and watched as he stabbed him and stabbed him and Callaghan was lying on the ground and he made this noise, like when someone's gargling or whatever ... and then he wasn't making any noise at all.'

Thorne stared across at Emily Mead, remembering what he'd seen on the bodycam footage the day before. Looking haggard and visibly distressed, she was no more than a shade of the young woman he'd watched on that screen, rising slowly from behind a tree, all bundled up in silver like she was a special surprise. Cocky even, as she'd pulled off her cap and stepped towards Adam Callaghan. 'What happened then?' he asked.

She shook her head as though she still couldn't quite believe it. 'It was like he was waiting for me to say *thank you* or something. *Well done*, maybe. He just hung around, wiping his knife, and then he saw the look on my face and he was making out he was disappointed. Like, what was wrong with me? I got a bit hysterical and I just kept asking him what the hell that was, what he'd just done.'

'What did he say?' Thorne waited, watching her fingers as they tapped against the table, the fingers bitten down to the quick. 'Emily...?'

'He asked me if I was stupid and hadn't I known that was the plan all along. I told him no way did I think that was the plan and what made him think I'd ever be happy about him killing someone. That was when he told me that he'd already killed three coppers. That it might even be four, because one of them was in a coma. He started talking about this one named Tully, who was the one he really had it in for, but I wasn't paying much attention because by then I knew I had to get out of there. I thought when I legged it that he'd try and stop me because of what I'd seen him do, but he didn't seem all that bothered. He just said "See you then" or something like that and carried on wiping the blood off his knife.'

'You said you didn't know that was the plan,' Thorne said. 'To kill PC Callaghan.'

'Of course I bloody didn't.'

'So what did you think the plan was?'

She blinked. 'I didn't—'

'Why were you there at all?'

'I just wanted ...' She hesitated, her breathing quick and ragged. 'I needed to ...'

'What did you need?'

'To *confront* him.' She spat the word out, then immediately sank back into herself. She hunched slowly over in the chair and her voice dropped to a whisper. 'I just wanted to confront him, that's all.'

Thorne looked at Tanner, who picked up the cue, and when she asked the question, she spoke almost as softly as Emily Mead. 'About what, Emily?'

They waited.

After a few seconds, Thorne repeated the question, and when it got no response he changed tack. 'How did you and this man communicate with each other?'

'It's all done online,' she said, eventually. 'There's this place he set up on the Dark Web where we can message.'

'How do you know about all that stuff, about accessing those sites?'

'Someone showed me,' she said. 'A drug dealer I used to

know.' She looked up at Thorne and there was a glimpse of defiance suddenly. 'I went through a hard time a while back, OK?'

'We don't need to know about that stuff,' Tanner said.

Thorne leaned forward. 'Your description of events after PC Callaghan arrived in the park was very helpful,' he said. 'The circumstances of his death, I mean. Thank you. We're well aware just how difficult that must have been.' The young woman was about to speak, but Thorne didn't give her the chance. 'Only it wasn't straight after he arrived, not quite.'

'What do you mean? Callaghan came to the park and—'

'Something happened before the man appeared with the knife, and I know that because I've seen it on PC Callaghan's bodycam.' Thorne let that sink in, but, despite his best efforts, the woman would not meet his eyes. 'What that camera captured before he turned it off.'

'Nothing happened.'

'There was a moment between you and him.'

'No.'

'We saw it.'

'I don't know what you're on about.'

'There's no reason to be scared,' Tanner said.

'I'm not scared.'

'What did you think was funny?' Thorne asked. 'When he said you were unhurt.'

Emily Mead shook her head again.

'You seemed to find that funny for some reason.'

She turned her head away and began to moan softly.

'The plan was to confront PC Callaghan,' Thorne said. 'You just told us that, but you'd be helping us a great deal if you told us what you wanted to confront him about.' Thorne and Tanner exchanged a glance while they waited. 'You knew him, didn't you, Emily?'

Now, she looked at him, and suddenly her eyes were filled with tears again. She scrunched them closed, shaking her head more violently. 'I just wanted him to put his hand up to it. To ... confess.' She could barely get the words out now, spluttering them as the snivels became sobs. 'I wanted him to admit what he did and turn himself in.'

'What did he do, Emily? You need to tell us.'

She raised an arm to wipe away the tears and snot on her sleeve, then brought both her arms up to cradle her head before they slid slowly down to cover her face and muffle the sound of her keening.

That was when Tanner spotted the small tattoo, delicately inked in red, blue and green on the inside of the young woman's wrist.

A butterfly.

When she understood exactly why Adam Callaghan had turned off his bodycam.

She immediately spoke the words necessary to terminate the interview and, though Thorne would not understand why she'd done so until afterwards, he sat and watched her lean across the table towards Emily Mead and reach out her hand.

'It's OK,' Tanner said. 'I know what he did.'

PART TWO

PREVENTING ALL OFFENCES

EIGHTEEN

He still *had* the name he'd been born with, and it was bound to be there on a few official documents, though not on anything current that could lead to him if anyone came looking. He knew how people got traced. He'd picked a different name and had the necessary IDs knocked up so he could get phones and driving licences, benefits and what have you, but there were no bank accounts in his proper name any more, no credit cards, nothing like that.

It wasn't that he thought of himself as LoveMyBro – even if it was that person's life he was living most of the time now – it was more that if he heard anyone shouting his real name on the street, he'd presume it was someone he'd been at school with.

There simply wasn't anyone else left who might use it.

He wasn't kidding himself that he'd ever had loads of mates, but there had been a few once upon a time. They'd backed away one by one after it had happened and he'd started to talk about it. He'd talked about it a lot, he knew that. He thought it was only natural; that talking about such a terrible thing to as many people as possible whenever he got the chance was what anyone in his position would do. The way those around him had reacted, though, you'd have thought he was constantly banging on about chemtrails or the earth being flat or whatever. Like he was one of those conspiracy theory nutbags.

So, friends had gradually melted away, and even though it had been upsetting at the time, now he just thought good riddance.

Now, they'd only get in his way.

His parents had gone too, but he knew exactly who was to blame for that.

He thought about the people he'd lost a fair bit and for obvious reasons, the ones he'd cared about anyway. Now, staring out of the car window into the rainy dark, watching for the man he was waiting on to arrive, it struck him that despite everything he'd been thinking a couple of nights before when she'd ignored his messages, it would be sad if he never heard from ButterflyGrrrl again.

It would be a waste.

They'd suffered in very different ways, of course, but it had all kind of overlapped and he'd thought there was a bond. Something. Even though it was tricky to know what people were really thinking or feeling when you only talked to them online, he'd definitely sensed a connection.

Maybe she just needed a bit of time, some breathing space, whatever. Obviously, *her* mission was done with – thanks to him – but maybe once she'd had a chance to think about it for a while, she might decide to step up and give *him* a hand with things. He reckoned they'd make a good team—

And then, perfectly on cue, the man he was there to have a

look at lumbered into view. Yes, he was carrying a little more timber than was good for him, but he looked fit enough for his age.

He was frankly amazed that any copper lasted long enough in the job for retirement to even be a thing. He certainly wasn't surprised that most of them got the hell out as soon as they'd done their thirty years and, if they'd been stupid enough to join up when they were relatively young, it meant that they'd still have a fair amount of life left ahead of them to enjoy.

At least, some of them would.

Running pubs, wasn't that what a lot of them used to do back in the day once they'd turned in their warrant cards? These days there were websites advertising jobs specifically aimed at ex-coppers. He'd seen them. Jobs as prison officers, or cybersecurity consultants or even private investigators for the ones who still fancied themselves as super-sleuths.

He reckoned a good few just sank like stones or wasted away, which was no less than most of them deserved. A broken marriage, then a few unhappy years lying awake every night, eaten up by guilt and despising themselves. Drinking far too much to blot it all out and occasionally meeting up with former colleagues to talk about the good old days until the inevitable early stroke or heart attack.

He supposed working as a security guard was as good a way as any of killing time while you were waiting for that to happen. Night shifts, especially. Just you and a head full of horrible memories and as many sudokus as you could manage.

The man in the high-vis jacket walked slowly across the street, which was dimly lit and – happily – deserted. He watched him reach for keys as he approached the gates of the builders' yard and was sure he saw the poor bugger's shoulders drop as he fumbled with the padlock.

Was he unhappy? Bless him, was he feeling unfulfilled?

Did he think that sitting in a Portakabin all night and keeping a watchful eye on a few piles of bricks and assorted bags of sand and cement was below him? A comedown for an experienced thief-taker people once looked up to? For someone who had proudly worn the Queen's cloth and a cunt's pointy hat and used to have actual *power*?

LoveMyBro watched the man step into the yard then turn to close the metal gates behind him, and even though he'd be back again the following night to ensure this was a regular routine he could have faith in, he wondered if, when the time came, he might actually be doing him a favour.

The poor, powerless old bugger wouldn't have to dwell on former glories for very much longer.

NINETEEN

There were two unmarked squad cars parked nearby, their occupants with eyes on the entrance to the building. Thorne and Tanner walked past both vehicles on their way to the front door, but took care to show no sign that they recognised any of their fellow officers.

Having rung the bell, they held their IDs to the camera on the entryphone and were buzzed in from the street. They exchanged meaningless pleasantries with the uniformed officer in the lobby, signing in next to their names on a list of approved visitors before being allowed access to the stairs. Two flights up, Thorne and Tanner raised their faces to a second camera, then knocked quietly on a door and waited for the building's only resident to open it.

It was called a 'safe house' but was actually a single-bedroom apartment in a bog-standard block of flats in Edgware. There were eight rooms in the place and, at any one time, these might be housing protected witnesses, vulnerable refugees or victims of domestic violence and people-trafficking. To find this one unoccupied had been a major stroke of luck, as similar properties managed by the UK Protected Persons Service were considerably busier. The Modern Slavery Unit had just brought down a large Romanian gang in Harrow and more than forty young women who'd been forced into sex work had been housed in protected accommodation across three different boroughs.

When she'd begun ringing around, Tanner had, coincidentally, been offered space in a building currently playing host to the man who'd grassed up Nick Cresswell. The former member of Cresswell's firm who would, when the time came, be giving evidence against him.

'I hope it's damp,' Thorne had said when Tanner told him. 'I hope it's got rats.'

Emily Mead just nodded when she opened the door, then immediately turned back inside. Thorne and Tanner followed her through to the small sitting room. A beige carpet and a two-seater sofa Thorne guessed would be described as oatmeal.

'It's nice,' he said.

Tanner nodded, though she'd seen it the day before when she'd dropped Emily off, so already knew how bland and depressing it was.

Emily Mead stood next to the low pine table in the middle of the room and stared around as though this was the first time she'd seen it. 'It's boring as fuck,' she said. 'Clean, though, and I've got tea- and coffee-making facilities.'

'Coffee sounds good,' Tanner said.

Emily walked across to the galley kitchen. 'Instant, obviously.'

'Fine with me,' Thorne said. 'I like instant coffee.'

'What?' Tanner looked horrified, as though he'd just confessed to some unspeakable perversion.

'You're such a snob,' Thorne said. The truth was he drank instant coffee now and again because it's what they'd drunk at home when he was growing up and it reminded him of his parents. The Mellow Bird's his mum had loved, made with hot milk once in a while as a treat. 'Why don't you fire off a strongly worded email to the PPS and insist they supply cafetières?'

'I'll just have tea,' Tanner said.

When Emily had brought the drinks across, she sat down next to Tanner on the sofa. Thorne took a small hardback chair that was leaning against the wall and sat opposite them. The young woman looked a lot better than she had when Thorne had last seen her. She was showered and wearing fresh clothes that had been brought from her home address in Brixton. The silver Puffa jacket was hanging up just inside the door, though Thorne guessed she wouldn't have the chance to wear it for a while.

Not unless she agreed to the proposal they were there to make.

'How're you settling in?' he asked.

'Yeah, fine.'

'Did you sleep OK?' Tanner asked.

Emily shrugged then turned to stare at the wall. 'It's weird not having windows,' she said.

'Trust me, you're not missing much,' Thorne said.

Tanner sipped her tea. 'No, it's not the loveliest view.'

'Unless you like gazing out at scaffolding and the odd skip.' Thorne saw a smile appear and for the first time he got a good look at Emily Mead's teeth, or what was left of them. He remembered the drug problems to which she'd alluded during the interview. Meth, he guessed, or maybe a serious cocaine habit that had led to a poor diet and excessive teeth-grinding.

He sometimes wondered if drug dealers and dentists were in cahoots.

'Are they worried about snipers or something?'

'You don't need to worry about anything,' Tanner said.

Thorne remembered an occasion five or six years before at a safe house in Enfield that *did* have windows, when Kalashnikov-wielding associates of a particularly nasty oligarch had shot the shit out of the place from a passing car, but he decided that now was not the time to share.

'So, what's going to happen?' Emily asked.

'You stay here,' Tanner said. 'That's it. You stay here, where you'll be safe, while we try to catch the man who killed Callaghan and those other officers.'

'I mean after. What's going to happen to me when you've caught him?'

'We can talk about that—'

'And what if you don't catch him?'

Tanner looked at Thorne. The fact was that Russell Brigstocke had not been altogether convinced by the proposal that their suspect should become a protected witness and had only agreed after Tanner had pushed, hard. Even then, he had made it clear that Emily Mead might yet end up facing charges, though he couldn't say for sure at this stage what those might be.

'There's no point us not being straight with you,' Thorne said. 'If recommendations are made, the Crown Prosecution

Service could still decide to press charges against you once this is all over.'

'*What?*'

'We just don't know,' Tanner said. 'That's the truth.'

'Who makes those recommendations?' She looked in desperation at Thorne and then at Tanner. 'You?'

'Probably not, no,' Thorne said.

'It's not fair,' she said.

'No, it isn't.'

'I didn't do anything.'

'I believe you.' Tanner put her mug down and moved closer to her. 'I know this is not what you wanted to hear, but what I can say for sure is that the likelihood you would face any serious charges would be considerably reduced if you worked with us.'

Emily sat back. 'How do I do that?'

'We want you to help us by reaching out to the man who killed Callaghan,' Thorne said. 'The man you know as LoveMyBro.'

Tanner raised a hand when she saw Emily begin to shake her head. 'It's just a few messages, that's all. You start a conversation and then ask if he'd meet you somewhere.'

'Are you serious? I saw that mad bastard stab someone to death and people like that don't tend to like having witnesses knocking around. He might say he wants to meet up just so he can use that knife on me.'

'You'll be perfectly safe,' Tanner said. 'If a meeting was arranged, we'd obviously be there to make sure of that.'

'So, I'm what . . . like bait?'

'No,' Tanner said. 'It's not—'

'Yes, *exactly* like that,' Thorne said. 'So we can catch this man before he has the chance to kill anyone else, give some kind of closure to the relatives of the people he's already killed and, as a nice little bonus, maybe keep you out of prison. So yeah, bait.'

Emily barked out a laugh, but she still looked horrified. She dropped her head back and closed her eyes. Half a minute later she opened them and sat up. 'I haven't got a computer,' she said.

'We'll supply all the equipment you need,' Tanner said. 'And someone to help you with it. To talk you through everything.'

'When?'

'As soon as I can get it all set up. Maybe we can start tonight?'

She took another minute or so, stared at the wall where the window should be, then shrugged. 'I've got sod all else to do, have I?'

'Thank you,' Tanner said.

Thorne nodded thanks of his own, then raised his mug. 'Coffee's pretty good, too.' He gave another nod towards Tanner. 'Whatever the Duchess of Hammersmith here might think.'

TWENTY

On their way to Brigstocke's office, Thorne and Tanner were waylaid by DC Steve Pallister.

'I just wanted to say sorry again for that gaff at the briefing the other day. What I said about a good news story.'

'Don't worry about it.' Thorne remembered thinking back then that as a relatively new member of the team, Pallister had simply been trying to make his presence felt. That he'd actually been making a fair point, however clumsily he might have put it. He was thinking now that when it came to horror stories about coppers 'dropping the ball', there might well be another one about to break.

'I don't think before I speak sometimes,' the DC said. 'Stupid ... '

Tanner nodded towards the file Pallister was carrying. 'What's that?' It had been all hands to the pump since the poisonings, and the murder of Adam Callaghan had ramped things up still further. In a crowded and frenetic incident room, it was easy to lose track of who was supposed to be doing what and Tanner was always keen to ensure that actions had been allocated efficiently. Even if the likes of Tom Thorne believed that cases were rarely solved by spreadsheets, she knew that one stupid admin glitch could be the difference between a good result and a very bad one.

Left hand, right hand, all that.

'Oh.' Pallister held the file up. 'I'm just assisting DI Holland with his suicide.'

'There you go again,' Thorne said. 'Speaking without thinking.'

Five minutes later, having filled Brigstocke in on their meeting with Emily Mead at the safe house, they watched the DCI remove his glasses and pinch his nose as if he had a bad headache coming on.

He said, 'I'm still not completely happy about this.'

'We went through it all yesterday,' Tanner said.

'Yes, we did.'

'I thought you were on board.'

'I am, but I just want it noted that I have reservations.' Brigstocke put his glasses back on. 'We're placing an awful lot of confidence in this woman.'

'Because it's the right thing to do.'

'So you keep saying, and *I* keep saying that, however this goes, Emily Mead might still end up being charged. Conspiracy maybe, or even worse. Because she's the one who made the call which got Callaghan to that park, under joint enterprise regs they might even want to push for murder.'

'That's ridiculous,' Tanner said. 'You know it is.'

'I'm just laying out the possibilities.'

'For God's sake, she's the victim.'

'We only have her word for that,' Brigstocke said. 'For obvious reasons, Adam Callaghan won't be standing trial and the fact is that, apart from a bunch of bootprints, we've no actual evidence there was ever a man in that park with her at all.' He looked at Tanner and Thorne. 'I mean, have we?'

Tanner looked to Thorne, who could see that she was struggling to stay calm, to stay in her seat.

He knew that part of Brigstocke's job as the Senior Investigating Officer was playing devil's advocate in situations such as this, and it was not something Thorne envied. He kept his mouth shut, happy for Tanner to take the lead in pushing a course of action based solely on trusting Emily Mead because he sensed that her commitment would get them over the line. He also thought that the voice of a female officer would carry more weight, as it should, considering the offences that were beginning to look like being central to the case. On top of which, he did not want Brigstocke to feel he was being ganged up on.

'I believe her,' Tanner said. 'That's the beginning and end of it.'

Brigstocke nodded, finally conceding it was enough to be getting on with, and reached for the phone that had begun to ring on his desk. When he put it down again, having said no more than 'Right' and 'Thank you', it looked as though that headache was seriously beginning to kick in.

'What?' Thorne asked.

'Jeremy Walker's just arrived,' Brigstocke said.

'Lucky you.'

'He wants an update, apparently.'

'Can I tell him about Tully? You know, if you're too busy.'

There were not very many occasions when Thorne would relish giving an operational update to a senior officer, especially one he was already at loggerheads with, but the opportunity for a little payback was irresistible.

'Tell him *what* about Tully?'

'Well, we know now why Walker's officers were poisoned, don't we? We know that it was one officer in particular who was the target. So, based on what LoveMyBro wrote on that message board and the strong possibility that Adam Callaghan was killed because he was a rapist, we can hazard a pretty good guess as to why Tully was the one being targeted.'

'Seriously, Tom?' Brigstocke was fiddling with a stapler. 'That's what we're doing now, is it? Guessing.'

'Oh, come on, Russell.'

'No, I get it. Evidence is so old school.'

Now Thorne was the one who was finding it hard to retain his composure. He stood up, waited for Tanner to follow suit and walked towards the door. 'Give DCI Walker my best.'

He was immediately presented with the opportunity to do so himself, when, stepping out of Brigstocke's office, he all but bumped into the DCI from Wood Green.

They stared at each other somewhat awkwardly, while Tanner took the opportunity to slide past them both into the incident room.

'You here to see DCI Oldfield, then?' Thorne clicked his fingers, as though he'd realised the mistake he'd deliberately made. 'Sorry, I mean *Brigstocke* ... DCI Brigstocke.'

Walker's thin smile immediately made an appearance. 'Yes, you're right, DI Thorne; what I said to your DCI the other day was out of order.' He adjusted his tie, which today, was a rather more muted colour. 'Heat of the moment, or whatever.

I've already apologised to Russell.'

'Oh, right,' Thorne said.

'I think I owe you an apology too.'

Thorne stared past him and saw Tanner watching from across the room, clearly curious as to what was being said.

'We definitely got off on the wrong foot,' Walker said.

'Yeah, just a bit.'

'And that may well have been my fault. So, I'm sorry if anything I said to you was upsetting, or offensive.'

Thorne had no idea how to react, being every bit as bad at accepting apologies as he was at making them, even if neither happened particularly often. Tanner was still staring, and he was aware that Brigstocke was now behind him, waiting in the doorway of his office. As Thorne struggled for something to say, a man whose presence he hadn't yet registered moved up to stand at Walker's shoulder as though waiting to be introduced.

'Oh . . . this is DI James Greaves,' Walker said.

Thorne leaned forward to shake the dry hand that was swiftly proffered. He leaned to peer at the DI's lanyard, but the man spared him the trouble. He was tall and broad with thinning sandy hair and there was an apologetic smile when he spoke, clearly well aware of what some people's reaction might be.

'Counter Corruption Unit,' he said.

'No need to panic,' Walker said.

'I'm not,' Thorne said.

It was widely acknowledged that the establishment of the CCU as a specialist unit within the Directorate of Professional Standards had been directly inspired by the TV show *Line of Duty*, but what had initially been a relatively small department had, for obvious reasons, expanded its operations somewhat in recent years. Restoring public confidence was now a major priority. The officers tasked with investigating the activities of their colleagues were predictably unpopular with the rank and file, but to describe their efforts to weed out extreme criminality as 'half-arsed' would be over-generous.

Frustrated by a lack of cooperation, possibly; hamstrung by procedure almost certainly. Ineffectual, without question.

Thorne had certainly had his run-ins with the DPS, but while his wrist had been slapped a good few times for overstepping or wilfully ignoring regulations, he had never come under the rather more intensive spotlight of those investigating serious corruption and abuse. He was wondering what Greaves was doing there when the name finally registered.

'James Greaves? Jimmy ... ?'

'I've heard all the jokes,' Greaves said.

Thorne didn't care. 'Best centre-forward Spurs ever had.'

'Like I said—'

Thorne turned at the sound of Brigstocke clearing his throat and it was clear that the DCI did not want to be kept waiting any longer. He looked back to Walker and Greaves. 'I'll leave you to it, then,' he said.

Standing next to the coffee machine in the corner of the incident room, Thorne stared at Tanner, who seemed to be thoroughly enjoying the skinny latte for which she'd paid a frankly ridiculous £1.75.

'Well, I have to say I'm very surprised,' he said.

Tanner looked at him.

'No, I'm actually *shocked*. Shocked that you can even stomach that slop, I mean. From a machine. A connoisseur of the bean such as yourself.'

Tanner sighed, refusing to rise to it. 'I don't get it,' she said. 'How can Russell not believe her? Sometimes you just know when someone's telling you the truth, right?'

'I'm sure he does believe her,' Thorne said.

'He bloody well should, because I can't remember a witness that was any more credible. He was watching that interview, wasn't he?'

'He's just covering all the bases, Nic. Covering bases, covering arses, it's more or less the same thing. It's why I've never put in for a promotion.'

'That, and the fact that you probably wouldn't get it.'

'Yeah, fair point. Seriously, though—'

'I was being serious,' Tanner said.

They looked up as Holland walked quickly across to join them. 'So, this suicide ...'

'Not been too successful by the look of it,' Thorne said.

'Pallister told us he was trying to help things along,' Tanner said. 'Did you lose your bottle, then?'

Holland looked confused, but chose to press on. 'You remember the basics, right? This bloke Daniel Sadler going off the viaduct in the middle of the night.'

Thorne and Tanner told him they did.

'Well, I did a bit of digging because, for whatever reason, it all felt a bit ... off. Now, I'm pretty sure that his wife Karen doesn't know about this because it happened before they were married, but twelve years ago Daniel Sadler was nicked for having indecent images of kids on his computer.'

'There you go, then,' Thorne said.

'Right,' Tanner said. 'So, it's not really "off" at all.' She tossed her empty coffee cup into the bin. 'Plenty of convicted paedophiles kill themselves sooner or later. They're something like a hundred times more likely to do it than anyone else.'

Holland was already shaking his head. 'That's the thing, though. He *wasn't* convicted. He wasn't even charged in the end. Looks to me like there was plenty of evidence, it was all very straightforward, and then for some reason it just went away. He's arrested and then ... nothing.'

'That doesn't sound right,' Thorne said.

'Could just be some cock-up with the records,' Tanner said.

'Yeah, could be,' Holland said. 'I've talked to the guvnor and he says he's going to have a look, see what he makes of it.' He turned when Thorne nodded, to see Brigstocke heading towards them. 'Odd, though, on top of everything else. What the wife said about Sadler's general disposition and the palaver in even getting to that viaduct. Oh, and his phone still hasn't turned up, by the way.'

Thorne asked the question as soon as Brigstocke had joined them. 'Who brought the CCU in, then?'

'Well, it certainly wasn't me,' Brigstocke said. 'Wasn't Walker either, according to him.'

'So how did they get wind of what we're doing?'

'No idea, but they do tend to keep their ears to the ground.'

'There's an anonymous tip line,' Tanner said. 'Or maybe they're looking at the same websites we are.'

Not knowing precisely how the Counter Corruption Unit had become involved would nag at Thorne, he knew that. Right then, though, the fact of DI James Greaves being there was probably the only one that counted. 'So, what was he after?'

'Just getting the lie of the land, seemed like,' Brigstocke said. 'He took a lot of notes, put it that way. They're clearly aware of certain accusations that have been made and they're interested in the irregularities around Callaghan's actions when he arrived in Hendon Park.'

'Turning off his bodycam.'

'Yeah. Fair to say that rang a few of their alarm bells.'

'How did it go with Walker? It's just struck me that you've only got to change one letter of his name ...'

Brigstocke's smile was thin, there and gone. 'It was about as much fun as I thought it would be,' he said. 'I brought him up to speed with the developments in the Callaghan case and our current lines of enquiry. I have to say DCI Walker shares some of the doubts about Emily Mead that I had.'

'Did you talk about Tully?' Thorne asked.

'Yes, we talked about Tully. We talked about all the victims.'

'I take it he's still not willing to consider the possibility that Tully might have been a rapist.'

'Nobody's considering that, Tom, not until there's any evidence.'

'Well, something made this bloke want him dead,' Thorne said. 'Made him want it badly enough that he was willing to kill two other coppers to make sure.'

'Make that three other coppers,' Brigstocke said.

They all looked at him.

'That was actually the main reason Walker was here.' Brigstocke turned, preparing to address the rest of the team. 'He came to inform us that Catherine Holloway died a couple of hours ago.'

TWENTY-ONE

Tracking the delivery on her phone, Helen announced that the pizza they'd ordered was five minutes away. Thorne laid out plates on the kitchen table and they both looked up at the sound of footsteps on the stairs.

'Shit,' Helen said.

'Looks like there's going to be three of us.'

'Oh, well.' Helen fetched a roll of kitchen towel from the worktop.

'Good idea,' Thorne said. 'He *is* messy.'

'I know, bless him.' Helen crammed an imaginary slice of pizza into her mouth and chewed noisily. 'There'll be more of it on his face than there is on his plate.'

'I *can* hear you,' Hendricks said, ambling into the kitchen and making straight for the fridge.

'It's why we were talking so loudly,' Thorne said.

Helen checked her phone again. 'Pizza's nearly here, by the way.'

'Great, because I'm starving, but more importantly did you remember to ask for extra sausage?'

'I doubt they can actually fit any more meat on to it.'

'Well, they're obviously not trying hard enough.'

'You any idea what that stuff's doing to your arteries?'

'If only there was a doctor around we could ask.' Hendricks brought two beers across to the table. He handed one to Thorne and opened his own as he sat down. 'I'm wiped out, mate.'

'You were up there ages,' Thorne said.

'Yeah, he wanted a story and he'll be too old for them soon. What was I supposed to do?'

Helen came across to join them and poured herself a glass of wine. 'Was it *James and the Giant Peach*? I probably know that bloody book by heart now.'

Hendricks shook his head. 'Alfie was adamant that he wanted something a bit more challenging, so I told him one of mine.' He leaned, grinning, towards Thorne. 'That brilliant one about the body they found tangled in fishing nets in the Gulf of Mexico. Soon as they popped the poor bastard on the slab, there were live shrimp and loads of little crabs crawling out of his mouth and nose.' He laughed and took a swig of beer. 'Alfie thought it was hilarious.'

'I'm too scared to ask if you're making that up,' Helen said.

'On my life,' Hendricks said. 'One of the crabs pinched the pathologist's glove.'

'No, I meant that you actually told that story to my son.'

The doorbell spared Hendricks any further questioning. 'I'll get that,' he said, jumping up and snatching a knife from the table on his way to the door.

'What's that for?' Thorne asked.

'Well, obviously I'm hoping that's our pizza, but if it's Jehovah's Witnesses, I may not be responsible for my actions . . .'

While they ate, Helen talked a little about her day at Citizens Advice: a shift on the helpline dealing with calls from those anxious about benefits, immigration status and, most commonly of all, the misery of spiralling costs and crushing debt. It was a day she would be only too happy to forget, but she was well aware that for others it had been significantly worse. As someone who'd only too recently been a copper herself, she knew what the death of a fellow officer meant.

Another fellow officer.

'It's horrible,' she said. 'I don't know if there was ever a chance she'd come out of it, but . . .'

'It was always unlikely.' Hendricks had not performed the post-mortem on Catherine Holloway himself, but he'd spoken to the pathologist who had earlier in the day. 'She never stopped bleeding internally. All the major organs were damaged beyond repair. Just a matter of time, really.'

'That's five then,' Helen said. 'If it was the same bloke who killed Adam Callaghan.'

'It was the same bloke,' Thorne said. 'And I'm not sure he's finished either, so if the operation we're trying to put together with Emily Mead doesn't work out, God knows where this could all end up.' He had not stopped thinking about his conversation with the uniformed officer at the Callaghan scene. The suggestion that he and some of his colleagues were ready and prepared to fight back, that they would refuse to be the enemy.

Bring it on . . .

Police officers taking collective action was nothing new.

It was less than two years since more than a hundred Met firearms officers had stepped down from their duties and handed in their weapons, in protest after one of their number had been charged with murder. Taking what was effectively strike action was one thing, though. What that PC in Hendon Park had been hinting at smacked of something altogether more sinister.

'Well, if you reckon it's rapey coppers he's after, it sounds like he's got a fair few to choose from,' Hendricks said.

'It's starting to look that way.'

'Come on,' Helen said. 'It's not like there are *that* many.'

'That's not what you were saying the other night,' Thorne said. 'You were making out like it was some kind of epidemic.'

Helen looked annoyed. 'That's a stupid exaggeration of what I said.'

'Yeah, OK,' Thorne said. 'Sorry.'

'Look, don't get me wrong. It's unacceptable that there are *any* police officers who would abuse their power, or that a single woman should become a victim of it.' She looked at them both. 'But surely there are still more good coppers than bad ones?'

'Like you said, though, one's too many.'

'This bloke clearly had some personal issue with Tully, right?' Hendricks said.

Thorne nodded, chewing. 'Because Tully was a rapist.'

'I don't want to sound like Russell—' Helen said.

'Yeah, I know, but we'll get the proof eventually.'

Hendricks clearly had a point to make. 'He didn't have any axe to grind with Callaghan, though, did he?'

'Not as far as we know.'

'No, but Emily Mead did. This LoveMyBro nutcase killed

Callaghan because she told him Callaghan was a rapist. So it's starting to look a bit like it's some kind of crusade or whatever. I mean, when you think about what's been happening, there are people who might think he's a bit of a hero.'

'Tell that to Catherine Holloway's family,' Thorne said.

'Yeah, course, I was only saying—'

'And the families of Kazia Bobak and Asim Hussain.'

Hendricks just nodded and reached for another slice of pizza, and after a few seconds Thorne did the same.

If Callaghan and Tully had done the things he believed they had, while he would still much rather have seen them tried and put away for it, Thorne was not going to pretend he was hugely sorry two bad coppers were dead.

It wouldn't stop him trying to catch their killer, though.

For the families of the good ones.

Dave Holland sat on the edge of the bath in his underwear, while his wife took the antiseptic ointment from the cupboard.

'I'm sure it's fine now,' he said.

Pippa slowly removed the plaster she'd put on herself two nights before and lifted the dressing that covered the graze on his palm. 'It's looking a lot better.' She took the dressing off then leaned down to examine his hand more closely. 'We can leave the dressing off now and let the air get to it. It was definitely starting to get infected, though.'

'I think I was very brave,' Holland said.

'*Very* brave, and also a bit stupid.'

'Can't we just focus on the brave thing?'

'I mean, climbing over bloody fences?' She began gently rubbing the ointment onto the wound, rolling her eyes when Holland winced.

'I went back,' he said.

'Went back where?'

'To the place Daniel Sadler got access to the railway line. Only I don't think that *is* how he got access.'

Holland's wife worked as a civilian staff member on a homicide investigation team based in Islington and they had already discussed his concerns about the Daniel Sadler suicide several times. 'Go on, then.' She laughed when Holland sucked in a breath and yanked his hand away. '*So* brave!'

He told her how hilarious she was, then reluctantly let her carry on. 'I wanted to have another look in daylight,' he said. 'So I went back and walked around a bit and I found part of the fence that had been bent and pulled away. He could easily have got in through there and then up the slope to the tracks.'

'There you go, then.'

'Or . . . he could have been *taken* in through there.'

Pippa stopped what she was doing and looked at him.

'There were a lot of footprints on that slope,' he said. 'I mean, I know that doesn't prove anything, because chances are kids have been up there. Kids love messing about on railway lines, don't they?'

'Do they?'

'Well, I did,' Holland said. 'Squashing pennies on the tracks, you know, or playing dare if there was a train coming. Like I say, it's probably nothing to get worked up about.'

'You are, though,' Pippa said. 'I can tell.'

'It doesn't feel kosher, that's all.'

'So, talk to your guvnor.'

'He's on it,' Holland said. 'But I'm not sure an iffy suicide is high on his list of priorities right now. With everything that's going on.'

Pippa grinned. 'I tell you something *else* that's going on . . .'

'Is it that time?'

'Yep, I'm about to start ovulating, so the fertility window is officially open.'

Now, Holland grinned. 'The fertile window of opportunity.'

'Time to get about your business, detective inspector.' She took his wrists and pulled him to his feet, putting the tube of ointment back in the cupboard on their way out of the bathroom. 'Don't worry, you won't have to take any weight on your hands.'

TWENTY-TWO

If Emily Mead was at all curious as to why Tanner had brought her down to an empty apartment on the ground floor she didn't say so, but the reason became obvious when the man Tanner had asked to help her send a message to LoveMyBro finally arrived.

'Emily, this is Greg,' Tanner said.

Hobbs reached up to shake Emily's hand, then wheeled himself past her and across to the large desk that had been set up in the corner of the sitting room. This aside, the apartment was identical to the one Emily was staying in; clean and tidy if somewhat spartan and with no view beyond its walls.

'Nice place,' Hobbs said, looking around. 'Someone likes beige, don't they?'

'Maybe it's supposed to be calming or something,' Emily said.

Tanner was watching her. The woman looked a little less jittery than she had been, but it was hard to tell. 'Is it working?'

'Have a guess.'

The two of them sat down on the oatmeal sofa and watched as one of Hobbs's DFU colleagues carried in his equipment in a series of metal flight cases, then, while Hobbs issued instructions, immediately began to assemble it. Hobbs himself was brandishing a black leather bag, which he unzipped to reveal a collection of cables and portable hard drives, with separate compartments for power banks, memory cards and a row of colour-coded thumb-drives.

'That your "special" bag then, Greg?' Tanner asked.

'Oh yes.' Hobbs stroked the leather, lasciviously. 'Everything I need in here, plus there's room for my sandwiches.'

Emily looked at Tanner. 'Where d'you get *him* from?'

Once everything had been set up to Hobbs's specifications, the DFU worker left and Hobbs beckoned Emily over. She carried a chair across and sat next to him. She nodded; she was ready.

Hobbs smiled and told her there was nothing she needed to be ready for, at least nothing she had to be nervous about. 'DI Tanner tells me you're already familiar with the mysteries of the Dark Web,' he said.

'I don't know about that.' Emily looked over at Tanner, who was watching from the sofa. 'Someone I used to have a few dealings with showed me the basics. So I was able to get on there and buy a few things I shouldn't have done.'

'Don't worry,' Hobbs said. 'I might have bought a few things I shouldn't have done myself. Like maybe some painkillers a bit stronger than the ones you can get from Boots.' Now he looked at Tanner. 'Not going to nick me, are you, DI Tanner?'

'I couldn't give a stuff,' Tanner said.

Emily laughed. It was a little nervous certainly, but she

seemed to be relaxing a little. 'And I can find the place where me and this bloke used to message,' she said. 'The room or whatever you call it.'

'OK, show me,' Hobbs said.

Hobbs's fingers flew across the keyboard as he followed Emily's instructions, his eyes flicking between the three different screens on the desk. It wasn't long before Emily pointed and said, 'Yeah, there,' and they were both looking at a series of unanswered messages to ButterflyGrrrl from two days earlier; a matter of hours after the man sending them had murdered Adam Callaghan.

> <<It went exactly the way you wanted, didn't it? The way I thought you wanted, anyway. Talk to me . . .>>

> <<Helloooo . . . ??>>

'Well, he certainly knows what he's doing,' Hobbs said. 'Getting this private chatroom set up for the two of you shows he's got some proper chops. There *is* a more straightforward way of getting here, mind you, a few shortcuts. I'll show you once we're done.'

Emily just nodded, staring at the messages.

'The key question is, how would you reply to him?'

'I don't know . . . I didn't think I'd ever have to.'

'Well, just sit and think about what you're going to say and, when you're ready, I'll do the typing.' He smiled at her again. 'Don't worry, he's not going to know it isn't you.'

'You sure?'

'He's good,' Hobbs said. 'But he isn't as good as me.'

Emily thought for half a minute or so, then began to dictate her reply.

> <<Sorry for being a bit shit and not getting back. Yeah, I was a bit freaked out by what happened. Feeling ok now though and glad that copper got what he deserved. So thanks.>>

'Let's pause there for a minute,' Hobbs said. 'So it doesn't look like something you've rehearsed, you know? You don't want to seem too confident.'

'Right.' Tanner, from the sofa. 'We're not going to suggest meeting up yet, anyway. We just need to re-establish a dialogue with him, make sure *he's* feeling confident.'

'Oh, he's seriously confident,' Emily said. 'I can tell you that for nothing. Confident what he's doing is right and that nobody's going to catch him.'

'Yeah, I'm sure,' Tanner said. 'But thanks to you he might be about to find out that confidence is misplaced.'

Emily nodded and turned back to Hobbs. 'OK, let's go again ...'

> <<So, what's next?>>

'Oh, I like that,' Hobbs said. 'It tells him you're onside, but it's putting the ball in his court.'

'Yeah.'

'So now we wait and cross our fingers.'

Tanner stood up and came across to look at the screen. 'That's very good.' She laid a hand lightly on Emily's shoulder. 'That's perfect.'

'You sure?'

'Thank you.'

Hobbs wheeled around and raised his arms, wearing a mock 'what-about-me' expression. 'You're welcome.'

'Yes, obviously you, too.' Tanner smiled. 'Tell me about those dodgy painkillers again . . .'

It was after nine o'clock by the time Hobbs had left with all his kit and Tanner had escorted Emily back upstairs to her own apartment. They were both hungry, so one of the plain-clothes officers on surveillance outside brought in some hot food from a nearby chicken shop.

'Better than a hotel,' Emily said. 'Cheaper, anyway.'

Taking her appetite to be a good sign, Tanner watched Emily devour her food while she explained what would happen next. They were obviously hoping to get a response to the messages Emily had sent, but any further exchanges would be handled remotely by Hobbs from the DFU.

'They'll be your words, but we won't have to go through all that rigmarole again.'

'It was good to get out and about, as it goes,' Emily said. 'Even if it was only two floors down.'

When they'd finished eating, Tanner said, 'Listen, I want you to know I'm here if you ever feel like talking about what happened with Adam Callaghan.'

'Oh . . .'

'What happened before, I mean.'

Emily slowly lowered her head and shook it, staring down at the mess of chicken bones on her plate.

'Of course. That's absolutely fine.' Tanner stood up and reached for her coat. 'Whenever you're ready, and only if you want to.'

'You could stay a bit, though.' Emily looked up. 'You know, unless you need to be somewhere else.'

Tanner dropped her coat back on the chair. 'I'd like that.'

TWENTY-THREE

Brigstocke was definitely looking more worn out and ground down than he had been a couple of days earlier, but to be fair, Thorne couldn't see too many people around the table he could describe as fresh-faced and chipper. A case like this could do that – the long hours and the growing number of victims – and Thorne had no doubt that Helen was thinking much the same thing about him.

'Right, let's crack on,' Brigstocke said.

The growing number of victims and the motives for their murder.

'On the first page of your briefing notes, you'll see a transcript of the encrypted messages that were sent, via a private chatroom on the Dark Web, yesterday evening.' Brigstocke waited while everyone opened the folder in front of them. 'These are messages from someone our prime suspect knows only as ButterflyGrrrl. She is actually Emily Mead, who we are no longer treating as a suspect and who is now working with us as a protected witness.' He gave a small nod in the direction of Nicola Tanner. 'There's been no response to these messages as yet, but the DFU are monitoring the chatroom, so if and when there is, we'll know about it straight away.'

DC Charita Desai raised a finger. 'When you say "prime suspect" ... ?'

'Only suspect,' Thorne said.

'We're definitely saying they're linked, then?' DC Dipak Chall looked across at him. 'The poisonings and the stabbing in Hendon Park?'

'I can't imagine any scenario in which they aren't.'

'The press are going to have a field day—'

Brigstocke cut in. 'I'll be coming on to that in a minute,' he said. 'But yes, we're now working on the assumption that Adam Callaghan was killed by the same individual that poisoned Catherine Holloway and her fellow officers five days ago. According to Emily Mead, the man she met in Hendon Park was keen to claim responsibility.'

'*Keen?*' Chall shook his head.

'Emily Mead was raped by Adam Callaghan,' Thorne said.

Brigstocke nudged his glasses. 'Well, she's certainly making that allegation.'

'Yes,' Thorne said. 'She is.' He was still talking directly to Chall and Desai, but he knew he had the attention of everyone else in the room, most particularly James Greaves from the CCU who was sitting on a chair against the wall, 'observing' and scribbling notes. 'Emily Mead was the victim of rape at the hands of a serving police officer and the man who killed him has made similar accusations about PC Christopher Tully.' He glanced across at Brigstocke, wanting to be sure the DCI would appreciate how nice and carefully he was about to tread. 'So ... whether that turns out to be true or not, we're definitely starting to see some kind of motive.'

'Something personal?' Chall asked.

'Got to be.' Thorne was thinking about what Hendricks had said the night before, but still found it hard to believe that what this individual was doing was any kind of crusade. He hadn't killed those coppers because of some twisted calling. 'This is a reaction to something.'

'Right.' Brigstocke looked down at his notes. 'Thanks for that, Tom.'

Thorne decided he should keep quiet for a while, knowing his boss well enough to tell that he was anything but grateful.

'In an effort to manage this "field day" Dipak was talking about, there's going to be a press conference this afternoon. We'll be letting them know about Catherine Holloway's death and Catherine's mother has generously agreed to take part, so it should be pretty powerful. We will be taking questions, but we will not be talking about any connection between the murders of Catherine Holloway and her three colleagues, and the death of Adam Callaghan. That is strictly operational information which, for the time being, stays in this room.' Brigstocke looked around. 'We clear about that?'

Everyone appeared to be.

'What if someone asks you directly?' Pallister had clearly thought quite carefully on this occasion, before asking what was a perfectly reasonable question. 'Some smart journo putting two and two together.'

'Luckily there aren't too many of them,' Tanner said.

Almost everyone around the table seized the welcome opportunity to laugh, just a little.

'That'll be dealt with if and when it happens,' Brigstocke

said. 'Besides which, it won't be me answering the questions. DCI Walker will be hosting the press conference.'

'Walker?' Thorne could not keep the distaste from his voice. 'Why?'

'Because I asked him,' Brigstocke said. 'He's as well informed about the investigation as anyone here and, more importantly, Catherine Holloway was a PC at his station. It seemed like the right thing to do.'

There was little else Thorne could say.

'One other matter which *isn't* in your notes ... a suspicious fatality which came in overnight. A fifty-six-year-old security guard named Stuart Needham was the victim of a hit-and-run in Stoke Newington. The car, which turned out to be stolen, was found burned out a couple of hours afterwards, so it's obviously being treated as murder. The team in Hackney that's caught this can't say yet if it was premeditated, but the key factor, for us, is that the victim was a retired officer.' Brigstocke let that sink in. 'I've told them to keep me posted.'

'Coincidence, maybe?' Pallister said.

'Quite possibly, but until we know more there's no reason we should jump to conclusions.'

Thorne didn't need a reason. 'So, that's a nice round half-dozen.'

Tanner caught up with him in the corridor outside the briefing room and said, 'Sounds like Russell's finally on board.' She checked to make sure Brigstocke was nowhere within earshot. 'Took him long enough, mind you.'

'I think he was always on board.' Tanner muttered something about 'trust' and 'experience' but Thorne was only half listening. He was still thinking about that hit-and-run and what was almost certainly their killer's sixth victim. 'He's just got to weigh up all the options, cover the bases, like I said. I mean, if things go pear-shaped, he's the one who'll get it in the neck.'

'I thought shit always rolled downhill,' Tanner said.

'Don't worry, it'll get to us eventually.'

They turned at the sound of a door opening to see Brigstocke coming out of the briefing room. He walked past them without a word, then stopped and came back, though he appeared somewhat reluctant.

'We've worked together a long time, so you know I've always valued input from every member of my team.' He was talking directly to Thorne, leaving Tanner a little embarrassed on the sidelines. 'You, more than most, Tom ... but I don't think it's hugely helpful to contradict me, however subtly you think you're doing it. And I really don't need you to run my briefings.'

'Come on, Russell, I didn't—'

'Let's say no more.' He shook his head sadly, and now he looked at Tanner. 'This is a pig of a case and we're all capable of getting a bit fractious.'

They watched him walk away.

'What was that?' Thorne asked.

'I can sort of see his point,' Tanner said.

'I mean, I've got no issue with an honest-to-goodness bollocking ...'

'Right, because you're used to it.'

'... but I really can't stand the whole "I'm not angry, I'm just disappointed" thing.'

Brigstocke stopped at the end of the corridor to talk to one of the civilian staff. He glanced back at them.

'He looks done in, don't you think?' Tanner asked.

'I do think,' Thorne said.

Tanner touched her face. 'His skin's gone all chalky and there's loads more lines than there used to be. It's why they're called worry lines, I suppose. I know *I* can hardly talk, but I reckon it's a good job he's not the one going in front of those cameras later on. He'd need a fair bit of concealer.'

Thorne saw Brigstocke pause in the doorway of his office and look back at him, before disappearing inside. He said, 'How fast does Botox work?'

TWENTY-FOUR

There'd been an instant, no more than a fraction of a second really, when it had seemed as if Stuart Needham was looking right at him. Like their eyes had met through the spiderweb of the windscreen's cracked glass, right before he'd rolled off the bonnet into the road.

Hello, goodbye, *thump*.

It wasn't like Needham would have recognised him and the arsehole might well have been dead by then anyway, because the car was going at a fair old lick, but it was a nice moment, all the same. He'd remember it for sure, same as he'd remember the look on Callaghan's face when he realised where he'd seen that girl in the park before. And Tully, of course, *especially* Tully, when him and his mates finally opened that box and saw what he'd left them.

A small token of appreciation from a grateful member of the public.

Grateful, hateful, close enough.

He'd been watching from behind the tape. The four of them grinning like idiots and high-fiving each other like it was the best thing that had ever happened to them. It was only doughnuts, for Christ's sake.

Funny thing was, he hadn't even intended to do Needham the night before. He'd gone along to check the bloke's routine again, that was all, have another look for cameras and what have you, but everything had lined up so perfectly, he would have been daft not to take his chance. Needham had come trudging across the road – which was every bit as dark and deserted as it had been the previous night – bang on time, so he'd decided he wasn't about to look a gift horse in the mouth. He *did* have one final look to make doubly sure there wasn't anyone around and then he'd put his foot down.

He'd actually been wondering where that expression had come from – was it something to do with a horse's teeth? – when Needham had turned, far too late, obviously, and seen how comprehensively fucked he was. Then there was only him shouting, with that high-vis jacket making him impossible to miss. Frozen to the spot and screaming something nobody would hear, his last words drowned out by the roar of the engine before he was flying across the bonnet and their eyes had met.

Might have met.

He'd never believed any of that 'life flashing before your eyes' stuff, but he knew that if former PC Needham had been granted a super-quick recap of his old life on the thin blue line, it would not have made for comfortable viewing. A proper little horror film.

What was the name of that album his old man used to play? *Power, corruption and lies.*

He decided to google the gift horse thing and was pleased to discover that he'd been right. All about looking at a horse's teeth to figure out its age. As he was there anyway, he googled 'hit-and-run Stoke Newington' and 'fatal car accident Hackney' but nothing had made the news as yet. So he googled 'awkward family photos' and looked at a few of those for a while, because they made him laugh.

His tea was all but cold, but he downed what was left of it anyway and rolled his chair across to a different screen. Half a minute later he was happily scrolling through the latest posts in FUCK THE FILTH and STAB UP DA COPZ when he got an alert from his private chatroom. It only took a few more clicks before he was looking at the series of messages that had arrived overnight from ButterflyGrrrl.

<<Sorry for being a bit shit
and not getting back.>>

He didn't know what to think, because even though he was pleased enough to find himself smiling, he was also pissed off. Considering everything he'd done for her, 'being a bit shit' really didn't cover it. Not even close. He'd reached out to her and she'd chosen to ignore him, so he didn't care how sorry she was, because it wasn't sorry enough.

What the hell had she been doing for the last three days, anyway?

Granted, he hadn't got a clue who she really was. He didn't know what she got up to when she wasn't online or watching him stab rapists in the park. She might have family commitments or a full-on job that kept her busy, though he seriously doubted it. Judging from the look of her that night, she'd have spent all the time since walking the streets, or off her face on something or other.

She wasn't a high-flyer, he knew that much.

It had crossed his mind, of course, that she might have decided to tell someone, but he wasn't losing too much sleep over it. He was fairly sure she wouldn't, because of how involved she'd been, which meant she'd only be getting herself into serious trouble. If she decided that she'd do it anyway, and more fool her, what could she actually tell anyone?

She knew no more about him than he knew about her.

While he made himself another tea, he tried to make up his mind about whether or not he'd respond. If he chose to ignore her, it would be no less than she deserved, a taste of her own medicine. If he banged out a reply right now and was all 'hey, it's great to hear from you', he'd be letting her off the hook and she'd never learn to appreciate him properly. By the time he sat down again, he'd decided, after carefully weighing it all up, that he *would* get back to her.

Not yet, though.

It wouldn't hurt to leave her hanging for a while.

He read through her messages again and thought he could smell a bit of desperation. He'd always had that feeling about her and guessed that she didn't have a lot of people to turn to. Nobody she could trust. He did understand that it would be hard to trust anyone after what she'd been through, but even so, he didn't have her down as much of a party animal.

She wasn't a social ButterflyGrrrl.

<<So, what's next?>>

To be fair, it was a very good question.
Though *who* would have been a better one.

TWENTY-FIVE

Tanner got to Kentish Town a few minutes before the ten o'clock news and, after a dash to the toilet – from where she delivered a seriously sweary report about traffic on the Westway – she dropped on to the sofa and began emptying the plastic bag she had with her.

Crisps, pistachio nuts, a box of Maltesers and two sausage rolls from the petrol station.

'I brought snacks.'

Thorne dived straight for the Maltesers. 'What's this, movie night?'

'I didn't really have time for proper dinner.' Tanner leaned forward as the news started. 'Here we go.'

'They're only going to show a few minutes anyway,' Thorne said. 'The same few minutes I've already watched three times on Sky News.'

'Yeah, I've watched it too,' Tanner said.

'So why schlep all the way up here?'

'What, aside from the pleasure of your company?'

Thorne grabbed another handful of Maltesers. 'Well, yeah, obviously.'

'I'm here so we can watch it again,' she said. 'Together. With snacks.'

The press conference wasn't the first item on the programme, which was hardly surprising given the terrible events taking place worldwide on a daily basis. They had always known it would end up being sandwiched somewhere between the latest terrorist atrocity and a dog barking the national anthem. In the studio, there was a brief introduction from the BBC's home affairs correspondent who – as the faces of Christopher Tully, Asim Hussain and Kazia Bobak appeared on-screen behind him – recapped the murders that had taken place almost a week earlier. The precise manner of their deaths remained a matter of conjecture, he explained, as police had not yet released details to the media. This had left reporters and concerned members of the public hopeful that today's press conference might shed a little more light on exactly how those officers had died.

'No bloody chance,' Tanner said.

DCI Jeremy Walker stepped on to the makeshift stage at Scotland Yard, a few paces ahead of the woman who Thorne and Tanner already knew was Catherine Holloway's mother. She sat down and immediately reached for a glass, nodding her thanks as Walker filled it from a water jug.

Walker took a piece of paper from his pocket and unfolded it. He leaned towards the microphone in front of which his name was printed on a strip of folded card.

'Six days ago, three police officers lost their lives in a cowardly and unprovoked attack.' Walker glanced up, towards the gathered crowd of reporters brandishing mobile phones and mics, towards the cameras. 'The investigation into those murders is ongoing and apprehending the individual responsible remains our highest priority. As you already know, a fourth officer, PC Catherine Holloway, survived the attack and has been fighting for her life ever since. Today, I have the sad task of informing you that Catherine tragically lost that fight yesterday afternoon and passed away at 1.06 p.m. in St Thomas' Hospital. Catherine was a very fine officer and, along with her three colleagues, will be deeply missed by all of us who knew and worked with her.'

He turned, grim-faced, to look at the woman next to him and leaned away from the microphone to mutter something. She nodded and took out a piece of paper of her own.

'Catherine's mother, Sylvia Holloway, has very kindly agreed to be with us here today, and would like to read out a statement...'

'I still don't know how people can do this,' Tanner said. 'Doesn't matter how many times I see a parent or a husband or whatever.'

Thorne said nothing. He knew that Tanner was thinking about her own partner, Susan. The teacher she had loved and lived with, who'd been murdered on their own doorstep five years before.

He reached over to lay a hand on her arm.

'I don't know how they keep it together,' she said.

'Catherine always wanted to be a police officer. Ever since she was a little girl. It's a small comfort to myself and her dad that our daughter died doing a job she loved.' Sylvia Holloway looked up and managed a wobbly smile. 'Only a small one, but it's something... something that helps.' She took another drink of water, gulped it down. 'There's been a great deal made in recent months about the behaviour of some police officers. About those who have committed unspeakable crimes. That's as it should be, of course, and Catherine was the first to condemn those people, because she hated the thought of any police officer abusing their power. Of any police officer breaking the oath they'd taken to faithfully discharge their duty with integrity and respect. That was what my daughter did every single day. That was all she ever wanted to do. She was one of the good ones and so were the three officers she was on duty with that night.'

'Maybe not all of them,' Thorne said.

'So, if there is anyone watching this who has any information, please come forward, so that Catherine's colleagues can catch the man responsible for their deaths. Whatever it is ... any information at all.' She sat back, her hands shaking as she folded her piece of paper up again.

'Amazing.' Tanner's voice was barely above a whisper. 'Doesn't matter how many times I've seen it.'

Thorne gave her arm a small squeeze.

'Once again, we're hugely grateful that Catherine's mother has taken the time to talk to you today.' Walker turned to the woman and nodded to acknowledge her bravery. 'And I can only endorse what Sylvia had to say. With that in mind, we're sharing an e-fit today of a man we'd very much like to talk to in connection with the investigation. It's there in the press packs, but it's important to get it on camera, so ... '

Walker gave a signal to someone at the side of the stage, and a few seconds later the Met Police logo on the screen behind him disappeared and was replaced by the computer-generated image of their suspect's face.

'This image is based on a description given to us by an eye witness on the night Catherine and the others were attacked.'

'Pants on fire,' Tanner said.

The e-fit had actually been compiled from a detailed description provided by Emily Mead. In the belief that the man portrayed may well be watching, and not wanting him to know that Emily Mead was now working with the police, there was a justifiable need for Walker to be economical with the truth.

'He's a pretty good liar,' Thorne said. 'I almost believe it myself.'

Walker announced that he would take a few questions and pointed as soon as a hand was raised. A woman stood up, gave her name and said that she was from ITV. 'You haven't made any reference to the more recent murder of a police officer in Hendon Park.'

'Here's that smart journo Pallister was on about,' Thorne said.

'I just wondered if that was deliberate and, if so, is it because that murder is now part of this same investigation?'

Another journalist stood up and spoke without being invited. 'Are we seeing a series of concerted attacks on police officers?'

'See the look on Walker's face?' Tanner said.

'Rabbit in the headlights,' Thorne said.

'I hope you understand that I cannot comment on any ongoing operation. I will say only that the murder of any police officer, for whatever reason, is a tragedy. I want to assure you that our investigations are starting to bear fruit and that the public can be confident those responsible for these terrible crimes will be brought to justice.'

Walker turned to deal with more questions and they cut back to the studio.

'Did he really just talk about public confidence in the police?'

'I'm still trying to work out the fruit thing.' Tanner reached for the remote.

'What are you doing?'

'It's only going to be that home affairs bloke wrapping it up, so ...'

'Don't you want to know the football results?'

'Not especially.'

'Come on, you and Fiona can cuddle up later on in your torture room and talk about Brentford's lack of form away from home.'

Tanner told him he was a bell-end and turned the TV off.

'Tomorrow's going to be a sod.' Thorne had moved from Maltesers to pistachios and grabbed another handful. 'More of a sod, I mean.'

Tanner groaned. They both knew that televised appeals for information inevitably led to several days of fielding phone calls, of dealing patiently with those swearing blind that the man police were after lived next door or had once painted their shed or was working in their local chip shop. She stood up and, after announcing that she was taking the sausage rolls home with her, told Thorne that she'd see him in the morning. 'Maybe something'll come in from Hackney.'

He walked her to the door. 'I'm not holding my breath.' While Thorne remained convinced that the killing of the ex-copper in Stoke Newington was no coincidence, there had been no further updates from the team handling the case. They'd spent the rest of the day digging into Stuart

Needham's career on the Job, but there were no red flags. His service record was spotless, he'd been commended numerous times by members of the local community, and he'd barely taken a day off in thirty years. To all intents and purposes, he'd been the perfect copper.

Then again, so had Callaghan and Tully.

TWENTY-SIX

Emily Mead turned the TV off and trudged through to the bedroom. She removed her trainers and the grey trackies that needed a wash and sat on the edge of the bed in T-shirt and knickers, crying for Catherine Holloway's mother. And for Adam Callaghan's. She knew that was a somewhat strange thing to do, all things considered, but the agony Sylvia Holloway had clearly been going through while she'd sat there in front of those cameras, was probably no greater than the pain Callaghan's mother would be feeling. Pain which was no less valid because of what her son had done. What he'd been. Emily chose to believe his mother could not have known that, but wondered if her grief would have been any less crippling if she had.

You stood by your kids, no matter what, didn't you?

There had been a time when Emily believed she'd find out for herself one day. Kids of her own had definitely been part of a future she'd once imagined, even if she hadn't met anyone she'd considered having them with, but now all that happy-ever-after stuff seemed like a stupid dream she'd been shaken from. Like winning the lottery or becoming a film star. That future – *any* future worth thinking about – had been stolen from her the day PC Adam Callaghan had come knocking on her door a second time.

Sorry . . . yeah, hi. Just took me a moment to . . .

That's OK.

I'm still a bit jumpy and, you know, because you're not in uniform.

Well, I'm not actually on duty.

Right. So, what . . . ?

I just wanted to see how you were doing, that's all.

Oh, that's so nice of you . . .

Emily got up to fetch some toilet paper from the bathroom, then walked back to the bed and sat wiping her eyes. She knew that the tears weren't just for those grieving mothers, because Emily had done plenty of crying before that. Lying awake when all she wanted to do was sleep; arguing with the voices in her head when all she wanted was peace and quiet; screaming as the black knot in her stomach tightened still further when all she wanted was for the pain to stop.

Then crying a whole lot more, angry and ashamed because of the stupid shit she'd smoked or snorted or popped to try and *make* it stop.

Slowly devoured by guilt for all the things she could have prevented.

Guilt about Adam Callaghan's death, the sordid and brutal manner of it, because however many times at her lowest ebb she might have wished for him to suffer, that was not what she'd wanted to happen.

Guilt about the other women – maybe a couple or maybe dozens – who he might well have gone on to hurt after her. Women who could have been spared the agonies she'd endured if only she'd gone to the police and told them what he'd done.

Guilt because she hadn't been brave enough.

She stood up and leaned against the wall and told herself that was all in the past, because now she was actually doing something. Whether or not you could call it *brave* was debatable, what with her being holed up in this perfectly nice little box, with coppers stationed outside twenty-four hours a day. Invisible to snipers *thank heavens*, and rather more significantly, safely hidden from a man who she didn't think would stop what he was doing any time soon.

So no, not brave exactly, but she had finally stepped up, at least.

Brave was what Catherine Holloway's mother had been, staring out at those journalists and making her appeal, and even though Emily didn't recognise the detective who'd been up there with her it was obvious that he'd been trying to make it easier for her. Thinking about it, she'd met dozens of coppers in the days since she'd walked into that station in Clapham, but the only ones she'd spent any real time with had been Tanner and Thorne, and she counted herself lucky, because they were both OK.

She trusted them, as far as she had it in her to trust any copper.

It wasn't as though she'd ever been a massive fan of the police, but she hadn't been *anti* them either. Before the attack, she'd never really thought about it one way or the other. Nobody loved seeing coppers, did they, because the police weren't normally showing up if something good had happened, so a degree of ... nervousness was only natural.

Do policemen normally drop in on people when they're not on duty?

Well, I think they should, if they can. I always try to, if I'm passing or whatever, especially if there might be a cup of tea or something in it. That was a hint, by the way.

OK, I think I can run to tea ...

But she'd never actually been scared of them.

At least the e-fit they'd shown on TV was a pretty good likeness and that had to be down to the description Emily had given. It was something she could feel good about. Having said that, the man who'd murdered Adam Callaghan wasn't particularly distinctive looking. He definitely wasn't the kind of bloke you'd look twice at, so they just had to hope that somebody who knew him saw the picture and came forward.

When the only relationship you'd had with someone was online, they never turned out to be like you'd imagined when you finally got to meet them IRL. LoveMyBro certainly hadn't, though to be fair Emily wasn't sure what she'd been expecting. Maybe not someone who looked so ... ordinary, even if he'd turned out to be anything but that.

She'd always suspected that most people online – herself included – were just weird, phantom versions of themselves. Spirit identities haunting their own little corners of cyberspace while their physical selves mooched around in the real world, unsatisfied.

Emily smiled when the idea came to her.

She walked through to the living room, having decided that if this plan of Thorne and Tanner's was ever going to stand a chance of working, she needed to take the initiative.

To provoke some reaction, at least. She picked up the secure mobile that Greg Hobbs had given her, which was charging on a table near the door, and sent him a text.

Another message from ButterflyGrrrl to LoveMyBro.

<<So, now you're the one that's ghosting ME!? Fair enough, I suppose, but I didn't think you were that childish. Or maybe, YOU'RE the one that's scared now. #AreWeDone?>>

It took Hobbs less than a minute to reply. *It's been posted. That should shake him up!*

Fingers crossed.

Everything crossed. Well, except my legs, obviously. Someone has to do that for me.

Emily wandered across to the kitchen and flicked the kettle on. *I thought you might be asleep.*

Don't do much of that.

Me neither. She opened the jar of instant coffee and took milk from the fridge.

I'm just sitting around staring at a computer screen, if you want to talk for a bit.

About what?

Anything you like.

Why are you in a wheelchair?

SHOCKED FACE EMOJI

You said anything.

Because my legs don't work.

Smartarse.

I'd always presumed it was fairly obvious.
Obviously I mean, HOW?
You don't waste any time, do you, Emily?
She carried her coffee back into the living room and sat down. *Wasted far too much already.*

TWENTY-SEVEN

A working day that began and ended with positive developments on any case was a rarity in itself, but had Tom Thorne known it would be their last for some time, had he had the slightest idea what lay ahead, he might have appreciated it even more than he did.

He'd have got down on his knees and thanked God.

'Looks like your girl's done what we wanted.' Brigstocke handed over a piece of paper for Thorne and Tanner to examine as soon as they'd sat down in his office. 'She's got him talking, anyway.'

Thorne and Tanner studied the transcript of the online exchange between protected witness and prime suspect, which Emily Mead had instigated late the night before.

<<Why would I be scared?>>

<<I didn't really think you were.>>

>><<You were trying to wind me up?>>

>><<Just strange that you weren't talking to me.>>

<<THEY'RE the ones who
need to be scared.>>

>><<I'm sure they are.>>

<<And I don't know about
WE but I am not done.>>

'I hate to say I told you so,' Tanner said.

'I know for a fact that you love it,' Brigstocke said. 'But you can't say it anyway, because we're not there yet. Nowhere near there. Yes, she's managed to get him communicating again, which was the first thing we needed, but we're not going to push it.'

'Course not,' Tanner said.

'I see that,' Thorne said. 'Nobody wants him getting suspicious and we don't want to scare him off, but the rate this bloke's going, I don't think we've got a lot of time.'

Brigstocke nodded, thinking about it. 'There's still nothing that links the ex-copper in Stoke Newington to any of this, by the way.'

'There will be,' Thorne said.

'Maybe, but yeah ... I take your point. We'll have to get Emily to push for a meeting sooner or later.'

'I vote for sooner.'

'I hear what you're saying, Tom, but if our suspect does

smell a rat and backs off, it's all been for nothing. We'll *have* nothing. Now, obviously, if there's any further contact between them, I'll let you know and we can take a view on it, but for the time being . . . softly softly, right?'

'Let me talk to Emily again,' Tanner said. 'See where her head's at and try and come up with an approach that's likely to work.'

'Sounds like a plan.' Brigstocke leaned back and sighed heavily. 'So, what did you make of the press conference?'

'Walker did a good job,' Tanner said. 'Catherine Holloway's mother was amazing.'

'Yeah, she was.' Thorne could not quite bring himself to add to the praise for Jeremy Walker. 'Has anything useful come in?'

'I don't know about useful,' Brigstocke said. 'But we've had plenty of calls already. You two need to get out there and start answering a few.'

'Can't wait,' Thorne said.

'Got to be done.' Tanner waved the transcript in Thorne's face. 'And *this* is not nothing.'

Thorne couldn't argue. With many hours of what some officers referred to, somewhat insensitively, as the *nutbags' phone-in* stretching ahead of them, it was nice to be greeted with some good news.

'Nicola's right,' Brigstocke said. 'And you never know, if one of these tip-offs from a member of the public comes good, we might not even need Emily Mead to do anything else.'

'And where would that leave her?' There was no need for Thorne to add that he was talking about possible charges against Emily Mead.

'Remains to be seen,' Brigstocke said.

Tanner stood up, ready to go to work. 'She's done everything we've asked of her up to now, though, right?'

'Nobody's saying she hasn't.'

'She's doing a good job, Russell.'

'Listen, if this pans out, you can spell out *I TOLD YOU SO* in big shiny balloons and hang them up over my desk.'

'I'll take pictures,' Thorne said. 'Should make the front page of *The Job*.'

'But until such time . . . ' The DCI stared down at a copy of the transcript on his desk. 'Yes, this is looking good.'

Tanner waved her own copy again. 'It's looking like progress.'

'Happy days,' Brigstocke said.

All calls received following an appeal to the public were screened by the Met's central call centre before being put through to the requisite incident room. This would, theoretically at least, avoid the kind of time-wasting that could seriously jeopardise an investigation. The fact was however, that the civilian members of police staff manning the phones on a major case like this one, could be somewhat . . . risk averse. While they would weed out the most obvious of crank callers – those who insisted the killer was an alien or a ghost or Paul McCartney – almost anyone else ringing the tip line stood a decent chance of being put through to a member of the investigation team. It was annoying, but ultimately forgivable. Nobody was trying to make extra work for detectives, but equally, nobody wanted to dismiss a caller only to discover down the line that the killer *was* that creepy-looking man who'd built their shed or was working in their local chip shop.

Nobody wanted to be the person who didn't put the crucial call through.

Nobody wanted to screw up.

None of this was of any comfort to Thorne, Tanner and the rest of the team as they dutifully logged every detail provided by a caller: the times and locations of every possible sighting; the names and addresses of any named individuals; makes and registration numbers of vehicles that might be significant; mobile phone numbers, clothing descriptions, train timetables and, on more than one occasion, the breed of dog that the 'man in the picture' had been spotted walking.

Surprisingly, the morning passed quickly enough and at lunchtime Thorne and Tanner each grabbed one of the sandwiches that had been delivered to the incident room. Tanner had plumped for a tuna salad and said she thought it was a decent gesture by Brigstocke – or whoever else had organised it – to provide lunch for a team that was already overworked when the day started. Thorne, who was using his teeth in an effort to extract his ham and cheese from its impenetrable plastic packaging, was rather more cynical.

'Yeah, and also it means we don't have to leave the building.'

For the duration of their foreshortened break they talked about some of the more outlandish tip-offs they'd received, but, grumpy as Thorne was, he certainly didn't need Tanner to remind him that the job needed to be done, or that what they'd been doing all morning – and would be doing again all afternoon – was only the start of it. In the days to come, hundreds of officers, the majority of them uniformed, would be out on the streets doing the legwork; following up on every single lead, however flimsy, because it was important.

Because a break in the case could come from anywhere.

Tanner saw the look on Thorne's face as he continued the struggle to release his sandwich and decided to remind him anyway.

'Dennis Nilsen was only caught because one of his neighbours called in a plumber when the drains started to smell.'

'I know,' Thorne said. 'The only time in history an extortionate call-out charge turned out to be worth it.'

'Son of Sam was caught because a woman spotted a man hanging around in the middle of the night, near a place where the police had been handing out parking tickets.'

Thorne sighed in satisfaction, having finally managed to get his sandwich out. He brandished it at Tanner. 'I know what you're saying, I know any snippet could turn out to be vital, but even so ... if the man we're after turns out to be the owner of a distinctive-looking Schnauzer, I'll give you a hundred pounds.'

There was no let-up for the rest of the day, as people who had only just seen the e-fit in their newspapers or on the afternoon news called in with information. The time didn't pass quite as quickly as it had in the morning, but Thorne kept his head down and did what was required of him.

He understood why Brigstocke's optimism had been so cautious.

Without some kind of break, via the conversations with Emily Mead or as a result of information provided by the public, they had nothing. They had a reasonable description of the killer, they knew his online alias and – if those prints lifted from the park turned out to be his – they knew what size boot he wore.

It was nowhere near enough.

It was not evidence.

So Thorne saw out the day with as much hope and enthusiasm as he could muster, thinking about Catherine Holloway, Asim Hussain and Kazia Bobak. About the ex-copper run down in Stoke Newington who, until he learned otherwise, was another innocent victim of the man Thorne wanted to catch as badly as any killer he had ever hunted.

Preventing all offences against people.

That was part of the oath *he* had sworn many years before.

All that said, Thorne was still thinking about home – about beer and bed – when Dave Holland came marching across the room, clutching a sheet of paper as if it was a winning lottery ticket.

'Who's a clever boy, then?'

'What?'

Tanner was moving across to join them as Holland slapped the piece of paper down in front of Thorne and pointed to the key information. 'Those fag ends you thought we should collect from Hendon Park? They ran all the DNA and we got a hit.'

'Right.' Thorne was trying not to get over-excited. The cigarette end that had provided the DNA match could just as easily have been discarded by someone who'd been nicked for drink driving or once been done for shoplifting. Then he looked at Tanner, who had already read the first few lines of the report and begun to grin.

'A big, fat, fucking hit,' Holland said.

TWENTY-EIGHT

He'd been thinking about his parents, on and off, all day.

Three years gone now, both of them, and it hadn't got any easier, and the most terrible thing of all was that, when he tried to picture them, he could only see them as they'd been in those first few days of the trial. His mum in her best blue dress and his dad in a suit and tie, because they thought that was important. Because you dressed up if you were going to court and they understood those things.

'It isn't like we haven't had to do it before,' his mum had said.

He'd dressed up, too, worn a jacket his mum had picked out for him.

Not that he'd lasted very long in that courtroom.

They were pinched and pale, the faces he remembered. Unsmiling, for obvious reasons, and it was so unfair because both of them had smiled a lot before that. He doubted very much that either of them had ever smiled or laughed again. Just hard stares and harder silences for the three poxy months they had left after that verdict came in. Picking their way quietly through the wreckage of it. Martin and Diane, fading away together in a few small rooms, with her dress and his suit both dry-cleaned and hanging up in the wardrobe.

Forty years married, then gone within a fortnight of each other.

They'd stayed all the way through the trial, his mum and dad, even when it had become fairly bloody obvious which way things were going. They wanted to be there, because it was the right thing to do, they'd told him, the loving thing. So, day after day, they'd sat there, helpless, and listened to all the lies. They'd watched, saying nothing while one bullshit witness after another had sworn a sacred oath then cheerfully perjured themselves; scientific experts and copper after filthy copper, all of them conspiring to destroy his parents' world while they sat holding hands in the gallery.

He hadn't been able to keep quiet or behave himself like they had. He'd had plenty to say, right from the off, which was why he'd only just managed to dodge a contempt charge and ended up making his protests on the street outside. He'd known that badgering journalists and shouting at passers-by about justice wasn't going to make any difference to what was happening in that courtroom, but he had to tell people the truth. Someone needed to do it, didn't they? To let everyone know what was being done in their name, in the crown's name, whatever, the complete and utter disgrace of what those bastards were doing.

But a placard and a loudhailer were never going to measure up against barristers in their stupid wigs and the so-called indisputable forensic evidence. So, in the end, after he'd watched his parents wither and die, he'd gone searching for some evidence of his own and found a different way to do things, in a different place.

To protest and then, eventually, to punish.

He wasn't what you'd call squeaky clean before then, never really had been. He'd hung around with bad lads and occasionally he'd been one himself. *Rape*, though . . . that was something else entirely.

Rape was ridiculous.

Rape was worse than murder.

Rape was disgusting and the people that did it were animals.

Obviously, he had a very particular reason for feeling quite so strongly about it, so driven to mete out his own version of justice. He understood that his take on it was what some people would call extreme, especially where rapists in uniform were concerned, but he didn't much care because it was the only way to make things fair again. To dull the pain caused by everything they'd done to him, and to Martin and Diane, and worst of all to the only person left in the world he cared about.

Peter . . .

He could feel the rage starting to bubble, the acid in his stomach, so he sat down at his computer and logged on. It was strange, but an hour or so browsing through the posts on **FUCK THE FILTH** or **ROASTING THE PORK** almost always calmed him down. He could happily lose himself in other people's disgust for a while, take some comfort from it, and, when he logged off, he would not be feeling quite so alone.

The fact that he *did* feel so strongly was why he'd reached out to ButterflyGrrrl to begin with. He hadn't done so straight away, but he'd known he was going to as soon as he'd seen her first message. How could he ignore it? They'd been coming at things from very different angles, obviously, but they shared the same hatred.

It was why he'd offered to help, even if she'd pretended not to understand exactly what that help would entail and wasn't as immediately grateful as she might have been. As she should have been.

It sounded like she was coming round, though.

TWENTY-NINE

'Say hello to Peter Samuel Brightwell.' Tanner stared at the mugshot on her computer screen.

'Looks like a charmer,' Holland said.

The individual to whom they now had a familial DNA match was easy enough to locate on any number of Met systems and databases. Tanner had gone down the obvious route by logging straight into the Police National Computer and calling up the details of a man who had been arrested multiple times for a series of offences.

A man who had been in prison for the past three years.

'Three guesses what he got sent down for,' Tanner said.

Thorne nodded. 'Name's ringing a bell.'

Tanner, Holland and Thorne were gathered around a single monitor as Tanner switched between programs, swiftly accessing arrest records, photographs and court reports; providing a running commentary as she scrolled through multiple pages of information.

'Brightwell was sentenced to life three years ago for the rape of a woman named Siobhan Brady and is currently doing his time at HMP Woodhill in Milton Keynes.'

'Life doesn't get handed down for rape too often,' Thorne said.

Tanner nodded at the screen. 'There were aggravating circumstances.'

Thorne needed to read no more than a few lines before he sucked in a breath. Siobhan Brady had suffered a vicious and prolonged attack.

'Pleading innocent didn't do him any favours, either.' Holland had moved across to the printer on an adjacent desk and was gathering up pages, doing his best to read them as fast as they spewed out. 'Maintained he didn't do it from start to finish, even with rock solid DNA evidence.'

Thorne walked over to join him, while Tanner carried on scrolling through different databases and printing out any documents that she thought might prove useful.

'OK, it's a familial match,' Thorne said, 'and I doubt the man we're after is Brightwell's father, so . . . his son, you reckon?'

'Peter's forty-four, so it's certainly possible.' Holland scanned the page he was holding. 'He was married . . . in fact his wife gave him a false alibi for the night the rape took place and ended up getting six months herself . . . but there's nothing anywhere to suggest he ever had kids, so—'

'It's his brother,' Tanner said.

Thorne turned to look at her, thinking: *Of course it is.* 'Love my bro . . .'

Tanner gave him a thumbs-up. 'Loves him a bit too bloody much by the looks of things. She nodded as the printer began whirring again. 'Here he comes now . . .'

Several photographs emerged, which Thorne and Holland gathered up and laid out on the desk.

'Emily Mead did a pretty decent job,' Holland said. 'He's lost some hair since these were taken, but that e-fit's pretty spot on.'

'Alex Brightwell,' Tanner said. 'He's our killer.'

Thorne picked up one of the photographs. A man shouting at a small crowd gathered outside a building.

'Thirty-three when those were taken, so thirty-six or thirty-seven now.'

Thorne lifted up another picture, a photo and a short article; a press cutting from the *Wandsworth Guardian*.

'He tried to kick up a big stink at the time of his brother's trial,' Tanner said. 'Local papers, local radio, waving placards around outside his MP's surgery, all that. Didn't do any good, obviously.'

'What's killing coppers got to do with any of this?' Holland asked.

Thorne began to read aloud from the newspaper article. '"My brother is innocent," says Alex Brightwell (33). "I'm not going to claim he's never broken the law, but he is not a rapist. Obviously people will claim I'm biased, but I know for a fact he did not commit this terrible crime. The police have known the truth all along and there's a very good reason why they've done everything they can to hide it. There's a reason why they've lied right from the start and why they're continuing to lie and that's because the truth is not in their interest. My brother was fitted up, it's as simple as that, and I won't rest until everyone knows what really happened and Peter is released."'

Thorne handed the article across to Holland as though the answer to his question had now become obvious.

'Looks like he ran out of patience.'

'Oh, *yes*,' Tanner said, suddenly. 'Get *in*.'

'What?'

Tanner was staring open-mouthed at whatever information was now in front of her and pointing at her screen. 'A fortnight before Peter Brightwell was arrested for the attack on Siobhan Brady, he was nicked for assaulting a sex worker.' She glanced at Holland. 'A charmer, like you said. She alleged that Brightwell refused to pay up once they'd finished their business and that he got a bit rough with her.' She read on, her smile broadening. 'As it was, nothing much came of her allegation, because for whatever reason she eventually declined to press charges, *but* . . . ' She turned to look at Thorne, beaming. 'Who do you reckon the arresting officer was?' She didn't wait for an answer. 'I'll give you a clue—'

'Come on, Nic—'

'He won't be eating doughnuts again any time soon.'

'Tully?'

'Police Constable Christopher fucking Tully.'

Thorne turned and leaned back against the desk, trying to work out where this new information left them. 'OK, so it's pretty clear that Alex Brightwell thinks Tully was a rapist, which he might well have been and maybe we'll never know, but . . . what? That's the sole motive for killing him? Alex Brightwell kills Tully, along with three other officers as collateral damage, just because he thinks Tully did something he believes his brother *didn't* do . . . ?'

Thorne wasn't convinced.

Tanner thought about it. 'Unless he's just planning to kill anyone who ever nicked his big brother for anything.'

'Hang on, though,' Holland said. 'We checked Tully's arrest

record days ago. We checked all those officers' records, but we had a really close look at Tully's. I mean, didn't we ... ?'

'Who was on it?' Tanner asked.

Thorne knew exactly whose job it had been and was already marching across the office. A few seconds later he was slapping his hands down on DC Stephen Pallister's desk.

'Fine, so you open your mouth when you'd be better off keeping it shut,' Thorne said. 'That's not against the law, and obviously you haven't been on the team very long so maybe you're still feeling a bit awkward or whatever, but are you *actually* a moron?'

Pallister just stared for a moment or two, then looked to others in the room as if one of them might come to his aid.

'Apologies if that sounds harsh, DC Pallister, but it's the only explanation I can come up with.' Thorne leaned across the man's desk. 'I really can't think of any other reason why you'd have checked Christopher Tully's arrest record and *not* thought the fact he'd arrested someone two weeks before the same individual was subsequently arrested and charged with aggravated rape was a *fucking red flag*.'

'I don't understand,' Pallister said.

Making at least some effort to keep the expletives to a minimum and struggling not to smack the DC in the side of the head with a stapler, Thorne walked Pallister through Tully's arrest of Peter Brightwell at the home of the sex worker following her accusation of assault.

'Shit ... I don't know,' Pallister stammered, and reddened.

'You don't know?'

'I must have missed it, that's all.'

'Right,' Thorne said. 'You must have.'

'I'm sorry ... '

Thorne turned when Tanner called his name, to see her heading in the direction of Brigstocke's office. He held up a finger to signal that he was right behind her. Shouting the odds when someone screwed up always got Thorne's blood pumping, but it couldn't quite compare with reporting a major break in a case to the Senior Investigating Officer.

There was still time for a parting shot.

'Never mind thinking before you speak.' Thorne stepped back from Steve Pallister's desk and shouted as he walked away. 'Just try *thinking*.'

Heading towards Brigstocke's office, he caught sight of DI James Greaves standing in the corner of the incident room. They exchanged nods. Greaves had clearly seen the aggressive dressing-down Thorne had given Stephen Pallister and Thorne could not help wondering which of them the CCU officer had been most interested in.

'This job does my head in sometimes . . .'

Done in or not, Brigstocke was shaking his head as he thumbed through the assortment of documents that Tanner had brought into his office with her. 'It's like you have days . . . *plenty* of days when you don't get anywhere at all, when it's like wading through treacle, and then there are days like this one, when a case just breaks wide open out of nowhere.' He looked up at Tanner and Thorne. 'It's days like this that make it worth coming into work.'

'Speak for yourself, Russell,' Thorne said. 'I'm excited every day I come in. I'm like a puppy chasing bog roll.'

'Right.' Brigstocke flashed a smile, which might well have been the first one Thorne had seen since this case had begun.

'Now we've just got to find Alex Brightwell,' Tanner said.

'On the hurry-up, for obvious reasons.'

'Should be the easy bit.'

'It *should* be,' Brigstocke said. 'We'll start with all the obvious searches. DVLA, voters register, banks ...'

'I don't think he'd be that careless,' Thorne said.

'Probably not, but we still need to tick all those boxes—'

There was a knock before Holland stepped into the office, looking as fired up as he had been when the DNA results had come in and starting to speak before he'd even closed the door behind him. 'I've been doing a bit more digging into the Siobhan Brady rape case,' he said. 'Turns out that when Peter Brightwell was nicked for it, one of the two arresting officers was our hit and run victim.' He nodded, pleased with himself. 'PC Stuart Needham.'

A few seconds passed while that sank in.

'Not a coincidence, then,' Thorne said.

Brigstocke was on his feet. 'What about the other officer?'

'Yeah, he's still on the Job,' Holland said. 'Working out of a station in Surrey somewhere.'

'We need to warn him straight away,' Brigstocke said. 'Maybe get him into protective custody. In fact, we should make efforts to contact every officer who worked on that case. Every uniform at whichever station Brightwell was held at, the desk sergeant who booked him in ...'

'Witnesses at the trial,' Tanner said. 'Prison officers, maybe?'

'It can't hurt.'

'We could be talking hundreds of people here,' Thorne said. 'There must be some way to narrow that list down.'

'I don't see how,' Brigstocke said. 'Needham was killed just because he happened to be the unlucky sod who slapped the handcuffs on Peter Brightwell three years ago, so why shouldn't everyone else connected with that case be at risk?' He leaned down and started scribbling notes to himself. 'I'll get the late shift to make a start and let's see where we are in the morning, when we've all had a few hours off.'

Brigstocke carried on writing while Thorne, Holland and Tanner drifted towards the door.

'You might want to think about getting shot of Pallister,' Thorne said.

Brigstocke looked up. '*What?*'

'He's a liability.'

'Seriously, Tom?' Brigstocke took off his glasses and wiped a hand across his face. 'Bearing in mind everything we've just been discussing, you think now's a good time to be losing a member of the team?'

'No, obviously not, but if he messes up again—'

'You never messed up, Tom?'

It was a question Thorne was able to ignore, as everyone present knew the answer.

'Russell . . .' Holland stopped at the door. 'I just wondered if you'd had a chance to look at that Daniel Sadler stuff I emailed to you.'

'Your suicide?' Tanner said.

'*Possible* suicide.' He looked back to Brigstocke. 'That weird business of the child porn charges never materialising, remember?'

'I told you I would, didn't I, Dave?' Brigstocke said.

'Yeah, I'm just—'

'And I will . . . only right now I'm a *bit* too busy to be wasting time on what still sounds like a straightforward suicide. We're all a bit too busy, don't you think?'

Holland nodded and mumbled his agreement, having clocked the look from Tanner suggesting that he should stop pushing it.

'Right, good, now you can all piss off home.' Brigstocke waved them away. 'Have a few drinks, because you've earned them, and most importantly, get some sleep. Tom, Nic . . . ' He reached for his mobile. 'I need to make a few calls, but presuming I can twist an arm or two, you'll be heading to Milton Keynes first thing tomorrow.'

THIRTY

Thorne was almost home when Hendricks called to ask him if he'd eaten. Liam was away, he'd said, but had cooked the night before and there were leftovers. Thorne turned immediately towards Camden.

'Away where?'

'Some conference in Edinburgh,' Hendricks said. 'Species Specific Rapid Identification Using Probe Technology.'

'Sounds like a bag of laughs.'

'It's going to be a riot, mate. There's a particular focus on blowflies.'

'Course there is.' Liam Southworth was a forensic entomologist, so it wasn't all quite as strange as it sounded. 'Your pillow talk must be riveting.'

'There isn't much time for talking.'

'Don't start that again,' Thorne said. 'You'll put me off my dinner.'

Fifteen minutes later, Thorne was sitting in Hendricks's

front room; a minimalist arrangement of chrome and leather with several new additions to the somewhat idiosyncratic décor. The skull of something with horns was sitting on a shelf near the enormous home cinema system and a stuffed weasel perched on a branch had been mounted above a doorway. Or maybe it was a polecat. Thorne shouted through to the kitchen where Hendricks was preparing the food.

'Fuck's that thing on the branch?'

'I'm not sure,' Hendricks shouted back. 'A stoat, maybe?'

Thorne looked around. There was also a stuffed magpie, a fox's head and a barn owl in a glass display case. It obviously wasn't a surprise that Hendricks was at home with dead things, but Thorne knew most of them had come courtesy of his boyfriend; the buying if not the actual stuffing.

'Liam really loves all this weird shit, doesn't he?'

'It's very on trend, mate.'

'Is it?'

'You're such a philistine.'

'I thought the latest trends in interior design were about how many cushions you should have on the bed, or what colour you should paint your wall.' Thorne looked again at the beady-eyed magpie. 'Not which dead animal was all the rage. Oh, and just so you know, the answer to how many cushions you should have on your bed is obviously *none*.' He heard the *ping* of the microwave and, a minute or so later, Hendricks carried through a tray; a beer for each of them and a bowl of something.

'Your cassoulet, monsieur.'

Thorne looked at it. 'It's a casserole, yeah?'

'A cassoulet.'

'Right. A casserole with beans.'

'Just eat it.'

Thorne looked at the tray, then at Hendricks. 'Salt and pepper?'

'Oh, for fu—' Hendricks stomped back to the kitchen, shouting. 'It's already seasoned. Liam would go apeshit ...' He quickly reappeared with the condiments, as requested. 'Oh, I forgot, you're the bloke who puts HP sauce on a carbonara.'

'What, and you've suddenly got a sophisticated palate, have you, Phil?' Thorne added salt and pepper while Hendricks sat down shaking his head. 'I watched you eat a pizza with half a pig on it the other night, remember?' He took a mouthful of the cassoulet and moaned appreciatively. 'It's very nice.'

'I'll tell Liam,' Hendricks said. 'Not about the salt and pepper, though, because to him you might just as well have pissed in it.'

Thorne spooned in a few more mouthfuls, then looked up. 'You going to sit there and watch me eat?'

'I've got a high boredom threshold. Plus I've already had a plateful.'

Thorne grinned. 'You put salt and pepper on, right?'

'Course I did,' Hendricks said. 'I love Liam to bits, but when it comes to food the bloke's a Nazi.'

They opened their beers and Thorne ran Hendricks through the last twelve hours. From the frenzied tedium of the tip-line calls and the contact between Emily Mead and LoveMyBro, right through to the DNA match that had pointed them towards the 'bro' in question, and finally the identification of Alex Brightwell as their prime suspect.

Hendricks said, 'Sounds like you had a busy one,' then sat back. 'You not going to ask me about my day, then? You aren't the only one whose job is a never-ending thrillfest.'

'Go on, then.'

'So, this morning I was elbows deep in an old woman whose heart looked like it had bacon wrapped round it, and this afternoon it was a sixty-six-year-old alcoholic with a liver that even a cannibal would have sent back. Oh yeah, mate, I'm properly buzzing.'

'Glad to hear it.' It would have taken descriptions far more disgusting than either of those to prevent Thorne finishing his food.

'Sounds like you've got another fun-filled day lined up for tomorrow,' Hendricks said. 'What are you hoping to get out of Brightwell the elder?'

'His brother's current address would be good, but I might be being optimistic.'

'You think he knows what his brother's up to?'

'We'll find out.'

'Do *you* know?'

'I think I know what it started as,' Thorne said. 'A reaction to the offence his brother was convicted for, which obviously Alex thinks he didn't do. Revenge against the cops generally, but with a specific thing about the ones who are rapists themselves. I really don't know what his motivation is now. He thinks Tully was a rapist, and we know Callaghan was. Holloway, Hussain and Bobak were in the wrong place at the wrong time and Needham was just doing his job. So, God knows ...'

'Maybe he's enjoying himself.'

It was something Thorne had been afraid of. 'That's always the worst,' he said. 'When they start to get a kick out of what they're doing and eventually doing it becomes reason enough in itself.'

'Strange, though, don't you reckon?' Hendricks said. 'That Tully, who just happened to have arrested Alex's brother right before he was arrested for raping Siobhan Brady, turns out to have been a rapist himself.'

Thorne was still struggling to work any of it out. As yet, there wasn't a shred of evidence that Tully *had* been a rapist, but Thorne remained convinced that he was, and the fact that Alex Brightwell believed it was all that mattered in terms of the investigation. If it turned out that Brightwell was wrong, Thorne would live with it.

You never messed up, Tom?

He would make some kind of penance to Chris Tully and his family. He'd do what he could to honour the memory of a good officer.

Right then, though, he was fairly sure he'd never have to.

Hendricks carried the tray back into the kitchen, then spoke from the doorway. 'Does Helen talk much to Alfie about his father?'

Thorne looked up. 'Did he say something?'

'No, but I was thinking about it the other night, when I was telling him that story.'

'Oh yeah, once upon a time there was a crab-infested corpse . . .'

'You think I'm a maniac?'

'I think it's a possibility,' Thorne said.

'I told him the one about the giant peach, *obviously*.'

'Look, he knows his dad's not around any more, but I'm not sure how much Helen's told him about why.' Alfie's father had been a police officer called Paul Hopwood, who'd been killed while Helen was pregnant. 'It's between them, isn't it?'

Hendricks nodded. 'Yeah, and I mean, it's not like the lad

hasn't got any positive male role models, is it? He's got you . . . OK, so maybe not all that positive, but he's got me, right?'

'The poor little bugger's definitely going to need therapy,' Thorne said.

THIRTY-ONE

Pippa had gone to bed, but Holland was not quite as tired as he had every right to be, so he stayed up to watch TV for a while. He tried to get into some Netflix thriller about a woman whose husband was secretly a psychopath, but it was too ridiculous for words. In all his years on the Job he'd only encountered one – the sort to give Hannibal Lecter a run for his money – and that individual was thankfully no longer around, but if TV dramas were to be believed, if you weren't living with or next door to one, you were undoubtedly a psychopath yourself.

He changed channels but couldn't concentrate.

He couldn't stop thinking about an abandoned motorbike and a man stumbling along a railway line, high up in the dark.

He turned off the TV and made the call.

A man who he presumed was the son – Nathan, was it? – answered and Holland apologised for calling so late.

'It's fine,' the man said. 'Mum isn't sleeping much, anyway.'

Holland waited.

'Hello, there . . .'

Karen Sadler sounded so stupidly pleased to hear from him that Holland immediately began wishing he'd never picked up the phone, feeling the guilt gain a little more weight. 'I hope I'm not disturbing you,' he said.

'You're really not.'

'I wish I had better news.'

'Oh . . .'

'Any news, really.'

'Meaning you still haven't been able to make . . . what did you call it . . . a determination? About Daniel.'

'I'm afraid not.' He heard the sigh. 'I'm still working on it, though. I suppose that's what I called to tell you, really.'

'Only I'm sort of in limbo here,' she said.

'I do understand—'

'I can't organise the funeral, or deal with the awful legal stuff and what have you, and all the time I'm sitting here asking myself, if it's not suicide, then . . . what is it?'

'I don't know, Mrs Sadler.'

Her voice dropped to a whisper. 'I mean, obviously I've thought all sorts, because you do, don't you? And all I'm left with is *why*?'

'I will find out,' Holland said. 'I promise you.'

'I know I've already said this to you, so I'm sorry for repeating myself, but anyone who thinks Daniel killed himself is wrong. They're plain wrong, simple as that. I've never been more certain of anything in my life, because I knew Daniel better than anyone.'

Holland said nothing, thinking about the side of her husband for which he had once been arrested; those disturbing and highly illegal tendencies about which he could only assume

Karen Sadler knew nothing. Then he considered the likely circumstances of that arrest. He pictured officers removing a computer and other materials from the house she still lived in, and wondered if perhaps she did know, or at least suspect.

He certainly didn't feel able to ask her, not yet at any rate. More importantly, he didn't see how finding out what his widow did and didn't know about her husband's past would further the investigation into Daniel Sadler's death.

'You're working very late,' she said.

'I'm at home, actually.'

'Oh. Well, it's very kind of you to call in your own time.'

'It's honestly not a problem.'

'Are you married, Detective Holland?'

Holland was momentarily taken aback, before happily telling her that he was, that in fact he'd been married just under a year.

'Well, do me a favour, will you? Stop wasting your time trying to make me feel better and go and kiss your wife.'

Holland felt himself redden. 'Right ... '

'Promise me.'

'OK, I will. And just to say that as soon as I get to work in the morning I'm going to be back on your husband's case. I'd hoped to have got a bit further with it, but things have been a bit hectic.'

'Yes, of course,' she said. 'You must all be very busy. It's dreadful what's happening ... I saw it on the news.'

Holland said that he'd call again if there were any developments. Or even if there weren't. Then he said goodnight, turned off the lights and went upstairs to do what Karen Sadler had told him to.

THIRTY-TWO

Brigstocke had clearly twisted enough arms to bypass the normal protocol for prison visits. He had managed to get a visitation order arranged at only a few hours' notice and to secure a private visits room, but the final decision as to whether or not the visit would go ahead had rested, as always, with the prisoner himself. Peter Brightwell would have been perfectly within his rights to simply decline, but had, by all accounts, been entirely comfortable with the arrangement.

He seemed every bit as relaxed now, when he was led into the room and sat down opposite Thorne and Tanner as though he were joining them for lunch.

'Thanks for agreeing to see us,' Tanner said.

'I didn't have a lot on.' Brightwell sniffed and looked around. Aside from the small collection of brightly coloured armchairs, a low table and a selection of safety notices pinned to a cork board, there wasn't a great deal to look at. 'Plus there was always the slim possibility that you might be here to say sorry.'

'Sorry for what?' Thorne asked.

'What d'you think?'

'That's not why we're here.'

'Like I said, a slim possibility.' Brightwell smiled, showing a far from complete collection of small, yellow teeth. 'They talk about "pigs might fly", don't they, because that's something that's never going to happen, but there's more chance of that than ever getting one to apologise.'

Three years into his sentence, Peter Brightwell looked very different from the man Thorne and Tanner had seen on that mugshot the day before, but the change in his appearance was not unusual. He was as prison-pale as they'd been expecting, as every other prisoner would be, but while some altered their shape through hours spent working out and a few wasted away, Brightwell was one of those who'd become bloated and jowly after years of stodgy food and no exercise at all. His gut bulged beneath the green tabard he wore over a sweatshirt and his neck had all but disappeared.

'We'd like to talk to you about your brother,' Tanner said. 'About Alex.'

'I do know my brother's name,' Brightwell said.

'When did you last see him?' Thorne asked.

'Not sure ... a couple of months ago, maybe.'

'He comes to visit you fairly regularly, does he?'

'Yeah, he's been in a lot.'

'He believes you're innocent.'

'He knows I'm innocent. Because I am.'

'But he hasn't been to visit recently?'

'Well ... I suppose he's been busy.'

'Oh, he's been very busy,' Thorne said.

Brightwell looked from Thorne to Tanner. 'What's all this about?'

It had become clear fairly quickly that the confidence Brightwell had been keen to display when he'd first come in was no more than an act. Thorne wasn't remotely surprised. HMP Woodhill was a place where the only thing anyone could be confident about was how much danger they were in on an almost daily basis. The prison housed some of the country's most notorious and high-profile violent offenders. The suicide rate was higher than in any other prison and, only a few years before, three inmates had been convicted of murder after attempting to behead a fellow prisoner in full view of CCTV and in front of prison guards.

So-called 'vulnerable' prisoners were even more vulnerable here than they would be anywhere else, and, as a sex-offender, Peter Brightwell would not have been given an easy ride. Thorne looked at him – at the shrunken eyes blinking a little too rapidly and the hand sweeping back and forth across a shaved head – and, though he felt no sympathy, it was apparent just how hard that ride had been.

Rapists were always a target.

So were those who had once been coppers.

Thorne could only guess at how much tougher life behind bars would be for men who ticked both those boxes.

'Did your brother ever mention someone named Christopher Tully?'

Thorne wanted men like that put away for as long as possible, but that was the beginning and end of it. He didn't want them shanked in the shower or doused with boiling water. He was not even comfortable at the thought of them drinking tea that had been pissed in, but knowing that some or all of these things might well happen, he still struggled to summon up any great compassion.

'He was a police officer,' Thorne said. 'Tully.'

Brightwell nodded slowly, one bristly chin sinking into the others. 'Yeah, I remember Tully, and I know what's happened to him an' all because I saw it on the news. I can't say I was particularly upset because the arsehole nicked me once.'

'When you assaulted a sex worker,' Tanner said.

'I was released without charge.'

'Lucky for you.'

'I should have done them for wrongful arrest.'

'Not quite so lucky for Siobhan Brady.'

'I did not rape Siobhan Brady.' Brightwell shifted forward in his chair and looked hard at Tanner. 'I never raped anyone.'

'Did Alex ever mention Tully?' Thorne asked. 'When he was visiting.'

'I don't know ... maybe. We talked a lot about the case, obviously.'

'What's Tully got to do with the Siobhan Brady case?'

'His name must just have come up, that's all. We talked about coppers all the time. About how you couldn't trust any of them, how totally rotten and rancid they all were.'

'None taken,' Thorne said.

'Where's this going, anyway? Why are you so interested in Alex?'

'Because he murdered Christopher Tully,' Tanner said.

Brightwell laughed, then sat back and stared. Then he laughed again.

'If you saw it on the news, you'll know that he actually

murdered three other police officers at the same time, but we know Tully was the one he was interested in.'

'You lot have lost the plot,' Brightwell said.

'A few days later he stabbed an officer named Adam Callaghan to death,' Thorne said. 'Then the night before last he ran over and killed an ex-police officer named Stuart Needham.'

'You seriously expect me to believe any of this?'

'He's been very busy, like I said.'

Brightwell was starting to get worked up. 'It's a sick joke, that's what it is. Like you're not content with fitting me up, so now you want to fit my brother up as well. What's wrong with you people?'

'Nobody's getting fitted up,' Thorne said. 'We were able to identify your brother's DNA at the Adam Callaghan crime scene.' That wasn't strictly true, of course. The fag-end that had provided the incriminating DNA had been found *in the vicinity* of the crime scene and Thorne was well aware that as a piece of evidence it could be dismantled by any half-decent brief in a few sentences, but he wasn't about to split hairs.

'Oh, right, *DNA* ... well, now I know this is bollocks.' Brightwell began to rant as he mounted what was clearly a hobbyhorse. 'DNA's the reason I'm in here and I didn't do anything. A nice handy bit of DNA trumps everything, right? Alibis, witnesses ... whatever. Like that stuff's the holy fucking grail, like it's never wrong and the people in those labs can't possibly make a mistake.'

'Your DNA was found in Siobhan Brady's rape kit.' Tanner sounded frosty suddenly. 'There wasn't any mistake.'

'You any idea what it's like to be falsely accused of rape?'

'No, I haven't, and I don't think we should get into this.'

'It's as bad as *being* raped.'

'You should stop before you start to seriously piss me off,' Tanner said.

'We're not here to talk about your case, Peter,' Thorne said.

'Well, *I* want to talk about it. I've spent the last three years talking about the fact that I'm innocent, even if nobody wants to listen, and so has my brother.'

'Yes, he has,' Thorne said. 'But now he's done talking. He's murdered six people so far and there's nothing to suggest he's finished.'

Brightwell mumbled, grim-faced, 'So you say.'

'We're saying it because it's the truth.' Tanner appeared to have calmed down a little. 'Whatever the circumstances of your arrest and conviction, all we're concerned about now is finding Alex before he kills anyone else.'

'And you think that I can help you?'

'We're hoping that you might.'

'That I *would* help you, even if I was able to?'

Thorne and Tanner both understood that this was an entirely different question, but they had little option but to try. 'Have you had any contact with your brother since he last came to visit?' Thorne asked.

Brightwell leaned back and, for half a minute or more, it seemed as though the conversation might have come to an end. Then he looked up and shrugged. 'I talked to him on the phone a couple of weeks ago.'

'And how did he sound?'

'He sounded pretty happy,' Brightwell said. 'Excited.'

Thorne nodded, wondering if Alex Brightwell had called his brother when he'd first had the idea for the doughnuts, or right after he'd taken delivery of the arsenic. 'Do you know where he was living at that point?'

Brightwell shook his head. 'He never said. Actually, now I think about it, we didn't talk about my case or anything like that, which I suppose is a bit strange because we usually do. Appeals and whatever. We mainly talked about our mum and dad. You know they both died just after I was sent down?'

Tanner glanced at Thorne. 'Sorry to hear that,' she said.

'We were both pretty cut up about it . . . I mean, obviously, but Alex was the one who had to organise everything. He was in bits for a long time.'

'I asked about where he might have been living because, for obvious reasons, he's gone off the grid,' Thorne said. 'Have you got any idea where he might have gone?'

Brightwell might still have been thinking about his parents or he might simply have had nothing to say.

'Any friends he might be staying with?' Tanner asked.

'I don't think Alex has got any friends,' Brightwell said. 'He doesn't really see anybody. He spends all his time trying to get me out of here.'

'If he gets in touch again, we'd very much like to know about it.' Thorne leaned towards Brightwell, but it didn't look like he would be getting a positive response any time soon. It didn't much matter. Any calls made or received by Peter Brightwell from now on would be monitored and recorded, on the off chance that if his brother did make contact, he might let slip something to give them a clue as to his whereabouts or what he was planning to do next.

Thorne doubted that Alex Brightwell would be quite so careless, but it was worth a punt.

'Apart from my wife, he's the only person in the world who

has any faith in me,' Brightwell said. 'The only one. Everyone out there who even remembers me and every fucker in this place thinks they know what I am. So that's how they treat me. Like a piece of shit. Alex has always stood by me, though, which is why I'm finding it so hard to believe what you're telling me.' He looked up at Thorne and Tanner and tried to blink away a film of tears. 'Why I don't *want* to believe it.'

Driving south on the M1, Thorne said, 'Interesting what he said about Tully, don't you reckon?'

Tanner nodded, staring out of the passenger window. 'Why's Tully's name coming up at all when Peter and Alex are talking about the Siobhan Brady case?'

'Right. Peter's arrested for raping Siobhan Brady and the only link to Tully is that a fortnight before he nicked Peter for an offence that's completely unconnected.'

'Then a few years later, his little brother's making accusations on that message board.'

Thorne thought about the message Alex Brightwell had posted: *Chris Tully and Craig Knowles. Two peas in a pod.*

'Something we're not seeing,' he said.

'Or something that just hasn't become visible yet.' Tanner turned from the window. 'The parents dying might be important, too.'

'Yeah. If Alex blames the police for Peter's conviction, then his parents die soon afterwards ...'

'He probably blames the police for that as well.'

'Sounds like a motive to me,' Thorne said.

They drove on, the regimented outskirts of Luton drifting past and giving way to scrubby brown fields and patches of woodland. Thorne turned the radio on and tuned it to

Absolute Country, but after a minute or so Tanner leaned across to turn it off again.

'Come on, that was Merle Haggard.'

'I don't know if Brightwell was deliberately pushing my buttons in there or what,' Tanner said.

'Yeah, I could see he was winding you up.'

'All that false accusation stuff. You do know that's bollocks, right?'

'It's what I'd expect him to say.'

'It's a convenient myth put about by rapists, that's what it is. The whole idea of women "crying" rape. Do you know how many men are actually falsely accused of rape every year?' She didn't wait for an answer. 'It's one in every two hundred allegations, like ... half a per cent of all cases. A man's more likely to be raped by another man than be falsely accused of it by a woman. He's got more chance of being eaten by a shark—'

Thorne's phone rang and, while Tanner was still quietly cursing, he touched a button on the dash to patch the call through to the speakers.

'Hey, Dave ...'

'How did it go with Brightwell?' Holland asked.

'Well, Nic's his new BFF.' Thorne turned to see Tanner giving him the finger. 'But yeah, a couple of things we need to talk about. We can fill you in when we get back.'

'OK, but it's a bit of a madhouse here, just so you know. Emily Mead's managed to persuade Alex Brightwell to meet up with her, so Russell's putting a big op together.'

'What?' Tanner sat up a little straighter. 'When?'

'Eight o'clock tonight. Whittington Park.'

'*Tonight?*'

'That's why it's such a kick-bollock-scramble.'

'Shit . . . I'd better talk to Emily.' Tanner was already reaching for her phone.

'I spoke to her myself about an hour ago,' Holland said. 'And she's doing OK. I mean, she's nervous, you know . . . but she's up for it. To be honest, I think she just wants to get out of that flat.'

'First rule of a bait operation,' Thorne said. 'Always put your bait up somewhere with a beige colour scheme.'

THIRTY-THREE

Whittington Park was a relatively small green space at the north end of Holloway Road, midway between Archway and Upper Holloway tube stations and, as it happened, only two miles from Thorne's flat in Kentish Town. On a side street opposite one of the park's entrances, Thorne sat next to a unit driver in the front of a people carrier with blacked-out windows. Emily Mead was next to Tanner in the seat behind and, at the back of the car, a tactical firearms commander named Chowdhury sat marshalling his officers via a laptop computer.

This was the operation's command post from where all movement would be monitored and all orders given.

'That's supposed to be his cat, right?'

Tanner turned round. 'What?'

Chowdhury looked up from his laptop and nodded towards the large, leafy cat that had been sculpted from a bush at the park's entrance. 'Like in the pantomime. Turn again, Dick Whittington, all that.'

'I suppose.'

'Yeah, but that's just a story,' Emily said. 'He was actually a real person, you know, a merchant or something. I don't think he even had a cat.'

'But there's a statue of the cat up the road, outside the hospital.'

'Like I said, mate, he was a real person.'

'Yeah, I get that.'

'He was Lord Mayor of London.'

'Probably because he helped get rid of all the rats.' Chowdhury nodded to himself. 'Well, his cat did.'

'I already told you, that was just a story.'

'Can we forget about the fucking cat?' Thorne said.

Emily took a final look at Chowdhury, then leaned close to Tanner and whispered. 'I can't say I'm overly confident about *him*.'

'Don't worry,' Tanner said. 'He's here because he's good at his job, not because of what he knows about local folklore.'

There were several other entrances to the park, with a plainclothes officer stationed to have eyes on each. Further officers, each armed with a concealed Glock 19 pistol had been positioned in or around the playground at which Emily had arranged to meet Alex Brightwell; two undercover as a young couple, with a third playing the part of an evening dog-walker. There were more firearms officers hidden in the trees on either side of the playground. These carried Sig Sauer carbines with night scopes and, along with every other officer taking part in the operation, were in permanent radio contact with the TFU commander as well as Thorne and Tanner.

'It's all going to be fine,' Tanner said. She hadn't needed to hear Emily snapping at the firearms commander to know how nervous she was. 'I promise. You're doing brilliantly.'

'I haven't done anything yet.'

'Just getting this far.'

Emily nodded, shrinking a little inside her silver Puffa jacket.

'I mean it. The way you got him here was seriously smart.'

'If I *have* got him here.'

Thorne turned round to look at her. 'Nicola's right. Whatever happens, it was bang on, how you handled him.' Having seen a transcript of the conversation she'd had with Brightwell first thing that morning, he had no doubt that Emily Mead was very smart indeed, and not just because she knew Dick Whittington didn't really have a cat.

<<I know about another copper like Callaghan.>>

<<*How?*>>

<<Because Callaghan told me. They were mates. Used to compare notes on the women they'd done it to. Mark them out of ten. Fucking animals.>>

<<*What's his name?*>>

<<Is this place really safe? Throwing names around.>>

<<You weren't worried when you told me about Callaghan.>>

<<His name's Marsh, works out of Clapham station. He's a sergeant, I think.>>

Emily had explained that Marsh was actually the officer she'd first spoken to when she'd turned herself in five days before. 'I thought I'd better give Brightwell a real name,' she'd said. 'In case he checked.'

Thorne and Tanner both agreed that Emily had been right to play it safe, although knowing how quickly Brightwell had moved in the past, the officer she'd named had been immediately taken off duty.

<<I want to help.>>

<<I don't need any help. You should know that by now.>>

<<I can be involved though. Let's meet up and talk about it at least.>>

<<. . .>>

<<I won't freak out again I swear. I already said sorry about that.>>

<<Fair enough.>>

<<Same place as last time? The park.>>

<<Not there. Might still be filth around.>>

<<Fine, you pick somewhere . . .>>

Thorne looked at his watch. 'Five minutes,' he said. 'You should go.'

Emily nodded, breathing a little more heavily than she had been.

'Don't worry.' Tanner leaned across to give the woman a hug. 'We'll be with you the whole time and if you're worried about anything, anything at all, just say the word.' Like everyone else, Emily had been fitted with a hidden earpiece and microphone. 'We'll call it off and pull you out straight away.'

'OK.' Emily reached for the door then stopped. 'Do you know any more about what's going to happen to me when it's over? If he does turn up and you catch him, I mean.'

'I'm afraid we don't,' Tanner said. 'But I can promise we'll be fighting for you. Just try not to think about it.'

'Oh yeah, course.' Emily looked at Tanner as if she was mad, then took a deep breath and opened the door.

Thorne and Tanner watched her waiting at the pelican crossing, bouncing on the balls of her feet, before walking quickly across the Holloway Road and into the park. They saw a plainclothes officer move to follow her fifteen seconds later.

'All units from TFC,' Chowdhury said. 'Standing by . . .'

'She'll be grand.' Thorne turned around. 'Nic . . .'

Tanner said nothing, peering through gaps in the traffic at

Emily Mead's silver jacket as it shrank into the distance and then disappeared from view.

Emily walked fast, but not too fast, like they'd told her. It was a reasonably straight path with tall trees on either side and she could see the outline of buildings up ahead in the distance. It was seriously cold. She asked herself why the hell she was doing this, why she was on her way to meet up with a murderer, especially when she might well end up in prison for her trouble anyway. Fine, so there were coppers everywhere, but she knew how dangerous the man she'd arranged to meet was.

What he was capable of.

'Don't think about it, just keep walking.'

'Everything OK, Emily?' Tanner's voice was tinny in her ear.

'Sorry, talking to myself.'

'No problem. Just try and keep calm. I know that probably sounds stupid.'

'I just wish it wasn't so dark.'

'Not for long,' Tanner said. 'Where you're supposed to be meeting, there's spill from the football pitch up by the playground and there are some outside lights at the community nursery.'

'Hang on . . .' Emily watched as a figure loomed into view. 'There's a man coming towards me.'

'Don't worry, it's not him. We've got officers watching every entrance and he hasn't been spotted.'

The figure got closer, his face illuminated by the light from a phone screen. 'It's fine,' Emily said. 'It's just an old bloke. Sorry.'

'Don't be sorry,' Tanner said. 'You're nearly there, OK?'

Tanner had been right about the lights, and by the time Emily reached the bench at the edge of the playground she could see her surroundings much more clearly. She spotted the young couple sitting together on the slide. She knew they were coppers, same as the man with the dog mooching around by the nursery.

'OK, I'm in position,' she said.

'Still standing by,' Chowdhury said.

Each of the armed officers quickly acknowledged the message.

Ten minutes later, Emily was starting to shiver, jumping at shadows and struggling to breathe normally. 'How long are we going to give him?' she asked.

'Just hang in there,' Thorne said.

'That's easy for you to say.'

'I know.'

'It's bloody freezing out here.'

'I think we should wait at least—'

Thorne was cut off by a message from one of the officers manning the park's perimeter. 'IC2 male matching suspect's appearance has just entered park via the west entrance next to the community centre.'

'Shit,' Emily said.

'Try not to panic,' Tanner said. 'We've got officers on him every step of the way.'

'All units, move to code amber,' Chowdhury said. 'Suspect approaching playground . . .'

Emily turned to see the man walking towards her. He was wearing a dark jacket over a hoodie, his face obscured.

She stood up and raised a hand.

The figure was no more than twenty feet away from her. It was still possible, of course, that he was going to walk past, that he was simply someone out for an evening stroll through the park. She didn't even know if she wanted it to be Brightwell or not.

What she wanted was to turn and run.

'All units from TFC. Prepare to move to code red . . .'

Then the man lurched suddenly across to her side of the path and quickened his pace, heading straight for her.

'All units go!'

'Armed police! Stay where you are and put your hands in the air.'

Emily looked to see the young couple running towards her with guns in their hands; the dog-walker doing the same.

'Hands in the air!'

The man stared for a few seconds as if he couldn't see them, then slowly raised his arms. 'Yeah, all right, I'm doing it. I'm doing it . . .'

Thorne and Tanner were out of the people carrier and sprinting into the park as soon as the firearms officers took their weapons out. Within thirty seconds they had reached the playground to see one of the officers standing close to the suspect, while the others kept their guns trained on him from a few yards further back.

Emily was watching from the bench, her hands across her mouth.

'Fuck's going on?' the man asked.

'Lift your hood up so we can see your face.'

Still looking somewhat dazed, the man did as he was told.

'It's not him,' Emily said.

Thorne and Tanner stepped forward and Thorne told the armed officers to put their guns away.

'All units stand down,' Chowdhury said.

'Who the fuck are you?' Thorne asked.

'I'm Billy,' the man said. 'How you doing?'

He sounded slurry and, even from several feet away, Thorne could smell the alcohol on him. 'What are you doing here?'

The man lowered his arms. 'I've got something for *her*, haven't I?' He pointed at Emily. 'Some bloke came up outside the tube and paid me twenty quid to give her a message.' He reached into his jacket and the armed officers immediately produced their weapons again.

'I'd do it slowly if I was you, Billy,' Thorne said.

'I mean ... twenty quid's twenty quid, right?' The man gingerly produced a crumpled piece of paper and Thorne moved quickly to snatch it off him.

Tanner watched as Thorne unfolded it and leaned in to look.

'What is it?' Emily asked.

'Can I keep the money?' Billy asked.

'It's nothing,' Thorne said.

'I want to see.' Emily walked across and held out a hand.

Thorne turned to Tanner, who took a few seconds then nodded. Thorne handed the message across.

Emily stared down at the elaborate drawing and stifled a scream.

A butterfly, splayed and mounted on a bloodied pin.

THIRTY-FOUR

By the time they had driven Emily back to the safe house in Edgware, Tanner had already received a message from Greg Hobbs at the DFU. The text of a message Alex Brightwell had posted to Emily in the usual place, sent within a few minutes of the operation being wound up at Whittington Park.

> <<You must think I'm an idiot, Emily. Did you really think I didn't know what you were up to, and do you honestly believe you're SAFE?>>

Tanner waited until Emily was in the bathroom and she could hear the shower running before showing Thorne.

'He was watching us.' Thorne began pacing the room; just a few strides between one bare wall and another. 'Watching us and laughing.'

'He obviously knew what was going on before we even got there,' Tanner said. 'When he was paying that pisshead to deliver his drawing.'

'Right, which begs an obvious question.'

'The same question we had when this started.' Tanner sat back on the oatmeal sofa and kicked her shoes off. 'How he knew about the Cresswell operation. How he knew exactly where Chris Tully was going to be that night.'

'Yeah, well we know he's got the capability to find *some* stuff out,' Thorne said. 'He told Emily, right? Specialist computer programs and databases, whatever.'

'This is more than him just doing his homework or having a fancy scanner. It's starting to look like someone's feeding him information.'

It was the same conclusion Thorne was fast coming to. 'Which begs an even harder question,' he said. 'We know *he's* not a copper, but he must be getting intel from police sources, surely? I can't see any other explanation for him being so far ahead of the game. I mean, unless I'm missing something.'

Tanner shook her head.

'If it's a copper who's giving him this stuff, a member of civilian staff maybe ... what possible reason have they got? Why the hell are they helping someone who's killing other police officers?'

Tanner was clearly struggling to come up with an answer every bit as much as Thorne was. She said nothing for half a minute, then looked across at him. 'If we're right about this, we should have a good look at the list of officers who've got access to this place.'

'We should come up with our own list,' Thorne said. 'And make it a very short one.' He was still puzzling it over, trying to process this horrifying new idea in any way that might make sense. 'Blackmail, maybe?'

'It's a thought.'

'If Brightwell was able to find out about Tully, maybe he'd already found another copper with something serious to hide.' The more Thorne considered it, the more it seemed like a decent explanation. Like the only explanation. 'Only instead of killing them, he's forcing them to provide the intelligence he needs to kill others by threatening to expose them if they don't. So they tell him about Tully working the Cresswell op. About Emily coming to us and about tonight.'

'It's got to be someone close to home,' Tanner said. 'Because there can't be too many people who had access to all that intel—' She stopped when she heard the shower shutting off and turned to look towards the bathroom door.

Thorne lowered his voice. 'We should take this to Russell first thing tomorrow. See if he can come up with the names of everyone who had access.'

'OK.'

Thorne reached for his leather jacket. 'I'm going to head off.'

'I think I'll stay here for a bit.'

'What are you going to do about food?'

'We'll get something delivered.' Tanner saw the question in Thorne's face. 'Don't worry, I'll get a lift home.'

'Call me later.' Thorne pulled his jacket on. 'Nic . . . ?'

Tanner was still waiting for the bathroom door to open, for Emily Mead to emerge. 'I think she could do with some company.'

Emily came into the living room a few minutes after Thorne had left. She was wearing joggers and a T-shirt under a well-worn dressing gown and rubbing at her wet hair with a towel.

'Warmed up a bit?' Tanner asked.

Emily nodded and sat down.

'You hungry?'

If the officer who'd been stationed outside the building resented being treated as a glorified Deliveroo driver, he showed no sign of it. When Tanner went down to collect the food, he said he hoped they enjoyed their dinner. He said it was a shame that the operation at Whittington Park hadn't panned out and asked if Emily was going to be all right.

'We'll see,' Tanner said.

Twenty minutes later, with the remains of a Chinese on the table between them, Emily said, 'What happens now, then?'

'To you, nothing,' Tanner said. 'You stay where you are.'

'Oh, great.'

'Look, it's not ideal, I get that, but we know who he is now, so it's only a matter of time.'

'You think?'

'Definitely. He makes one little slip and we've got him.'

'Or maybe that nerdy bloke in the wheelchair can do something magic with that special bag of his.'

'I wouldn't put it past him,' Tanner said.

'Fair enough.' Emily lifted her feet on to the sofa. 'It's boring as anything, but at least I'm safe stuck in here.'

Tanner said nothing. There was little point in sowing seeds of doubt or scaring the woman without good reason, so she had no intention of sharing the message Alex Brightwell had sent a couple of hours earlier.

'It's not like he's Spiderman, is it?' Emily managed the first smile since they'd brought her back. 'And there's no windows for him to get through even if he was.'

For half an hour or so, Emily talked about her family – a mum with MS and a father she hadn't seen for several years – and about an ex-boyfriend who'd cheated on her with a girl who worked in Aldi, then come crawling back a few months later saying he'd made a terrible mistake.

'He was fit, too, as it goes,' Emily said. 'But I'm not stupid.'

She talked about a few of the jobs she'd had and subsequently lost – receptionist, nursery assistant, telemarketer – and the drug habit that had been the reason more often than not. 'I've been clean for a while,' she said. 'I'm not going to make out like it's been easy ... so this is good, when you think about it. It's not as if I'm likely to relapse in here. Not unless the bloke who delivered my spring rolls does a sideline in skunk and Fentanyl.'

'You're doing brilliantly,' Tanner said. 'Everything you've been through, and what you're doing now, you should be proud of yourself.'

Emily cried after that, but not too much, and said nothing for a while.

Tanner was thinking that she should probably be getting home, when Emily looked across at her.

'It was actually the second time he'd been in my flat,' she said quietly. 'Callaghan.'

'OK ... '

'Him and another copper had been round a few months before when I'd been burgled. *Again.* Ground floor flat in south London, yeah?'

Tanner just nodded, but she was thinking that these days

you could count yourself very fortunate indeed if officers even bothered to attend following reports of a burglary. Thinking that in becoming known to Adam Callaghan in such circumstances, Emily Mead had been both lucky and horribly unlucky at the same time.

'That night, he just said he was passing. Said even though he wasn't on duty, he'd decided to pop in and see how I was doing, and I thought that was nice of him. Thoughtful.'

Tanner said nothing, sensing it would be better not to interrupt.

'So, I asked him in for tea.' She shook her head. 'I fucking *asked* him in ... and it was OK at first. We just sat in the kitchen and nattered about this and that, how there wasn't any progress on my burglary, but it wasn't like I was expecting any, not really, because the police have got other things to do, right?'

Other things ...

Tanner looked at the remembered horror that was already starting to etch itself across Emily Mead's face and it was impossible not to think about what some of those other things were.

'Then I'm thinking that he's on his way out, which is when he asks if he can have a quick look round. Check my security or whatever. It wasn't a big flat, so it didn't take long ... the windows in the kitchen which he told me needed better locks, the back door, all that.

'Then we go into my bedroom ...

'And when I turn round, he's standing between me and the door, and I need to sit down because I'm feeling a bit woozy and that's when I knew he'd slipped something into my tea. Roofies or whatever, like the girls get jabbed with in clubs.

Easy enough for someone like him to get hold of that stuff, I would have thought. I knew one hundred per cent he'd done it, but it didn't much matter because suddenly I could hardly stand up and when he pushed me down on the bed, I couldn't do anything about it. I knew exactly what was happening ... what was *going* to happen, but I couldn't do anything to stop it.' She swallowed hard and leaned forward, desperate. 'I couldn't do anything, I swear. I couldn't move.'

Tanner stretched out a hand. 'It's OK, Emily. You don't have to—'

'He wasn't in any great hurry.' She was staring straight ahead, the muscles working in her jaw. 'Took his time, you know? His hands were all over the place and when he'd done what he wanted with them, he started to do all the other stuff. My jeans came off and my underwear and then he was just ... on me. On me for a bit, then turning me over and pushing me down and doing it everywhere.'

'I'm so sorry,' Tanner said.

'That's when I heard the other man.'

'*What?*'

'I remember really clearly thinking that he'd left the front door open when he came in. While I was lying there and he was doing what he wanted I was thinking: *He didn't close the door behind him.* He'd left it open so this other bloke could come in.'

'There were two of them?'

'Yeah.'

'You were raped by Adam Callaghan and another man?'

Emily shook her head and squeezed her eyes shut for a few seconds. 'No, it was just Callaghan doing it, but there was another man in the room. Callaghan had his hands on my

217

neck, but I couldn't have raised my head to look anyway, the state I was in, but I heard him. I heard him clear as anything.'

'What was he saying, this other man?'

'Just . . . egging Callaghan on, you know? Telling him to try different stuff because I was obviously loving it.'

Tanner said nothing, because there was nothing she could say.

The tears had come again, but Emily just sniffed and wiped them away, as though now they were no more than an inconvenience. 'I think that's why I never said anything – why I didn't go to the police. Not just because Callaghan *was* police, but because I never did anything to fight back. I mean, obviously I couldn't, but you know what some people are going to think. It's stupid, because later on I realised that they could have found the drug he'd used on me, tested my blood or whatever, but it was too late by then.'

'You didn't do anything wrong,' Tanner said. 'Or even unusual. Five out of every six women who get raped don't report it and of the rapes that are reported, only two per cent result in charges.'

Emily nodded and half-smiled, took a few deep breaths. 'So yeah, obviously I hated Adam Callaghan for what he'd done to me. I'd lie awake wishing he was dead, even though I never wanted it to actually happen and certainly not the way it did. I'd take all sorts, anything I could get my hands on so I wouldn't have to remember how much it hurt.

'I started to cope with it all a bit better eventually and maybe now that he *is* dead, it'll get even easier.

'Because I'd like to sleep, I really would . . .

'But however many drugs I've taken or how much therapy I've shelled out for, I've never been able to stop thinking about that other man's voice. I can still hear it, every word he said. Gentle, almost. Half-whispered. It's the first thing I think about every day and it's the last thing going round my head at night.

'The voice of that man who was watching Adam Callaghan rape me and telling him what to do.'

PART THREE
RANK

THIRTY-FIVE

Brigstocke had not been in his office when Thorne and Tanner arrived at Becke House. He was on his way back from Wood Green, he'd said when Thorne had called, where he'd been liaising – as per their agreement – with Jeremy Walker. Thorne had too much else on his mind to further voice his reservations about the need to involve Walker at all, so he kept them to himself. Instead, with the call on speaker and Tanner listening in, Thorne asked Brigstocke to meet them in the coffee shop opposite Colindale station as soon as he got back.

'Something I should know?' Brigstocke asked.

Tanner looked at Thorne and shook her head. This was a conversation they needed to have in person.

'I'm buying the coffee,' Thorne said.

'Good enough.'

Thorne and Tanner were already on their second round when Brigstocke finally walked in, looking ready for some caffeine of his own. As soon as he'd had a shot, he sat back and looked at them.

'Before you say anything, yes I'm well aware that Walker's a bit of a knob, but these things have to be done and, luckily for you, I'm the mug that has to do them.' He waited, clearly a little surprised that the response he'd been expecting – from Thorne at least – was not forthcoming. 'Christ, this must be serious.'

'Just a bit,' Thorne said.

Tanner leaned across the table. They were not the only customers, so she lowered her voice as she told the DCI exactly what she'd told Thorne late the night before. The horrifying story that Emily Mead had told her.

Brigstocke looked as if he was struggling to find the right words, so settled in the end for one simple expletive.

'Sounds about right,' Tanner said.

'So, it wasn't an accident that Emily came up with that story when she was trying to get Brightwell to meet her,' Thorne said. 'About there being another man. Because she knows there is.'

Brigstocke shook his head like he was trying to take it all in. 'She told Brightwell that she knew about another rapist, right? Specifically, another copper who was a rapist, but this man you're talking about, he's not . . .'

'No, not a rapist, not literally . . . but what that man did to Emily Mead was worse.' Tanner's voice was barely above a whisper, but the disgust was clear enough. 'He *directed* it.'

'When she messaged Brightwell, she gave him a name which she knew wasn't kosher,' Thorne said. 'Because she needed a name to make it sound credible. The rest of it she wasn't making up at all, and that's how you make a good lie convincing, isn't it? You make sure there's an element of truth.'

'And Brightwell believed it,' Tanner said.

'Hang on—'

Thorne cut Brigstocke off. 'Which makes me think he already knows there's someone else. Maybe several someone elses. Brightwell agreed to meet up with Emily because he knew that basically, she was telling the truth.'

'Why didn't he show up, then?' Brigstocke stared at them both. 'If Brightwell thought Emily was being straight with him, if he had no idea what we were up to, why wasn't he there in the park last night?'

Thorne glanced at Tanner. Now, Brigstocke would understand just how serious things were and why they weren't having this conversation in the office. 'I think he knew exactly what we were up to. Not when Emily sent him that message, but later on, before it all went down in the park. He knew, because somebody told him.'

Brigstocke sighed and slowly removed his glasses. He wiped them with a serviette, put them back, then stood up. 'I think I'd best get another coffee.'

Ten minutes later, Thorne and Tanner had laid out their suspicions; suspicions that had been simmering since the Cresswell operation a week before. When Brightwell had known exactly where PC Christopher Tully would be and where to leave those fatal doughnuts. When Thorne had suggested that the killer might even be a police officer. Suspicions that had grown into the belief that their suspect was in possession of far more intelligence than could simply have been gathered online, or from close observation, or from monitoring sensitive police communications on some high-end piece of kit he'd picked up at Argos.

Brigstocke asked the obvious question. The same question

Thorne and Tanner had immediately asked themselves. Why would a police officer, or even a civilian working for the Met, provide assistance to someone who was targeting coppers?

Beyond the possibility of blackmail which he and Tanner had already discussed, Thorne still had no answer, but fumbled for one. 'It's not quite as ridiculous as it sounds when you remember that these were not exactly good coppers. We know Brightwell's got a personal motive, but maybe whoever's helping him has just got a thing about . . . I don't know, getting rid of the bad apples. Callaghan and Tully.'

'It wasn't any kind of police source that led Brightwell to Callaghan,' Brigstocke said. 'We know that information came from Emily Mead, and, in case you've forgotten, there's still no evidence to prove Tully was a rapist.'

'We just haven't found it yet,' Thorne said.

'What about the three innocent coppers he poisoned? Bobak, Hussain and Holloway. How does that fit in with your bad apples theory?'

Thorne was starting to flounder a little. 'Well, if I had to take a guess, I'd say that whoever tipped Brightwell off didn't know he'd be willing to kill them just to make sure he got Tully.'

'That's possible, of course, but this unknown informant, who for reasons of their own is just trying to clean up the Met, was still willing to carry on feeding him information, even *after* that? To tell him Emily Mead was working with us?' Brigstocke shook his head. 'I'm sorry, Tom, but I'm not buying it.'

'We're just thinking out loud,' Tanner said.

'Well, you might need to think a bit more clearly.'

Thorne had to concede that his boss had a point, that they

still hadn't come close to working out what Brightwell's source was up to, but it did not shake Thorne's conviction that there *was* one.

'Listen, Russell ... I know you don't want to believe that someone's passing on information—'

'Too right I don't.'

'Even so—'

'Like this isn't enough of a nightmare.'

'A bit worse for Emily Mead, I would have thought,' Tanner said. 'For all the other victims.'

Brigstocke nodded, reddening a little. 'Yeah, course.'

'It is happening, though,' Thorne said. 'There's a leak ... so I just think we need to be careful about who we're "liaising" with.'

'*Walker?* You're seriously—'

'No, I'm not suggesting it's him, because it'll be someone who isn't obviously such a twat, but it's definitely someone close to the investigation. I mean, it's got to be, right?'

Brigstocke's glasses came off again.

'Maybe even someone on the team.'

'Jesus ... '

'We need to tighten the circle a bit, that's all, choose who we share important information with. Until we catch Brightwell or manage to ID his source, we can never be sure who we're talking to.'

'We should start with exactly who has access to the safe house,' Tanner said. 'You saw the message Brightwell sent to Emily after what happened at Whittington Park. I'm sure she's in no danger, but even so, I reckon it should just be the three of us.'

'Fine, I'll get it sorted.' Brigstocke sat back and stared into his mug for a few seconds. 'Taking all that on board, where do we go next?'

They thought for half a minute or so.

Beyond exploring all the usual and as yet unproductive avenues in the hunt for Alex Brightwell, Thorne was not altogether sure what their next move should be.

'I think we should look a bit closer at the other rape cases that are connected to this,' Tanner said. 'Maybe what happened to Emily Mead wasn't a one-off.'

'Sounds reasonable,' Brigstocke said.

'I'll see if I can track down Siobhan Brady, find out exactly what happened when she was attacked by Peter Brightwell, maybe tap up a few other people who worked that case.'

'Be careful.' Brigstocke nodded at Thorne. 'Like Tom says, you'll never know who you're talking to.'

Tanner assured him that she would remain cautious. 'And I'll try and talk to the woman who was raped by Craig Knowles.'

'The wife, you mean?'

'Wasn't there an earlier case?' Thorne asked. 'I seem to remember he'd been accused before.'

'Really?' This was news to Nicola Tanner.

'Three years earlier,' Brigstocke said. 'Knowles was accused of rape and arrested for it. That case was dropped early on, though, which is why, when he was on trial for raping his wife, he could legally be described in court as a man "of previously good character".'

Thorne scoffed. 'Right.'

'I think I should talk to *that* woman then,' Tanner said. 'The one who accused him first time round.'

'I'm not sure that's a good idea,' Brigstocke said.

'Why not?'

'It's ... complicated. Well, you'll see, but I'm fairly sure you'll be wasting your time.'

Tanner waited, but Brigstocke did not elaborate. 'Look, I know Knowles is safely banged up, and as of now there's no obvious link,' she said, 'but we know he and Tully were at Hendon together, and Brightwell did mention his name in that first message, so I think any rape he was accused of is worth looking at, whether he was convicted or not.'

Thorne nodded. *Peas in a pod.*

'Priya Kulkarni,' Brigstocke said. 'That's the name of the woman you're talking about, but I'm betting she won't talk to you.'

Tanner waited.

'I wasn't anywhere near that case, so I don't know all the details, but I do remember it being something of a shitshow. For her, I mean.' Brigstocke downed what was left of his coffee. 'I'm not sure she's very keen on the police.'

'I'm starting to wonder if anyone is,' Thorne said.

THIRTY-SIX

Brightwell had always loved walking. Growing up, he'd gone on long, mad hikes with his dad, tramping through the woods at the back of the house, and across the fields even, if the weather was OK. They'd be out all day sometimes, lifting up logs to look for beetles and poking around in holes that his dad told him were made by badgers or foxes. They found a grass snake once, curled up in a rusty bucket; just a little one, which Alex's dad let him bring home even though his mum was horrified and refused to have it in the house. He'd kept it in a cardboard box in the shed, fed it frogs and baby birds, but for some reason the poor thing had died and shrivelled up in the end. Thinking about it, that might have been the last time he'd cried, at least until what had happened to Peter.

To Peter and then to his mum and dad.

Peter hadn't been quite such a fan of the outdoors, that's what he used to tell everyone, anyway. He'd pull a face and moan that it was too muddy or too cold or too much bloody effort, but Alex always reckoned that his big brother just wanted those few hours alone at home with their mum. *Their* time. Alex and Peter were as close as any two brothers could be, but still there'd always been this funny tension, because Alex was younger and played up to that, so yeah, looking back, he was probably a bit spoiled. It must have been hard feeling like you were being ignored or that you weren't quite as special as you used to be, so it was understandable that Peter took every chance to stay at home and let their mum do her mothering bit, until he started spending more and more time away for reasons of his own.

Hanging about with older kids and doing whatever he had to if he wasn't going to look like a baby. Heading for trouble ...

Walking in London wasn't quite the same, but these days, if Alex had the time, he'd head to one of the city's wilder open spaces that made him feel like he was in the countryside. Travelling to his favourite locations by bike, he could then happily spend hours getting lost in Trent Park up in Cockfosters, or roving around on Hampstead Heath. It wasn't like he wanted to forget what he was doing, or how important it was, but it was nice to clear his head every once in a while, because what was rattling around in there wasn't always ... pleasant.

His brother, bedding down with the nonces on the special wing.

His parents, dead inside and shrivelling up like that snake.

Tully and the rest of them ...

A nice clear head also meant that he was able to plan things, of course. To take stock and map out the next step. He hadn't known things would turn out this way when he'd started, but there always seemed to *be* a next step: a new name on the list;

someone else who needed to pay. He'd resigned himself to the fact that this was how it was going to be until the truth came out and Peter was released. If that didn't happen – and sometimes, laid low by a black mood, he worried it might not – then maybe there'd never be an end to it.

That was fine, too, because he knew now that it wouldn't be easy to stop.

Because he was doing the right thing.

He'd cycled down to Charlton, stopping for twenty minutes once he'd got there for a sandwich, and tea from the flask in his backpack. He'd pushed on to Oxleas Wood where he'd locked his bike before finally walking into the trees from Shooters Hill. This was one of the few areas of deciduous forest in the city, with some bits of it dating back to the last Ice Age. Trees that were thousands of years old, for Christ's sake. He knew because he'd looked it up, because he enjoyed knowing things. Now, drifting slowly through the raggedy network of oak and silver birch towards the big, slimy pond at the south end of the woods, he was thinking how much his dad would have loved it here, and that even if he couldn't get to Emily Mead he wasn't really too bothered.

It wasn't like he was too surprised that she'd done what she did, and it wound him up to think she could have underestimated him quite so much, but it wasn't the end of the world. He hoped his last message had put the wind up her a bit, all the same. He'd found out about the safe house the same way he'd found out about other things and that, along with all the rest of the information he'd been gifted, had been a rather more welcome surprise.

He was sure that, eventually, he could have done what he'd been planning to do without any help, but he certainly wasn't going to turn it down when it was offered, even if he still had no idea exactly where it was coming from.

That gift horse again.

Now, thanks largely to his mysterious benefactor, he knew all sorts of things. He knew the police had identified him and that his picture was doing the rounds, which was why he'd taken steps to disguise his appearance when he ventured outside. He knew they'd been to see Peter, though he wasn't sure what they could have gained from that. He was also well aware that they'd taken steps to protect anyone they suspected he might be going after. All manner of iffy coppers and auxiliary staff, prison officers and court officials had been warned and offered protection. Dozens of the scumbags up and down the country, wrestling with their consciences while they scurried to safety.

Brightwell stopped when he reached the pond and stared out across the green water. There was a smell coming off the algae like rotten eggs, but he didn't really mind it. He bent down to turn over a log, but there was only dirt and worms and a disposable vape, red and shiny among the leaves.

It didn't much matter what they knew or who they warned.

That next step would lead him to someone who wasn't going anywhere.

THIRTY-SEVEN

Thorne had already left the office by the time Tanner returned. Having met with officers on Rape and Serious Sexual Offences units in Hounslow and Notting Hill, she'd talked to both Brigstocke and Holland about what she'd discovered and, in a series of text messages, had agreed to bring Thorne up to speed later on, over fish and chips at Helen's place.

'We should eat first,' Tanner had said. 'It's enough to put you off your dinner.'

As it was, knowing full well where Tanner had been, and what she'd said to Thorne, it was Helen who raised the subject before they'd finished putting the salt and vinegar on. Neither Thorne nor Tanner was particularly surprised by her interest. After numerous scandals and high-profile failings, the Met's 'Sapphire' teams – which had been established specifically to support the victims of sexual assault – had ceased to operate under that name a decade earlier. Before being finally disbanded altogether, they had been merged with the force's

Child Abuse Investigation units to create a single, unified command.

Helen Weeks had worked for many years on one such unit.

'Russell wasn't lying.' Tanner looked at Thorne. '"Shitshow" is right.'

'Craig Knowles?' Thorne glanced up from trying to fit as many chips as possible between two slices of white bread.

Tanner nodded. 'As we know, Knowles was convicted just over a month ago,' she said. 'A twelve-stretch, and it couldn't happen to a nicer bloke ... but he was arrested for raping a woman named Priya Kulkarni three years before that.'

Helen grunted. She did not seem surprised.

'He should have gone down for it,' Tanner said. 'Should have, but didn't. If it hadn't been for his wife, who he'd been happily raping for years, Knowles would still be walking the streets.' She grimaced, like she was biting back something sour. 'Patrolling them.'

'Thank God for Mrs Knowles.' Thorne knew that the rape of a woman by her husband was still a divisive subject. He knew that whatever the law said, an awful lot of awful people – several of whom carried warrant cards – still refused to believe that non-consensual sex within a marriage *was* rape, and that accusing one's spouse remained an incredibly difficult thing for a woman to do.

'Why was the original case dropped?'

This was easily the most shocking element of what Tanner had discovered, and it intrigued her that Helen had asked the question, as though she could hazard a fairly good guess at what the answer might be.

'The circumstances of Priya Kulkarni's rape were very similar to Emily Mead's,' Tanner said. 'Knowles had been to her home before, when she'd made a complaint about her car being vandalised on the drive. He came back a few days later and assaulted her in her living room, in the middle of the afternoon. He didn't drug her, like Callaghan did with Emily, but if anything he was even more ... brazen. He knew that she could identify him and he didn't seem overly concerned.'

'With good reason, by the sounds of it,' Thorne said.

'With very good reason.' Tanner picked up a chip, then dropped it back on to her plate. 'Priya goes straight to the police in Notting Hill and makes a complaint. All the necessary forensic samples are taken, a rape kit is put together and Knowles is immediately arrested. Pretty standard stuff up to that point.'

'So, what went wrong?'

'Well, according to the paperwork they dug out for me this morning, it was a "freezer malfunction".'

Helen nodded, as if she'd guessed right. 'Yeah, there were one or two of those.'

'A *what*?' Thorne asked.

'A malfunction,' Tanner said. 'Specifically, affecting the freezer at the forensic lab where samples were being stored before being tested. Nobody seems quite sure what happened, but it was accidentally turned off overnight, or a fuse blew, or someone didn't shut the door properly.' She sat back and shook her head. 'Either way, a number of samples were destroyed, meaning that several rape cases, including Priya Kulkarni's, had to be dropped.'

'Similar thing happened once at a station I was at,' Helen said. 'Some moron left their lunch in one of the sample fridges and contaminated all the evidence. I'm using the word "moron" only because nobody could prove he hadn't known exactly what he was doing.'

'You're saying it was deliberate?' Thorne asked.

'I'm not saying it wasn't.'

'So what happened to Priya's sample might not just have been a malfunction.'

'It's impossible to prove,' Helen said. 'Certainly now, but there's a history of these units trying to bump up their clearance rates by making any cases that are difficult to prove simply go away. A couple of officers on a Sapphire unit in Southwark were caught deliberately suppressing evidence for precisely that reason.' She saw the look on Thorne's face. 'I know, and what's worse is I don't even find it shocking any more. A rape case is always going to be difficult to win when it's just he said/she said, and once you take the forensic evidence out of the equation, that's usually all you're left with.'

'Even better if the end result gets a fellow officer off the hook.'

'Absolutely,' Tanner said. 'The forensic evidence that would have put Knowles away was no longer valid thanks to ... whatever happened to that freezer, and Priya Kulkarni was gently persuaded to let it go.'

'Or not so gently,' Helen said.

'Worst thing is, I think Knowles knew all along that's exactly what would happen. Remember I said he was brazen? According to Priya's statement, he actually goaded her when he was finished. He stood there, grinning while he zipped up his jeans and told her to go to the police if she wanted, because it wouldn't do her any good.'

'It didn't,' Thorne said.

'No, because he knew he could rape her with impunity.'

Nobody said anything for a while after that, and Tanner had been proved right as far as the effect of the conversation on their appetites went, with the food going cold and largely uneaten.

'There was one other similarity between Priya's case and Emily's,' Tanner said.

Thorne looked at her.

'Russell was right about Priya not wanting to talk to me and I can't really blame her, bearing in mind what happened ... but it's there in the initial statement she gave. Obviously nothing was ever made of it, because the case was dropped once the evidence had mysteriously defrosted.'

'Another man at the scene?'

Tanner nodded. 'Priya didn't seem quite as certain as Emily was, but she mentioned that Knowles had left her front door open and that she thought she'd heard footsteps outside her bedroom. It's certainly not as definitive, but—'

'Fuck,' Thorne said. 'That's not a coincidence, is it?' Seeing that Helen was suddenly unclear as to what he and Tanner were talking about, he ran her through the story Emily Mead had told. The man who had shadowed her attacker and seemingly orchestrated her rape.

The disgust that washed across Helen's face was obvious.

'I suppose we should be thankful that some things are still shocking,' Tanner said.

'What happened to Priya?' Thorne asked. 'Afterwards?'

Tanner pushed her plate away and reached for the untouched glass of wine she'd been given when she arrived and which she suddenly felt in serious need of.

'Not good,' she said.

Six miles north in Clerkenwell, Dave Holland was discussing the same subject with his wife, though, as Pippa's fertility window was still theoretically ajar, the half an hour or so directly beforehand had been rather more enjoyable.

'She tried to kill herself,' Holland said. 'More than once.'

'Shit.' Pippa turned on the pillow to look at him. 'I didn't think Nicola had been able to talk to her.'

'She managed to track down one of Priya's friends. Apparently, she's had several breakdowns and been sectioned a couple of times. She's still under psychiatric care.'

Pippa tugged the duvet up a little. 'Something we never really think about, isn't it?' she said. 'Think about enough, anyway. What it's like for the victims later on.'

'Especially if the perpetrator gets away with it.'

'He did get convicted eventually, at least.'

'Yeah, that's something.'

'Hopefully that helped her a bit.'

'It doesn't sound like it,' Holland said.

'No . . .'

Holland stared up at a crack that zig-zagged from the central light fitting to the wall. 'He wasn't put away for what he did to *her*. Rather than stand there in court facing him, being put through the wringer and called a liar, then likely as not watching him walk away scot-free . . . she dropped it. Let them persuade her to drop it.'

'It must have seemed like the best option at the time.' Pippa reached for her reading glasses and picked up the prize-winning novel she'd been struggling with but was determined to finish. 'The best . . . worst option.'

'To all intents and purposes, as far as everyone except Priya is concerned, that rape never even happened.' Holland thought about what Tanner had discovered in the files at the RASSO unit; the manner in which Knowles had taunted Priya Kulkarni when he'd finished with her. It was some small consolation that the ex-copper wouldn't be feeling quite as cocky any more, locked up on the Beast Wing for what he did to his wife. 'Christ, no wonder she's . . . not well.'

After a few minutes, Pippa laid her book down. 'I was thinking about this other bloke, the one who creeps in and watches. He's obviously someone who knew Callaghan *and* Knowles.'

'Yeah, presumably,' Holland said.

'What about Tully? You already know that him and Knowles knew each other.'

Holland thought about it. They had not found any clear connection between Tully and Callaghan, but there was no denying that Tully seemed like the one Alex Brightwell had been most interested in. It was certainly something to consider, to talk to Thorne and Tanner about.

Could Tully have been the one Emily Mead had heard whispering instructions?

There were goose pimples on Holland's arms suddenly, so he tucked them beneath the duvet and reached to draw Pippa to him. They wrapped arms and legs around one another and, for a few seconds, Holland wondered if his wife was about to suggest having another crack at baby-making. He wondered if he should suggest it.

Neither of them said anything, content to leave it be.

'When are you talking to Siobhan Brady?' Thorne asked.

'I'm waiting for her to get back to me,' Tanner said. 'She still lives in London, so as soon as, hopefully.'

Helen came back in from the kitchen and handed Tanner

a Tupperware box containing the leftover fish. 'For Mrs Slocombe,' she said.

Tanner thanked Helen on behalf of her aged cat, and they both ignored Thorne when he began complaining, because he knew he'd find his appetite again and would have happily eaten the cold fish himself later on.

'I'm not quite sure what you're hoping to get out of Siobhan Brady,' Helen said. 'Her case is done and dusted and the man responsible is in prison. I mean, that's what all the killings are about, isn't it?'

'Right, because at least one person doesn't believe that man *is* responsible. I know there's rock solid DNA evidence that says he is, but I still think it might be worth getting the victim's take on it. I've looked through the trial transcript and she never gave evidence.'

'*Two* people,' Thorne said.

'Two people . . . what?'

'Two people who don't believe that Peter Brightwell raped Siobhan Brady. You're forgetting his wife.' Ever since they'd talked about Craig Knowles's wife coming forward to confirm his guilt, Thorne had been thinking about another wife who'd done the exact opposite. 'She gave him an alibi, remember?'

'Well, of course she did,' Tanner said.

'Yeah, but she stuck to her guns, even when the DNA evidence against her husband convinced everyone she was lying. Stuck to her guns so firmly that she ended up getting six months in prison for her trouble.'

'You think it's worth talking to her?' Helen asked.

'I can't see any good reason not to. For a kick-off, being one of only two people who protested Peter Brightwell's innocence, she might have something helpful to tell us about the other one.'

'The one who's now murdered ... how many people?'

'Six and counting, I reckon.'

'I suppose it's worth a try,' Tanner said.

'Mind you, I don't know if her and her brother-in-law were even close.'

'I *hated* mine,' Helen said, pouring herself another glass of wine.

Thorne hadn't thought about Tedious Tim in a while; the prick Helen's sister Jenny had been married to before she'd finally seen the light. Thorne's relationship with Jenny had improved considerably once she'd finally given him the heave-ho. 'But there's only one way to find out.'

'I'm guessing that Peter Brightwell's wife is someone else who's not going to be a big fan of ours.'

'It's unlikely, certainly.'

Tanner stood up and walked towards the door to collect her coat. 'Best of luck.'

'You don't need luck when you've got charm,' Thorne said. 'And a winning personality.' He ignored Helen's snort of laughter and watched Tanner pick up the Tupperware box from the table; its contents destined for an arthritic cat named after a terrible joke on a sitcom which nobody under forty could remember. He said, 'I don't suppose me and Mrs Slocombe could go halves ... ?'

THIRTY-EIGHT

They had been stuck behind the white van for ten minutes and the abuse scrawled in the grime on its back doors was certainly not interesting enough to merit a repeat reading. DC Charita Desai muttered, 'Sod this,' and moved out to overtake.

'So, how was your Sunday?'

Tanner had been very glad of the day off and, having spent the morning in bed, had done nothing more onerous for the rest of the day than cook lunch, watch the football on catch-up and worm the cat. The fact that she had shared these activities with someone she was growing increasingly fond of had made them all perfectly enjoyable. 'Not much,' she said. 'Just mooching around with my partner.'

'Sounds good.' Desai glanced at her. 'That's . . . ?'

'Her name's Fiona.'

'Right, yeah. Right . . .'

Tanner wasn't sure if Desai knew that she was gay or not and wasn't much bothered either way. She made no secret of the fact, but neither did she go out of her way to make it public knowledge. She wasn't like Phil Hendricks who – much as she loved him – seemed determined to let as many people know, in as much detail as possible, exactly what he'd been up to, where, with whom and for how long. The man did not so much trumpet his sexual proclivities as employ the services of a large orchestra.

And a choir.

'What does Fiona do?'

Tanner's girlfriend did all *sorts* of interesting things, many of which she'd roped Tanner into – quite literally – the previous day, but before Tanner had a chance to answer Desai's question and explain that Fiona worked as a nurse, the satnav announced that their destination was ahead.

'Doesn't sound like the nicest pub in the world,' Desai said.

'No?'

'I googled it.' Desai slowed when Tanner pointed out the sign and turned into a small car park. 'I was thinking we could maybe grab a sandwich or something afterwards.'

'Good idea,' Tanner said. 'We'll talk to the woman for half an hour about getting raped and then maybe she can rustle us up a couple of cheese toasties . . .'

Siobhan Brady had finally returned Tanner's message the evening before and said she'd be willing to talk. As long as Tanner was happy to come to her and they could get it done during her lunch break.

Brady worked at a pub called the Cromer Arms in Essex. It was tucked away behind Romford Greyhound Stadium and, true to the description Desai had found online, looked like the ideal place for someone who'd just pissed away a week's wages on the dogs and wouldn't be overly bothered about the décor or the clientele.

'I think I might skip that sandwich,' Desai said.

Having obviously been watching out for their arrival, Brady waved from behind the bar as soon as Tanner and Desai stepped inside. She moved quickly to collect her overcoat and led them back outside and around the side of the building, to the desultory garden.

They sat down on a damp bench and Brady immediately lit a cigarette.

There was still frost on the grass and scattered scraps of ice glittering on the patches of mud.

'Thanks for agreeing to talk to us,' Tanner said.

'No bother,' Brady said.

Charita Desai leaned forward from the end of the bench, so she could see Brady's face. 'Would you be happy to talk us through what happened three years ago?'

'Well, I don't know about *happy*.'

'Sorry,' Desai said. 'That was a bad choice of word.'

Brady shrugged and blew out a thin stream of smoke. 'No, I don't love talking about it, but I suppose you've got a good reason to ask. Talking about it's a piece of piss ... you know, in comparison.'

The woman had long dark hair with more than a hint of grey, and a face that was heavily lined thanks to years of a serious smoking habit. Her voice was low, with a trace of an Estuary accent, and even bundled up in a thick overcoat it was clear that she was somewhat thinner than she should have been. Without the benefit of pictures, it was impossible for Tanner and Desai to know if she'd been quite as skinny or grey-haired three years before.

'It was late,' she said, 'and I was coming home from the pub. Not this one ... a place in Wood Green. I'd had a few drinks, *more* than a few to be honest, which obviously his defence team tried to make a big deal about at the trial, but that doesn't matter, does it? Doesn't matter if I was thoroughly rat-arsed.'

'It absolutely doesn't,' Tanner said. 'Drunk or stone-cold sober, your condition when you were attacked is completely immaterial. Wouldn't have mattered if you'd drunk yourself unconscious.'

'Which I was for a lot of it.' Brady flicked away what was left of her cigarette and reached for a fresh one. 'By the time he'd smacked me in the face a few times.'

'This happened on a patch of waste ground, yes?' Desai asked.

Brady shook her head, lighting up again. 'Well, it's nothing really, just a grotty cut-through behind a block of flats. There's sometimes cars parked there, kids messing about on bikes. It's dark, that's the main thing. Which is why it was properly stupid of me to try and take a shortcut home up there. Why it was ideal for him.'

Tanner shook her head. 'Where the offence took place doesn't matter any more than how much you'd had to drink, or what you might or might not have been wearing.'

Brady took a drag. 'I was wearing dirty jeans and a knackered old anorak, so his defence couldn't pull that one.'

'Clothing is not consent,' Desai said.

'Thankfully, there aren't too many barristers who'd dare to try the "she was provocatively dressed" routine these days,' Tanner said. 'And, even if they did, it's meaningless ... a myth. A man doesn't rape a woman because she's wearing a short skirt. It's not about that.'

'He came up from behind me,' Brady said. 'Like I was

walking along and he was suddenly just . . . there. I didn't hear him coming because I had my headphones on. Again, stupid.'

'And irrelevant,' Tanner said.

'Still stupid, though.' Her head had dropped along with her voice, the memories clearly still raw and painful as they resurfaced. 'I must have sensed something, I suppose, because I turned round, and that's when he punched me. Then he bent down to punch me again when I was on the ground and after that there was nothing until I started to come out of it, and he was on me.' She drew hard on her cigarette. 'Fucker was *in* me.'

They sat in silence for a minute or so after that; Brady bent forward with her elbows on her knees, her cigarette smoke taken quickly away by the wind, while Tanner and Desai stared across the garden at the collection of upturned plastic chairs and a single, rusting swing.

'This might sound like a strange question,' Tanner said.

'A bit random,' Desai added.

'But while it was happening, did you hear anybody else? Any kind of voice that wasn't your attacker's?'

Brady sat up straight and looked at Tanner. 'How did you know about that?'

Tanner looked at Desai. 'I didn't,' she said. 'I don't.'

'I'm not even sure I heard it.' Brady closed her eyes for a few seconds. 'I was a bit all the over the place, when I started to come round. It was more a feeling that there was someone else there . . . someone watching, so at first it was like, thank God, because I thought they'd stop him or call the police or whatever, but they didn't.'

'You didn't tell anybody when you went to the police?'

'Because I thought maybe I'd imagined it.'

Tanner nodded. She'd read both the initial statement Brady had given and a fuller one taken later. Neither had made reference to any other individual being present while she was being raped by Peter Brightwell.

'I did mention it, when I was talking to my solicitor, but he advised me to keep it to myself. I think he was worried that I'd come across as being confused about what had happened. Unconvincing, he said. I think that was one of the reasons they suggested I didn't give evidence in court.'

'I wondered about that,' Tanner said.

'Trust me, I was happy enough not having to go through it,' Brady said. 'I knew who he was by then and I never wanted to clap eyes on Peter Brightwell again if I didn't have to. They said it wouldn't make any difference at the end of the day anyway – that me not going in the witness box wouldn't matter because the DNA evidence was so solid.'

'I understand,' Tanner said.

Brady dropped her cigarette and ground it out. 'And they were right, because it didn't matter, did it?'

'No,' Tanner said.

Brady turned to look back at the pub, said, 'Are we about done?'

Tanner thanked the woman once again for her co-operation, especially as it must have been so difficult. Walking back to the car with Desai, she was thinking that no, the victim not giving evidence herself had not made any material difference, because her rapist had been rightfully convicted. But she was also thinking that what Siobhan Brady had left out of her statements could end up mattering a great deal.

THIRTY-NINE

'If you're selling something you can piss off,' Mandy Brightwell said, when she opened the door.

Having established that, as a benefits claimant, Peter Brightwell's wife would not – or should not – be working, and that she would not respond favourably to any polite request for a chinwag, Thorne had decided that his best bet was to turn up at her home address unannounced. As predicted, he and Holland did not get the warmest of welcomes.

'We're not selling anything,' Thorne said.

'I'm joking.' The woman smiled, thin and sarcastic. 'Obviously not, because you're coppers. You can tell a mile off.'

'Could we come in for a quick chat?' Holland asked.

'As long as it *is* quick and you don't bad-mouth my husband.'

Thorne smiled, thinking, *Bad-mouth a convicted rapist, heaven forbid*, and said, 'That's not why we're here.'

'Good, because I'd have to ask you to leave,' Mandy said.

'That's entirely up to you.'

'By which I mean, tell you to fuck off.'

'Understood,' Thorne said.

She stepped back and waved an arm mock-theatrically. 'Then do come in, officers, and wipe your feet...'

It was a one-bedroom flat in a bog-standard block opposite Crystal Palace station. In many ways it reminded Thorne of the safe house in which Emily Mead was holed up; spotless laminate floors and simple furnishings, though there were at least a few pictures on the walls – abstract prints and black and white photos – and windows offering a view of the block opposite.

Following Mandy Brightwell into a small and overly warm sitting room, Thorne noticed the walking stick she was using. She leaned the stick against a low table and lowered herself gently on to a leather sofa.

'I'm registered disabled, in case you're wondering. Which you were.'

Thorne said nothing, but could not deny it.

'I wasn't before I went to prison, mind you.' She shrugged. 'But that's what happens when someone doesn't like the fact that you gave an alibi to a rapist and pushes you down a flight of metal stairs.'

'That's awful,' Holland said.

Thorne nodded. 'Sorry to hear that.'

She cocked her head and stuck out her bottom lip; like *poor me*, like she really didn't want anyone's sympathy and least of all theirs. 'A blue badge is a blue badge,' she said. She settled back on the sofa, then immediately leaned forward again, as if she'd remembered something. 'I should probably offer you tea.'

'Oh...' Holland looked keen to accept her offer.

She sat back again. 'But I really can't be arsed.'

Mandy Brightwell was in her late thirties; five foot bugger-all and stick thin, with peroxide blonde hair shaved at the sides and teased into spikes on the top. She wore a striped cardigan over a tie-dye T-shirt and camouflage trousers. She looked like a cross between a hippie and a punk, who'd kick seven bells out of you if the fancy took her. Or at the very least batter you with her walking stick.

'How much time did you do in the end?' Thorne asked.

'I was sent down for six months and ended up doing three. Most of that in hospital thanks to two crushed vertebrae. Those stairs, remember?'

'So why did you do it?'

'Why did I . . . ?'

'Give Peter an alibi?'

'You're seriously going to sit here in my living room and ask me that?'

'I thought I'd give it a bash,' Thorne said.

Her long-suffering sigh sounded more like a growl. 'Because it was the truth, still is the truth. Peter was at home with me that night, simple as that.'

'We're well aware that's your story—'

'Not a story—'

'—but why did you stick to it?' Thorne watched Mandy Brightwell's eyes narrow and, for a moment or two, he wondered if she might be about to reach for that walking stick. 'Once the DNA evidence had come back, I mean. If you'd held your hand up *then*, when it was obvious Peter was going to be found guilty, you might have got a slap on the wrist for making a false statement, but I don't think you'd have been sent down for it.'

'How many times?' She looked at Thorne and Holland as though they were idiots. 'Because it was the truth. Those DNA results were dodgy as you like.'

'Were they?'

'You do know they found DNA from someone else as well, don't you?'

Thorne did know, because he had seen it when he'd read the court transcript; an attempt by the defence to suggest that the forensics were not conclusive. It had been summarily dismissed in light of the fact that Siobhan Brady had freely admitted having sex with an on/off boyfriend a few days earlier.

'DNA from some other bloke on a mouth swab, but the fact that they found Peter's in traces of semen was enough, apparently.' She sneered and muttered something under her breath. 'So, yeah ... once those results were in, it was pretty clear to all of us that Peter was in trouble. I suppose I could have changed my statement, said I'd made a mistake or something – and, by the way Peter *wanted* me to because he knew what was going to happen – but it would have been like throwing him to the wolves and I wasn't prepared to do that. Yeah, maybe it was stupid.' She straightened her back, wincing a little. 'Sometimes, when the painkillers wear off or when I'm struggling to get out of bed, I know it was stupid, but I'd do it again any day of the week, because that's what you do, isn't it? You stand by the people you love.'

'So, in all that time, you never once thought you might have made a mistake?' Holland asked. 'Maybe got the date wrong or something? Once they'd identified your husband's DNA.'

'For Christ's sake.' She shifted, groaning a little and clearly starting to get irritated. 'Look, I'm the last person who'd ever claim Peter was a saint. I know he's done all sorts in his time, but even if he hadn't been at home that night, sitting watching TV with me, which he was, I'd never have believed for one second that he raped that woman.' She sniffed; shook her head. 'No, my old man is not someone who'll do an honest day's work if he can make a few quid more doing a dishonest one, and fine, when he's had a drink he can get a bit lairy, but attacking a woman in a dark alley is not something Peter would ever do. Never in a million years, OK?' She looked hard at both of them. 'It's not who he is.'

Thorne took a few seconds, waiting for her to calm down. 'When was the last time you had any contact with Peter's brother?'

She blinked. 'Alex?'

'We know he's always been very proactive when it comes to maintaining your husband's innocence, so we're presuming you saw a lot of each other. At one time, anyway.'

'Well, yeah, to begin with, at least,' she said. 'After I came out of prison, we sort of pooled resources. Got leaflets printed up, wrote letters or whatever. We supported each other, you know, especially after Peter and Alex's parents died.'

'Why only "to begin with"?' Holland asked.

'He got a bit full-on about it all. I was busy trying to find a job and somewhere to live, getting my life back. He had no time for anything except the campaign to get Peter released, and, seeing as that wasn't ever going to happen, in the end I just let him get on with it.' She cocked her head, suspicious. 'Why are you so interested in Alex?' When she didn't get an answer immediately she sat forward. 'What's he done?'

Thorne and Holland had talked about exactly how much information they were willing to share with Mandy Brightwell on their way over. While there was no need to tell her everything, they also needed her to understand the importance of anything *she* could share with *them*.

'We need to talk to him urgently in connection with the murder of a police officer,' Thorne said.

'Which one?'

It was a telling response. 'Is the name Christopher Tully familiar to you?'

Thorne could see that it was, even before she answered. 'Yeah. Alex mentioned him a few times, but— *shit*, was he one of those four coppers killed a couple of weeks back?'

'Ten days ago,' Holland said.

'So, what . . . you think that was down to Alex?'

Thorne had told her as much as he was willing to. 'Why did Alex talk about Tully?' He felt the same disconnect that he'd felt after he and Tanner had talked to Peter Brightwell at Woodhill prison. When he hadn't even worked on the investigation, why was Tully's name being mentioned in discussions about the rape of Siobhan Brady?

'I always thought it was about Peter being fitted up,' she said. 'Like maybe Tully was one of the coppers involved.'

One of the coppers . . .

'When was the last time you had any contact with Alex, Mandy?'

'I don't know.' She seemed nervous, suddenly. 'A few months back, maybe. He used to call after either of us had been in to see Peter, sort of compare notes on how he was doing. I don't think he's been to visit in a while, though.'

'Have you any idea where he might be living now?' Holland asked.

'Not a clue.'

'Have you got a phone number?'

'I did have, but it doesn't work any more.'

'OK. Well, if Alex does contact you, or you remember anything that might help us locate him, you need to let us know immediately.'

She nodded, said, 'Yeah, course,' but she was clearly thinking about something else. 'Your investigation, whatever it is ... will it change things for Peter? I mean, it's obviously connected, so is there a chance you'll be looking at his case again?'

Thorne was starting to think that there was every chance, but could not say as much. Sharing any further information with someone who might one day be called to give evidence was definitely not a good idea, so instead he made a few noises about being unable to comment further on an ongoing investigation and said, 'We'll get out of your way ... '

He stopped at the front door, and turned. 'You asked me which one,' he said. 'When I was talking about murdered police officers.'

'Did I?'

'Is that because Alex had talked about killing police officers?'

'No—'

'Did he tell you that's what he was planning?'

'No. I didn't know he was going to do anything like that, I swear.' She leaned on her walking stick. 'Look, I'm not a big fan of your lot, I'm sure you've worked that out already, but that's nothing compared to what *he* thought. So I can't say I was very surprised, that's all, because on top of how much he hates coppers he was always an oddball, you know? He can get a bit intense.'

Thorne had already changed his mind several times about exactly what manner of killer they were looking for. The poisonings pointed towards someone who was methodical and organised, who planned carefully and didn't take chances, but he also remembered Emily Mead's description of a man charging from the bushes and repeatedly plunging his knife into Adam Callaghan's neck.

Was Alex Brightwell frenzied or meticulous? Careful or reckless?

Ultimately it didn't much matter, and Thorne was happy to let prison shrinks work all that stuff out later on. But he also knew that understanding the man he was after might make him easier to catch.

'Don't get me wrong, Peter loves his brother,' Mandy said. 'But even he thinks Alex is a bit of a weirdo.'

Thorne thought that *weirdo* just about covered it, even if it wasn't a word that cropped up too often in psychiatric textbooks.

'He had this pet snake once, right?' Mandy Brightwell screwed up her face and feigned a shudder. 'Found it in the woods or whatever and took it home. He used to kill baby birds and frogs and stuff to feed it and then, when he got bored with doing that, he killed the snake, cut it up and fed it to a neighbour's dog.'

FORTY

Andre Campbell sat down and studied his visitor. He was confused, but also curious, so he decided to go with it. However the hell it panned out, it would be preferable to just standing up again and asking to be returned to his cell.

He sat back and folded his arms. 'Who the fuck are you?'

The visits hall was crowded and the dozen or so different conversations were taking place, as usual, in a variety of hushed tones. Every so often there might be a raised voice – were a loved one to reveal their plans for leaving the country, or announce to a husband or boyfriend who'd been inside for several years that they were pregnant – but by and large, whatever was being discussed, the room was filled with a gentle hubbub of murmurs and mutterings. Nobody in there wanted to be overheard, least of all those whose exchanges were of a rather more intimate nature.

So there was nothing unusual about the visitor leaning across to introduce himself nice and quietly.

Campbell shook his head, none the wiser. He said, 'That's not the name on the visiting order.'

'You might remember my brother,' the man said. 'You did some time together in Belmarsh a few years back, when he was on remand.'

Campbell thought for fifteen seconds or so, chewing his nails until the name came to him. 'Yeah, all right ... so?'

'So, we have a connection.'

'What do you want?'

Alex Brightwell leaned a little closer and said, 'It might be easiest if I tell you a bit about what I've been up to lately.'

He hadn't got all day, so he gave the man he was visiting the condensed version – the arsenic, the knife, the car, the *tally* – and, when he'd finished, he sat back and watched Andre Campbell pretend that he wasn't shocked; that he wasn't scared shitless. He watched his eyes dart nervously around for a while, and saw the effort it took to plaster on an expression he might wear if he'd been listening to the weather forecast or if someone had just told him the football scores.

'So ... what?' Campbell asked eventually. 'You want a round of applause or something?'

'Only if you want to.'

'Stab up the copper who put me in here and you might get one.'

'I'm telling you all this so you'll know who I am,' Brightwell said. 'So you'll understand what I'm capable of. I know that sounds like we're in some stupid thriller, but there we are.' He glanced up and caught the eye of a prison officer. He smiled, then turned back to Campbell. 'Because I need you to do me a favour.'

Brightwell had barely begun outlining the nature of the

required favour when Campbell started to shake his head, and he was shaking it even harder by the time it had been spelled out. 'Not going to happen, mate,' he said. 'Not even possible. Specialist wing, innit.'

'I'm sure you can find a way,' Brightwell said.

'Why the fuck should I?'

'Because you're in here and I'm not, which means I can always decide to branch out a bit from coppers and turn my attention to, I don't know . . . supermarket workers?' Brightwell saw Campbell's expression harden. 'That is what your girlfriend does for a living, right?'

Campbell glared, then lowered his head and talked quietly to the tabletop, doing his very best to sound menacing. 'What's to stop me calling a screw over here right now and telling him what you've just told me?'

'Nothing.'

'I'm sure the police are after you, yeah?'

'Yes, of course, so go ahead and fill your boots.' Brightwell looked across at the prison officer again and nodded. 'It'll only take one phone call, though, and I will be entitled to one, and a friend of mine will be waiting outside Ashworth Primary tomorrow afternoon when Marcus and Femi come out.' He waited until Campbell had raised his head. He ignored the naked hatred coming off the man like a stink, knowing full well that the understandable urge Campbell felt to fly across the table at him would come to nothing. 'Come on, Andre, why not? It's not like he doesn't deserve it and you're not getting out any time soon, so what have you got to lose?'

Campbell stared, his hands wrapped tight around the edge of the table.

'I'll make sure Marcus and Femi get something nice for Christmas.'

Thorne and Holland said very little as they drove north from Crystal Palace; little pertaining to the investigation, at any rate. Thorne asked Holland how married life was suiting him and, after saying that it suited him very well, Holland asked Thorne if Helen was still happy about her decision to leave the Job. Thorne told him that he thought she was, though in truth he wasn't altogether sure.

Eventually, as Holland turned on to Vauxhall Bridge, he said, 'I think I believe her.'

Thorne looked at him.

'Mandy Brightwell.'

'Right,' Thorne said. 'Fuck.' He slapped both his hands against the dash and leaned back. 'I believe her too, but things would be a whole lot easier if we didn't.'

Holland pulled out to take the pool car past a black cab. 'You mean we'd have a few less difficult questions to answer.'

'Yeah, just a few,' Thorne said. 'Like, if we're right ... if *she's* right and Peter Brightwell was fitted up, who did the fitting?'

'Not to mention why.'

'I can't see it being about Brightwell – someone having it in for him, I mean. I think he was just the mug who got unlucky.'

'The mug who gets put in the frame for the Siobhan Brady rape so someone else doesn't.'

It was exactly what Thorne was starting to believe; the only explanation that made any sense if Peter Brightwell was really innocent. 'Whoever did it was protecting someone,' he said. 'Coppers taking care of coppers, I'm guessing, but if we're going to have any chance of finding out who either of those people are, we'll need to explain how they did it.'

'The DNA,' Holland said. 'Supposed to never lie, right?'

'It can be economical with the truth, though.' Thorne was remembering what Peter Brightwell had said when he and Tanner had visited him in HMP Woodhill. *'Like that stuff's the holy fucking grail, like it's never wrong and the people in those labs can't possibly make a mistake.'* Yes, what had happened to Brightwell could have been down to human error, but Thorne thought there was more chance of Tottenham winning the treble.

The people responsible were inhuman and they did not make errors.

The same people who had inadvertently lit a murderous fire under Peter Brightwell's brother; whose efforts to protect one of their own had led to the deaths of half a dozen more.

It had started to drizzle as Holland weaved through the traffic; swanky hotels and showrooms full of expensive cars to one side and the expanse of Hyde Park on the other. 'We never really pay as much attention as we should to the wives and partners,' he said. 'We don't listen enough.'

'We listened to Brightwell's wife,' Thorne said.

'Not just her.' Holland sighed and shook his head, like maybe he was being stupid. 'I've been thinking about it, that's all.'

'I'm all ears, Dave.'

'Brightwell's wife, Craig Knowles's wife ... we think we know someone based on a couple of statements or an arrest report or a bloody interview, but if you've been living with someone for ten years, you're going to know them a lot better than we ever will.'

'You still thinking about your iffy suicide?' Thorne asked. 'About what Daniel Sadler's wife said?'

Holland nodded. 'I called her, for what it's worth. Yeah, I still feel guilty because I haven't followed it up. The boss said he was going to look into that arrest for indecent images that never went anywhere, but this case has just taken over. He's been too busy, I suppose.' He jumped a light at Portman Square and put his foot down. 'We're all too fucking busy.'

'The way it goes, mate.' Thorne was thinking that they needed to catch up with Nicola Tanner and find out how the interview with Siobhan Brady had gone; the woman who, in all likelihood, had *not* been raped by Peter Brightwell. He was thinking about that damning evidence, about those who had falsified it and the innocent men and women who had paid such a terrible price. 'And we're about to get a whole lot busier.'

FORTY-ONE

Emily Mead sat and had another little cry, thinking about the friends she was unable to see; might not see again for a very long time. In truth, she hadn't been the ideal friend for a while, hadn't really been anyone's idea of a proper mate since the night Adam Callaghan had dropped in. She could hardly blame the girls she used to hang around with when they'd decided to stop calling. She might well have done the same thing herself. How many times could you reach out to someone only to be told that they didn't really fancy a girls' night, or they didn't feel up to it, or they just weren't in the mood for coffee and a natter that day? How much time and effort could you put into a friendship before you gave up and cut your losses?

Too much for most people, as it had turned out.

She wondered if, when this was finally over, she'd have anyone left at all.

It wasn't like she'd had a lot of choice, though. How could

she have got herself dressed up and sat in some bar while Jade or Abby or anyone else for that matter asked how she was and what was happening, or – even worse – if she was seeing anyone? It wasn't in her to do it, simple as that. She couldn't pretend, she couldn't make stuff up and she certainly couldn't ever have told them the truth.

Well, yeah, there's been loads happening, as it goes. There was this copper who raped me and some other bloke who stood there watching and talking him through it, but it is what it is, I suppose. Oh, and now I'm off my tits on drugs most of the time. So, who's up for another piña colada?

Sometimes, she wondered if perhaps she *should* have put herself out there now and again after it had happened; the odd day when things weren't feeling quite as hopeless. Maybe if she'd spent just a little time with other people, heard a few more voices, she might have been able to drown out the one that was still echoing in her head morning, noon and night.

Look at her, she's loving it.

I think she wants it a bit rougher . . .

Emily picked up her phone. She scrolled through her contacts, past the names of people whose voices she *was* starting to forget. Jade, Abby, her parents who'd been told she'd gone travelling, and Will, the nice guy she'd been out with twice before Callaghan came knocking and who probably thought she'd ghosted him.

She stopped when she got to the name of the only person she was permitted to talk to. She could contact the police whenever she needed to of course, but the panic buttons in every room were a far quicker way of doing that. There was only one number she could actually *call*.

Why the hell not?

She needed to talk to someone. Anyone.

She prodded at the red call button. It wasn't very late, besides which she remembered him saying that he didn't sleep much anyway, and she could always leave a stupid message if he didn't answer.

'Emily? Is everything OK?'

'Yeah, fine ...'

'Do you want to send another message? I haven't heard anything from Tom or Nicola.'

'Right, yeah, no ... I just fancied a natter.'

'Fair enough.'

'It's no problem if you're busy.'

'Well, I *was* about to lay siege to the Icecrown Citadel,' Hobbs said.

'Oh, well ... sorry.'

'But I'm sure the other Elf Druids can do without me for ten minutes.'

'Have you got a girlfriend, Greg?'

Hobbs laughed. 'Is that question prompted by what I just told you I was doing, or is it more of a general enquiry?'

'A bit of both,' she said.

'Well then, yeah ... kind of.'

Emily lifted her feet up on to the sofa. '*Kind of* because she's a large-breasted alien queen or some even larger-breasted Lara Croft type? I *am* talking about an actual, three-dimensional woman, Greg.'

'Oh, she's definitely real,' Hobbs said. '*Kind of*, because I'm not actually sure she wants to be my girlfriend any more.'

'OK ...'

'Now you're waiting for me to tell you why, aren't you?'

'Yeah, obviously,' Emily said. 'And don't leave anything out.

I want all the lurid details, in fact the lurider the better.' She laughed. 'Is that even a word?'

'It is now.'

Emily carried on laughing and it took her a while to stop, because it wasn't something she'd done in a while. 'So, go on, then,' she said, eventually. 'Tell Auntie Emily all about it.'

'It might take a while.'

'Fine with me. I'm sure those Elf Lords can manage without you.'

'Druids,' Hobbs said.

Emily lay back and closed her eyes. 'Whatever . . .'

FORTY-TWO

Thorne stopped at the garage on his way home. He filled up, helped himself to a selection of three-for-two ready meals and drove to Kentish Town. An evening with Helen – not to mention a night – was very tempting, but sometimes heading back to his own place was just . . . simpler. Helen's flat in Tulse Hill was an hour's drive on from his own, longer even if there was heavy traffic, not to mention the extra time it would put on his journey into work the following morning.

He called her once he'd polished off his risotto.

She told him Alfie would be disappointed that he wasn't coming over, which Thorne was both happy and sad to hear. She said she'd had an interesting day 'advising citizens' and, while he didn't much fancy going into details, Thorne said he'd had an interesting day, too.

'You still pleased with the way things are going, then?' he asked.

'Doing this, you mean?'

'Yeah, and . . . chucking in the Job.'

'Couldn't be better,' Helen said. 'Why?'

'Nothing. Dave was asking, that's all.'

'I don't miss it, Tom. I really don't.'

Thorne said that he was happy to hear it, though he still wasn't entirely convinced.

When the call was done, he put on a George Jones and Tammy Wynette album and grabbed a beer from the fridge, because that's what George would have wanted. Later, he sat nursing another through the second half of a dreary Everton versus Bournemouth game, the highpoint of which was a studs-up tackle followed by five minutes of handbags and a flurry of yellow cards. Actually, it could well have been the game of the season, but Thorne's mind was elsewhere.

Brigstocke had not been in the office when he and Holland had got back, but he'd managed to catch up with Tanner and, after they'd put their heads together for half an hour, he'd found himself thinking about evidence and little else. The men it had cleared and those it implicated. He was already convinced that forensic evidence in the Siobhan Brady case had somehow been tampered with, so it was hardly a big leap to conclude that whoever had been responsible was also capable of simply destroying evidence when it suited them.

Thorne knew – or thought he knew – where to start digging for evidence of his own, but with the person passing information to Brightwell still unidentified and the leak yet to be plugged, he wasn't confident he'd be able to get what he needed alone. Not knowing who he was able to trust, he couldn't find the right person to answer the questions he wanted to ask.

But he thought he knew a man who could.

'What are you wearing?' Hendricks asked when he picked up.

'Not now, mate—'

'My money's on your old tracksuit bottoms and that faded Hank Williams T-shirt. God, that's *so* hot.'

'You done?'

Hendricks began to pant and moan. 'I will be in a minute.'

'I need a favour,' Thorne said.

'I know I'm going to kick myself, but go on, then.'

'Do you know the Fin-Cel lab in St Albans?'

'Yeah. I've sent stuff to them, tox and tissue samples whatever, but I've never been there.'

'That doesn't matter,' Thorne said. 'Do you know anyone who might have been working there three years ago?'

There were a few seconds of background noise on the line – traffic, music from somewhere – while Hendricks thought about it. 'Well, *know* might be putting it a bit strongly, but as it happens, I did cop off with one of the lab techs there a few times.'

Thorne grinned at his piece of good fortune. 'Course you did.'

'Right before I met Liam, actually—'

'Could you get in touch with him, see if he'll talk to me?'

'Yeah, I suppose,' Hendricks said. 'But why don't I just send you his number and you can talk to him yourself?'

'Because I don't want to take any chances.' Thorne explained that the investigation looked to have been compromised and that he needed to be sure he would be asking questions of someone he could trust. He might well be being over-cautious, but it was not beyond the bounds of possibility that those who had taken steps to engineer or destroy damning forensic evidence had done so with the help of someone working at the labs themselves.

Someone on hand to switch samples, say, or casually turn off a freezer.

'Ah ... best be a bit careful, then,' Hendricks said.

'So, can you contact him or not?'

'Leave it with me, mate.'

'Cheers,' Thorne said. 'Scotch eggs are on me next time we're in the Spread Eagle.'

'No worries. I'm always up for a Secret Squirrel kind of caper.'

'And don't let on what I want to talk to him about.'

'Got it.'

'Or anyone else, come to that.'

'Nothing on Twitter, then?'

'I mean it, Phil.'

'You think I'm daft?'

'No, but it's not like you're famous for your discretion, is it?'

'Cheeky bastard.' Hendricks sniffed. 'Fair point, mind you.'

Twenty minutes later, Thorne was in bed and struggling to sleep. Unable to get comfortable, a draught coming from somewhere. A George Jones song was running through his head, the mournful soundtrack to a series of images, remembered or imagined: Mandy Brightwell leaning on her stick and telling him about that snake; sugar and a sprinkling of something else around Catherine Holloway's mouth, right before she licked it away; Alex Brightwell, several steps ahead and laughing at them all dicking around in Whittington Park.

Priya Kulkarni.

Siobhan Brady.

Emily Mead.

A man watching and whispering from the shadows . . .

His last fully formed thought was that even the thinnest slice of good luck never hurt. That it could make all the difference, that in the end it might even save lives. He was, of course, well aware of his best friend's inability – when Hendricks was single, obviously – to resist anything with a pulse and a penis, but it had never come in quite this handy before.

FORTY-THREE

'Well, as acts of faith go, this one's pretty ... major,' Brigstocke said.

Tanner had emailed the DCI last thing the previous day, so he knew full well why she and Thorne had come knocking on his door before he'd had a chance to take his coat off.

'You're suggesting that we take this investigation forward based on the word of a woman whose husband was convicted of rape and sentenced to life in prison. A case based on forensic evidence so solid that the victim herself was not even needed in court.'

'That's about the size of it,' Thorne said. 'Yeah.'

'It's not that she wasn't needed,' Tanner said. 'Siobhan Brady was advised against giving evidence herself in case she talked about the other man who she believed was there while she was being raped.' She saw Brigstocke raise his hand, but wanted to finish. 'They were worried she might sound ... flaky.'

'I get it,' Brigstocke said. 'I get all of it.' He took a sip of the coffee he'd brought from home in a carry-cup and sat back, fiddling with a lever on his chair and swearing a couple of times until it reclined. 'So, obvious question. If Peter Brightwell didn't rape Siobhan Brady, who did?'

'Tully,' Thorne said.

'Based on...?'

Tanner was nodding. 'It all points to Tully. He was the one Alex Brightwell was after all along. Fine, so he got an appetite for it and widened things out to include Adam Callaghan and the poor bugger who arrested his brother for rape, but Tully's the one.'

'Why does Brightwell keep mentioning Tully when he's talking to his brother about the case?' Thorne said. 'Why does he talk about Tully to Peter's wife?'

'And to Emily Mead,' Tanner said.

'Tully's name just keeps coming up.'

Brigstocke nodded, accepting it. He thought for a few seconds. 'Well, obviously Alex Brightwell believed Tully was responsible, which is why we are where we are: why Brightwell killed him, along with three innocent coppers. So why the hell didn't he just go to the police? If he had any information that could help exonerate his brother, why didn't he come to us?'

'Because he believed the police were involved in covering it up,' Thorne said. 'Protecting the police offer who'd actually committed the rape by putting his brother away for it, and it looks like he was spot on.'

'We're the last people he'd have come to,' Tanner said.

Brigstocke took his glasses off and rubbed at his eyes, the shadows beneath them darker than ever. He seemed a little reluctant to put them on again, as if seeing clearly was the more painful option. 'So, why is it Peter Brightwell's DNA in that rape kit and not Tully's?' Brigstocke saw that Thorne was about to speak, but didn't give him the chance. 'If you're suggesting someone planted it, we'll need to explain how that someone *had* any DNA to plant. Brightwell's DNA was not taken when he'd been arrested previously. I know that, because I checked.'

Thorne had checked, too. It was something else he'd spoken to Hendricks about the night before.

'His profile was not on record before all this and he didn't provide a sample until he was arrested for raping Siobhan Brady, which was several days *after* her rape kit had been put together.' Brigstocke stared at them and raised his hands. 'So how the hell was it done?'

'Why *was* Brightwell arrested?' Tanner asked.

'Yeah, I mean, just out of interest,' Thorne said. 'Siobhan Brady never saw her attacker's face, so was there some other witness?' He was certain by now that there could not have been.

'An anonymous tip, if I remember rightly,' Brigstocke said.

'That's handy,' Thorne said.

Brigstocke shook his head. 'Either way, how was it done? The DNA—'

Thorne had not got the first idea, but he wasn't about to admit that. 'Look, Russell, we have to at least assume that whoever's behind this is the same mysterious individual who was present at the rapes of Emily Mead and Siobhan Brady.'

'And Priya Kulkarni,' Tanner said. 'She definitely hints at the same thing in her initial statement.'

'Right ... so, if this individual's in a position to be there during rapes committed by at least three serving police officers, namely Craig Knowles, Adam Callaghan and Christopher Tully, we can presume they've also got the capability to interfere somehow with forensic tests. To do whatever's necessary to cover for themself and their friends.'

'There's an awful lot of assuming and presuming going on,' Brigstocke said.

'What else can we do?'

Brigstocke's expression, the weary sigh that went with it, suggested that he didn't see any other option either. 'OK, then. Next step?'

'Phil Hendricks rang me this morning,' Thorne said. 'He's got an ex at the Fin-Cel lab and says this bloke's happy to talk to us.'

'Fin-Cel?'

'In St Albans. Seems like a good place to start without making a fuss and alerting the wrong people.'

'You know that's *not* where they ran the tests in the Brightwell case?'

'I do know that, yeah.' Having got in early and looked at the file, Thorne had discovered that Siobhan Brady's rape kit had been processed at a lab in Bracknell; a facility run by a completely different company. 'It's where Priya Kulkarni's rape kit was sent, though.'

'Where the freezer "malfunctioned",' Tanner said.

'We need to tread carefully,' Thorne said. 'At least until we find out where Brightwell's been getting his information from. Take one step at a time and, like I said, not make too much noise about it. Who's to say that people working in these places don't talk to each other or hang out together same as everyone else? All it takes is one stupid WhatsApp message about police turning up at different labs and asking questions.'

Brigstocke nodded. 'Sounds like a plan, but ...'

Thorne and Tanner waited.

'I still think we should be putting the majority of the team's efforts into finding Alex Brightwell. That has to be what we focus on.'

'Nobody's arguing with that,' Thorne said. 'If Brightwell turns himself in or he's nicked for speeding or gets spotted by some eagle-eyed member of the public, we'll all be happy. Until then, though, surely our best bet is to find out exactly why he's been doing what he's doing. How these people got away with umpteen rapes and who was protecting them.'

'It might even tell us who Brightwell's likely to go after next,' Tanner said.

Brigstocke thought about that. 'OK, makes sense ... but bearing in mind that we're all agreed we should be concentrating on apprehending our chief suspect, you *both* want to go down this ... forensic evidence rabbit hole?'

'I can't see it taking up too much of our time,' Thorne said.

'My two best DIs.'

Tanner tried not to smile. 'We won't tell Dave Holland you said that.'

'It's just one visit to one lab, Russell,' Thorne said. 'To start with, anyway. We'll be in and out of there like ninjas—' He heard the alert from his phone, took it from his pocket and read the message.

i'm in the car park now

He stood up and walked towards the door. 'I need to meet someone.'

Tanner appeared to be staying where she was for the time being, but the look she gave him made her curiosity clear enough.

'Go steady, Tom,' Brigstocke said.

Thorne smiled as he held up the phone before slipping it back into his pocket. 'OK, you can put a firearms team together if I'm not back in ten minutes, but I really don't think I'm in any immediate danger.'

'Generally, I mean ...'

FORTY-FOUR

While Alex Brightwell waited for the news he felt sure was coming, he walked, and wondered if there was anything else worth doing.

Any*one* else.

Though nothing he'd done had been very radical – that kind of business cost money he didn't have – he'd made an effort to change his appearance as best he could at least twice since they'd shown his picture at that press conference. Shaving or not, hats and glasses, all that. Even so, he knew they'd be looking at CCTV from outside Archway station where he'd paid that wino, and from the prison when he'd been in to see Andre Campbell, so there was always a chance someone might clock him.

They'd mounted a major operation, he knew that, so the possibility was always there, and if he was caught he'd already decided that he'd just have to suck it up. He wouldn't stop. He'd carry on making a noise in a different way, that was all.

These last few years, he'd learned a lot from Peter about how to survive in prison, and as someone who'd been put away for killing coppers he was bound to have things a damn sight easier inside than his brother ever had.

They'd be queuing up to pat him on the back.

Sometimes, when his mind wandered into even stranger places than it normally did, he wondered if fate had played a part and the pair of them had always been destined to end up behind bars: the Brightwell Boys together again, even if they were in different prisons. Had someone told him years before – when they were teenagers and Peter was going off the rails – that if and when that happened *he* would be the one who was actually guilty, Alex would have thought they were barmy.

It was funny how things turned out.

Not that he had any particular desire to spend the rest of his life in prison, so, while leaving the country was a non-starter – they'd be monitoring the borders – and he wasn't willing to hide himself away permanently, he did his level best to prevent that happening.

He kept out of the city, stayed off public transport and walked where there were very few people about.

The Olympic Park behind him, he trudged down to the river Lee, then along the towpath, moving under the series of decorated road bridges beneath the A12, before the traffic noise began to fade and he turned eventually into Wick Wood. Head down and hood up, he passed or was passed by a couple of dog-walkers and a wheezing jogger, but none of them paid him any attention.

He was feeling out of sorts, lethargic and at a loose end because, for the first time in a while, he didn't know who his next target would be. Since he had dealt with those directly responsible for Peter's conviction, there was nobody blindingly obvious. That said, Callaghan had just dropped into his lap, so it was always possible something similar would happen if he trawled through those message boards again. Maybe whoever had told him where to find Tully and warned him about Emily Mead would decide to be helpful again and suggest a name.

Someone would turn up eventually.

For ten minutes he walked parallel to the river, then turned on to a path and up a ramp until he reached Homerton Road. Staying under cover of the trees, he stared across the street, over a wall of wire and rusty iron sheets towards the changing rooms for Hackney Marshes playing fields. He knew that's what the building was because he'd been there several times with Peter. They'd watched a few games together, pissed themselves at some of the half-arsed antics of Sunday footballers, then had a fry-up afterwards at a greasy spoon nearby.

To be honest, the level of skill on display those mornings was far higher than when the two of them had kicked a ball about themselves. Peter was a better player than he was, but Alex had always got stuck in. And besides, it didn't matter how rubbish it was, because they were out in the back garden with their dad, getting out of breath and sweaty and having a laugh.

Their mum, watching from the kitchen window and clapping.

Making breakfast for her boys.

She'd even put a football scarf on once or twice, just to join in.

There didn't seem to be much happening over the road, not this early on a Tuesday morning, but just seeing the green of the pitches in the distance he could feel the anger rising up like sick in his throat. The determination that there would be someone else to go after.

It wasn't like there was any shortage of them.

Fate had nothing do with any of it.

Alex knew who was responsible for Peter being where he was, and that they'd do exactly the same thing to him given half a chance. Little men who'd been given a sniff of power and thought it made them big men. Twisted little sickos who thought they could get away with anything because they had a uniform or a badge, who did what they wanted and were willing to let others pay for it.

He turned away and walked back towards the woods.

He needed to get stuck in again.

FORTY-FIVE

When Thorne reached the bottom of the stairs, he turned and all but ran into DI James Greaves.

In typically British fashion, both said 'Sorry', neither of them meaning it.

'In a hurry?' Greaves asked.

'Kind of,' Thorne said. He carried on towards the exit, then stopped, unable to pass up the opportunity. He jogged back to the stairs and caught Greaves up. 'I meant to ask ... why are you actually here?'

'Seriously?'

'Well, this is a major investigation and we're trying to do our jobs, and having you hanging about the place is a bit disconcerting.' Thorne manufactured a smile. 'That's all.'

'OK, that's fair enough, I suppose.' Greaves nodded, serious. 'Look, I'm well aware that, above everything else, this is a murder case, but—'

'Six murders,' Thorne said. 'And counting, possibly.'

'Understood, and I'm not trying to get in anyone's way. But we both know what the background to these murders is and it obviously has implications that are well within the remit of the CCU.' Greaves waited until he was confident that had sunk in. 'I'm trying to do my job, too.'

They stared at each other for a few seconds. A female officer came down the stairs and they both stepped aside to let her pass, smiled and nodded.

'Who brought you in?' Thorne asked, when the woman had gone.

'Is that important?'

'I'm curious, that's all. How you found out about the *background* to these murders. Those implications you mentioned.'

'Nothing wrong with being curious,' Greaves said. 'But you must already know I can't reveal that information. When coppers are investigating coppers, they need to protect their sources more than anyone, don't you think?'

'Worth a shot,' Thorne said.

'Yeah, worth a shot.' The man from the CCU began walking up the stairs. 'Don't let me keep you.' He took a few more steps then raised a hand without turning round. 'Maybe catch you around . . . '

Thorne turned to head back down towards the exit, thinking that, if Greaves's investigative skills were on a par with others in the Counter Corruption Unit, he'd be lucky to catch a cold.

'What's with all the cloak-and-dagger bollocks?'

Thorne had been mooching around the car park for five minutes, getting increasingly chilly and annoyed, before he'd finally spotted Phil Hendricks emerging slowly from behind a police van, looking rather pleased with himself.

'Just being careful, mate.' Hendricks narrowed his eyes and tapped the side of his nose theatrically. 'Keeping everything hush-hush, like you said.'

'Yeah, but—'

'I *was* thinking about a disguise of some sort, going the extra mile, you know.'

'What do you *want*, Phil?'

'Well, you could bow down to me if you like, but that might be pushing it, so I'll settle for a sausage roll to go with that Scotch egg next time we're in the pub. Actually, a simple "thanks very much" would be nice.'

Thorne waited, growing ever more impatient.

'OK then, so ...' Hendricks leaned back against the van and folded his arms. 'Your DNA problem.'

'Yeah.' Thorne shoved his hands deeper into the pockets of his leather jacket and hunched his shoulders against the chill. 'Me, Nic and Russell were upstairs trying to make sense of that when I got your message.'

'It's definitely a conundrum,' Hendricks said. 'You're as certain as you can be that Peter Brightwell's DNA was planted by person or persons unknown, only you can't figure out how they came to have it in the first place.'

'Not as yet, we can't.'

The pathologist shook his head and sucked his teeth, milking it. '*I* can, though. I can and I have.'

Now Thorne himself checked to make sure there were no other officers nearby before stepping close. 'Go on then, genius.'

'I presume we're talking about a standard early evidence kit,' Hendricks said quickly. 'The one that was put together after Siobhan Brady was raped.'

Hendricks, being a medical professional, had used the correct and legally acceptable terminology. An early evidence kit (EEK) was a collection of forensic samples provided by the victim and assembled following an alleged sexual assault, though most coppers – Thorne included – still called them 'rape kits'.

'Far as I know.'

'So, urine sample, mouth swab, whatever ... and some kind of tissue or wipe used to collect traces of semen.'

The pause told Thorne that this was the crucial element. 'Right.'

'You told me that Tully had arrested Brightwell before.'

'Yeah, a couple of weeks before, after he'd allegedly attacked a sex worker. Tully was the first officer at that scene.'

'That would have been at the sex worker's home, correct?' Hendricks waited for Thorne to nod. 'Good. So, every chance there's going to be, I don't know ... packets of condoms dotted about, lube and toys and shit, all the usual bits and bobs your average sex worker might need. That kind of stuff, just lying around the place, while PC Tully's making a nice thorough job of checking the room out. Now, I don't know about you, but I'd be amazed if that didn't include a few used tissues tossed in a bin.'

'Fuck ... '

Hendricks nodded, seeing Thorne get it. 'Yeah, *fuck*. Tissues that our sex worker uses to wipe herself off once the client's finished. Specifically, in this instance, once Peter Brightwell's finished.'

'Hang on. What if he was wearing a condom?'

'I tell you who *was* wearing one and that's Tully, when he was raping Siobhan Brady. Which is the only reason they never found any traces of *his* DNA.'

Thorne had already reached the same conclusion himself. If Tully's DNA had been found, it would have been matched with the sample on record on the Police Elimination Database. 'But what about Brightwell? If he was wearing one . . .'

'I'm almost certain he was,' Hendricks said. 'Because otherwise the sex worker's DNA would have shown up on that tissue as well. So, the condom Brightwell used would have been knocking around somewhere in the sex worker's flat and – sorry for putting this picture in your head – it's not a big deal to transfer the contents on to a tissue later on. Either way, easy enough for Tully to pop the offending article into a plastic bag and stuff it in his pocket.' Hendricks shook his head. 'Now, PC Fuckface has got himself a get-out-of-jail-free card next time he fancies raping someone.'

'Him and his shadowy mate,' Thorne said. 'The one who likes coming along to watch.' He turned and stared into the distance, still trying to take it all in.

'You're welcome,' Hendricks said.

'OK, well, that's half the problem solved, but . . .' Thorne stopped speaking as a pair of uniformed officers walked past, twenty or so feet away.

When the officers had gone, Hendricks said, 'You seriously think your leak might be coming from someone at this station?'

'Could even be someone on my team,' Thorne said. 'Every chance, I reckon.'

'Why, though?'

'Fuck knows,' Thorne said. 'Blackmail's still a possibility. Someone with a serious grudge, been passed over for promotion, maybe. Or just someone with a screw loose. I don't really care why.'

A squad car nosed around the corner on its way out of the car park. The driver sounded his horn and waved at Thorne. Thorne waved back.

Hendricks waved too, though he had no idea who he was waving at. 'Half the problem, you said.'

'Yeah, it's all very well knowing how they got hold of Peter Brightwell's DNA – and rest assured, that sausage roll *will* be coming your way—'

'Now I've had time to think about it, I'd prefer the bowing—'

'—but how did they get it into Siobhan Brady's rape kit?'

'Buggered if I know,' Hendricks said. 'I can't figure it *all* out for you.'

Thorne paced back and forth, thinking aloud. 'Tully wouldn't have been there when the kit was being put together,' he said. 'And neither would any other copper, come to that. OK, an unconnected female officer, *maybe*, but it's normally done by healthcare professionals at a Sexual Assault Referral Clinic or a specialist Haven. So, how've they done it?'

Hendricks spun one of the large metal rings in his ear. 'Lab's the obvious place. I mean, you're already thinking along those lines anyway ... someone on the inside helping them out. That's why you're going to see this bloke at Fin-Cel, isn't it? His name's Matt Parkinson, by the way and it goes without saying that I'll want a full report.'

'Yeah, but hang on—'

'Mainly, whether he's still fit, obviously.'

'That particular rape kit didn't *go* to Fin-Cel,' Thorne said. 'Anyway, I think having people willing to help out rapists by tampering with evidence at two different labs might be stretching things a bit.'

'Well, they obviously did it somehow.'

They both turned at the sound of heels on tarmac, to see Nicola Tanner walking purposefully towards them.

'Hey, Nic,' Hendricks said.

'Phil,' she said.

'You're just in time for Tom to tell you how brilliant I am. Yes I know, nothing you weren't well aware of already, but—'

Tanner cut him off, staring at Thorne. 'We need to head back in, Tom.'

'Blimey, who's rattled your cage?' Hendricks asked.

Now, she looked at both of them. 'Somebody shanked Craig Knowles in prison.'

FORTY-SIX

The key members of the team had been gathered quickly enough, but it had taken a while for the CCTV footage to arrive from HMP Frankland in County Durham, so it was just shy of lunchtime when Brigstocke finally kicked things off in the incident room. By then, a two-page briefing document containing the few known facts had been handed out, DCI Jeremy Walker and two of his team from Wood Green had shown up and Craig Knowles had been transferred to an ICU unit at University College Hospital.

'As SIO, the buck stops with me anyway,' Brigstocke said. 'But I'm going to hold my hand up to this one.'

'You don't have to do that, Russell,' Tanner said.

'I do, because it's my cock-up. After Stuart Needham was killed and we talked about who our suspect might be going after next, I put together what I thought was an exhaustive list of anyone else who might be a target.'

'Looked like a pretty solid list to me,' Thorne said.

'Yeah, because it was,' Holland said.

Thorne looked around as other members of the team mumbled their agreement. He noticed DI James Greaves sitting with his notebook at the back of the room.

I'm trying to do my job, too.

Ignoring the show of support, Brigstocke stared across his team's heads at the large whiteboard on the far wall, on which the investigation had been mapped out in a series of photographs and scribbled names. 'All the officers involved in any capacity whatsoever with the Peter Brightwell case, the officers of the court where he was tried and every member of both the prosecution and defence teams. I made sure word was put out to all the prison officers at Whitehill, but it never crossed my mind that someone who'd already been convicted and put away would be in any immediate danger. That just didn't occur to me ... and it should have.' He looked back to his team and nodded, serious. 'So, this is on me.'

The voice that eventually broke the silence was a predictable one. 'Well, I don't think anyone's too broken up about it, guv. Some people get what they deserve in the end, right?'

It was probably not the most appropriate sentiment for DC Stephen Pallister to have voiced in front of his colleagues, not when a man was fighting for his life and no matter how many of the people in that room might have been thinking the same thing. All the same, though heads had certainly turned, only one person was ready to argue with him.

'Whatever you think of Craig Knowles,' Brigstocke said, 'he's got two teenage kids. So, if you don't want to get what *you* deserve, DC Pallister, you'll keep opinions like that to yourself.' He waited until he had the attention of everyone in the room. 'Right, let's have a look at what they sent us.'

Each member of the team moved to a computer or opened a laptop, a few sharing monitors. A link to footage from a camera in the visits room at HMP Frankland had been posted to all those present.

'A visit request for a prisoner named Andre Campbell was made online a week ago under the name Richard Silcox, giving an address in Maidenhead, which will almost certainly turn out to be fake, or at least irrelevant. The visitor, who we now know to have been Alex Brightwell, entered the prison yesterday afternoon with ID bearing that name. The visit itself lasted less than fifteen minutes and Knowles was attacked by Campbell first thing this morning.'

'Bloody hell, he didn't waste much time,' Dipak Chall said.

'See what you make of the footage,' Brigstocke said. 'But I'm guessing that Andre Campbell wasn't given a great deal of choice.'

Thorne watched, sharing his screen with Nicola Tanner.

Brightwell entered the room along with the rest of that day's visitors and was allotted a table by one of the prison officers. He was now bearded, with light, close-cropped hair and heavy glasses. It was obvious to Thorne and Tanner and presumably everyone else on the team that it *was* Brightwell, though he was no longer clearly identifiable as the man whose photo had been widely distributed to press and public.

He sat and waited until the prisoners were ushered in, looked up and smiled when Andre Campbell took the seat opposite.

To respect the privacy of visitors and prisoners alike, no sound had been recorded, but it appeared as if it was Brightwell doing most of the talking, while Campbell did not look very happy about what was being said.

It was Campbell who left first, signalling to one of the prison officers to let them know he was done before standing up and walking out.

Brightwell stood and watched him leave.

'What do we think?' Brigstocke asked.

'Threatened his family most likely,' Tanner said.

'A threat if Campbell didn't do what he wanted by taking care of Craig Knowles,' Holland said. 'Maybe a promise to look after them if he did.'

'Maybe both,' Brigstocke said.

'What *I* think is that this is getting bloody ridiculous.' Jeremy Walker stood up, and like well-trained dogs, the two officers he'd brought with him did the same. 'That's now six dead and another one who's heading that way and still you haven't seen fit to ask for our help. Let's not forget that this investigation began when the individual we've just been watching murdered four officers from my station.'

'Because one of them was a rapist,' Thorne said.

Walker turned. 'I must have missed the meeting where you presented the proof of that.'

'It's coming.'

'It needs to be,' Walker said.

'Brightwell began all this because Christopher Tully raped Siobhan Brady. We now know that at least one other individual was an accessory to that rape and we've good reason to believe they doctored evidence so that someone else would go down for it, leaving your boy Tully free to rape someone else. Which I'm willing to bet he did.'

Walker looked to his colleagues, said, 'We're aware of your theory,' then turned back to Brigstocke. 'I've already spoken to the Chief Superintendent and you're getting my team's help now, whether you want it or not.'

If Russell Brigstocke was annoyed by the development, he hid it very well. 'Fine with me,' he said. 'Whatever it takes.'

'Good, so where are we?' Walker didn't wait for a response. 'Let's start with what we know about Alex Brightwell. Fine, we have a working theory as to why he's committing these offences.' He threw a look in Thorne's direction, that icy smile again. 'But what do we actually *know*?' Now he looked to Brigstocke, but he wasn't quite finished. 'Pretty close to sweet FA, I'd say.'

'Not true,' Brigstocke said.

'So, correct me.'

'We know he has an online presence, which has been verified and which we're continuing to monitor via the DFU in case his activities on the Dark Web start up again.' He nodded to Tanner. 'Hobbs, right?'

'Nothing gets past him,' Tanner said.

'We know he uses at least one alias and has the documentation to go with it. We have images of him taken from CCTV pictures at Archway station which together with the footage we've just reviewed tell us that he's taking steps to change his appearance. Thanks to that footage, we now know what he looks like as of yesterday and this latest description, as with the previous photos we had, will be circulated widely through every media outlet at our disposal.'

Walker nodded, like he was impressed, and his colleagues nodded along. 'Oh, don't forget those boot prints from Hendon Park.'

'What?'

'You also know what size feet he's got.'

Now, Brigstocke looked annoyed. 'Are you trying to suggest that we've been sitting around on our arses?'

'You're putting words in my mouth, Russell.'

Thorne clenched his fists under the table, thinking that he very much fancied putting one of *them* in Jeremy Walker's mouth and wondering if Brigstocke had met with his opposite number privately to share what else he knew. The leak of key information that had enabled Brightwell to evade capture and cost a number of lives already.

'This team has been working flat out,' Brigstocke said. 'Eyes on the ball from start to finish, no corners cut and every lead and fragment of intel chased up.' Now it was the men and women on his own team nodding. 'If there's anything else you think we should have done, I'm dying to hear it.'

'So, why haven't you caught him yet?'

Thorne guessed that Walker had not been told about the leak.

'We will.' Brigstocke took a few seconds, visibly calming. 'And with your lot helping out, it's going to be sooner rather than later.' He turned to his team. 'This investigation remains our number one priority, and anything else ... *anything* not directly connected to the apprehension of Alex Brightwell, goes on the back burner.'

'Absolutely,' Walker said. 'Bang on.'

Thorne did not think it was accidental that Brigstocke looked at him a little longer than anyone else. 'Is that understood?'

FORTY-SEVEN

'You do know Russell's going to be seriously pissed off.'

'He'll get over it.'

'You reckon?'

Clutching the passes they'd been issued, Thorne and Tanner sat waiting in the palatial reception area of Fin-Cel Ltd. There was enough designer furniture on display to fill a showroom, large pieces of abstract art on the walls and some kind of atrocious ambient music leaking from speakers mounted on spidery metal stands. The forensic testing facility was housed in a large three-storey complex in an industrial park on the outskirts of St Albans, and if it felt like the headquarters of a decent-sized corporation, that's because it was.

It hadn't used to be.

A decade or so before, though the décor would have been far less impressive back then, the same building would have housed laboratories run by the Forensic Science Service, the origins of which dated back to the 1930s. Funded solely by the Home Office and working exclusively for police forces, the CPS and other agencies nationwide, the FSS had provided both scene-of-crime and testing services since the early nineties and had, most notably, established the world's first DNA database in 1995. The cutting-edge forensic techniques developed and the expertise that had solved thousands of serious crimes over many decades had ultimately been judged worthless, however, when the bean-counters had weighed them against the amount the FSS was costing the taxpayer. So, in 2012, David Cameron's government did what it was good at and, despite protests from scientific experts and victim campaigners alike, the FSS was abolished and sold off wholesale to a variety of private companies. Fin-Cel was one such; one among dozens of others currently providing forensic services to police forces, HM Coroners and the MoD among others, at a profit.

Looking around the lobby, Thorne marvelled at where some of those evidently sizeable profits were going. 'Look, I don't think what we're doing is *un*connected to catching Alex Brightwell, is it?'

'Back burner,' Russell said.'

'Whatever happened here with Priya Kulkarni's sample has to be linked to what happened with Peter Brightwell's DNA and that's why Alex Brightwell's been running around killing coppers. So, actually I think it's very much connected. It couldn't be more connected.'

'I hear you,' Tanner said.

'So, what's the problem?'

'Can I be there when you explain all that to Russell?'

Thorne looked away and stroked the soft leather arm of his

chair. 'We're not going to be here long. In and out, like I told him this morning.'

'Yeah, ninjas, I remember ... but you saw what he was like at the briefing,' Tanner said. 'Even if he shouldn't, he feels personally responsible for what happened at Frankham, so unless we go back with something earth-shattering ... well, I can't see him being very understanding, that's all.'

'We just need to ask this bloke if he can put together a list of anyone who had access to that fridge on the day of the malfunction. That's all. Lab techs, police officers—'

'DI Thorne?'

They looked up to see a man they presumed was Matthew Parkinson raising a hand, before touching a pass to the electronic barrier and walking through. He appeared to be somewhere in his mid-thirties; tall and what people a lot younger than Thorne and Tanner would call 'hench', with long hair and a tight AC/DC T-shirt.

Tanner nodded her approval. 'I can see what Phil saw in him.'

'I bet you can't,' Thorne said.

They walked across and introduced themselves and then, once the subtly produced warrant cards had been pocketed, they gently led Parkinson away from the main desk, out of earshot of the woman on reception.

'Phil didn't say exactly what it was you wanted,' he said.

Thorne explained.

'That'll all be on file somewhere in the records department,' Parkinson said. 'Work sheets and visitor logs.'

'Easy-peasy then,' Thorne said.

'I don't have much to do with them, but I've got a mate who works in there, so yeah, it should be doable.'

'We need it doing quietly,' Tanner said.

Parkinson began to look a little nervous. 'I don't suppose you want to tell me why you need the names?'

Tanner glanced at Thorne, who nodded. Though Hendricks's relationship with Matthew Parkinson had not exactly been professional, he'd been willing to vouch for him, which was good enough. 'It's in connection with an incident here three years ago. Samples that were destroyed when a freezer broke down or got switched off.'

Parkinson's eyes widened. 'Oh yeah, I remember all the memos flying about afterwards. A lot of people were very nervous that day.'

While Tanner carried on talking to him and handed over a business card, Thorne's attention was drawn to the man in motorcycle leathers who'd just walked in through the revolving door carrying a large refrigerated bag. Thorne watched him march up to the desk and exchange a few friendly words with the receptionist as he filled in paperwork.

When that was done, the man took out a sheet of paper and unfolded it. It appeared to be a poster or flyer of some kind. He asked if it would be OK to stick it up somewhere, and when he showed it to the receptionist, Thorne caught a glimpse of a face that looked familiar.

'Oh yes, I heard about that,' the receptionist said.

Thorne took out his warrant card as he walked across.

The receptionist shook her head sadly as the phone on her desk began to ring. She picked it up, said, 'Fin-Cel, can you hold?' and leaned back towards her courier friend. 'It's just awful, what happened.'

'Can I see that?' Thorne asked.

Clocking the warrant card, the motorcyclist immediately

handed the poster across, then threw a worried look at the receptionist, who was gawping, clearly curious, and continuing to ignore whoever was on the phone. 'I'm not in any trouble, am I?'

Thorne stared down at the poster. He saw the name and understood why he'd recognised the man whose photograph was underneath it. 'No, you're not in trouble.'

'It's just a GoFundMe, thing . . . to raise a bit of money for his family.'

'How did you know him?'

'Daniel and me worked for the same company.'

Thorne turned and waved Tanner across. 'Daniel Sadler delivered forensic samples?'

'We deliver all sorts,' the man said. 'But yeah, that's a major part of our business.'

'Just to Fin-Cel?' Thorne passed the poster to Tanner. He said, 'Dave Holland's suicide,' then, while she looked at what he'd given her, he turned back to the man in the leathers for an answer.

'No, we deliver to all the labs, and it's them that pay us, not the police in case you were wondering.'

That was definitely not what Thorne was wondering.

'Not that they pay us very much, mind you.'

'So Daniel Sadler would have delivered samples to the lab in Bracknell?'

'Yeah, like I said—'

Thorne was already turning away, shouting across the lobby as he and Tanner made for the exit; thanking Matt Parkinson for his time, apologising for having to leave in a hurry and reminding him to get in touch if and when he had any information for them.

Parkinson promised that he would, then shrugged and went back through the barrier, as the courier Blu-Tacked his poster to the desk and the receptionist finally picked up her call.

Thorne and Tanner pushed through the revolving door and walked quickly away from the building.

'Fuck.' Thorne was fighting the urge to run across the car park. 'Earth-shattering enough, you reckon?'

Tanner already had her phone out. 'You call Dave,' she said, 'and I'll call Russell.'

FORTY-EIGHT

The three of them met at the same coffee shop in which Thorne and Tanner had spoken to Brigstocke a few days before; where they'd told him about the voice Emily Mead had heard.

This new revelation was almost as shocking.

'That's how they got Peter Brightwell's DNA into Siobhan Brady's rape kit,' Thorne said. 'All the time we've been banging our stupid heads together, trying to figure out how they could have had the access they needed to make the switch, and they did it while the sample was on the way to the lab.'

'And who knows how many times they'd done something similar before?' Tanner said.

'Easy enough when you've got one of the couriers in your pocket.'

Holland just stared. He hadn't touched his coffee.

'Sadler picks up the kit,' Thorne said. 'Signs for it, pops it in his bag same as he's done a hundred times and he's away on his bike to the lab. Then all he has to do is pull over en route, wherever he's been told to stop and meet someone.'

'Someone who replaces the tissue in the rape kit with the one that Tully picked up from the sex worker's flat,' Tanner said.

'Someone who's got a tidy little system going.'

Thorne looked across the table at Holland, waiting for a response, some input, anything. He knew that ever since they'd told him what they'd inadvertently discovered while they were at Fin-Cel, Holland had been thinking about Daniel Sadler's wife. Processing this new information and reconsidering the woman's conviction that her husband had not been someone who would have taken his own life, that he had been a happy man and a *good* one.

Thorne knew that Holland was a diligent copper and a thoughtful one, but in this instance, he'd been wrong in believing that the spouses of suspects or victims knew them better than any police officer ever could.

Karen Sadler had not known her husband at all.

'You were talking about blackmail,' Holland said, finally. 'Remember? The possibility that whoever was leaking information might be being forced into it.' He picked up his mug of coffee, but still didn't look very interested in it. He looked gutted. 'All the time, Daniel Sadler was the one being blackmailed.'

'Seems that way,' Tanner said.

'Those child pornography charges,' Thorne said. 'Someone made them go away officially, but could also make them reappear whenever it suited them. If Sadler didn't do what he was told.'

'Still possible it was suicide then, do you think?' Holland looked at them both, but it was clear that he already knew the answer.

Tanner bit into a cookie. 'Possible, but I don't think it's very likely.'

'Be a bit strange to do it now,' Thorne said. 'When we know Sadler's been doing this for at least three years. His involvement in the Brightwell switch might have been a one-off, but I doubt it, so why suddenly decide to end it all? I think the decision was made to get rid of him once Tully was killed. Once it looked like it might all be starting to unravel.'

'He was called and told to meet someone, so he did what he was told, same as always.' Tanner brushed crumbs from her lap. 'Then he was taken to that bridge and either coerced into jumping or just pushed. Doesn't really matter which.'

'You think we can get Russell to open another murder investigation?'

'I'm not sure we have to,' Thorne said. 'Sadler's death is now very much tied to the one that already exists. We can just ... add him to the list.'

A waiter came to the table to take away Thorne and Tanner's empties. He saw that Holland's coffee was untouched, so left it.

'We keep talking about this "someone".' Holland leaned forward. 'Yeah, so we know there *is* a someone, and he's probably the same person who organised the various DNA samples being switched or destroyed and who turned up to whisper encouragement at those rapes, but as far as Daniel Sadler's murder goes, isn't there a more obvious suspect?'

'Obvious, as in Alex Brightwell?' Thorne asked.

'Makes sense, I would have thought. He's been knocking off anyone involved in framing his brother and now we know that Sadler was very much part of it, so why not? He's poisoned people and stabbed them, he's ... run them over, so why not add chucking someone off a bridge into the mix?'

'How could he possibly have known about Sadler?' Tanner asked.

'We only found out ourselves an hour ago,' Thorne said.

'How did he know about *Tully*?' Holland sat back hard and held out his arms. 'We certainly didn't.'

It was a good question and one that had not stopped bothering Thorne ever since those first four deaths. 'How the hell does Brightwell know *anything*?' he said.

'At least you can call Sadler's wife now,' Tanner said. 'Tell her she was right ... about it not being suicide, at least.'

'Yeah, course. Piece of piss *that's* going to be.' Holland grunted, shaking his head. 'Maybe I can pop round and give her the good news in person, she might bake me a cake.' He saw that Tanner was not best pleased by the sarcasm, especially when she had been trying to help. 'Sorry, Nic.'

'Don't worry about it,' Tanner said.

'It's just ... I tell her that her old man didn't top himself, she says so, was he murdered?'

'Whatever she says, it's got to be done,' Thorne said.

'I say yes, it looks that way and she says, by who? Or even worse, she asks why? How the hell am I supposed to answer that?'

'Maybe you're in the wrong job, Dave.' Thorne stood up, ready to crack on. 'Because the only easy answers are on *Tipping Point*.'

FORTY-NINE

While Helen knelt next to the bath to make sure Alfie was washing himself properly and that he didn't drown, Thorne sat on the bathroom floor, his back against the radiator.

'You think I was a bit harsh with Dave?' he asked.

'Telling him he's in the wrong job, you mean?' Helen leaned down with a sponge, but Alfie snatched it from her and said that he could do it himself, that he wasn't a baby. 'Yes, probably.'

'I didn't say that, exactly.'

'Maybe you're the one who thinks you're in the wrong job.'

'What?' Thorne laughed. 'I think I'd know by now.'

'You sure about that? Because it took me long enough.' She watched her son, who – even though he wasn't a baby any more – was doing as much playing as washing. She told him to hurry up before the water went cold, then couldn't help but grin when he gave himself a bubble-beard. 'It's called projection,' she said. 'We had a seminar about it at work, because someone decided it would help us deal with some of our clients better. Actually, it was pretty interesting.'

'Did you have to sit on beanbags?' Thorne had suffered through plenty of less than interesting seminars himself over the years. *Community Impact Awareness*, *Improving People-Facing Communication Skills*, and a particularly wanky 'de-escalation' workshop that still gave him nightmares.

'It's when feelings about yourself are diverted on to somebody else,' Helen said. 'It's a defence mechanism.'

'I know what projection is,' Thorne said.

'Yeah, but knowing what it is doesn't always mean you can recognise when you're doing it yourself. They said that in the seminar.'

'Did they?'

Helen turned back to Alfie, splashing him and laughing, then ducking away when he splashed her back. 'They're always looking to take on more people at Citizens Advice,' she said.

'Remind me why we're talking about this?'

'Just saying.'

'Because of what I said to Dave?'

'Maybe all those times you've been asking me if I'm happy that I quit the Job, if I miss it or whatever, it's because you're trying to work out how it would feel if *you* did. Projection again.'

'I promise you that's not what's going on,' Thorne said. 'Maybe I was a bit chopsy with Dave, but it's just this case. Whenever you think it can't get any more . . . disgusting, it—'

He stopped when Helen turned to give him a meaningful look. They'd discussed the latest developments when Thorne had got in, and while she was happy to carry on talking about it later, Helen certainly didn't want him going into any more detail in front of Alfie.

She stood up and reached for a towel. 'Right, let's get this little bugger out before he starts to go all wrinkly.'

Helen came down half an hour later, once Alfie was in bed. She made tea for them both and joined Thorne on the sofa.

'Who does something like this?' Thorne asked.

'Someone who gets off on power.' Helen said it like it was obvious, cradling her mug. 'Rape isn't about sex, it's about power.'

Thorne knew she was right. At one of the more useful seminars he'd attended, he'd sat and listened to a group of sexual assault survivors and each one of them had talked about being made to feel powerless, about their attacker's obvious need to be in control.

'So, this is the ultimate power trip.'

Thorne nodded. 'He *facilitates* it. He gets his kicks from watching his boys at work, then protecting them afterwards.' Then another shocking thought occurred to him. 'Christ, he might even have selected the victims.'

'Your average rapist is just a pathetic loser who thinks he's powerful,' Helen said. 'A rapist who's also a police officer must think he's fucking superhuman.'

'They might just as well have been,' Thorne said. 'Because whoever's making all this happen was able to keep them invisible.'

Helen leaned into him. 'Not any more, though,' she said. 'Now they're very visible, because thankfully they're dead, and *he* won't stay hidden for long, either.'

They sat in silence for a few minutes.

'Knowles and Tully and Callaghan,' Thorne said. 'They were all uniform, low status ... you know; in the scheme of things. They didn't have the access or the clout. They didn't have the capability to make criminal charges go away or interfere with forensic tests.'

'Sounds to me like the man you're after's a more senior officer.'

Thorne said nothing, because she wasn't telling him anything he hadn't already figured out.

'What was it Russell said to you?' She looked at him, waiting for him to look back. 'Go steady.'

Pippa picked up the remote and turned off the television. Holland sat up, as though the absence of sound had woken him somehow, even though he hadn't been asleep.

'I was watching that,' he said.

'No you weren't.' As soon as he opened his mouth again, she said, 'So, tell me what was happening, then. Or even the name of the programme.'

Holland sighed and fell back on to the sofa. 'Fine. I was just thinking about stuff, that's all.'

'Stuff?'

He sighed again and slapped the arm of the sofa, a little of the frustration and helplessness he'd felt earlier resurfacing. 'What am I supposed to tell Karen Sadler?'

'Look, I know it's not going to be easy,' Pippa said. 'But your boss was right, it's got to be done.'

He stared at her. 'Tom Thorne is *not* my boss.'

'Sorry, no ... course he's not.'

'We're both DIs, even if he sometimes acts like I'm not.' He thought for a few moments, remembering a time, years before, when the pecking order had been different; when, perhaps, things had been a little more comfortable. 'He *used* to be my boss.'

'Either way, you know he's right, so you need to call her.'

'Obviously he's right, he's always bloody right.' Holland was content to continue grumbling for a little while longer, happy to put off thinking about his conversation with Daniel Sadler's widow. 'Even when he's wrong he's usually right—'

'Just tell her the truth,' Pippa said, exasperated. 'You owe her that and chances are she'll thank you for it later on.'

'You think? After she finds out what her husband was arrested for? What they had on him?'

'You can't worry about that.'

'I definitely can.'

'The truth's always going to be the best option.'

Holland sat and wondered just how little of the truth he could get away with, while Pippa reached for the paper and began flicking through it.

'If I died . . .'

Pippa lowered the paper. 'I don't think she's going to react that badly.'

'I mean it. If I died and afterwards you found out something really bad about me . . . some very dark secret, what would you think?'

'Something you're not telling me, Dave?'

'Seriously, what would you think?'

'Bloody hell, *I* don't know.'

'What would you tell the kids? You know, if we were to . . . have any.'

'Well, if it was something *really* bad, I wouldn't tell the kids anything. If it was just, I don't know . . . you having a secret family nobody knew about or something, I reckon I'd get over it.'

'Really?'

'Just to be clear, I will still get your police pension, right?'

'Come on, Pip, I'd like to know.'

Pippa dropped the paper and turned to him. 'OK, if it was genuinely something horrible, I think ... I *hope* I'd try to understand.'

'Not much to understand about kiddie-porn, is there?'

'No ... that might be the only thing.'

'Yeah?'

'I think so, anyway.'

Holland nodded, seemingly satisfied. 'Why don't you put the telly back on? We can catch up with ... whatever it was we were watching before and you can fill me in on everything I missed.'

Pippa reached for the remote and flicked the TV on again. While Holland immediately began to ask questions, who was who and what they were up to, she stared at the screen, as though suddenly she was the one who had stuff to think about.

She said, 'I mean, everyone's got secrets, haven't they?'

FIFTY

Over the many years that he and Russell Brigstocke had worked together, Thorne had found himself in countless situations similar to this. Sitting in the DCI's office and sharing what he believed to be important insights. Of course, they'd also had more than a few conversations in that time about cases going nowhere, about brick walls and wild goose chases. Any time there had been genuine progress, though, when a breakthrough had taken a case in an unexpected direction, Thorne had become used to looking across that desk at his boss and seeing excitement. Resolve . . .

Now, whenever they'd dug deeper into the seemingly bottomless murk of the Alex Brightwell investigation and clawed out yet more evidence of rank corruption and criminality, Thorne saw only a terrible disappointment pass across Brigstocke's face. He seemed . . . crushed by each new revelation about the job he loved and to which he'd dedicated nearly thirty years of his life.

Thorne almost wanted to apologise.

This time, *rank* was a horribly appropriate word.

Brigstocke stared down at his desk, while Thorne and Tanner waited and exchanged glances. Finally, when the DCI looked up at them, it seemed as though, thankfully, he'd found another gear; that he'd summoned just what was needed from a well-stocked reserve of anger and determination.

'I'll need to take this higher,' he said.

Thorne and Tanner looked at each other again, having prepared for this response before coming in. 'I'm not sure that's a good idea,' Thorne said.

'Because?'

'Like we said, we're talking about a senior officer here. Maybe very senior.'

'You think the Chief Superintendent might be behind all this?'

'No.'

'The Chief Constable, maybe?'

'Well, I think he might have to resign when it all comes out,' Tanner said. 'But I doubt he's personally involved.'

'The point is, it could be anybody,' Thorne said. 'So can we not just hold fire for a while? Aside from anything else, we *do* know that someone's being a bit free and easy with operational intelligence.'

'And I'm still working to find out who that is,' Brigstocke said.

'We need to be careful, Russell, that's all. Look, I know it's highly unlikely that you'd inadvertently pass this information directly to the person responsible . . .'

'You're talking lottery odds, Tom.'

'Yeah, definitely, but even discounting the fact that there's someone passing on crucial intelligence, there's always a chance the man we're after might find out we're on to him anyway.'

'Memos getting passed around,' Tanner said. 'Meetings and supposedly confidential emails ... chit-chat at the Freemasons' Hall.'

'It's hard to keep things quiet at the best of times,' Thorne said.

Brigstocke nodded slowly, making it clear that he took the point. 'Fine, but at the very least we should bring the CCU up to speed. Talk to Greaves—' He stopped when he saw the look on Thorne's face. 'You don't think so?'

'Same argument applies, I reckon,' Thorne said. 'In fact, when you think about it, the Counter Corruption Unit's the perfect place to hide in plain sight. On top of which, I don't think they're doing a particularly good job, do you?'

'Obviously they're not,' Tanner said. 'Or shit like this wouldn't be happening.'

Most recently, one officer had been accused of sending 'dickpics' to female recruits and another of sexually assaulting a member of the public in his car. Both cases had been investigated by the CCU and passed up to the Independent Office for Police Conduct, but neither had resulted in anything more serious than 'gross misconduct' proceedings.

'What this bloke's done is definitely gross,' Thorne said. 'But I think we're a long way past *misconduct*. We don't want to see him slapped on the wrist or just dismissed from the force and barred from working in law enforcement. We don't want him suspended for eighteen months on full pay, then quietly encouraged to "retire". This fucker needs to go down, for a long time.'

'OK, I hear you.' Brigstocke tensed his shoulders then relaxed them again, that shadow of disappointment drifting briefly across his face. 'Fine, we'll keep it in-house for the time being, meaning just between us.'

'I think that's sensible.'

'Going back to this leak, though—'

'It's someone close to the case,' Tanner said. 'Has to be.'

'Is it possible that whoever's been leaking information is the same man you think is behind the rapes and the cover-ups? This same senior officer?'

Thorne had been asking himself that very question and couldn't see how that answer made any sense. 'Why would he pass information that could help Alex Brightwell when Brightwell's the one going after the rapists, the men who fitted his brother up? I mean, we don't know how much he knew before someone started helping him out, but surely this man wouldn't want to give Brightwell the advantage. Not when there's always the possibility Brightwell could come after *him*'

Tanner nodded. 'Whoever he is, he'd definitely be on Brightwell's list.'

'Top of it, I would have thought,' Thorne said.

'Yeah, I suppose.' Brigstocke fiddled with the troublesome lever on his chair and sat back. 'You know, I used to think this job had gone down the pan ten years ago,' he said. 'When filling in pointless forms and ticking off all the courses you'd been on became more important than solving cases and protecting victims.'

'And the seminars,' Thorne said. 'Don't forget the seminars.'

Brigstocke managed a half-smile. 'There was obviously a lot more of that stuff once I became a DCI . . . all the politics, whatever and even back then I was asking myself if I'd done the right thing. You know, climbing the greasy pole. *This*, though ...' He stared over their heads, eyes wide behind the thick glasses, looking all but stunned. 'It's no longer a force I recognise and certainly not one I'd want to join any more.'

'Unless you were a wannabe rapist,' Tanner said. 'Then it's pretty much tailor-made for you.'

They said nothing for a while. A peal of laughter rang out suddenly in the incident room; someone doing what – to the three in that office – seemed impossible at that moment and finding something to laugh at.

'Anyway,' Brigstocke said, eventually. 'Something a bit nicer.'

'Which would be anything,' Thorne said.

'I'm having a barbecue on Sunday, if you fancy coming. Nothing major, just a bit of a get-together. A few drinks.'

'A barbecue?' Thorne looked at Tanner. 'It's not exactly barbecue weather.'

'Bring a coat.' Brigstocke shuffled papers, looking a little sheepish. 'It's my birthday.'

'How old?' Tanner asked.

'Never you mind.'

'Come on.'

'Bearing in mind everything we've just been discussing, I think I'll treat that as confidential information.'

'A *big* birthday?'

Brigstocke ignored her. 'It'll be good to wind down and forget about all this for a few hours. I mean, we *won't*, obviously.'

'Speak for yourself.' Thorne rubbed his hands together. 'Give me a decent steak and I can forget just about anything.'

'I think it'll just be sausages and a few chicken wings.'

'Good enough,' Thorne said.

FIFTY-ONE

Thorne carried half a Guinness across and joined Holland at their usual table in the corner of the Oak. He saw that Holland had gone for the shepherd's pie, which was an act of courage surely worthy of the King's Award for Gallantry. That, or a sign that Holland was developing some serious psychiatric issues.

'Another morning to treasure,' Thorne said.

Holland rolled his eyes. 'Aren't they all?'

They – along with most of the other detectives on the team – had spent the last few hours ploughing through several dozen further sightings of Alex Brightwell. They'd been pouring in via phone and LiveChat since a still photograph from the Frankland footage had been distributed to the media the previous afternoon: a man seen buying fruit in Camberwell; a man waiting for a bus on Oxford Street; the ex-partners of at least two different women looking to make trouble for men who'd pissed them off.

'How's he getting around, d'you reckon? Brightwell?'

Holland looked up, gobbets of watery mince dripping from his fork.

'I mean, I can't see him hopping on and off the bus or the tube, can you? Too many people looking out for him.'

'And too many CCTV cameras,' Holland said. 'At stations, on all the buses.'

'Yeah. He *might* have a car, but only if he's nicked one. There are no records in his name at the DVLA which isn't much of a surprise, but there's nothing in the name of Richard Silcox either. Same with all the hire companies.'

'Well, we know he's got at least one set of fake ID documents,' Holland said. 'So it's possible he's got a bunch of them.'

'It's possible.' Thorne wasn't convinced. 'A bike's his best bet, you ask me. Quickest way to get around the city anyway, plus he can keep his head down most of the time, stay out of sight of the facial recognition cameras.'

'It's a thought,' Holland said. 'Maybe he's hopping on and off Boris Bikes. Might be worth a look.'

Thorne grunted. These days the bike-hire scheme was run by Santander, but most people still used the original term and the bikes themselves remained of far more use to Londoners than the self-serving idiot after whom they were named.

Holland appeared to have given up on his lunch. 'We could narrow it down to the areas we know he's been. Archway, Hendon Park ... check out the card payments at all the bike docking stations.'

'Bloody hell, and you thought this morning was a slog?'

'Actually, there's quite a few other bike-hire companies. Lime, and Tier, and Forest ... you know, if want a greener alternative.'

'I thought bikes *were* the greener alternative.'

'We should probably check them all out.'

'He might just have his own bike, Dave. Quite a few people do, apparently.'

'All right, smartarse, it's not like you're coming up with a lot of ideas.'

'I tend to wait until I've got a good one,' Thorne said.

Ignoring the finger from Holland, Thorne looked across and saw DC Stephen Pallister at another table, sitting with three uniformed officers he didn't recognise. Pallister nodded and Thorne nodded back, though they hadn't exchanged more than a few words since Thorne had bawled him out in the office for not picking up on Tully's arrest of Peter Brightwell.

He turned back to Holland. Said, 'I'm sorry about yesterday.'

Holland looked at him.

'I was a bit sharp. When you were talking about Daniel Sadler's wife.'

'No worries,' Holland said. 'I'm a big boy.'

'Bigger than you were, anyway.' Thorne still struggled sometimes to accept that the thoughtful and ballsy officer sitting next to him was the same overeager article that he'd felt lumbered with all those years before. Keen to impress, with a notebook on hand at all times and no idea of the horrors that lay ahead; on that investigation, certainly.

The 'Sleepyhead' case.

'We're trying for a baby,' Holland announced, from nowhere. 'Me and Pippa . . . well, obviously me and Pippa.'

'Oh, right,' Thorne said. 'You telling me that to prove you really are a big boy?'

'I just felt like telling you.'

'OK, well . . . that's great. Goes without saying, I'm expecting you to name the kid after me. You know, if and when.'

'I'll tell Pippa.'

'So, Tom or Thomasina.'

'Tom Holland's the name of the actor who plays Spider-Man.'

'Fair enough,' Thorne said. 'I'll be rooting for a girl, then.' He took a sip of Guinness and glanced at his watch. They didn't need to be back in the office for another twenty minutes. 'You seeing much of Chloe?' Holland's daughter was a couple of years older than Alfie, and Thorne knew that the opportunity to spend more time with her had been one of the main reasons for Dave's rejoining the Met.

'Not as much as I'd like,' Holland said. 'Sophie's being a bit tricky.'

'Your ex-wife was always tricky.'

'You only think that because she didn't like you.'

'Absolutely. She was a nightmare.'

Holland smiled. 'Let's be fair, she was very much in the majority.'

Thorne smiled back as he raised his glass and stared at Holland through it.

No, definitely not the man he was all those years back.

Then again, neither were a lot of people . . .

'Russell was a bit down in the mouth when I spoke to him this morning,' he said. 'I thought he was just depressed about the case, which is fair enough, but it sounded like more than that. He was talking as if he's about ready to knock it all on the head. Not the force he joined, all that.'

'He's right,' Holland said.

'Course he is, but is that reason enough to leave?'

'Maybe he's just knackered and had enough, or wants to go while he's still got the chance to do something else. People want to get out of the Job for all sorts of reasons.'

'The other night, Helen was suggesting *I* should think about it.'

'Was she?'

Thorne glanced across and saw that Pallister was still looking in their direction, as though he was worried they might be talking about him. 'She wasn't really serious . . . at least I don't think she was.' He swooshed what was left of his Guinness around in the glass. 'You ever think about calling it a day?'

Holland shook his head.

'You'd have a lot more time to spend with Thomasina.'

'Now's not the time,' Holland said. 'Yeah, everything about this job's pretty horrible right now . . . worst it's ever been, I reckon. I mean, we're seeing it with this case, aren't we? Close up and seriously personal, but that's exactly why we need to stay put and fight it out. It's the straight coppers that need to stick around until things are put right . . . or until they're better than they are now, at least.'

Thorne said nothing, thinking that passionate speeches in the pub were all very well.

'We've got to try and get a bit of trust back.'

'Still "glass half full", then, Dave?' Thorne downed what was left of his beer. 'Glad to see they haven't knocked that out of you.'

'No, and you're exactly the same,' Holland said. 'However much you like to make out you're not. Mind you, you did once tell me that your glass was half full of hot piss.'

'Did I?' Thorne turned, catching movement and watched

as Pallister and his uniformed friends got up to leave. Another nod, when Pallister got to the door.

Thorne reached for his jacket. He remembered sitting at the same table with Holland and Tanner the day after the poisonings; the two uniformed officers who'd nervously approached them to offer support and show solidarity.

What those coppers said back then, even if it was a little gung-ho and par-for-the-course, had at least sounded sincere.

'We're all on the same side.'

Now, it just sounded fucking ridiculous.

FIFTY-TWO

Brightwell thought that the whole 'enemy's enemy' thing made a fair amount of sense, so under normal circumstances he'd see anyone who hated the police as being worthy of a decent hearing. Those whose pain seemed genuine and whose grievances sounded as heartfelt as his own. The men and women – and there were always plenty of women – gleefully professing an urgent desire to 'stab up da copz' or 'roast the pork'.

Christ, though, *some* of them . . .

Digging just a little deeper into the threads on those message boards where he'd first lurked and then posted, where he'd been thrilled to discover that he wasn't alone, he couldn't believe the reasons people gave for being there. The nature of their complaints.

Not being respected.

A burglary that remained unsolved.

Being done for speeding.

Now he could see that they were idiots, all of them, and it

annoyed him that they were taking up space somewhere serious people like him could meet to exchange serious views. Of course, he had sympathy for those who had acceptable cause to feel aggrieved – who'd been stopped and searched for being the wrong colour or beaten up by thugs in uniform for no apparent reason – but not paying your road tax did not give anyone the right to feel the same hatred he did.

It was an insult to him and to Peter, to anyone who'd actually *suffered*.

He got angrier, the more he trawled.

How could anyone think that these people were anything more than moaners and time-wasters who were only on the Dark Web at all because they had a bit of IT nous and thought it made them edgy or alternative? Gave them hard-ons they couldn't get sounding off in all the regular, vanilla places. They belonged on Twitter or Facebook. Better yet, on one of those nauseating neighbourhood forums where people complained that their bins hadn't been collected or that there was never a copper around when you wanted one.

Righteously furious as he was, Brightwell smiled to think he'd done his level best to make *that* problem just a little worse.

As it was, he hadn't been in the best of moods when he'd logged on. He was still irritated that Andre Campbell had only done half a job on Craig Knowles. The injuries sounded reasonably bad, mind you, so there was always the hope Knowles would die eventually and even if he didn't, he'd probably never be able to shit properly again.

That thought gave Brightwell some comfort as he began posting a few messages of his own. Letting these imposters know just how pathetic they were, reminding them what real hatred was and what serious people did about it. Hinting, at any rate. It wasn't like he was about to confess online, however secure his VPN was.

He was still receiving information, so he knew they were continuing to monitor his online activity. He knew they'd reviewed the footage from the prison and that a new photo had been sent out. He was still none the wiser about who was sending those very helpful messages, even if lately they hadn't included anything he could really use. They were more like operational updates really, but he remained grateful for the support, all the same.

There was at least one other serious person out there somewhere.

While his cursor blinked expectantly at him, Brightwell sat and thought about the only person to whom he had actually confessed. Now, *she'd* had a proper grievance, and it had been dealt with, thanks to him.

And then what had she done?

The worst thing Alex Brightwell could ever imagine; the worst betrayal.

He began to type.

If his enemy's enemy was his friend, what did that make his enemy's friend?

FIFTY-THREE

Once he'd been given the go-ahead by Nicola Tanner, Greg Hobbs had sent instructions to Emily Mead on how to download a secure application that would enable them to video-chat. As soon as she'd messaged him to confirm that she'd installed the app, he called her.

'Well, that works then.' Hobbs grinned and gave a thumbs-up, then, seeing the image of himself in a small box on the bottom right of his screen, he instinctively straightened his collar and made a few quick adjustments to his hair.

'Yeah.'

Hobbs enlarged the main image and could see immediately that Emily Mead had been crying. 'You OK?'

'I've definitely been better, Greg.'

'We can do this another time, if you want.'

'It's fine.' She almost smiled. 'I've been a lot worse as well.'

'Do you want to talk about it?'

She clearly needed no further invitation and, while Hobbs

had no idea if she was telling him the things she did because she specifically wanted him to know or because he was the only person she *could* tell at that moment, he quickly stopped caring either way. He just listened and tried not to look too shocked. Too horrified.

'Fuck, that's . . . awful,' Hobbs said. Emily had paused and turned her face from the camera on her phone, breathing hard as though fighting to keep a lid on her emotions. He wasn't sure if there was more to come, but struggled to imagine that it could get any worse.

'Yep.' She turned back to look at him. '"Awful" is about right.'

'I never knew,' Hobbs said. 'Any of it.'

'Why would you?'

'I'm just the nerd who gets paid to do the IT stuff. They don't actually tell me anything.'

They stared at each other for a few seconds. The bare wall behind the sofa on which Emily was sitting was a suitably bland backdrop and Hobbs realised that he should have thought a little more about what *she* could see behind *him*.

'It'd be fine if it wasn't for that voice,' she said, eventually. 'The other man's voice. I mean, no . . . not fine, but maybe bearable. I know I can't really claim I'd come to terms with what Callaghan did . . . not when I was part of that stupid hate forum and considering what I let Brightwell draw me into. Hopefully it's going to get easier anyway now he's dead, but all I'm saying is it's not him that keeps me awake at night. Never really was. I can still remember what that piece of shit smelled like and the noises he made while he was doing it, but they're just like . . . flashes, you know?'

'If you smell something similar,' Hobbs said. 'When you hear those kinds of noises.'

'Right. But that voice has never gone away, never left me alone.'

'Maybe when they've caught him.' Hobbs knew it sounded trite, unconvincing even, but he didn't know what else to say. 'You've got good people on the case. Nicola and Tom Thorne.'

'I know,' she said.

'So . . .'

'Is there a reason you wanted to talk?' she asked. 'I don't mind if there isn't.'

Hobbs had already cleared it with Nicola Tanner. Once he'd given her the update, she'd said that she had no intention of sharing the news with Emily Mead. It was information that no longer made any difference, she'd said, operationally or otherwise, but Hobbs had told Tanner that he'd like to pass it on.

He thought that Emily had a right to know.

'Brightwell's been online again,' he said. 'On your "hate forum".'

'Saying what?'

'It was weird, like he was showing off. Letting everyone else in the group know that they were lightweights, basically.'

'Well, he's right, isn't he? I mean, compared to him, everything he's done.'

'It also felt a bit like he was touting for business, you know? Angling for suggestions . . . names of coppers he could go after.'

'Did he get any?'

'Not as far as I could see.'

'That's good news for somebody.'

'Oh yeah.' Hobbs was trying to sound nice and casual, like it was no big deal. Because it really wasn't. 'And he sent you another message.'

Emily blinked and turned away again, just for a second or two. 'What did he say?'

'Hang on ...' Hobbs executed a few swift strokes on his keyboard so that Emily would see the screenshot he'd taken.

<<Stay safe ...>>

He did what was necessary to get Emily staring back at him again.

'Fuck's that supposed to mean?'

'Like I said, he's just showing off. He must know we're seeing it, that it's all being monitored, so it's just ... posturing or whatever.'

'Course it is, because I *am* safe.'

'Absolutely,' Hobbs said.

'Safe *here*, I mean. Aren't I?'

'Safe as houses.'

'You know, unless he's got a missile launcher or he's planning to burn the building down or something.'

'It's all just for our benefit,' Hobbs said. 'There's nothing he can do, you know that, right?'

'Yeah ... thanks.' Emily nodded and leaned down out of shot. Hobbs heard the tell-tale hiss.

'Are you *vaping*?'

Emily reappeared on-screen, chugging away at the disposable vape and grinning like a naughty child when she puffed the vapour out. 'One of the coppers outside smuggled it in for me.'

'That's a government building.' Hobbs was grinning, too. 'I doubt very much that the use of e-cigarettes is permitted on the premises.'

'They're hardly going to kick me out, are they?' She started chugging again. 'I could sit around in here smoking crack if I wanted to. Wouldn't make much difference, as there's every chance I'm getting sent down anyway when this is all over.'

'I doubt that's going to happen.'

'You couldn't get me some, could you? Crack, I mean. Maybe from that site where you bought those iffy meds.'

'Almost certainly,' Hobbs said. 'But I know you're joking.'

'Half joking.'

Hobbs leaned across to adjust the volume on his computer and heard Emily laugh. He leaned back again. 'What?'

She pointed. 'What the hell is *that*? Behind you.'

Hobbs turned to look at the object mounted on the wall, the one he'd paid nearly nine hundred pounds for at a gamers' fair and really should have thought about covering up before he made the call. He turned back and did his best to look dignified. Unashamed. 'It's a life-size replica of Frostmourne,' he said. 'The two-handed longsword which bestows eternal power on the Lich King.'

'Oh, right . . . and he lives in that citadel you told me about, does he?'

'It's his last bastion,' Hobbs said.

Emily sat back, unable to get the vape into her mouth because she was laughing so much. Hobbs watched her and decided that he'd made the right decision in making the call because, if nothing else, he'd certainly cheered her up.

'Well, Greg, the good news is that it's actually pretty cool.'

'Yeah . . . I know.'

'But the bad news is, I don't think your on/off girlfriend will be on again any time soon.'

FIFTY-FOUR

Thorne doubted that he had a greater number of imaginary conversations than anyone else, but he was pretty sure that, by and large, they were rather more interesting than most people's.

The odd chinwag with a notorious serial killer.

Chit-chats with any number of madmen and murderers, dead or alive.

Quite often, of course, these conversations – the ones at the more extreme end of the spectrum – were simple exercises in wish-fulfilment. An after-the-fact mind game during which Thorne got to say all those things he'd neglected to come out with at the time; in the interview room, in court, whatever. Insults and home truths and a decent collection of brutal one-liners.

A bit sad, quite probably, but satisfying nonetheless.

Other imagined exchanges were rather more fantastical, such as those Thorne firmly believed would have changed the course of musical history for the better. Telling Hank Williams that he really didn't need to play that show in Canton, Ohio and to get out of the Cadillac he would otherwise be found dead in the back of. Persuading Elvis to cut down on the drugs and cheeseburgers. Urging Phil Collins to stay behind the drums ...

Even if he didn't want to dwell for too long on what it said about him, the majority of these conversations that should have taken place but never did were with fellow officers. The one he imagined having with James Greaves involved the man from the CCU answering *all* Thorne's questions before taking a nasty tumble down those stairs, and over the previous ten days or so he'd imagined any number of encounters with DCI Jeremy Walker. Several of these were even more heated than those they'd actually had, with a few containing little in the way of actual dialogue and rather more in the way of punching, or worse.

More than a bit sad, and *enormously* satisfying.

Not altogether surprising, though, all things considered.

Over the course of his career, Thorne had witnessed a good deal of violence; the act itself or its aftermath. It was virtually an occupational hazard when the deeds of violent men – and it was *almost always* men – paid his wages. Yes, he'd meted out a fair amount of low-level violence himself but, on balance, he thought he'd been on the receiving end of it more times than he'd dished it out.

He'd been shot and stabbed and badly beaten. There were any number of visible scars and plenty more that nobody would ever see.

He remembered what Helen had said to him a few nights before and the question he'd asked Dave Holland in the pub.

'You ever think about calling it a day?'

It was a wonder they talked about anything else.

Helen was out for the evening with some colleagues from Citizens Advice, so Thorne had gone back to Kentish Town. He'd eaten cheese on toast with tomato soup and listened to Johnny Cash's 'Ragged Old Flag' and mooched around the flat, trying to tidy a little. Now he sat staring at a TV he couldn't be bothered to switch on and thought about the anger etched across Nicola Tanner's face when they'd been talking about the abject failings of the Counter Corruption Unit. The 'shit that wouldn't be happening': that *shouldn't* be happening. Their conversation with Russell Brigstocke about a job that none of them recognised any longer.

Then he imagined a couple more.

The one he was going to have when he finally arrested the police officer who had enabled others to commit terrible crimes and subsequently protected them would be predictably non-verbal. Thorne couldn't quite decide on the location, but it would definitely *not* be in an interview room. Somewhere away from the cameras, for obvious reasons.

It wouldn't last very long.

His second conversation was rather more straightforward – a simple phone call – and had to be imaginary because, with the investigation still ongoing and with no authorisation whatsoever to do so, it was certainly not one he could actually have.

He imagined calling Mandy Brightwell to apologise.

'I'm sorry I didn't believe you ... and I'm sorry on behalf of all the other officers who didn't believe you. And the ones that put you in this position in the first place by lying, and worse. All the lawyers and everyone else responsible for sending your husband to prison for a crime I know he didn't commit. I'm sorry you got

sent to prison when all you did was tell the truth, and for what happened to you afterwards. When all this is over, I'll do anything I can to help you sue every one of those bastards for wrongful imprisonment and obviously the same goes for Peter. Whatever it takes, we'll get his conviction quashed and get him out of there as soon as we can. I understand why you're angry because you've got every right to be, and I'm not expecting that this will make you any less angry, but I'm sorry anyway. For what it's worth.'

'Well, it's about bloody time. Thank you.'

Ten minutes later, Thorne had a beer open and was looking for the number. There was rather more shouting and swearing during the *actual* conversation, which was fair enough all things considered, but it went more or less the way he'd imagined.

FIFTY-FIVE

While Tom Thorne tried to work out how much trouble he might eventually be in relative to how little he cared, Dave Holland sat three miles south in Clerkenwell clutching his own phone; summoning up the courage to make the call and have the conversation he'd barely *stopped* imagining for the previous twenty-four hours. Since Thorne and Tanner had got back from Fin-Cel and passed on the news about Daniel Sadler and what kind of items he'd been paid to deliver.

He got up and walked into the kitchen. A quick cup of tea and *then* he'd do it . . .

It wasn't as if he had to make the call at all. The case – to which Karen Sadler was no more than peripheral – was still far from put to bed and there was no compulsion for him to pass on any updates whatsoever to her. Even when it was over, it didn't have to be *him*, besides which nothing he told her was going to bring her husband back, was it?

Her face, though, when she'd handed him that photograph.

Her voice, the genuine gratitude in it when he had called to let her know there was no news at all and promised that he'd call again as soon as there was.

With the kettle still grumbling, he marched back into the living room and snatched his mobile from the table.

'Oh, hello, Mrs Sadler, this is Detec—'

'Detective Holland. I recognise your voice.'

'Right, good.' Pippa was in another room, but Holland took a quick look over his shoulder anyway. He wasn't sure why he didn't want her to overhear the call. Maybe it was just that he didn't want her to see him struggle. 'How're you doing?'

'Well, you know. Things aren't easy, but you've just got to keep going, haven't you?'

'I was calling because there has been a development in the case ... in our investigation into Daniel's death.' He waited, but her silence suggested that she was happy for him to continue, or would be if happiness and dread meant the same thing. 'We're now as sure as we can be that Daniel did not take his own life.' He waited again.

'Oh ... '

'There's not much more I can tell you at this stage, I'm afraid, but I thought you'd like to know.'

'Well ... thank you, I suppose.' She sniffed. 'I knew I was right about Daniel not killing himself, and I should probably be ... well ... not *relieved* exactly, but this makes even less sense. You see what I'm saying? I mean, God alone knows why he'd even have been up there, but I presume you don't think it was an accident.'

'No, we don't think that's a possibility.'

'So ... ?'

There they were, the questions Holland had known would

follow; unasked but clear enough above the slight hiss on the line and the sound of Karen Sadler sniffling.

Who killed my husband?

Why was he killed?

'I'm sorry that I can't really give you any further information,' Holland said. 'I can assure you that the case is still very much ongoing.'

'I understand.'

'Are you OK?' Holland closed his eyes and shook his head. Maybe he didn't want Pippa there listening to him asking ridiculous questions. 'Would you like me to arrange for the Family Liaison Officer to come over?'

'It's fine. I've still got Nathan with me.'

'Let me know if you change your mind. It's really not a problem.'

'We'll manage,' she said.

'OK, then ...'

'Thank you for letting me know, David.'

'Like I said, it's not a problem.'

'For taking the time ...'

When he'd ended the call, Holland walked back to the kitchen and straight to the fridge. He poured himself a glass of wine from the bottle Pippa had opened earlier and carried it back to the living room.

He sat on the sofa, downed half the glass and let his head drop back.

Karen Sadler would have all her questions answered soon enough, and when all the details emerged would almost certainly wish she'd never asked them.

What had he said to Pippa a few nights before?

Not much to understand about kiddie-porn, is there?

Unless of course Karen Sadler already knew about her husband's arrest twelve years before. Unless Holland had misread her every bit as much as they'd all misread Mandy Brightwell. More than anything, he hoped that wasn't the case.

He lifted his glass again, listening to Pippa talking in the next room, making a phone call of her own. He wondered how things were going as far as the fertile window was concerned and asked himself if he really wanted another child at all.

Finishing the wine, he reminded himself – not that he needed any reminding – that he was an idiot. Having a baby with Pippa would be amazing ... *better* than amazing. He couldn't wait, but it was only natural to have a few ... concerns, wasn't it? Things being as they were.

How would Chloe react?

How would Chloe's *mother* react?

Even thinking about that was ridiculous, of course. He and Pippa were married, for God's sake, so if they chose to have a child, or a dozen of them, it was no bloody concern of his ex's. All the same, it was definitely worth keeping in mind, because Thorne had been spot on when he'd been talking about her in the pub. 'Nightmare' was about right and he had to remember that Sophie could make his and Pippa's life difficult if she chose to. With Chloe and what have you.

Holland turned when he heard the door open to see Pippa nodding towards the empty glass in his hand.

'You left any for me?'

'There's half a bottle left,' Holland said.

'That'll do.' She walked across, leaning down to kiss him on her way to fetch some wine for herself.

A few seconds after she'd disappeared into the kitchen, Holland shouted through. 'Listen, I know I'm getting a bit ahead of myself here. I mean, I don't want to jinx it, but presuming everything goes the way we want it to on the baby front ... have you given any thought to names?'

Pippa reappeared in the kitchen doorway and leaned against it, her own glass in one hand and the bottle in the other, ready to top up Holland's. She grinned. 'Maybe.'

'OK, great. I was just wondering if *Tom* might be anywhere on the list.'

'Only if it's a really long list,' she said.

FIFTY-SIX

Overcooked sausages, undercooked chicken and the lurking spectre of botulism would not normally be Thorne's idea of a Sunday afternoon out, but after a couple of beers and a few sharp nudges from Helen he'd actually begun to enjoy himself.

He was glad he'd worn a coat, though.

There were perhaps thirty people gathered in Brigstocke's small back garden and Thorne knew most of them, by sight at least. Charita Desai was there and Dipak Chall. Thorne was quite surprised to see Stephen Pallister enjoying the DCI's hospitality, even if he looked a little sheepish when Thorne caught his eye. A good few of the guests were former colleagues Brigstocke had worked with before joining his current MIT and Thorne presumed that those he didn't recognise were friends or neighbours. He chatted briefly to several of the guests he didn't know, did his best to sound interested in golf and gardening, but gravitated eventually to the group he felt most comfortable with.

Phil Hendricks and his boyfriend Liam seemed to be engaged in a competition to see who could eat the most chicken wings. Tanner had brought the not remotely freaky-looking Fiona along and Holland was there with Pippa.

Everyone was making an effort not to talk shop.

'See that bloke over there?' Hendricks nodded towards a man spooning salad on to a paper plate; the same man who'd talked at Thorne for ten minutes about the problems with his swing and the fantastic new putter he hoped would improve his game on the greens.

'Keen golfer,' Thorne said.

'Keen drinker an' all . . . look at the colour of him. His liver's knackered, I reckon. I give him six months at the most.'

Some people were making less of an effort than others.

'Bloody hell, Phil,' Tanner said.

'I'm telling you. If he's booked himself a summer holiday, that's money he might as well have flushed straight down the shitter.'

'Nice.'

Next to Tanner, Fiona grinned and leaned in to whisper something.

Hendricks was a picture of innocence. 'What?'

'Just . . . you're exactly like I'd thought you'd be,' Fiona said. 'That's all.'

'Oh yeah?' Hendricks dropped the remains of another chicken wing on to his plate and stared at Tanner. 'Been telling you all about me, has she? I mean, obviously I'm even more impressive in the flesh.'

Liam rolled his eyes at Thorne.

'Definitely,' Fiona said. 'Nic's description didn't do you justice.'

'I've heard a fair bit about you, too.' Hendricks smirked, ignoring the glare from Tanner.

'OK, and am I what *you* were expecting?'

'Yeah, I'd say so.' Hendricks shrugged and wiped his mouth with a serviette. 'Give or take the odd nipple clamp.'

Thorne almost spat his beer out as Fiona laughed, providing the cue for Holland and the others to do the same, while Tanner stepped smartly across to punch Hendricks on the arm.

Brigstocke walked across to join them, carrying a plate of predictably blackened sausages. 'Sounds like everyone's enjoying themselves,' he said.

'Yeah, it's a good do,' Thorne said.

Everyone nodded and murmured their agreement.

'I did have one bit of chicken that was a bit pink,' Hendricks said. 'But I don't think I'll sue.'

Brigstocke bit into a sausage and told him that he couldn't give a toss either way.

'Thanks for inviting us,' Pippa said.

Tanner leaned to touch Brigstocke's arm. 'Yes, and happy birthday by the way.'

'You still haven't told us how old you are,' Thorne said.

Brigstocke smiled. 'It's nice to get together away from ... everything, don't you think?' He looked at Thorne and Tanner. 'Just for a few bloody hours?'

'Shit, were we supposed to bring presents?' Hendricks asked.

'Well, yeah, it's a birthday party and unless you're ignorant northern scum that's what people normally do,' Thorne said. He and Helen had brought a bottle, same as most of the other guests had done, judging by the sizeable collection of bottle-shaped parcels on a table inside.

Hendricks nodded. 'Well, in which case my present's going to be the whole not suing you for food poisoning thing. Fair enough?' He leaned across, touched his beer can to Brigstocke's. 'Many happy returns, mate.'

'I think I might get a bit teary,' Brigstocke said.

Thorne looked across to see Brigstocke's wife, Sally, moving between the guests, handing out fresh cans and topping up glasses. He walked across to join her, gave her a hug.

'How's life, Tom?'

'I'm good,' Thorne said. 'This is great, by the way. I'm guessing it was your idea.'

She smiled, nodded. 'You warm enough?'

'Well—'

'A very stupid idea. A barbecue, I mean.'

They stared across at the group Thorne had just left. Brigstocke was laughing at Hendricks's usual twisted cabaret turn.

'How's your old man doing?' Thorne asked.

Sally looked at him. 'I was going to ask you the same thing.'

'Oh.' Thorne remembered what Holland had said about spouses knowing their other halves better than anyone else. That said, coppers often chose to leave the darker elements of their days behind them at the office, to keep work and home lives separate. So it was perhaps unsurprising that Russell Brigstocke's wife might know less about her husband's state of mind than those he worked with every day. 'He's a bit stressed,' he said.

Sally was still watching her husband. 'Yeah, he's definitely not himself.'

'We've got a pig of a job on.'

'Dead police officers, right?'

'Right,' Thorne said. Thinking: *Well, that's how it started.*

She nodded and twisted the wine bottle in her hand. 'It's got to him, you know?' She leaned in close to whisper. 'He's actually been dropping hints about retiring. He probably won't, knowing him, but all the same ...'

Thorne said nothing, not altogether surprised considering some of the things Brigstocke had said recently. The force he no longer felt part of.

'One of the reasons I wanted to do *this*,' Sally said.

They carried on staring for a few seconds before Thorne felt the need to change the subject. 'Kids not here?'

Sally laughed. 'No bloody chance.'

Their eldest boy was just finishing his second year at university while their youngest was about to start his first. Their daughter was training to be a teacher somewhere up north. They'd lost a fourth child to meningitis fifteen years before. Thorne knew just how devastated the family had been, though Brigstocke had not talked about it for a long time.

Work life, home life ...

'We all had a little Zoom get-together the other night,' she said. 'But even if they were around, I doubt very much they would have come. A party with your parents' friends is every teenager's nightmare, isn't it? I think the music would have given them the heebie-jeebies for a kick-off.'

'Yeah, I suppose,' Thorne said. They'd brought a speaker out on to the patio and Thorne's reaction to some of the music had been no less extreme than the kids' would have been. Why was 'easy listening' always so bloody difficult? Ed Sheeran and the fucking Eagles. There had been a Coldplay track a few minutes earlier, about which, Thorne decided, he would have serious words with the DCI when the chance presented itself.

There was no need to spoil his birthday party.

Thorne was about to say something else when he saw Tanner and Holland walking towards him, a phone clutched in Tanner's hand and expressions that told him their break from shop talk was well and truly over.

'I'd best let you get on,' Thorne said.

Sally squeezed his arm and took a step away, then turned back and nodded towards the jaundiced golfer. 'Try and avoid Alan from next door,' she said. 'He's dull as fuck.'

Tanner pointed towards a quiet corner.

'Greg Hobbs just called,' she said, once Thorne had joined them. 'Alex Brightwell's posted another message to Emily Mead.' She tapped at the screen on her phone then held it out for Thorne to look at.

> <<A safe house isn't always safe as houses.>>

'What's he playing at?' Thorne asked.

Holland shook his head. 'It's like Hobbs said. He must know we're monitoring this stuff, so he's just winding us up; winding Emily up. What the hell can he actually *do*?' He looked from Thorne to Tanner. 'Nothing, right?'

'Right,' Tanner said.

'It's solid,' Thorne said. 'She's safe.'

Holland was nodding. 'Talk me through it.'

'Really?' Tanner said.

'I mean, it can't hurt to go over this stuff, can it?' Holland had not visited the safe house in Edgware. Since the list of approved visitors had been cut down, only Thorne and Tanner had been granted access. 'Just run me through the set-up then we can all relax and go back to the barbie and a few more of Phil's dirty stories.'

Tanner looked at Thorne and shrugged. 'Other than that visit to the ground floor when Hobbs came over, Emily's not left the flat since she was first taken there. Not for a minute. She has access to one phone and that's only to call us or Hobbs. She's got no access to a computer and nobody in her family knows she's there.'

'They've been told she's travelling,' Thorne said.

'There's a rotating team of officers stationed outside the building, front and back, and more officers inside. Umpteen ID checks and CCTV cameras inside the building. Food is delivered twice a day directly to the officers outside, as per a rota which we agreed on when Emily was first taken to the flat. Nothing gets to her door until the officer carrying it has passed through all the ID and camera checks.' Tanner held out her arms. 'I don't think she could be any safer unless we locked her up in our incident room. Actually, scratch that... she's way safer.'

'OK,' Holland said. 'Never a bad idea to talk it through.'

'No, you're right.'

'I wish I could have food delivered every night.' Holland leaned in, conspiratorially. 'Cooking isn't exactly Pippa's strong point, though please don't tell her I said that.'

'Not a word,' Tanner said.

'So, what's on the menu in Edgware tonight?'

Tanner thought for a moment. 'Sunday is... burgers. Large cheeseburger, fries and a Diet Coke with no ice. Emily's *very* demanding.'

'What d'you reckon, Tom? I don't think you'd miss home cooking, would you? Not the stuff that *you* cook, anyway.'

Thorne wasn't listening. He was looking across at the others, thinking about Hendricks's non-existent birthday present; what he *wasn't* going to sue Brigstocke for. Trying to stay calm as the prickle took hold at the nape of his neck and began to spread.

From nowhere; sudden and shocking, all too familiar.

Like the softest brush of cold, thin fingers against his skin.

FIFTY-SEVEN

There was always a way.

He thought about how things had played out with Tully. It would have been easy enough to do what he'd later done with Callaghan, to study the shift patterns then put out a call and wait for the dutiful bobby to come trotting along. He would have done exactly that, had not something a little more inventive occurred to him.

The day he'd come up with the doughnut idea had definitely been what you might call a good day at the office, and he hadn't lost too much sleep over the other three who'd died. He was already struggling to remember their names. 'Innocent', that's how they'd been described in the papers and on TV, but he knew better. There was no such thing as an innocent police officer, only one who hadn't turned yet.

There was always the *right* way.

Putting a plan together, then executing it perfectly was immensely satisfying, of course it was, and Peter deserved no less. It was even better, though, when the opportunity simply fell into your lap.

He'd got there good and early and sat waiting outside the burger place, on the second-hand moped he'd picked up for less than a grand on Gumtree. He'd watched the delivery riders pulling up every ten minutes or so and collared each of them when they came out, checked the address until he knew he'd got the right one.

Waving a twenty pound note around and telling the bloke his story.

Now, I know this is going to sound a bit weird . . .

The delivery was actually for his girlfriend, he'd said, and he was planning a special way to propose. She wouldn't know it was him because he'd keep his helmet on and he wanted her to find the ring when she took out her burger. Maybe even *inside* it, though on second thoughts he didn't want her to choke on the flipping thing. It was sort of an 'in' joke because she *lived* on bloody takeaways. Fingers crossed and all that, but she'd definitely find it funny . . .

So, what do you think? Can I deliver this one for you?

The driver had said it was sweet. Romantic, you know? He'd actually been grinning as he handed over the delivery boxes and wished him luck as he was pocketing the twenty quid.

Aww.

He turned into a side street a quarter of a mile or so away from the Edgware address, stopped and removed the delivery package from his rucksack. He needed to be quick; didn't want the butterfly's dinner going cold, after all. He snapped on rubber gloves before taking out the small glass bottle and carefully adding the 'extras'. He smiled as he watched it dissolve into the burger, at the fact it just looked like a bit of added salt on the chips.

Definitely not good for you.

Ten minutes later he drew up behind the unmarked car he knew all about, climbed off the moped and carried his rucksack across. He tapped on the window, then stepped back as the copper in the driver's seat opened the door and got out.

'Here you go ... ' He lifted the brown bag from his rucksack. 'Large cheeseburger, fries and a Diet Coke. Still nice and hot.'

The copper nodded but said nothing as he took the bag.

'Smells seriously bloody lovely, that does. Actually, I quite fancy a burger myself now.' He waited for a reaction, but the copper was stony-faced. He said, 'You're welcome,' and turned back towards the moped ...

... to find himself staring at two men and a woman pointing guns, while behind him the other copper scrambled out of the car and the one who was still holding the cheeseburger began shouting, telling him to raise his hands.

By the time Thorne and Tanner had got out of the car from where they'd been watching and run across the road, the man who'd delivered the food had been searched and was now down on his knees, his fingers laced behind his head.

'He's all yours.' The copper to whom the food had been handed had already put it into a large evidence bag. He stepped forward and passed it across to Tanner. 'He was right, though, it does smell good.'

Thorne walked up to the man kneeling on the pavement. 'Take the helmet off,' he said.

'There's been a mistake.'

'Take it off. Slowly ... '

The man on the ground did as he was told, setting the helmet down on the ground next to him.

'Hands back behind your head.' Thorne waited until the man obeyed, then leaned down, good and close. 'Hello, Alex.'

'Sorry, *who?*'

Thorne peered at the face he'd seen daily for almost a fortnight, in innumerable photographs and CCTV stills. The face that stared down from the wall of the incident room, instantly recognisable despite the various attempts to disguise it. 'You look better without the beard.' He turned to Tanner. 'You think?'

'I can't make my mind up,' she said.

'I don't know who you think I am, but—'

'I know exactly who you are,' Thorne said. 'And as of a couple of hours ago, I knew exactly where to find you.'

Thorne had known, back in Brigstocke's garden, as soon as he'd felt that terrible itch taking hold; its tell-tale creep. He'd known there was a flaw in the security protocol and exactly how it could be exploited.

He'd stood there as the laughter and conversation had faded around him, wondering if that information leak had extended to Emily Mead's home-delivery rota.

If Alex Brightwell had used up all his arsenic...

Now, he let Tanner do the honours.

'Alex Brightwell, I'm arresting you on suspicion of the murder of Christopher Tully and several others we will be talking to you about at a later time.'

Brightwell was shaking his head and muttering. 'This is ridiculous—'

'You do not have to say anything, but it may harm your defence if you do not mention, when questioned—'

'You've got the wrong bloke—'

'—something which you later rely on in court.' Tanner began to speed up as the suspect grew more agitated. 'Anything you do say may be given in evidence.' She looked at Thorne. 'Got there in the end.'

'I can prove it.'

'Well, obviously if we *have* made a mistake I can only apologise,' Thorne said. 'We'd best get you down to the station, hadn't we, see if we can get to the bottom of this.'

'I can prove I'm not Alex Brightwell.'

'If you say so.'

'I've got ID.'

'Course you have,' Tanner said. '"Richard Silcox", is it? Or is that just one of many?'

Thorne was trying hard to keep a straight face. 'There's really no need to get worked up,' he said. 'We can settle the confusion easily enough. Once we're at the station, all we need to do is take a few samples. Won't take five minutes, just a quick swab and then, thanks to the miracle of DNA, we can get this little mix-up well and truly sorted out.'

Brightwell lowered his head and laughed, but when he looked up again, the fury was clear enough. 'Have you any idea how fucking ironic that is?'

Thorne was happy to let the smirk come as he took out the handcuffs, then moved quickly to apply them. 'I never really thought about it.'

FIFTY-EIGHT

Brigstocke wanted to run the interview, which was fine by Thorne.

There was clearly competition though as, just a few minutes after Jeremy Walker arrived, everyone in the incident room had become aware of the raised voices coming from Brigstocke's office. When the two of them eventually emerged, at the same time that Alex Brightwell was being escorted from his cell to the interview room at Colindale station, the rest of the team did their best to look busy; as if they weren't overly concerned either way.

Like one or two of them hadn't been laying bets.

Thorne thought that Brigstocke showed remarkable restraint in not punching the air, but his expression – not to mention Walker's – made it clear enough which DCI had come out on top.

'I'll be conducting the Alex Brightwell interview together with DI Thorne,' Brigstocke announced. 'DCI Walker will observe via video link ...' Walker stared at his perfectly polished brogues. ' ... alongside DIs Tanner and Holland, together with DI Greaves from the CCU.' A few looks were exchanged at the mention of the officer from the Counter Corruption Unit, but Brigstocke ignored them. He nodded at Thorne and the two of them began heading for the door.

They were watched all the way. It was several hours into a late shift already, but every member of the team still working knew that, even though a murder charge was all but a foregone conclusion, this first interview with their suspect would nevertheless be hugely important.

A suspected cop-killer.

There were words of encouragement as they went, a few shouts, a fist or two banged on a desk.

Tanner winked at Thorne as they passed her.

Steve Pallister said, 'Good luck, sir,' though the look on his face suggested that he might have had a few quid on Walker.

Fifteen minutes later, Thorne and Brigstocke removed their jackets and took their seats opposite Alex Brightwell. Brigstocke ran through the formalities while Brightwell picked at a fingernail and the on-call solicitor – a corpulent hack named Fisher – scribbled notes.

Thorne watched and tried to keep his expression blank, thinking that, for all the good it would do him or his client, the solicitor might just as well have been making a shopping list.

'Let's start with the events leading to your arrest earlier this evening,' Brigstocke said. 'Could you tell us why, when as far we know you are not and never have been a food delivery driver, you were attempting to deliver food to an address in Edgware.'

Brightwell did not even bother with a dramatic pause.

'No comment.'

'This was a meal scheduled to be delivered to a woman named Emily Mead. Is that name familiar to you?'

'No comment.'

The solicitor locked eyes with Thorne and shrugged. *Just doing my job.*

'It should be,' Brigstocke said. 'Emily Mead's the young woman you met in Hendon Park almost exactly two weeks ago, isn't that right? The woman who until then you'd known by her online alias ButterflyGrrrl. You met up with her the night you stabbed a police officer named Adam Callaghan to death, isn't that correct?'

Brightwell looked up and across at them for the first time before he spoke and suddenly it sounded as though he was starting to enjoy himself. 'No comment ... whatsoever.'

Thorne leaned towards him. 'Obviously we're still waiting on the test results from the food you were attempting to deliver, but we know it's going to contain arsenic, Alex.' He waited. 'That from the same batch you used to kill Christopher Tully, was it?' Thorne saw another no comment coming, so pressed on. 'Let's talk about the murder of Christopher Tully, shall we?' He removed photographs of Asim Hussain, Kazia Bobak and Catherine Holloway from the folder in front of him and spread them out in front of Brightwell. 'These were the three other officers you killed at the same time.'

Brightwell glanced at the pictures, but his expression didn't change.

'They were just collateral damage really, weren't they?' Brigstocke said.

'It was Tully you wanted.' Thorne stared across the table. 'It was Tully you blamed for what happened to your brother, wasn't it?'

Brightwell looked back at Thorne, eyes narrowing.

'We do know *why* you've been carrying out these killings, Alex.'

'No comm—'

'We understand,' Brigstocke said. He glanced down at his mobile phone when it buzzed, saw the message from Walker in the viewing room above.

Ask how he knew about the Cresswell op.

Brigstocke turned the phone so that Thorne could see the text, just as another one arrived. Brightwell peered, trying to read them.

We need to ID the leak.

'It was very ingenious,' Brigstocke said. 'The business with the doughnuts. I bet you were pleased with that, weren't you?'

'No comment.'

'How did you know where to leave them, though?'

'Yeah ... that's still bothering us,' Thorne said. 'We were hoping you might be able to clear that up.'

'I mean, it wasn't just luck, was it?' Brigstocke said.

'No comment.'

'How did you know, Alex?' Thorne reached to scratch his shoulder, glancing towards the camera in the corner of the room. 'How did you know where Tully was going to be?'

'Who told you, Alex?'

Brightwell leaned forward suddenly. 'Seriously? You think I'm going to *help* you?'

Fisher looked up from his scribblings and now it was Thorne's turn to shrug. *Bad luck, mate. Sometimes they just want to chat.*

Brightwell shook his head, laughing quietly. 'You say you know why these murders happened. Why those coppers had to die. So, bearing that in mind, what on earth makes you think I'd say anything that might help you?'

Brigstocke nodded, like it was a perfectly fair question.

'Because you'd be helping Peter,' Thorne said.

The laughter stopped, because now, Brightwell was interested. 'How?'

'Well, let's just say that during the course of our investigation, we've come across information that leads us to believe your brother was not the man who raped Siobhan Brady.'

'You *believe* he wasn't?'

The phone buzzed again. Another message from above.

Go steady.

'I know he wasn't,' Thorne said. 'And you choosing to help us, might provide the impetus for us to do something about it.'

'Who was it?' Brightwell asked.

Thorne said nothing, as though this was a card he wasn't ready to play just yet, though the truth was that he wasn't actually holding it. He wasn't remotely bothered about upsetting DCI Jeremy Walker, but however much he wanted to, he couldn't say Tully's name. They still did not have the proof. There *was* sufficient evidence, however, to have Peter Brightwell's conviction marked as unsafe, and Thorne knew that would be good enough.

'We can get your brother out of prison,' Brigstocke said. 'How quickly that happens depends on how much you decide to help us.'

Thorne and Brigstocke were happy to let Brightwell think about that offer for a while. Brigstocke turned pages. Thorne smiled at Fisher then let the smile drift up to the camera; to Walker.

'Who fed you the information about the Cresswell operation?'

Thorne asked, eventually. 'We're presuming they also passed on intelligence about Emily Mead turning herself in, the sting in Whittington Park and the location of the safe house. You were even told what Emily Mead had ordered for dinner tonight—'

'It was all done online,' Brightwell said.

'Not *how*, Alex. *Who*.'

'It was anonymous.'

'I don't believe you.'

'That's how it works online.'

'So, just out of the blue someone decided to send you the information you needed?'

'Yeah, pretty much.'

Brigstocke's phone buzzed again. *Push him. He knows who it is.*

'We're talking about a police officer, yes?' Brigstocke said. 'You must have worked out that much.'

'Yeah, it had to be,' Brightwell said. 'How else would they know?'

'What does "online" mean, exactly?'

'Well, they weren't Facebook messages.'

'A private group, then. Like the one you used to contact Emily Mead?'

Brightwell nodded, then raised his hands. 'Look, that's as much as I can tell you. Trust me, if I knew any more ... if anything I could tell you would get Peter out any quicker, I would. I didn't know who was sending me this stuff and I've got even less idea why.' He sat back and smiled. 'Whoever he is, though, I'd like to buy him a drink.'

'That's unlikely to happen.'

'Maybe you can share a tea in the prison canteen,' Thorne said.

There were a few seconds of silence until the phone jumped on the table.

We've got enough ...

While Brightwell was being taken back to his cell, Thorne and Brigstocke were joined in the corridor by Walker, Tanner and Holland. There was no sign of James Greaves, who presumably had other places to go and other implications to investigate.

'Nice job,' Tanner said.

Thorne grunted a 'Cheers', but he did not seem convinced.

'You going to have another crack at him in the morning?' Holland asked.

'I don't see the need,' Walker said.

Thorne turned to him. 'The *need*?'

'I think DCI Walker might well be right,' Brigstocke said. 'No, we didn't get an out-and-out confession, but we've got enough forensics, we've got an eyewitness to at least one of the murders in Emily Mead and a solid motive our suspect isn't arguing with. As soon as the tests on that food come back, we can charge him.'

'It's the perfect result.' Walker was smiling as he reached to lay a hand on Thorne's arm. 'And one we wouldn't have got at all if DI Thorne hadn't put the whole food delivery thing together. It's all down to him.'

Thorne, Tanner and Holland were fifty yards or so ahead of Walker and Brigstocke as they walked the short distance from the station back to Becke House. Tanner was trying to move quickly and urged Thorne to do the same, keen to get out of the cold. Thorne's silence and the slump of his shoulders made it clear that – unlike the senior officers behind them – he wasn't thinking about the congratulations that would undoubtedly be offered when they got back to the office, or the drink that would be all but compulsory before they finally got the chance to go home.

She didn't need to ask him the question.

'It's not the perfect result, is it?' he said. 'Fuck's he talking about?'

'It's a bloody *good* result, Tom,' Tanner said. 'Six murders, one attempted, one conspiracy to murder if Knowles doesn't recover . . . that's not nothing, is it?'

'That's a seriously dangerous individual we'll be putting away,' Holland said.

'Right, and one we won't be.'

'No, but—'

'We've got a senior officer who's been overseeing multiple rapes then covering them up. We've been telling Russell not to pass this on because someone's leaking information and all the time we've been talking about the *same person*. It's got to be, surely. Right from the off, we've been asking ourselves why anyone would give information to Brightwell and it's patently obvious. He's covering his tracks, isn't he? He's cleaning house.'

Tanner looked at Holland then glanced behind her, but Brigstocke and Walker were well out of earshot. 'So, he gives Brightwell what he needs to get rid of Tully, because Tully can identify him?'

'Yes, and it doesn't much matter if three other coppers are killed in the process. He tells Brightwell about Emily Mead and the safe house, because he'd rather she was out of the way, too.'

'What about Callaghan?'

'I think Brightwell did that one off his own bat, once he'd hooked up with Emily Mead, but it certainly did the man we're after a favour.'

'You think Brightwell killed Daniel Sadler as well?' Holland asked.

'Maybe, but either way *someone* decided he had to be got rid of.' Thorne turned to him, stepping carefully across a perfectly curled dog-turd that was already glistening with frost. 'Look, obviously I'm happy we've got Brightwell, but we need to know who was giving him the intel he needed.'

'The man whose voice Emily Mead heard,' Tanner said.

'And Priya Kulkarni,' Holland said. 'And Siobhan Brady.'

'That's who we need to take down.' Thorne's fists were clenched, deep in his pockets. 'That's our perfect result.'

They walked on in silence until they reached the main entrance to the Peel Centre. They showed their IDs at the gate and walked across the car park towards Becke House.

'I do think Brightwell was telling the truth, though,' Tanner said. 'He doesn't know who was sending him those messages. He'd have no reason not to tell us, if he did, because he wants his brother out of prison.'

They pushed through the doors into the lobby and stopped briefly to enjoy the warmth; to undo coats and loosen scarves.

'One quick drink to celebrate?' Holland asked.

'Nothing to celebrate yet,' Thorne said.

FIFTY-NINE

Every instinct told Thorne that he should be heading straight for the nearest bed – which was his own – and collapsing into it. He needed to see Helen, though. After he and almost everyone else there with a warrant card had gone charging out of Brigstocke's garden, she had left several messages, the concern in her voice a little more apparent each time she'd called.

He rang to let her know he was on his way, so she was up and waiting for him when he eventually got to Tulse Hill just before eleven o'clock. There was tea and there was toast. There was a nice, long cuddle which she correctly guessed he needed even more.

Thorne settled down and told her what had happened; the highlights at least, from the moment he'd approached Brightwell on the street outside the safe house to the final look they'd exchanged as Thorne had left the interview room. He accepted her words of congratulation – one (ex) copper to another – with rather better grace than he'd received Tanner's.

He parroted a few of the job-well-done speeches that Tanner, Holland and even Walker had trotted out, and tried to hide his lack of excitement at how things had panned out a little better than he had an hour or so earlier.

The fact that Helen immediately began trying to cheer him up was enough to tell him he hadn't made a very good job of it.

'Well, Phil was *very* chuffed that you all buggered off,' she said.

'Course he was,' Thorne said. 'More burnt sausages for him.'

'It was like Man v. Food.'

They both laughed, but Hendricks had left several messages of his own after Thorne had outlined his theory about the arsenic and gone tearing across to Edgware.

Don't touch Anything! If you do, it'll probably cause no more than minor irritation and changes to skin pigmentation, but benign arsenical keratoses CAN turn malignant.

Then:

Seriously, mate, be careful.

And:

On a cheerier note, these chicken wings are fucking awesome.

'Some good news,' Helen said.

'Tell me.'

'It sounds like the Counter Corruption Unit might finally be getting their act together.'

Thorne waited, though the crinkle around Helen's eyes told him that there was a joke coming; an *actual* joke as opposed to what the CCU did *all the time. Didn't* do.

'They took some swift and decisive action against an officer in East London last week.'

'Oh yeah?'

'They demoted him after discovering that he'd sold a pair of Met Police-issue trousers on eBay.' She saw the look of disbelief on Thorne's face and shook her head. 'Seriously.'

'Nice to know they've got their priorities sorted out,' Thorne said.

'Well, it's certainly restored *my* faith.' Helen slid across the sofa, picked toast crumbs from the front of Thorne's shirt and leaned her head against his shoulder. 'The man you're after thinks he's untouchable,' she said. 'That he's got enough power to keep getting away with what he's doing.'

'It looks like he's right.'

'For now, maybe. But they're always the ones that slip up.'

Thorne thought about it for a minute or so. 'It shouldn't be like that, though. We shouldn't have to sit around and wait for his sort to make a mistake.'

'You've hardly been sitting around.'

'That's what it feels like,' Thorne said. 'It feels like he's been running rings round us, and I don't understand how he's done it. Fine, so thanks to Brightwell, some of the people who might have been able to testify against him are out of the picture now, but there have to be others, right? Others he's protecting.' He looked at Helen. 'Don't you think?'

She nodded. 'Even if there isn't anyone you can identify right now, there will be.'

'Because he'll do it again, you mean?'

'Rapists don't stop, whether they're wearing uniforms or not, and if someone gets their kicks from enabling them, they won't stop either. You just need keep your ear to the ground and find one copper who's willing to give him up.'

Thorne said, 'Yeah . . . ' but his eyes were beginning to close.

'Come on, you need to get some sleep.' Helen stood up and

waited, smiling at the groan as Thorne hauled himself to his feet. 'And remember what Walker said. Brightwell wouldn't be in custody at all if it wasn't for you.' She saw the face Thorne pulled at the mention of Walker's name, sighed and pulled one of her own. 'For God's sake, Tom, take the win.'

Looking back later, Thorne would remember that it had all begun with a phone call from Russell Brigstocke in the early hours and that, just over a fortnight later, it had ended – the Brightwell part of it at least – in very much the same way.

It was just shy of four in the morning this time, but the DCI's tone was every bit as serious. A weight in the short silence after Brigstocke said his name that told Thorne there was nothing good coming.

'Tom . . . look, there's no point going round the houses here.'

'OK . . .'

'Alex Brightwell was found dead in his cell half an hour ago.'

'*What?*' Thorne sat up. Now, as then, he felt Helen stir next to him, though she did not wake.

'Was found unresponsive in his cell, I should say. He was pronounced dead at the hospital.'

'Jesus, Russell. How?'

'You know as much as I do.'

Thorne climbed out of bed and began feeling for his clothes. 'So, he killed himself?' He staggered back against the bed, trying to step into his trousers. Helen moaned quietly and asked what the matter was, still half asleep. 'It'll all be on camera anyway, right, so I suppose it'll be pretty obvious—'

'I'll see you there,' Brigstocke said.

SIXTY

The sun was just coming up and the grass at the front of Colindale station was starting to emerge from beneath its blanket of frost. With the cacophony of the rush hour still an hour or so away, the only soundtrack came courtesy of birdsong, the footsteps of early morning commuters on their way to the underground and the growl of an occasional vehicle turning in or out of the car park.

The scene inside the station was predictably noisier and way more hectic; as hectic as any crime scene would be with the dust yet to settle, but with rather more police officers in situ.

The custody suite itself had been sealed off, as had the corridor in which the cell most recently occupied by Alex Brightwell was located. Every other cell in that and the adjacent corridors had been cleared and all those detained within them hurriedly transferred to other stations.

Thorne had to show ID three times before finally being allowed access.

The first person he saw was DCI Jeremy Walker talking to a shell-shocked custody sergeant. Then he spotted Brigstocke, grim-faced and deep in conversation with DI James Greaves and several others who Thorne immediately marked down as officers from the Directorate of Professional Standards. He wasn't remotely surprised that the DPS were already on site in numbers. The men and women from the Dark Side could move quickly enough when they really had to.

While Thorne was waiting for Brigstocke, he drifted around; exchanging cursory greetings with those he knew, shaking his head when necessary to acknowledge the seriousness of the situation, but largely for the purpose of earwigging. There were half a dozen or more informal interviews being conducted, though he couldn't tell if any of those officers making statements had been on duty overnight; if any could be classed as witnesses. He watched still photographers and others with video cameras recording at the booking desk and in the open office area behind, and saw others emerging from one corridor in particular, having presumably finished documenting the scene in and around Alex Brightwell's cell.

He had a hundred questions, but knew he was unlikely to find anyone willing to answer them.

Finally, Brigstocke stepped away from the CCU officer and Thorne caught his eye. Brigstocke nodded towards the door leading out to the yard, then walked towards it, waiting for Thorne to follow. The implication was obvious.

They needed to talk privately.

As soon as they were both outside in what was earmarked as an exercise area, but was basically smokers' corner, Brigstocke stepped close.

'We are in major trouble,' he said. 'Not *us*, specifically

but ... well, all of us.' He looked around quickly to make sure there was nobody indulging in a crafty cigarette who might be able to overhear. 'He didn't kill himself.'

'How d'you know?' Thorne asked. 'Have you seen the footage?'

'I know because there *isn't* any footage.'

Thorne stared. He had studied footage from custody suite cameras on countless occasions and knew that in addition to a standard CCTV set-up in the booking area, or *bridge*, there was a high-tech system monitoring every inch of the corridors and, crucially, the interior of each cell. There were audio and visual recordings of all these areas 24/7. In fact, the only places where there wasn't unfettered coverage were the toilets, and even then the cameras had been programmed in such a way as to black out only the faces of those using the facilities. 'How's that possible?'

'Well, there *is* footage, but not covering the seven minutes during which Alex Brightwell met his death.'

'You're having me on, right?'

'All the cameras covering the corridor he was on and those inside the cell itself were switched off for just over seven minutes.'

'Switched off?' Thorne's mind was already starting to race, ideas careering wildly, until he suddenly found himself thinking about fridges; about 'malfunctions'.

'The system shut down ... someone shut it down.'

Thorne thought for a few more seconds. 'OK ... but even if all the cameras went off for whatever reason, why didn't the custody assistants notice there was a problem? Weren't they a bit concerned about the fact that suddenly they were staring at a bank of blank screens?'

'They were ... distracted,' Brigstocke said. 'Some kind of major fracas on the bridge.'

'According to who?'

'According to everyone who was there at the time. A couple of PCs brought a drunk in around two a.m. A drunk or a junkie ... but either way he started to kick off big time, going properly berserk. Lashing out, you know, smacked a few people. It was all hands to the pump by all accounts, with every available body dragging this bloke kicking and screaming on to the corridor and finally, into a cell. A cell which happened to be on a different corridor to the one Brightwell's cell was on.'

'That was convenient.'

'Yeah, wasn't it?'

'So, this ... *fracas* means nobody's looking at the monitors and, more importantly, gives someone enough time to access the other corridor,' Thorne said. 'Enough time to get into Brightwell's cell and out again.'

'That's what it looks like,' Brigstocke said. 'Then whoever turned the cameras off switches the system back on again. By which time ...'

'How was it done?' Thorne asked.

'The cameras? Not a clue, mate.'

'No, how was Brightwell killed?'

'Oh ... well, I've heard whispers, but we won't know anything else until Hendricks has finished the PM, so best not to speculate.'

Thorne leaned against a wall, trying and failing to process it, any of it.

'For obvious reasons he's been told it's a rush job.' Brigstocke took the spot against the wall next to Thorne and let out a long, tired breath as he leaned back. 'Phil was *not* happy about being woken so early.'

By mid-morning they were back at Becke House, having left the station once Brigstocke had rightly pointed out that there was little more they could usefully do at the crime scene. Now, having been joined by Dave Holland, they were gathered around a laptop in an empty office, waiting for Nicola Tanner.

'She'll get what we need,' Thorne said.

'Let's hope so.' Brigstocke was reading through an email that had arrived on his phone a few minutes before.

Holland nodded. 'Nic can be very persuasive when she wants to be.'

Brigstocke put his phone down and removed his glasses. 'The DPS want to talk to us this afternoon.' He looked at Thorne. 'You and me.'

'Why? What happened at the station's got nothing to do with us.'

'They'll want to make sure our interview with Brightwell had no bearing on his death.'

'That's crackers,' Holland said.

'What kind of bearing?'

'I know, it's ridiculous,' Brigstocke said. 'But they'll need to cross all the t's and dot all the i's, however pointless it is.'

'Why do they need to talk to us?' Thorne asked. 'Can't they just look at the interview room footage?'

'Oh, I'm sure they'll be doing that, too.'

Thorne shook his head. 'Yeah, definitely best to check we didn't wink knowingly at Brightwell, or slowly draw our fingers across our throats before we left.'

'We don't have a lot of choice,' Brigstocke said.

They sat in silence after that and watched the door, waiting and hoping that the conversation Nicola Tanner was having elsewhere would give them the chance to look at a more recent recording. A private viewing. This was footage that definitely *did* have a bearing on the death of Alex Brightwell and to which they knew they would not be granted immediate access were they simply to ask.

The look on Tanner's face when she came through the door was enough to let them know they were in business. She sat down and moved her chair to give herself a good view of the laptop. 'He's sending a link. Should just be a couple of minutes.'

Tanner had spent the last twenty minutes on the phone to Greg Hobbs, ostensibly to get his opinion on how the CCTV system in the Colindale custody suite could have been taken down remotely. Once he had explained how it might have been done, she'd then asked if he'd use his own expertise to access the footage from the custody suite immediately before the cameras had been turned off. Yes, it was unorthodox, she'd explained when Hobbs had asked the understandable question, but she wouldn't be asking if it wasn't important, besides which they'd see the footage eventually anyway. It was just a question of needing to move fast, she'd said, because things would inevitably slow up now the DPS was involved. It was evidence they urgently needed to see.

'He took a bit of persuading,' she said. 'We definitely owe him several drinks, and I had to promise that if it comes to it we won't be letting on how we came to view the footage.'

'What did he say about the cameras?' Brigstocke asked.

'Well, he said quite a lot that was way over my head. I started to zone out when he was on about "overwriting the host server", but he thinks it's a straightforward backdoor hack, whatever the hell that is. Not massively difficult, that's what he was basically saying. Told me he could take control of the entire system remotely inside five minutes.'

'Bloody hell,' Holland said.

'Basically, somebody paid somebody.'

'Yeah, and we all know who that first somebody is—' Thorne stopped when an alert from his laptop signalled the arrival of an email. 'Here we go . . . nice one, Greg.' He leaned forward to open the link Hobbs had sent and they sat back to watch.

They fast-forwarded through the minutes leading up to the fracas; a few minor comings and goings, some inane chat between the custody sergeant and his colleagues. Nothing out of the ordinary.

Then the drunk was brought in; shouty in the way some drunks can be, but seemingly manageable. He was led to the desk by a pair of uniformed PCs, both grumpy enough to suggest that he'd already given them a hard time. He started to resist when he was instructed to empty his pockets, and all hell broke loose when one of the PCs moved forward to grab his arm.

He lashed out, catching the PC in the face, and when others moved from behind the desk, it quickly escalated. The man kicked and spat, and by the time he was trying to bite the custody sergeant there were half a dozen officers and civilian staff attempting to restrain him.

'Doesn't look like he's acting to me,' Holland said. 'He's definitely pissed.'

'Yeah, but someone got him pissed,' Thorne said. 'Told him to kick off.'

'Easy enough,' Tanner said.

'Probably just bunged him twenty quid, same as Brightwell did with that bloke at Archway station. Gave him some cash and a bottle and promised him a night in a nice warm cell.'

'We'll find out once the DPS have talked to him,' Brigstocke said.

Thorne watched. 'I don't think they'll get very much.'

There was only another fifteen seconds after that as the prisoner, still flailing and loudly threatening to 'kill every one of you cunts', was hauled up from the floor and dragged out on to the corridor towards the cells.

Then the screen went black.

Thorne scrolled back so they could watch it all again.

Half a minute in, just after the drunk had hit the PC in the face, Thorne paused and went back. He pressed *play*, then quickly hit *pause* a second time and pointed to one of the uniformed officers who had brought the prisoner in. '*Him*.'

'What?' Tanner leaned forward to peer at the screen. 'You know him?'

'His name's Healey,' Thorne said. 'He was one of the uniforms working the perimeter at Hendon Park, the night of the Callaghan murder.'

'So were a lot of other coppers. I don't see—'

'What are you thinking, Tom?' Brigstocke asked.

Thorne wasn't *thinking* anything. He knew without needing any further information that they were looking at the man who had murdered Alex Brightwell at Colindale station eight hours earlier. He quickly told Brigstocke and the others what Healey had said to him that night at Hendon Park; the suggestion that he – and others like him – were ready and more than able to fight back against anyone who targeted police officers.

How else are we supposed to react?

Thorne leaned down to move the footage on a few seconds. '*There* . . . see him turning round, see his hands? It looks to me like he's doing something on his phone.'

'Like he's sending a text or something,' Tanner said.

'He's messaging whoever has control of the CCTV system, letting them know it's time to hit the off switch.' He jabbed at the screen. 'There's your killer, and even the useless twats in the DPS shouldn't have much trouble proving it.'

'I wouldn't be too sure about that,' Brigstocke said.

'Come on, they're going to find his DNA in Brightwell's cell, aren't they? All over the body, likely as not.'

'I'm sure they will.' Brigstocke shook his head. 'Unfortunately, it's not going to mean anything, because Healey was still there when they found Brightwell's body.'

Thorne swore quietly, knowing what was coming.

'He was one of the officers who rushed into that cell and checked for vital signs. His DNA isn't going to prove a thing.'

SIXTY-ONE

A report had come back confirming the presence of arsenic trioxide in the meal Brightwell had been attempting to deliver to Emily Mead, but now it felt almost irrelevant, and the final hour of a very long day proved to be every bit as frustrating as those that had preceded it. Thorne sat at his desk working through the service record of police constable Michael Healey and found only exemplary reports from superiors and public feedback that marked him out as a conscientious and hard-working officer.

Another model copper . . .

It wasn't as though Thorne had been expecting a note on Healey's file saying *watch out for this one* or *murderous tendencies*, but it made him feel like going at his computer with a lump-hammer nonetheless.

Even the call from Phil Hendricks did little to improve his mood.

'You're only getting sloppy seconds,' Hendricks said.

'I forgive you.' Thorne knew very well that whoever was leading the DPS investigation would have had first dibs on the PM report. 'So, let's have it.'

'Alex Brightwell died of heart failure.'

'OK...'

'Not the sort of bog-standard, too much red meat/too little exercise heart failure that *we're* going to die of – you before me quite probably. Oh no, it's a bit more interesting than that.'

'Is this how you presented your report to the DPS?'

'Just trying to jazz it up a bit.'

'Yeah, well you know how much I hate jazz. Come on, Phil.'

'OK, long story short... his heart gave out after a sustained electric shock. The killer used pepper spray to incapacitate him, then basically zapped him to death.'

'You talking about a Taser?'

'Well, I very much doubt there was time to wire him up to the mains, so yeah, a Taser... but I don't mean the killer fired the darts. Judging by the scorch marks, we're talking at least two or three minutes on "drive-stun" with the Taser pressed directly to his neck. Not a nice way to go.'

Thorne said nothing, remembering his encounter with Michael Healey; the PC with his hand on the butt of his Taser like it was a Glock 17.

'Mind you, this is the bloke who killed all those coppers, right, so I'm guessing you don't give a stuff.'

'They were very bad coppers,' Thorne said. 'Most of them, anyway. So I'm... conflicted.'

A few minutes later, he managed to catch Tanner who, with her coat over her arm, looked as if she was on her way out. He told her what Hendricks had told him. 'For what it's worth,' he said.

'It's proof of murder,' she said. 'So it's worth something.'

'He's going to get away with it, though, isn't he?'

'The DPS aren't quite as useless as you think, Tom. They'll know it had to be someone in that custody suite at the time. They can work out who was dealing with the drunk and who wasn't, so somebody's going to figure out it was Healey.'

'Yeah, for sure,' Thorne said. 'You'd have to be stupid not to work it out eventually, but even if they're one hundred per cent convinced, I don't see how they can prove it. So, *he* walks away and so does whoever set the whole thing up. Fucking ... Teflon-coated same as always.'

'Is it not at least worth considering the possibility that Healey was acting alone?'

Thorne began shaking his head.

'Well, not quite alone, obviously, but you know what I mean. You've already said he had a bit of a vigilante vibe or whatever.'

'Not a chance,' Thorne said.

'It doesn't make sense, though. If whoever set this up *is* the same person that was leaking information to Brightwell—'

'It is—'

'Why go to all the bother of killing him? Brightwell already said he didn't know *who* was sending him the intel.'

'Well, that's assuming the man we're talking about is somehow privy to what was said in that interview. Even if he was, there's a big difference between what's said in an interview room and what might come out in the course of a long, drawn-out trial. He can't take any chances.' Thorne watched Tanner thinking about it. 'Brightwell being killed right after we take him into custody is not a coincidence and the man we're after made it happen, simple as that. Yeah, it was quite an operation he put together, but we already know what he's capable of.'

'Tom . . .'

Thorne could see that Tanner was a little concerned at how worked up he was getting, how easily his accusations could be overheard. He lowered his voice, but there was still plenty of anger in it. 'He can waltz into labs and destroy forensic samples. The courier in his pocket meant that he was able to plant evidence. I don't think it's much of a stretch to imagine he's got IT experts whose arm he can twist when he needs to.'

Tanner nodded.

'Maybe it was Healey who told that drunk what to do, but everything else was put on a plate for him. The cameras . . . an electronic passkey for Brightwell's cell.' Thorne lowered his head, watched his own knuckles whitening around the edge of a chair. 'And all we can do is stand by like idiots while the man who's pulling all the strings walks away, same as always and goes back to work. Sitting behind a desk somewhere, thinking about the next rape, his next chance to watch and whisper . . . and polishing the fucking pips on his shoulder.'

Tanner watched him for a few seconds, waiting until his breathing had slowed. As soon as he raised his head, she moved forward and drew Thorne into a hug. 'I'm going to see Emily Mead, if you fancy coming.' She stepped away from him and put her coat on. 'I think I should tell her about Brightwell anyway, but I wanted to see how she's getting on. She's staying with her brother for a while, so . . .'

'I think I'll just head home.' Thorne manufactured a smile. 'Listen to some depressing country tunes and think about an alternative career.'

'Sounds like a top night.'

That was when Thorne remembered what Helen had said to him the previous evening and suddenly began to feel a lot more positive. He grabbed his jacket and walked out to the car park alongside Tanner thinking that now, at the very least, he had something to do. It wouldn't be possible immediately, but it was a way forward and, with luck, a direct route to the end of it all.

As soon as Tanner had peeled off towards her own car, Thorne called Helen. She didn't pick up, so he left a message. He told her that he'd be going back to Kentish Town, that he'd call again in the morning and that he'd been thinking about what she'd said.

'... about just needing to find one copper who might be willing to give him up? Well, I think I've got one. Someone who knows who the man we're after *is*, anyway.'

Thorne would need to let those investigating the death in custody of Alex Brightwell have first crack at Healey. Let them do their best, or more likely their worst, and come away with nothing.

Then it would be his turn.

His line of enquiry would be quite distinct from theirs, of course. He was after very different information, for a start. It was just a name, so it would all be over a lot quicker, and PC Michael Healey would find Thorne's methods somewhat less polite than those employed by the DPS.

SIXTY-TWO

Emily Mead's elder brother, Patrick, lived in a small, converted worker's cottage in Bethnal Green. Tanner stared down at the shiny wooden ramp that led up to the front door and hoped she wasn't smiling too much when Emily finally opened it. Clearly she was, though.

'*What?*'

'Just . . . no, nothing.' Tanner was still looking at the ramp. It was evidently a recent addition to the property; the wood varnished and as yet unmarked.

'Greg said he might pop in, that's all,' Emily said. 'So Patrick knocked that up for me.' She held out her arms, mock-affronted as she stepped back from the door. 'Is that OK?'

Tanner said it was absolutely fine, that it was none of her business, but the smile was still flickering as she stepped into the house. It had more or less gone by the time Emily had switched on the kettle and they stood facing one another in the kitchen.

'Where *is* Patrick, anyway?' Tanner wasn't just being nosy.

Emily had told her she was going to be staying at her brother's place for a while because she thought the company would be nice for both of them. Tanner knew it was her own way of saying that she didn't want to be alone.

'Gone to get us a takeaway,' Emily said. 'He'll be back in a minute and I'm sure there'll be enough for all of us if you want to stay.'

'What are you having?'

'Well, it's not cheeseburgers, I can tell you that much.' Emily laughed a little nervously and shoved her hands into the pockets of her baggy grey joggers. 'I don't think I'll ever be able to look at a cheeseburger again.'

'Understandable,' Tanner said. 'I'm a bit like that with Southern Comfort.'

'Eh?'

'Not because anyone tried to poison it or anything. I just got horribly pissed on the stuff when I was seventeen. Even thinking about it makes me feel a bit sick.'

Emily nodded enthusiastically, and now the laughter that went with it sounded a little more natural. 'It's Tia Maria for me. Drank a bottle of it on my sixteenth birthday and was chucking up for two days.' She shuddered and leaned back against the worktop. 'That Brightwell bloke's a proper maniac, though, I swear.' She looked at Tanner. 'He will get life, won't he? I mean, he's got to, right?'

'*Was* a maniac,' Tanner said. She glanced down at her phone when the message alert sounded and saw that it was a message from Brigstocke. 'And he won't be going to prison at all, because he's dead.'

Emily took a few seconds. 'What?' She screwed up her eyes and shook her head. 'How . . . ?'

'He was killed this morning – early. At the police station.'

'What the fuck?'

'Yeah, what the fuck is about right.' Tanner had already said more than she needed to, more than she should have done quite probably, but she didn't care a great deal.

'Who killed him?'

'It's not our case.' Initially, Tanner had been wary of telling Emily Mead anything that might exacerbate her trauma. She had come to learn, though, that despite all the damage the woman was a little more resilient than she'd first appeared. A survivor and not a victim. That said, only twenty-four hours on from an attempt on her life, she did not need to know any more about the man they believed had orchestrated the murder of Alex Brightwell. The same man whose voice she had heard while she was being raped. The man who was responsible for almost everything. 'They're keeping us in the dark.'

Emily said nothing for a few seconds, just stared, unblinking over Tanner's head until she suddenly turned away, having remembered why they'd come into the kitchen in the first place. 'Tea.'

'Right,' Tanner said. 'Lovely.'

The kettle had already boiled, but Emily flicked it on again. 'Actually, I need a quick wazz . . . '

'I'll sort it,' Tanner said, reaching up for mugs from the cupboard while Emily hurried away to the bathroom. When the kettle boiled again, she laid her phone down on the worktop, pressed the speaker button and listened to the message from Russell Brigstocke as she made the tea.

'Hey, Nic . . . I know you're going to see Emily, so I just wanted to make sure you thanked her on my behalf for all her help. What

she did was hugely brave and I'm really sorry I never actually got to meet her personally, but please pass on my thanks.

'More importantly, you can tell her that there won't be any further action taken in regard to the Adam Callaghan murder. I talked to a CPS lawyer late last night, after we'd interviewed Brightwell . . . before everything kicked off this morning. Anyway, they've reviewed Callaghan's bodycam footage and based on that, and Emily's agreement to become a protected witness, they're not going to pursue any kind of case against her. So, feel free to give her the good news.

'Right, back to this latest disaster . . .'

Tanner dropped a used teabag into the bin, then turned at the sound of a ragged breath behind her to see Emily frozen in the doorway.

She was ashen; trembling.

Tanner took a step towards her, but Emily immediately recoiled and cried out. 'OK . . . I'll stay where I am,' Tanner said softly. She could do nothing but stand and watch as the young woman clawed fingers through her hair, her eyes tight shut and her skinny chest heaving. 'Emily . . . what's the matter?'

This case, or rather the circumstances of its significant developments had only confirmed what Thorne already knew: that phone calls in the dead of night never brought good news. Crimes were not timetabled for his own convenience, so it was something he was well used to.

Someone at his door was a very different matter.

There were any number of people he'd put away over the years who – if and when they were out again – might decide to pay him a visit in the small hours. They had friends and relatives who could do the same thing any time they felt like it.

So, being afraid was perfectly natural.

The only reaction, in fact, that made any bloody sense.

He was wide awake within a second or two of hearing the doorbell, pulling on a T-shirt and moving slowly out into the hall. It was full dark outside and the flat was freezing. He switched on the light and took a quick look to ensure that the antique wooden truncheon he kept behind the front door was where it should be.

'Who is it?'

He couldn't quite make out what his visitor was saying, but he recognised the voice and knew that the truncheon would not be necessary.

He opened the door. Said, 'Fuck's sake, Nic . . .'

Tanner tried to speak, but nothing came out. She seemed even more apprehensive than Thorne had been a few seconds earlier and it looked as if she'd been crying.

Thorne stepped back to let her in. 'OK, well, it's obviously something important, but couldn't you have called?'

'No—'

'It's three o'clock in the morn—'

'*No* . . . I couldn't have called.'

Thorne closed the door and turned to look at her, decided she'd definitely been crying. 'What's happened?'

'It's Russell,' she said. Whispered.

'What are you on about . . . is he OK? What's—?'

Tanner was already shaking her head violently and the noise, which shut Thorne up immediately, was somewhere between a growl and a sob. 'I'm saying . . . it's *him*.'

'Well, either you're very drunk or I am,' Thorne said. Then he saw the look on Tanner's face and began to shiver.

'The man we're after is Russell.'

PART FOUR

THE NIGHT JUST BRINGS SORROW

SIXTY-THREE

They talked until the sun came up.

Talked, shouted and shed a few more tears between them. There were long periods of silence too, when they did nothing but stare; at the walls, at the floor, at one another. Each of them struggling to make sense of a situation that, to Thorne at least, still seemed unbelievable.

That had certainly been his initial reaction when Tanner told him what Emily had said after hearing the message Brigstocke had left. The young woman's certainty that his was the voice she'd heard while Adam Callaghan was raping her. The urgent conversation had quickly become heated while Thorne made coffee, the two of them snapping back and forth between hallway and kitchen.

'She's wrong,' Thorne had said. 'She must be.'

'Trust me, I wish she was.'

'It's just... a voice, on a crappy phone speaker. A voice that sounds similar to one she thinks she can still remember.'

'It's a voice she's never been able to forget—'

'And Russell has a voice that sounds a bit the same, that's all.' Thorne was trying not to sound desperate. 'That's all it *can* be, right?'

'You didn't see her.'

They reconvened in the living room, the pair of them shivering not only at the cold, but at the thought of what might lie ahead if Tanner was right.

'OK, let's try to imagine for just a minute that Emily's not ... mistaken.' Thorne looked at her. 'That it *was* Russell's voice she heard while she was being raped six months ago. That it's actually Russell who's been behind all of this. Let's go completely mad and put everything together and say that it was Russell who did the same thing while Priya Kulkarni and Siobhan Brady were being raped, who arranged for those rapes to happen. Who planted the evidence that got Peter Brightwell imprisoned and destroyed the evidence that might have got Craig Knowles convicted.' Thorne was ranting now, gabbling every bit as frantically as his mind raced. 'Russell who aided and abetted Alex Brightwell in the murder of Christopher Tully and three innocent officers, who was almost certainly involved in the staged suicide of Daniel Sadler and subsequently arranged to have Alex Brightwell murdered in custody. Have I left anything out?'

'Needham,' Tanner said quietly. 'The security guard.'

'Oh, yeah, my mistake. Needham. It's quite hard to keep track when your boss ... your *friend* is apparently such a master fucking criminal, but—'

'Tom—'

'Let's just see if we can get our heads around that little lot, shall we?'

'What do you think I've been doing for the last few hours?' Tanner said.

'Well, forgive me if I'm finding it the teensiest bit tricky to catch up, all right?' Thorne stared hard. 'So, you're saying that's where we are?' He waited. 'That's the current state of play, is it, Nic?'

'I wish it wasn't.' Tanner was on the verge of tears again. 'Christ, have you any idea how much I don't want this to be true?'

Thorne shook his head, closed his eyes and waited until his breathing had settled a little. He said, 'I'm sorry for getting . . . worked up.'

'We're both worked up,' Tanner said. 'Course we are.'

'Right, but in terms of actually doing something about it . . .'

'We *have* to.' Tanner stared at him. 'Tom, we have—'

'What Emily says about the voice she heard isn't enough. It isn't proof.'

'I know that.'

'It's nowhere near enough.'

'There's more,' Tanner told him. She took a sheet of paper from her bag and showed him.

There wasn't anything said for a while after that. Thorne went into the bedroom to fetch a sweatshirt and dressing gown. He flicked on the heating and made more coffee. Then he sat down again and the two of them avoided looking at one other, trying separately to process the shock and to manage their apprehension of what was to come; a wholly unexpected resolution to an investigation that had grown steadily darker and more dangerous at every turn.

The end of the uncertainty and suspicion.

The end, however things panned out, of so much more than that.

'How long have you worked with him?' Tanner asked eventually. She had been part of the team for a fair few years herself, but knew that Thorne's relationship with Russell Brigstocke went back a good deal further.

'Twenty years, give or take,' Thorne said.

'I'm sorry ...'

'And nothing, in all that time. I mean, not a sniff of anything that was even remotely ... off. He's always been ...' Thorne stopped speaking and shook his head, well aware that he sounded like any number of thunderstruck individuals he'd interviewed over the years. The family, friends and neighbours of those who'd committed the most terrible of long-undiscovered crimes, whose nearest and dearest subsequently pronounced themselves entirely amazed.

Each one of them shocked, all of them deluded.

He seemed like such a nice bloke.

He was always lovely with me.

Bloody hell, you think you know someone ...

There was a time when Thorne had considered himself a decent judge of character. It was, he'd believed, a handy gift to have as a detective. He'd thought himself better than most at marking out those who lied or dissembled, at seeing why the men and women who did so skirted around the truth or actively sought to bury it.

He'd been lying to himself; or, at the very least, had simply been an idiot.

It was less than a year since he'd fatally misjudged the woman with whom he was having a relationship. Her betrayal had ultimately cost Melita Perera her life and had very nearly cost Thorne his own, but it had certainly put paid to the notion that he was any better than the next mug at working people out.

There were those to whom it came naturally and those who learned it as a matter of necessity, but the simple fact was that some people were horribly skilled at hiding their true nature.

Even so ...

It didn't make Thorne feel any better, knowing he was far from being the only one Russell Brigstocke had fooled.

Once the light had begun to bleed into the room, milky around the edges of the living room curtains, they talked tentatively, with as much purpose as they were capable, about what they were going to do.

An immediate plan of action.

The innumerable *ifs* and *buts* that might easily derail it.

When they'd got as far they could usefully get, Tanner announced that she was going home to change. 'I'll see you in a couple of hours,' she said.

'I'll send a message to Dave,' Thorne said. 'Tell him we need to meet good and early.'

They hugged fiercely on the doorstep and, once they'd released each other, Tanner apologised again. Thorne told her not to be stupid. 'No point being sorry until we've got something to be sorry for,' he said. 'It might be sooner than we think, but let's see what happens in the morning.'

He watched Tanner head towards her car, a somewhat forlorn figure against a brightening sky streaked with red and amber, then went back inside and walked straight through to the bathroom, shedding his clothes as he went. He stepped into the shower and turned it up good and hot.

Tried and failed to scald away some of the horror.

SIXTY-FOUR

Dave Holland was not in the best of moods – or was making a good job of seeming so for comic effect – when he slumped into the small conference room that Thorne and Tanner had commandeered on the floor above their own. It was half an hour before any of them were officially due to start work and the offices of the various Major Investigation Teams were still relatively quiet. Holland had encountered a handful of officers winding up their own shifts on the late turn, but it seemed that few were hugely keen to get in early for a day that would be spent managing the aftermath of Alex Brightwell's death at Colindale station.

Not as keen as those who worked for the DPS, anyway.

Clusterfucks were their bread and butter.

'This better be good.' Holland was carrying a coffee and appeared to be half asleep, but he still looked less knackered than Thorne or Tanner. 'Pippa and me had ... plans for this morning.'

Thorne remembered what Holland had told him about he and his wife trying for a baby. It couldn't be helped.

'You'd best sit down, Dave.'

Somewhat nervously, Holland did so. 'Sounds serious.'

Starting with what Emily Mead had told her the night before, Tanner began to lay out just how serious it was. Holland appeared to wake up very suddenly and took a hearty slurp of coffee. '*What?*'

'He never met Emily in the flesh,' Thorne said. 'Not once.'

Tanner was looking at Holland. 'He even said that on the message. He recognised her on the footage from Callaghan's bodycam, so he knew he could never meet her. Never speak to her in case she recognised his voice.'

'It's why he monitored her initial interview remotely,' Thorne said. 'And why he was happy to let Walker run that press conference. He knew Emily would be watching.'

'Maybe Emily's got it wrong.' Holland looked from Thorne to Tanner and back again. 'I mean, it wouldn't be her fault, but—'

'She's not wrong, Dave.' Thorne knew that Holland was hoping Emily Mead was mistaken every bit as much as he had been the night before and for the same reasons. Now, it just felt like clutching at straws.

'It was Russell who was feeding Brightwell all the information,' Tanner said. 'Setting up Tully and everyone else. Even setting up Emily in the end.'

'How?'

'He contacted him the same way we did,' Thorne said. 'Encrypted messages on the Dark Web.'

'He learned how to do it,' Tanner said. 'I checked with Greg Hobbs and Russell was one of those "powers that be" he told me about that first time I went to see him at the DFU. He'd requested that all the anti-police sites and message boards be monitored, found out how to do it himself from home. He saw the message Brightwell had left about Tully before we did. The one accusing Tully of being a rapist.'

'That's when he knew he was in trouble,' Thorne said.

'From that point on he was sending messages of his own, passing on all the intelligence Brightwell needed to get rid of all the people he blamed for what had happened to his brother. Conveniently for Russell, they were the same people *he* wanted out of the way.'

Holland was still shaking his head, but he knew better than to doubt Thorne and Tanner's obvious conviction, so by now it was shock rather than disbelief. 'What about the forensics?'

'He had access to that lab.' Tanner was shuffling papers on her lap. 'I got an email back from Hendricks's ex, who finally managed to come up with a list of officers who were there on the key date.' She passed a printout across to Holland. 'Russell visited Fin-Cel the day that freezer "malfunctioned".'

'Fuck.' Holland stared down at the printout, at Brigstocke's name highlighted on what was a very short list. He looked up at Tanner. 'I presume this means he arranged for Daniel Sadler to be killed.'

'I don't know,' Thorne said. 'Sadler was definitely someone else he'd have wanted out of the way.'

Tanner produced another list and handed it to Holland. 'Twelve years ago, Russell was one of the officers involved in the child pornography case against Sadler. Not directly, but he was certainly across it.'

'He said he didn't even remember it.'

'He lied,' Thorne said. 'He's been lying all the time.'

'Promised me he'd look into it.' Holland's voice was low and the anger was obvious. 'Well, now I know why he never bothered.'

'He made that case against Sadler go away,' Tanner said. 'Which meant he now had a courier in his back pocket. Once Alex Brightwell crawled out of the woodwork and started making accusations, Sadler had to go and it was made to look like suicide. It might have been Brightwell who chucked him off that viaduct or else Russell lined up someone else to do it, same as he did when he finally got rid of Brightwell.'

'Right now, we'd only be guessing,' Thorne said. 'I certainly don't think he did it himself. He always got someone else to the dirty work. Brightwell, Healey ... the prisoner in Frankland who tried to kill Craig Knowles. I'm sure it was Russell who pointed Brightwell in *his* direction.'

'What about the victims, though?' Holland looked from Thorne to Tanner and back. 'He gave Brightwell the address of the safe house, which means he was willing to see Emily Mead be killed, so why didn't he try to get rid of the others? Siobhan Brady and Priya Kulkarni?'

'My guess is that he was getting desperate by the end,' Thorne said. 'When it was all coming apart. Up to that point, I don't know ... he didn't see the need because he was getting away with it? Or maybe he was just deluded and didn't even see himself as the bad guy. Like he was above it all, somehow.'

They sat in silence for a minute or more.

'So, what now?' Holland asked eventually. He sounded like someone who very much did not want his question answered.

Thorne looked at his watch. 'He should be getting here in ten minutes.'

'And then what? Look, I'm not saying that this doesn't all add up, because it does ... but it's circumstantial, all of it.'

'We know that,' Tanner said.

'We haven't got any *proof*.'

'It's enough to nick him,' Thorne said. 'To ask questions. To get him in an interview room and make things seriously difficult.'

'Right, and he just denies it. He lawyers up and brings a federation rep in, or he tells us we're idiots then does whatever he can to fuck up the rest of our careers.'

Tanner leaned towards him. 'You don't have to be involved if you don't want to, Dave. Tom and I brought this to you. We won't have a problem if you'd be more comfortable stepping back from it.'

Holland did not even blink. 'No fucking chance,' he said.

Forty-five minutes later, the three of them reconvened in a corner of what was now a busy incident room.

'I've called down and he hasn't rung in sick.' Tanner glanced around to make sure they could not be overheard.

Thorne nodded. 'He's not answering his mobile.'

'Have you tried him at home?' Holland asked.

'They don't have a landline.' Thorne thought for a few seconds. 'Maybe we should just go round there.'

Tanner looked dubious. 'Arrest him in front of Sally?'

'Hang on, though.' Holland stared at them both, like they were all being stupid. 'Aren't we forgetting the small matter of a death in custody? He said yesterday that the DPS would be talking to us all. He's probably in with them.'

'Makes sense,' Tanner said.

Thorne had to concede that it did, but he couldn't help but

feel anxious nonetheless. As though they had a serious problem. 'We can't just call them up and ask,' he said. 'There'll be twenty minutes of *"Could you tell me what it's regarding?"* and *"I'm sorry but I'm not at liberty . . ."*'

'So, we just tell them it's urgent,' Holland said. 'It's an operational emergency and we need to talk to our DCI.'

'Problem is, they don't think anything can possibly be as urgent as whatever it is they're doing.'

'Desai's got an "in".' Tanner looked across to where the DC was busy at her desk. 'She kept it quiet for obvious reasons, but she used to go out with someone at the DPS.'

'She must have been desperate,' Holland said.

'Maybe she could call him, just to catch up, you know.'

'Worth a try,' Thorne said.

Tanner went over to confer with Charita Desai and, when she turned to give a thumbs-up, Thorne and Holland walked back to their desks, with little option but to wait.

It was nearly lunchtime when Desai beckoned Thorne from the door of the incident room. Tanner wasn't in the room, so Thorne moved across on his own. Holland clocked what was happening and followed.

'Sorry,' Desai said. 'He's only just called me back, but he did tell me that DCI Brigstocke isn't with them.'

Thorne and Holland exchanged a look.

'I think they've got their hands full anyway, mind you. Sounds like there's progress on the death in custody. The Brightwell murder.'

Thorne waited, feeling that prickle at the back of his neck again. The sign that something important was coming, for good or ill.

'That PC who was at the station when it happened. Healey?' Desai looked at them.

'Yeah, we know who he is,' Thorne said.

'Turns out the DPS has been looking at him for a while, got evidence against him for all sorts. So, once they laid everything out, Healey conferred with his rep and they started talking about a deal. My ex reckons he's being pretty talkative.'

Thorne thanked Desai for her help and he and Holland stepped away.

'Well, if Russell knows about *that*—'

'Why wouldn't he?' Thorne had been hoping PC Michael Healey might turn out to be a weak link, but he hadn't banked on it happening quite this quickly. He moved to grab his jacket from the back of a chair. 'He knows about every other fucking thing.'

Holland ran to fetch his own. 'His home address?'

'I doubt he's there, but it's as good a place to start as any.'

They hurried towards the door. 'I'll drive,' Holland said.

SIXTY-FIVE

The Brigstockes lived in Loughton, on the border of Epping Forest, twenty miles and about as many minutes away from Becke House in deepest, darkest Essex. Thorne and Holland drove up through Edgware and turned on to the M25 at South Mimms, using blues and twos to cut through traffic as and when.

Holland had barely paused for breath since they'd set off, clearly still trying to process the staggering turn of events.

'The whole thing's just incredible.' He slammed his hand against the steering wheel. 'It's ... *sick*. All that time we were racing around like twats, trying to work out why anyone would be helping Brightwell. Why an individual we knew had to be close to the case, who was quite probably a copper himself, would be aiding and abetting someone who was targeting other coppers. Fine, so these were not exactly good coppers, not all of them anyway, but Christ on a bike ... even so.

'I mean, it never made any sense. Why the hell would this

person be passing key information to our prime suspect? Stuff about Tully and where to find him, then about Emily . . . all of it?' He growled and stamped on the accelerator to take the car past a line of vehicles on the inside lane. 'Banging our heads against a wall, and all the time it was the man in charge of the investigation screwing us all over . . . screwing *everyone* over and doing whatever he thought was necessary to save his own skin. To get rid of anyone who could implicate him, because he knew the game was up. Or that it might very well be, which meant he couldn't take any chances.

'Hiding in plain sight, while he as good as signed death warrants for the rapists *he'd* enabled and for those other poor bastards like Kazia Bobak and Catherine Holloway who'd done nothing . . . and all the time he was drawing Brightwell in until he could do whatever it took to get rid of him, too. He even made sure he'd be in there interviewing him, so he could find out exactly what Brightwell knew about where the information was coming from before having him killed.' He looked across at Thorne. 'It's fucking . . . unbelievable.'

Thorne wasn't about to argue, but just nodded and turned away to stare out across the hard shoulder at the blur of fields rushing past. He was thinking, as he had been since they'd left, about the last time he'd made this same journey. Two days before on the way to Brigstocke's birthday bash.

His conversation with Brigstocke's wife.

'Yeah, he's definitely not himself.'

Now, Thorne understood exactly what Brigstocke had been so 'stressed' about, why developments in the case had appeared to affect him so adversely, and just how repugnant that *self* actually was.

'You remember when you and Nic went to him?' Holland

looked at Thorne again. 'When you decided the man we were after had to be a senior officer?'

Thorne nodded, remembering Brigstocke's reaction, how crushed and disillusioned he'd been. Had *appeared* to be.

'He told you he'd have to take it higher up, right?' Holland shook his head, tightened his grip on the steering wheel. 'Sounding like he was horrified, you know? Like he was on board with it all and ready to take steps, only because the sneaky fuck knew very well that you'd talk him out of it.'

Thorne recalled the DCI's sorrowful expression that day and his heartfelt little speech about a 'force he no longer recognised'. It had all been for show, that was obvious now, but the sentiment was one Thorne could no longer take issue with and that was down to the activities of Brigstocke himself and others like him.

Though it was almost unthinkable that there *were* any others like him.

'How's this going to be for you?' Holland asked.

Thorne looked at him.

'Just . . . you know.' Holland took a few moments, searching for the right way to voice his concern. He slowed at the turn off for Loughton, then put his foot down again.

'What?'

'I'm happy to be the one who makes the arrest,' Holland said.

'No.'

'More than happy, actually.'

'No need.'

'If you're going to find it . . . difficult.'

'Why would I find it difficult?'

'I don't mean *difficult*.' Holland shifted in his seat. 'But you and him are friends, right?'

Thorne turned to look out of the window again. '*Were*,' he said.

When the traffic began to snarl up around the town centre Holland hit the siren again, then switched it off when they were within a few streets of the one they were heading for. Thorne didn't question it, but couldn't help thinking that Holland was being over-cautious. Under normal circumstances, it was not a good idea to let your suspect know there were police approaching, but Thorne guessed that if Brigstocke *was* at home and already knew about the deal Michael Healey had struck with the DPS, he wouldn't be surprised that someone was coming for him.

It would not be Thorne he was expecting, though.

Holland swore under his breath as he was forced to pull up hard at lights.

'Relax, Dave,' Thorne said. 'He'll be there or he won't, so a few more minutes isn't going to make any difference.'

Holland nodded and leaned back. He let out a long, slow breath then threw Thorne a glance as the lights began to change. He said, 'I'm going to bloody *love* watching you nick him.'

As they pulled away, Thorne caught the car that was approaching from their right in his peripheral vision. He turned just in time to see it jump the lights, to clock how fast it was coming. Instinctively, he raised his arms to protect his head, but he did not even have the chance to cry out before the impact.

Before the deafening bang and the blackness.

SIXTY-SIX

It was dark, and smelled of disinfectant, and he could only get around slowly, because the air was thick and gloopy. His mouth tasted bad, as though he'd swallowed something sour. There was a loud, low hum and pressure on his ears as if he was underwater, so he couldn't make out what Helen was saying to him, or Nicola or Phil who seemed keen to tell him something, and when he tried to speak to them nothing came out.

They were all smiling, but when they'd drifted away others appeared through the murk who stayed silent and seemed a lot less happy to see him.

Melita Perera and Stuart Nicklin.

Brigstocke...

Then it was just... nothing again, until the hum began to fade and he struggled his way to the surface.

Thorne slowly opened his eyes and squinted into the light.

'Hey...' Nicola Tanner's voice.

When he tried to turn his head, he realised immediately that he would need to do so very carefully. Tanner and Hendricks were sitting together by his bed.

'About bloody time,' Hendricks said. 'Christ, hospitals are boring.'

Tanner put down her magazine and moved her chair closer. 'How you feeling?'

Thorne intended to say 'I've been better', but managed no more than a croak. Tanner reached for the plastic jug, poured water into a paper cup and leaned in so that Thorne could take a sip. He lifted his head, just a few inches from the pillow, and as he drank he saw the plaster running from his thigh on one leg and from knee to foot on the other. There were several different tubes snaking from his hand and he could only guess that one of them was delivering a healthy supply of morphine because, although it wasn't easy to breathe with strapping of some kind across his chest, he wasn't in any particular pain.

He said, 'Helen . . . ?'

'She's just outside with the doctor,' Tanner said.

'Who I couldn't help noticing was extremely fit,' Hendricks said. 'I reckon your missus is after him, and it's not like you can blame her, what with you at death's door and all that. But if she isn't, I might have a bash at the dreamy doc myself, ask for a thorough examination. I haven't had my prostate tickled in a dog's age.'

Thorne laughed, then winced because *now* it hurt.

'Shit . . . sorry, mate,' Hendricks said.

'OK, so what's the damage?'

'You really want to know *now*?' Tanner asked. 'You should be resting.'

Thorne managed a small nod.

'OK, well . . . one broken leg, a broken ankle, several broken ribs and a fractured pelvis.'

'Is that all?'

'Well, there's quite a lot of bruising.' She pointed to his face. 'Down to the airbag, most of it.'

'It's a definite improvement if you ask me,' Hendricks said.

Tanner ignored him. 'It could have been a lot worse.'

'If you say so.' Thorne stared up at the pale-yellow ceiling. He listened to the drip of saline and the hiss of some machine for a few seconds, the clatter of a trolley outside the door, then turned back to Tanner. 'Brigstocke?'

She shook her head. 'Gone . . . but he can't hide for long.'

'Right.'

'You'll still get the chance to nick him, Tom.'

Thorne wasn't quite as convinced as Tanner that he would, but it was still as good an incentive to make a quick recovery as he could wish for. He remembered the last thing Holland had said to him before the crash. 'How's Dave doing?'

The look that passed between Tanner and Hendricks was momentary, no more than that, but it was enough.

'Tom . . .'

Thorne felt a powerful jolt of pain that no amount of morphine would ease and, as it began to spread and settle, he closed his eyes and pressed his head back into the pillow.

He wanted only to find his way back to that thick and quiet dark.

SIXTY-SEVEN

Two weeks earlier, there had been another funeral.

Thorne had still not recovered sufficiently from his injuries to attend, but he knew that then, as now, there had been a good deal of Met Police pageantry on display. All the bells and whistles laid on. There had been a far larger attendance that day, but that was only because *three* officers were being laid to rest; three coffins removed simultaneously from shiny hearses and carried slowly towards the crematorium.

Coffins containing the bodies of Kazia Bobak, Asim Hussein and Catherine Holloway.

Today, there was just the one.

Thorne could only stand – with some difficulty – and watch as Dave Holland's coffin made its final journey. He had very much wanted to be one of those bearing it, but the lingering pain in his ribs, not to mention the crutches, made it impossible. Phil Hendricks had taken his place, alongside Holland's brother, and father and three of his oldest friends.

Standing next to Nicola Tanner, Thorne looked on as the procession moved through an honour guard of constables, all of them stock-still in their dress uniforms. Buttons gleaming and white gloves pristine. As the coffin passed him, Thorne stared at the Met Police flag draped across it, the enormous wreath sent by the Brass and the card that read *In Memory of Our Fallen Colleague*. And the hat.

There was always a stupid fucking hat.

He wasn't even sure it was Holland's hat, though he'd certainly have worn one like it at some point in his career.

It was the hat that set Thorne off...

The bearers finally came to a halt at the crematorium doors and waited, a little awkwardly, for the Deputy Chief Constable – in his own dress uniform complete with braid and medals – to step forward and give the salute.

There was half a minute of silence.

Then they all went inside.

The humanist celebrant – a smiley, middle-aged woman named Bryony – had been Pippa's choice, to the mild disappointment of her in-laws. She said that Holland would not have wanted a religious ceremony, would have wanted as little fuss as possible in fact, though they had never actually discussed any arrangements in detail. 'I know we should have,' she'd told Thorne. 'Considering the Job and everything. But you don't, do you?' She'd been half-smiling as Thorne had passed her a tissue. 'Because it feels like you're tempting fate...'

Bryony explained that although there would be no hymns or prayers, the beliefs of all those gathered would be respected as they said farewell to David Anthony Holland.

Anthony. Thorne had not known that.

She talked about Holland's career and his family. She

stressed how devoted he'd been to his wife and daughter and, smiling broadly, described the affection and esteem in which he was held by his friends and colleagues. She said a lot more after that, as did Holland's brother and one of his friends from school, but Thorne was struggling to take it all in above the noise in his head; to cope with the nerves as he sat clutching Helen's hand and waited for his turn to speak.

'I'd like to invite you all to take just a few minutes for quiet reflection . . . '

Thorne straightened as the celebrant introduced a song that Pippa had chosen because it was one of her husband's favourites.

Thank you for the days . . .

It was a song Thorne loved, too, though he was surprised to learn that Holland had been a Kinks fan. They'd talked about country, Holland gently taking the piss while Thorne banged on about Hank Williams or Johnny Cash, but they'd never talked about the music Holland liked. Something else Thorne hadn't known or taken the trouble to find out.

Holland's brother read a poem after that. It wasn't one Thorne recognised, but he couldn't help but be slightly irritated by the final line which he thought was mawkish, not to say inaccurate.

'I was not there, I did not die.'

I know you died, Dave. I was sitting next to you . . .

Then Thorne heard the celebrant say his name and felt Helen squeeze his hand. He grabbed the chair in front and used it to haul himself, a little clumsily to his feet. Helen leaned close and offered to help him get to the podium, but Thorne shook his head. When he eventually reached the front, the celebrant took his arm and guided him up, but now Thorne didn't mind the helping hand, relieved at having managed to make it without going arse over tit.

At least I'd have given you a good laugh.

He stood his crutches up against the lectern then leaned on it, hoping it would support his weight. It felt a little rickety, but he didn't have a lot of choice. Thorne stared out for a few seconds at the sombre assembly of black suits and blue uniforms and, as he opened his mouth, he wondered why he hadn't listened to Helen when she'd urged him to write it down.

He told himself it would be fine, because what he wanted to say wasn't going to take long.

'When you lose someone suddenly ... actually, even if you've been expecting it, you end up thinking about all those things you never talked about. You can't help but wish you'd made more of an effort when you still had the chance, but most of the time people just don't. We should talk to each other more about important stuff ... because we're rubbish at it.' He looked across to where a group of male PCs were sitting; Hendricks in the row behind them with Liam and Greg Hobbs. 'Blokes especially, I think.' He watched Hendricks lower his head while Liam nodded next to him.

'There are so many things I never talked to Dave about and I'm always going to regret that. I missed out ... and I know that now, because talking to his friends and family these last few days, there was so much more to him than just the copper I was lucky enough to work with.' He glanced down at Holland's wife, at his parents who simply looked pale and shellshocked. 'Most of you here today already know that, obviously, and I feel very sorry – very *stupid* – because I found out too late ...'

Thorne talked for a few minutes more, echoing the celebrant's words about how much Holland had loved Pippa and doted on Chloe, the high regard in which he was held by his colleagues. The fine officer he was and the even finer one he'd have gone on to be. He spoke about how he would never forget the look of determination and commitment on Dave's face right before the accident and how much that said about him. He made a joke about the terrible haircut he'd had when they first met.

'I worked with Dave for a while,' he said, 'and then for a long time I didn't. It wasn't until he came back to London and we started working together again that I realised quite how much I'd missed him. As a colleague and as a friend.'

He was almost done, feeling pleased with himself that he'd managed to get through it, when he felt his eyes began to fill. He reached out for one of his crutches.

'Now I have to miss him every day.'

As everyone milled around outside the crematorium, a few smoking much-needed cigarettes and all grateful that the rain had held off, Thorne and Helen made their way over to where Tanner was standing with Hendricks and Liam.

Tanner reached over to rub his arm. 'That was very nice. What you said in there.'

'Was it all right?' Thorne leaned on his crutches. 'I should have thought about it a bit more.'

Hendricks stepped forward to pull Thorne into a hug. 'Yeah, it was.' He was smiling when he finally stepped away again to take his boyfriend's hand. 'You big soppy bastard.'

'Cheers,' Thorne said.

They chatted for a few minutes: about how nice the ceremony had been; who would be travelling with who to the Oak to get hammered and how it might be sensible to grab some food on the way. They talked about the sales rep who had been running late for a meeting, who had walked away from the crash with no more than a few cuts and bruises and would soon be standing trial for causing death by dangerous driving. In hushed voices they talked just a little about the man Thorne and Holland had been on their way to see when the accident had happened and whose whereabouts remained unknown.

A manhunt that was now being run, nominally at least, by the DPS.

'Do you think there are any more?' Tanner asked. 'Like him.'

'I'd be amazed if there weren't.' Thorne turned and spotted Pippa talking to Holland's parents. 'I don't really want to think about it. Not today, anyway.'

He told Helen he wouldn't be long.

Pippa saw Thorne coming and walked to meet him. She held out her arms once he'd got to her, and the hug was no less tricky to manage than the one he'd received from Phil Hendricks; crutches dangling on either side of her while she held him upright.

'Thank you,' she said.

'Don't be daft.'

She smiled. 'I'd really like to see that haircut you were on about.'

'Oh, yeah. His Hugh Grant phase.'

'He never really showed me any photos from back then.' Her smile became a cod grimace and she held up her fingers, crossing them as though warding off evil. 'The "Sophie years" ... '

'I'll see if I can dig one out,' Thorne said. 'So ... how're you doing?'

'Well, it's all phenomenally shit, obviously ... but I've had to spend most of the day making sure everyone else is all right, you know? So, far too busy to fall apart.' She turned to look back across the neatly cut lawn at Holland's mother and father, who were already walking slowly towards the car park. 'Worse for them, I reckon.'

'I don't know about that,' Thorne said.

'No, it is.' She turned back to him. 'We aren't supposed to bury our children.'

Thorne said nothing, thinking about the unborn child he and his then girlfriend had lost fifteen years earlier. It had been hard, but it wasn't ... this.

'We were trying for one.' Pippa was staring at her shoes. 'A baby, I mean.'

'Right ... ' As always, Thorne's expression gave him away.

'You knew, didn't you?'

Thorne saw little point in denying it. 'I was glad he told me,' he said. 'Flattered, I suppose.'

She smiled again and shook her head. 'I swear, if he was here, I'd bloody well kill him. I told him not to say a word to anyone.'

'I don't think normally he would have,' Thorne said. 'It was just about ... having something nice to talk about at a really bad time.'

'OK, well, in that case I might think about forgiving him.'

'He was excited. Talking about names and all that—'

No, it hadn't been Thorne who had raised the subject, but even so, he knew straight away that it had been a very stupid thing to say. Stupid and insensitive. He watched her fight to keep her emotions in check, sensing that it was a battle she really needed to lose.

Pippa Holland began to sob.

*

They were working their way slowly along the seemingly endless line of wreaths – Thorne beginning to tire a little, while Helen leaned down to read out the messages on the cards – when Thorne felt his mobile vibrate in the pocket of his jacket.

He could not have explained how, but he knew who was calling.

Without a word to Helen, he limped away until he could not be overheard, struggling to fish out the phone as he went. He could see that the number was withheld.

He leaned against a corner of the crematorium and answered the call.

'Tom . . . ?'

'What do you want?'

'I just—'

'Do you know where I am?' Thorne waited, but not for very long. 'Do you have any idea what's happening today?'

'You can't put that down to me. It was an accident—'

'Oh yes I fucking can, because it *is* down to you.'

'Fine, if that makes you feel better.'

'*Better?*' Smashing the phone against the wall would have made Thorne feel an awful lot better, but he didn't. 'I asked you what you wanted.'

'I don't want anything.'

'I mean, I hope I'm wrong, obviously, but I doubt you're calling to tell me you're handing yourself in.'

'I . . . no, I can't do that.'

'Of course you can't, because you're a fucking coward. Actually, that's not even the worst thing you are, not by a long way.' Thorne lowered his voice and hissed his disgust into the handset. 'I'm not even sure there's a name for what you are.'

'You need to understand that I'm not well ... my mental health—'

'*Rapist*. Let's go with that for a kick-off, shall we?'

'I never raped anyone.'

'Course you didn't, same as you never killed anyone. You just helped other people do those things while you got off on making them happen.'

'Will you at least let me try and explain?'

'I don't want your piss-poor explanations, because there aren't any.'

'But you *know* me, Tom.'

'I thought I did,' Thorne said. 'I know you *now*, though.'

There was silence for a while. From where he was standing, Thorne could see the next funeral cortège approaching. He watched the hearse turn in at the entrance.

'So, what now? How do we ... ?'

'Move forward? Well, how about you do the honourable thing? Maybe you could pay a visit to that viaduct you chucked your kiddy-fiddling courier off.'

'That wasn't me—'

'You're pathetic.' Thorne was making no effort to keep his voice down any more, spittle flying on to the screen. 'You don't deserve to live.'

'Tom, listen—'

Thorne hung up and watched the hearse draw closer. He felt numb and helpless. Beaten. Only an idiot believed that life was fair, but he could not recall it being quite so capricious or desperately cruel. A good officer, a good man, reduced to a few wisps of smoke from a crematorium chimney, while another – as bad as any he had ever come across – was still breathing and free to try and justify his unspeakable actions.

He leaned against the wall for few minutes, until the scream inside his head had died down a fraction.

When he hobbled back round the corner, Nicola Tanner was waiting for him.

'I heard you shouting.' She pointed to the phone Thorne was still struggling to stuff back into his pocket. 'It was him, wasn't it?'

Thorne nodded and began heading back to where he'd left Helen.

'Nothing that's going to help us, I'm guessing?'

'No.'

Tanner stepped over to walk alongside him. 'Don't worry, Tom.'

'I'm not worried.'

'However long it takes, we'll get him.'

'You'll have to do it on your own.'

'What does that mean?'

'I'm sorry, Nic.'

Tanner slowed, then stopped, but Thorne kept on moving. He saw Helen waiting for him, the flicker of concern on her face as she raised a hand to wave. He planted his crutches, drove himself forward and spoke again without turning round.

To himself as much as anybody else.

'I'm done,' Tom Thorne said.

ACKNOWLEDGEMENTS

I should begin by thanking (in advance) those readers who choose *not* to post any spoilers, specifically those relating to the double whammy of shocks and reveals at the end of *What the Night Brings*. Believe it or not, there are those who delight in such mean-spirited activity. The sort who would gleefully spoil *The Sixth Sense* by telling everyone that Bruce Willis is actually a ghost.

I know that you would never do such a thing, so thank you.

Of course, you may be the type of weirdo who turns to the very end of a book first, in which case you will have no idea what I'm talking about. So, hello and forget I said anything.

It's been fantastic to spend time with Tom Thorne again and, as always, I owe a huge debt to the amazing team at Little, Brown who – despite the dark places to which I took the miserable old bugger this time – made that process such a joy. So thank you to David Shelley, Charlie King, Catherine Burke, Lucy Malagoni, Robert Manser, Callum Kenny, Nithya

Rae, Tamsin Kitson, Duncan Spilling, Hannah Methuen, Rachael Jones, Tom Webster, Gemma Shelley and Sarah Shrubb. Outside of LB, I am once again grateful for the eagle eyes of Wendy Lee and Jon Appleton, and the bacon-saving copy-editing attentions of Nancy Webber.

Thank you to Brian Price for knowing a frightening amount about poisons, Graham Bartlett for his generosity with police procedural expertise and to Kate Bendelow, whose unique experience as a CSI plugged more than one plot hole. If the conversation between Thorne and Hendricks about tissues in Chapter Forty-five made you go '*ecch*', it's entirely Kate's fault.

As always, special thanks are due to my brilliant editor Ed Wood, my fantastic agent Sarah Lutyens and my peerless publicist Laura Sherlock. As a one man/two women combo, I have previously compared them to Boney M, and even though it has since been pointed out to me that Boney M *actually* comprised of one man and *three* women, I stand by the comparison, because Laura and Sarah easily do the work of three women. This is the eleventh and sadly the last of my books to be immeasurably improved by the editorial nous of Ed Wood. Good luck and thanks for everything, Ed, not least enough spicy chicken to sink a battleship.

I'm enormously grateful for the continued support and enthusiasm of my US publisher and agent. I remain indebted to Morgan Entrekin, my editor Joe Brosnan and my publicist Jenny Choi at Grove Atlantic, and to my agent David Forrer at Inkwell.

Because I've been given strict instructions, *special* thanks must go to the JBE for knowing far too much about long-swords, Lich Kings and Icecrown citadels than is strictly necessary. Thank you, Jack. Get a job.

What the Night Brings is my twenty-fifth novel in as many years, so it feels like an appropriate time to thank you, the reader, for sticking with Tom and with me for a quarter of a century. Twenty-five years! I know, right? Hard to believe, isn't it, what with me being so youthful-looking and fresh-faced.

Isn't it . . . ?

Here's the thing. I've heard some writers say that they don't really care what readers think; that they write purely for themselves or because they 'simply must' or some such twaddle. I write to be read, pure and simple. So how can I be anything but inordinately grateful that, thanks to you, I am?

And finally, I want to thank my incredible wife Claire, for continuing to put up with me, and with Tom Thorne, Declan Miller and the hundreds of other characters that live inside my head. I've just popped downstairs to ask her the same question I posed to you. The thing about me being fresh-faced and what have you.

Oddly, she was equally non-committal.

Oh, well . . .